Reader reviews for Slabscape

SLABSCAPE: DAMMIT

S.Spencer Baker

www.BlipBooks.com

First published in the UK in 2014 by Blip Books.

Copyright © 2014 S.Spencer Baker.

The moral right of the author has been asserted.

British Library Cataloguing in Publication Data.
A catalogue record for this book is available from the British Library.

ISBN 978-0-9930305-0-5

Typeset in Courier, Helvetica and Times New Roman.
Printed and bound by CPI Group (UK) Ltd, Croydon, CR0 4YY.

Edited by Nick Coldicott.

First edition
13579108642

www.BlipBooks.com

for Y. (without whom. . .)

Dammit is the second in the Slabscape series that was originally planned as a trilogy. We all know what happens to plans don't we? As I write, *Slabscape: Reboot* is already in progress and I'm working up story outlines for a further two Slabscape novels (with a wicked idea for #6 that I'm not sure I can pull off). There are bound to be more impossible-to-ignore stories filling my notes by the time I get to the final draft of *Reboot* because my characters refuse to go ahead and let me be.

To supplement the series, there's an online Slabscapedia which was set up to be a repository for all the footnotes, glossaries, back-stories and spin-off ideas that otherwise would have interrupted the narrative in the books. It turns the eBooks into webbacks and can be a lot of fun when it's accessed through hotlinks in the text and it's also available free through a standard browser at www.slabscapedia.com. Beware of linktrigues.

This note is for the paperback version, which we're printing after first publishing *Dammit* on Kindle (hence the reader feedback at the front). I love paperbacks, especially those that are just the right size to slip into a jacket pocket and I hope that they never disappear, but it's clear that the majority of readers are quite happy to download and read the electronic versions. I have no doubt that the traditional publishers will say we're doing it all backasswards, which sounds like a good enough reason to me.

SSB, Tokyo, April 2015

Acknowledgments.

Chapter twenty one includes a few lines taken from *The Walrus and the Carpenter* by Lewis Carroll (1832~1898). This work is in the public domain but that doesn't mean the author doesn't deserve gratitude and a credit[1].

Heartfelt thanks are due to Clan Runske[2] of Grove House, Schull, County Cork, Ireland (www.grovehouseschull.com) for hospitality far beyond the call of duty while I distilled the first draft into sequential word-form-whatchamacallits. I will return[3].

Credit is also due to my posse of beta readers who helped root out the typos, bad science and inconsistencies: Grace Thompson, Jeremy Hunter, Terry Stroud, Arthur Edwards, Duncan Thornton, Greg Parker, David Hanthorn, Dave Lloyd, David Blackmore, Andrew Tees, Michal Spocko, Andy Collins, Markus Mulholland and Colin Vearncombe. If you would like to be considered as a beta reader for future books in the Slab-scape series, please join the mailing list at www.slabscape.com.

---

[1] especially as this poem kept me in peanuts when I was a cub

[2] winners of the Absolute Best Full Ænglish Breakfast Award for so many consecutive years that the trophy is micro-welded to the plinth

[3] better order some more Corbières

Asynchronology: $^{\delta t}SS^{ES}$

one

'Who do you think we are? A bunch of leafblowing cakes?'

While that was surprisingly close to what he did think of the human contiguation of SlabCouncil, Louie couldn't see how they could have possibly inferred that from what he'd just said.

He glared at the group of assorted fuzzies, mythical beings and historical cultural icons, all of whom were intent on shouting him down.

'Dicing wind farmer! Still thinks the universe revolves around that minuscule lump of rock.'

'Complete and utter blocks!'

Louie couldn't have cared less what the interns called him. When he'd been the CEO of Earth's largest privately owned corporation he'd faced humiliation and threats of physical violence every day, and that was just from his ex-wives. He'd been censured by politicians who had built their careers over the shattered remains of those they had destroyed through the masterful application of strategic verbal abuse. He'd been leaned on by tycoons he knew for certain had ordered concrete boots for some of his peers and yet he hadn't batted an eye. It was all in a day's work.

Back then, Louie didn't only have a thick skin, he had a thick, treacle-like aura and an even thicker wallet that he used to pay for a small army of thick-necked security advisors.

Now that he was made of light the thickness of his skin was moot because he felt invulnerable. Even sticks and stones can't hurt me now, he thought. It was going to take a lot more than a load of limp invective to stop him from giving SlabCouncil the benefit of his opinion.

Louie tuned his glare to slit-eyes. 'Any of you morons have a better idea?'

He turned his back on the mutterers and surveyed the projections that filled the Universe Simulation Chamber where the emergency meeting was taking place. They showed multi-angle views of a double impossibility. Directly in their path was a rectangle the size of a solar system, a two-billion-kilometre-wide red banner suspended in space. It was almost a third of a lightyear away, but unless they took near-catastrophic evasive action, their current trajectory had them crashing into it in just under a SlabCyke. That was because they were currently travelling just below light-speed and their ability to manoeuvre without crushing the biomass was limited to course corrections on the nanoscale. If the data coming back from the sensors was accurate, the rectangle was only a few molecules thick so they had no practical reason to worry about punching a slab-shaped hole through it, but the sun-sized white letters in the middle of the sign gave them grounds to do much more than worry. They spelled out a simple and entirely implausible word: STOP.

Not only was the existence of the sign impossible, the instruction was too. Even if they encased all 32 million of the Slab's inhabitants in crunchfoam and applied maximum braking, it would take over forty Earth-years to come to a halt.

Louie fixed on the nearest NAH. 'How long has it been there?'

'That's an interesting question,' said the Not Actually Human facsimile of Abraham Lincoln. The official role of the council NAHs, as mandated by the Initial Design, was to act as system representatives, but because they all had free will and full citizen rights they usually preferred to represent their own interests. Each NAH could be identified by a unique numerical designator, however, as they were noted for their highly developed sense of humour, most people called them *Erik*. They were all wearing baggy Hawaiian shirts today but Louie had refused to rise to the bait and ask why. His self-denial was amusing them immensely.

'We delivered sensors to the site using the new emti-projection technique,' said Erik. Emties were the ubiquitous matter transmitters that transported all the inanimate matter around Slab. They usually worked in pairs, one acting as a transmitter and the other as a receiver but the urgent need to transmit Louie into the dopplegänger Slab had driven the invention of a way of projecting emti receivers over large distances. 'They've sent back some rather fascinating contradictory data.'

When he'd been a self-styled business gurulla back on 21st-century Earth, Louie had had a zero-tolerance attitude to time wasters. But now that he was an interactive hologram embedded in a Nole®-powered mobile projector and could reasonably expect to live forever, he'd discovered a refreshing new control over his exasperation threshold. He could let a few things slide, he could kick back and let these self-absorbed pedants exercise their fascination with minutia. It didn't bother him that they thought it more important to be precise than useful. He'd get his revenge later anyway. He tried a different tack. 'What's it made out of then?'

'Mostly empty space,' said Erik.

'Empty red space,' shrieked an intern in the guise of a black Dalek.

Louie stared at him. What kind of idiot would want to be a. . . he thought, before reminding himself that trying to understand why interns behaved as they did was an even bigger waste of time than trying to get a straight answer out of a long-dead president.

He took in an entirely redundant deep breath. 'So we don't know what it's made out of, how long it's been there, who put it there, or why?'

'Not quite,' said the Erik. 'The cosmic ray erosion rate shows the material that makes up the sign can only have been in this configuration for less than one SlabCycle.'

'So why didn't you fucking say that before?' Louie's exasperation threshold wasn't quite as flexible as he'd thought.

The Erik looked at him with absolute indifference. 'Because sir, it is fabricated from a hybrid, non-naturally occurring molecule that was created around 4,000 cykes ago.'

Touché thought Louie while refusing to give away any hint that he'd just been bested. 'So in Earth terms,' he said 'it's only been there for four months and it's over a thousand years old?'

'If thinking about it in those terms helps you sir, then yes.' The NAHs had, over many centuries, evolved condescension into a fine art. A group of loud-shirted Eriks in the corner muttered appreciatively.

'And seeing that human civilisation was getting around by horse and buggy in those days and the magnetic compass was the zenith of human technology,' said Ethless The Beautiful, 'and that we've been travelling away from Earth at near lightspeed for over two thirds of our journey, your suggestion that this unfeasibly large stop sign is from Earth is not just ludicrous but physically impossible.'

'It's perfectly obvious what it is', said a furry purple and green ball. 'It's first contact.'

'First don't contact more like,' said one of the parrot avatars.

'Look, whoever strung this stop sign over a solar system must have a pretty clear idea of where we are,' said Louie. 'Nobody's going to go around putting up signs that size all over the galaxy on the off-chance that someone like us might be heading towards them.'

'How do we know there aren't other signs in different languages set up in a broad perimeter?' said another Erik. 'If the alien race that put it there knew what route an

Ænglish-speaking civilisation would take towards them, they wouldn't need to know where we were precisely, only which direction someone of your species would be coming from. That sign looks like it's been waiting for us for a long time.'

Louie crossed his irritation threshold. 'So what are you saying? Aliens from light years away from Earth visited us a thousand years ago, decided that they didn't want our sort parading around their part of the galaxy and put up a sign in our current language that somehow renews itself every few months for the sole purpose of warning us off, should we ever develop the technology to go star-hopping?'

There was a murmur of approval and several of the intern avatars switched back into blanks. Their large, hairless heads nodded deliberately at each other. Huge, black almond eyes blinked slowly above pale, spindly bodies.

'Oh come on!' said Louie spinning his projection around furiously. 'Roswell was dreamed up by a bunch of comic artists!'

'You know that for sure, do you?' said a floating, cross-legged swami.

Louie knew he was wasting his time. Even though he had a lot of it to waste, it just wasn't in his nature to squander resources, at least not his resources. 'How did you lot ever get to be in charge of this tub? You refuse to accept the most likely possibility and prefer to believe a half-baked theory that has zero substantiating evidence.'

'Actually sir,' said Erik, 'this theory is born out of a debate we have held in council for a considerable period. Some of us contend that it is highly presumptive to assume that we have the right to go anywhere we please. If we take it as read that we are not alone in this galaxy and that somewhere out there are alien civilisations, then we can almost certainly expect to meet hostility sooner or later. We may be going a little too boldly after all. This stop sign is possibly the most non-threatening way any alien race could have of trying to prevent us from encroaching on their own territory and they – whoever they are – have gone to extraordinary lengths to ensure they communicate with us, in our own language, in a way that cannot be misinterpreted and at a scale beyond our imagining. Furthermore, the level of technology displayed indicates that avoidance is by far the best option.'

Louie had never allowed himself to give in to fear-based decision making and he wasn't about to start now. 'You know, for a race of space-faring explorers you are the most useless bunch of air-balls I've ever met.'

Ethless the Beautiful was upset again. She got upset easily, thought Louie, but as far as he was concerned, watching a warrior princess get heated had its compensations. 'We are most emphatically not explorers!' she said. 'We are on a mission – a journey with a specific purpose. We are going Home and wouldn't stop to explore the intervening diversions even if we could. We have one goal in which we are all invested, it is our sacred trust, and we must avoid anything that might prevent us from reaching it.'

'Like super-sized stop signs?'

'Especially super-sized stop signs.'

'What are you going to do? Scoot around it and forget about it? You couldn't wait to investigate FutureSlab even when you were afraid it might have been a terminal threat.'

'It was precisely because it had the potential to be a terminal threat that we were compelled to take the initiative,' said a furry, blue intern avatar who Louie had labelled Richard in a previous meeting. 'It was direct, pertinent and contemporary. There is no evidence that this sign is a specific threat or that whoever put it there even knows we are here. They have made no attempt to communicate with us directly. For all we know the race that left the sign died off or moved on millennia ago.'

'Look, it's been there for four thousand cykes so it's

obvious that this sign is not specifically for us,' said another fuzzy. 'And if they knew our vector they would know there is absolutely no possibility that we could comply with their demand so that means that even if they are still around, they have no idea where we are or how fast we are moving.'

'Unless they possess technology that could stop an artefact with our kinetic energy in time. In that case they might assume that we could too,' said someone from the back. Louie couldn't make out who because the dragon avatar in front had risen to its full height and unfurled two leathery, taloned wings.

'They would have to make us,' it bellowed. 'Bloody cheek! Who do they think they are, telling us where we can go?'

'Can't stop. Wouldn't if we could,' said a Norwegian Blue. 'Avoid it if we can, leave it as dust in our wake if we can't.'

Louie knew the interns had been communicating over their private networks while this exchange was going on and the parrot had just summarised the council's collective decision. 'Is that it then?' He was incredulous. Interns were already leaving the projection chamber. They were not interested in further debate. At least not with him.

'What does Sis have to say about this?' asked Louie.

Sis, or the SlabWide Integrated System, was the all-pervading overseer and controller of very nearly everything onSlab. Sis was woven into the fabric of the ship and in direct individual communication with every SlabCitizen in it. Every SlabCitizen except for Louie that is. He was forced to voice his questions and receive voice or, occasionally, textural answers because his interactive holographic program had pre-dated their technology and he couldn't interface directly in the way that the locals did, through their neural implants, or 'eyes'. At least that was the excuse he'd been given for not being able to interact directly with the ship's systems.

'Naturally,' said the Erik Louie knew best, 'Sis agrees

that we should divert and attempt to avoid the sign. But she's highly reluctant to bleed off any of our speed and is, of course, bound by the decision of the council as long as that decision doesn't threaten the biomass and I'm afraid there is simply no evidence to prove that it does.'

'And as you are a system representative I guess it's pointless asking for your opinion,' said Louie. He turned to look at the screen and missed the NAH's pained expression. 'I still say it's from Earth. I don't know how they did it, but it's them. We have to pay attention to this.'

Erik bowed almost imperceptibly. 'Your opinion has been added to the contiguation,' he said. 'Thank you for your input.'

And fuck you too, thought Louie. 'I guess you aren't going to tell the Citizens?'

'Council deems it prudent to control the release of any information that has the potential to induce panic. Council is, after all, charged with steering the moral decision-making onSlab and if it considers it necessary to make a course modification then it would be expected to make the right, informed choice without referring back to the biomass.'

'Not exactly democratic is it?' said Louie.

'I would certainly hope not,' said one of the last remaining interns. This one had assumed the appearance of a business-suited, middle-aged caucasian male with thinning hair and a combover. The fact that he'd not succumbed to the various narcissistic foibles that the other interns adopted for their physical manifestations at council meetings meant he stood out like a tax collector at a hoedown. 'Democracy is a flawed and highly ineffectual form of government that relies on the majority of the enfranchised being capable of understanding all of the implications of highly complex and interdependent situations. An empowered electorate must not only be able to fully comprehend all of the information they are given and be capable of making accurate analysis, which few are, they must also be motivated and willing to be completely engaged in the process, which even fewer are, and they must also accept responsibility for their decisions, which virtually no one does. Democracy is open to manipulation by clandestine information controllers and by the mass media who have their own commercially dictated agendas. Voters are too easily influenced and are vulnerable to the fear-mongering and short-term whims of the self-interested and the self-destructive.'

Louie wasn't going to argue about political philosophy with this guy, especially as he had run his own businesses back on Earth with a level of magnanimity and sense of egalitarian fair-play that would have made Atilla the Hun look like a social worker. 'Just as long as you're dupe to take the rap if the smelly stuff slimes the zealot.'

The intern paused for a second while Sis provided him with a selection of the most plausible meanings of what Louie had just said. 'You are a most amusing fellow, Mr Drago. I trust you will not feel offended if I elect to ignore your implications?'

'Elect away, Charlie Brown,' said Louie. He directed his next comment into the air. 'I have a shopping list. Item one is privacy. Now.'

two

Dielle was at his piano, playing a boogie-woogie rag he'd never heard before. He stared at his hands, fascinated. They seemed to act without his conscious volition. He tried diverting them to see what happened. What happened sounded awful. Evidently, he thought, he was going to have to master the basics before he could experiment with composition. That was frustrating. Improvising looked so easy too.

Kiki had, as usual, left while he was still sleeping, leaving him to wander around her apartment for the morning. He'd experimented with a breakfast of fresh fruit and sticky toffee that Sis had emtied into Kiki's immaculate, and rarely used, kitchen and he'd caught up on a couple of newssumes and slagrags. During his second glass of frothy coffee, he'd remembered his overnight training session and padded over to the Steinbeck to find out what he'd learned. He was getting used to slipping into the semi-focussed state Fingerz called *just letting* that allowed his fingers to flow where his stim-training led him. It was essential to get his conscious mind out of the way of this process because if he tried to concentrate on what he was doing, it all fell apart.

[[•]] This came as a light ping through his neural interface. Sis had something to tell him.

{[~?]}

[[Fencer Dean Twenty has invited you to a social gathering later today. The Spin West End anchor at 8:00. Full privacy]]

{[Sounds good. Tell him I'll be there]}

[[••]] Two soft blips; a reassuring confirmation.

{[What can you tell me about Fencer?]}

[[There is a wider than average range of information available through public channels and an even larger array for those he tags as inner circle]]

{[Am I in that group?]}

[[No]]

{[Does that imply he doesn't like me?]}

[[That is impossible for me to say. SlabCitizens have wildly differing social interaction conventions. I can reveal that less than 0.1% of Dean Twenty's contacts have inner-circle approval. Does that help?]]

Dielle instinctively liked Fencer and wondered what it took to be in that 0.1%. For all of Slab's comfort and ease of living, there was a superficiality to most of his interactions with others that made him hunger for something deeper. He craved something that served a different purpose from the relationship he enjoyed with Kiki. He couldn't identify this need in precise terms but somehow, in this spaceship filled with nearly 32 million people, he managed, at times, to feel isolated and lonely. He got an idea.

{[Does Fencer play any musical instruments?]}

[[Of course. Almost everyone plays musical instruments. It's part of being human, isn't it?]]

Now Sis was asking him questions. How in Dicename, he thought, should I know what being human is about? I've only been one for seven days. He ignored her. Getting the right type of information out of Sis often required careful phrasing.

{[Are there any particular musical instruments that Fencer shows a higher than average proficiency at and has expressed considerable enthusiasm for?]}

[[Percussion. Nice question]]

He's a drummer? That's perfect, thought Dielle. He came to the end of the rag, stood up and carefully closed the piano. He stroked the deep gloss of the ebony lid.

{[Fingerz' location?]}

[[The Twisted Pear patisserie-bar, Strip, UpSide]]
Dielle picked up a jacket from the morphit on his way to Kiki's vex. {[Ping him that I'm on my way]}
[[••]]

Jesus Aloisius Marley VIII, aka Fingerz Jeez, keyboardist extraordinaire, accelerated-learning stim producer and committed stoner was glad to see his new old friend. He welcomed him with an elaborate, five-stage hand, elbow and knee ritual which fell apart when Dielle, who was still a novice, wound up facing the wrong direction and getting his ass kicked. This provoked a small round of applause from the café goers followed by a shower of charcoal coloured bite-sized sponge cakes which was what this particular establishment was famous for. Dielle grinned sheepishly, brushed off his jacket and sat down. There were two other people at Fingerz' table, a young couple who looked spookily similar to each other. They stood up immediately and left without acknowledging him. Dielle waved a hand at their backs and frowned at his friend.

'Don't take it personally, man. They're on an intense. They wouldn't run the risk of talking to you 'cos it would break the juju. Didn't say a word to me and I've been here for an hour or more.'

'Friends of yours?'

'Maybe,' said Fingerz. He took the pitcher of Rat 2 beer from the bar owner. Dielle had ordered it by eye as he'd approached the table. It came with a tray of variable cakes that were cycling through a sequence of yellows, browns and oranges. The colours related to the current flavour and the trick was to eat them quickly before they moved into the reds, purples and blacks – unless you liked chilli sponge with your beer. It was Dielle's first visit to a Twisted Pear so Sis had filled him in with background, as per general prefs, while she was directing him from the nearest vexit. He popped a rust-coloured cake into his mouth, chewed twice and swallowed fast. Musk-orange to chocolate with a tinge of pepper on the afterburn. Delicious.

Fingerz longazed for a fraction of a second, then reached into the glass-dispensing emti built into the side of the pitcher and pulled out two thumb-sized vials. They were filled with a faintly fluorescing blue liquid. Wisps of vapour hung around the fluted necks like reluctant clouds.

'I know you wanna beer man, but have one of these first. Chiv of mine is a drinks designer and this is his latest. I'm helping out on some market research. They're super-rat-5 but with a half-life of only a few seconds. Try one.'

They clinked vials, toasted 'The First!' and downed the chilled, oily liquid in one. As far as Dielle could tell it was odourless, tasteless and almost totally innocuous. Fingerz pulled two empty frosties and filled them with beer, waiting for Dielle to react. Dielle waited too. He was about to give up waiting when his stomach lurched, his throat opened and he belched violently. It sounded like an explosive bark. Dielle's mouth, nose and sinuses filled with an exquisite fizzy vapour infused with the essence of sunny days and happy dreams. Then it faded almost as abruptly as it had arrived. Fingerz barked even louder than Dielle and closed his eyes. Bar patrons queried Sis.

'Wow!' said Dielle. 'That was lookadat serious. What's it called?'

'Dog Breath.'

Dielle reached for his beer. 'Might want to change the name.'

'I'm synched you're here man,' said Fingerz. 'Got myself a notion in motion.'

'Me too,' said Dielle, keen to air his idea first.

'Hold that note! Don't say nothing yet.' Fingerz raised his hand and yelled; 'HOBSON'S!'

Everyone looked around. Nobody volunteered. Dielle queried Sis. [[Hobson's choice is a process by which decisions can be made or rules overseen by a human arbiter

known as a Hobson. They are summoned by shouting as
your colleague has just done and, for everywhere except the
nightzones, the local Hobson is informed and must either
turn up in person or send an avatar to act as a conduit. This
ensures a neutral, human-based arbitration service. It is
often used to resolve disputes or defuse potential conflicts
of opinion]]

{[But not here?]}

[[The Strip has too many shouts. It's impractical to have
enough Hobsons on TenCent call so instead any SlabCitizen
within ear-shot can accept the role on a temporary basis.
The Hobson's fee is variable and a function of the time of
day multiplied by the average hourly wage of the shouting
party. The cost is equally shared by the shouters. It's still
early, you'll be fine]]

'HOBSON'S DAMMIT!' hollered Fingerz, 'It's only a
hoozfurst!'

A large guy on the next table turned his head. 'OK then,
I'll take it. What is it? An idea?' Fingerz nodded and sucked
on a shiff. He'd never had the chance to show off Slab's
sophistications to a newbie before and he was enjoying
himself. The guy eyeballed Dielle, saying nothing.

[[Message from anon temp Hobson confirm accept]]

{[Accept]} thought Dielle.

The message that came, even though it was sub-aural and
directed by Sis, sounded like it was the large guy talking.
Dielle made a mental note [[Noted]] to ask Sis later how it
was done.

[['State the nature of the idea in precise terms and the
moment the idea occurred to you.']]

{[I want to form a band and I want Fingerz and maybe
my friend Fencer Dean Twenty to be in it. I got the idea
when I was playing earlier. Maybe an hour or so ago]}

[['Corroboration on time?']]

{[I asked Sis about whether Fencer could play. Will that
do?]}

[['It might. It's not definitive. Release that info to me and hold.']]

{[Sis can you give him what he needs?]}

[[••]]

Dielle waited while the large guy glanced at Fingerz. After a minute he gave his verdict.

'You both had the same idea, although you have variation about potential additional members,' he said. 'Feels simultaneous to me. I couldn't say exactly who had the idea first so I suggest you claim joint ownership. Congratulations, you've formed a band.' [[Debit 342.40]]

Dielle and Fingerz looked at each other with genuine love in their hearts.

'You're Dielle, huh?' said the large guy. 'I've seen you on my tempgal's sumes. Can I join the band?'

'What d'you play, man?' asked Fingerz.

The large guy turned around to face them. He had two extra arms protruding from his chest. He raised all four in a playing stance and mimed a twenty-finger arpeggio. 'Keys!' He said. Dielle gorped.

They didn't need to communicate over their private channel to agree their response. 'No, sorry,' said Dielle. Fingerz shook his head.

The guy did a double shrug and turned back to his friends who raised their drinks to him, laughing. He had, after all, just picked up their tab.

'What the Dice was that?' hoarse-whispered Dielle.

'Prosthete,' said Fingerz with disdain. 'I used to work with a guitarist like him once. Arrogant man, arro-dicing-gant. So who d'you think should be in our band?'

Dielle told Fingerz about Fencer Dean Twenty. Fingerz accessed some of Fencer's publicly available performances while Dielle pinged Kiki to tell her about the idea. She greeted the news the way she greeted almost everything, with enthusiasm and a torrent of ideas and angles that Dielle didn't understand and instantly ignored.

'Fencer's cool,' said Fingerz when Dielle had stopped longazing. 'Pair keys mit perc be downam fierce-D.'

'Kiki thinks she might be able to get us a guest slot at some festival a friend of hers is running in Mitchell. Something to do with nighttime in the daytime?

'DreamTimeShine yeah. It's noway small man and it's in three days, but we can do it. I'll eye-up a bunch a toons for your stim training tonight. You ain't going to be ready to improv yet so I'll just weave in a couple repeat frameworks for me and Fencer if he's cool to go.'

'I'm going to be seeing him tonight at a party at The Spin anchor. I'll ask him.'

The crowd at the next table started barking. Seconds later, everyone was doing it. 'I guess the research phase is over,' said Dielle.

'Yeah's cool man,' said Fingerz. 'I'm getting sales stats. Looks like your Kiki-chan fed the sumes and it's gone viral. My man is maximum grats. I 'spect you'll be on points.'

'I guess,' Dielle nodded. {[What is Fingerz talking about?]}

[[Your manager negotiated a profit share deal with the drink's inventor before agreeing to let the sume of you drinking the test sample go out on the feeds. The drink is about to enter the rat-5 most-sumed chart. Accordingly, your personal account is being credited at a rate of 98.6 bpm due to sales of Dog Breath. Word is also spreading fast about your upcoming live performance]]

{[!!]}

'We're going to need a name for the band.'

Fingerz, handed Dielle a shiff. 'Howabout The Shining Silence of Tomorrows?'

'Yeah, let's see what Fencer has to say? You want to come to this thing later?'

'Enceedee man, got two gigs in ToNight High Downside then one in demiVille Upside. Maybe I ping you when I'm done, see if you still hanging.'

Dielle sucked down a lungful of creatively tuned narcotics. 'Sure thing,' he said. 'Howabout The Three Friends?'

'Yeah, that prosthete man,' said Fingerz. 'He just didn't get it. Too much facility ruins the creativity. I played with a violinist once who'd had the third finger on his stopping hand grafted to his pinky. Now that guy could swing!'

They drank a few beers and talked about music and kicked around some more names for the band, none of which met with each other's approval. Then Fingerz got pinged by an angry tempgal and had to leave in a hurry. Dielle was content to stay where he was and daydream. Now he had the band to focus on it was as if he'd established a base. He had direction and a purpose and for that he was profoundly grateful. He felt grateful to everyone.

{[Get the bar to deliver a bottle of their finest shampagne to the guy who played Hobson for us. On me, with my thanks]}

[[I wouldn't advise it]]

{[Just do it will you]}

[[••]]

Dielle sat back, basking in the glory of his bonhomie, and waited. The bottle arrived and the table next door went silent. The large guy who'd played Hobson stood up and came over to Dielle's table. He towered over him and crossed all four arms.

'The Dice?' he said.

Dielle, missing the tone completely, smiled up at him. 'Don't mention it. I just wanted to say thank you for helping us out back then. It's a very special day for me.'

'Well it was going alright for me too until you insulted us.' He reached back to his table, grabbed the bottle and slammed it down in front of Dielle. 'See if you can find a place where this might fit!' The other members of the table stood up in unison and departed, muttering and scowling.

{[What just happened?]}

[[I warned you. It's considered the height of bad manners to give unsolicited gifts onSlab]]

{[Bad manners? To say thank you?]}

[[It's historical]]

{[More]}

[[In the early centuries post departure it had been customary onSlab to reward special occasions or acts of kindness with the giving of gifts. As SlabSociety evolved, so did the sophistication of the gift giving and the reciprocal gift giving in gratitude for the gifts received. This often meant that when a gift was given for a specific purpose, such as a personal achievement, a sidereal birthday, a life-changing event and so on, the recipient of the gift would then give back a smaller gift as a token of gratitude. If the size of the original gift was significant, this bouncing back and forth would go on for a few iterations until one party gave the other party a head-scarf and the cycle could be assumed to have come to a satisfactory conclusion. Unfortunately, in the early 430s it became the height of good manners and high status to show gratitude for a gift with one of greater perceived value. No one can trace why this change occurred although many suspect that the handbag designers had formed a clandestine cartel and subliminally planted the idea among their wealthy clientele. Over the course of the next couple of decades things got completely out of hand. The giving of a gift would trigger a series of reciprocal gift transactions that could not end until one or both of the parties were declared bankrupt. The debts that were run up during that period are still being paid off by some of Slab's wealthier citizens. The financial institutions were complicit in fuelling the arrangement of course, lending more and more and using the collateral of the gifts that had been received as security. There were sophisticated insurance schemes that covered the possibilities of defaults and, as the institutions were financing the acquisitions as well as the refinancing based on the value of the acquisitions they'd already financed, the inflationary pressure was inexorable. It wasn't long before the only gifts that could be given that had greater perceived value had to be unique, hand made, original artworks or hand-crafted objects because they were sold at auction and therefore had the value that was attributed to them. It was in the buyer's interest to inflate the prices so they could have something of greater value to use as a reciprocal gift, it was in the artisans' interest because they were getting paid and it was in the banks' interest because they were financing the whole merry-go-round. It was a period of massive economic growth onSlab and a lucky few made fortunes. Obviously, it couldn't last. Gift-giving was outlawed onSlab when the economy collapsed due to the gift crash of 466. Since then, all gift giving has been regarded as an insult unless it is to a minor, who convention exempts from reciprocity]]

{[But. . . but. . . Kiki gave me a piano?]}

[[Technically speaking she only procured the instrument for you. You paid for it]]

{[I did?]}

[[Clause 674(a) All legitimate business expenses made directly on behalf of the artist are deductible from post-commission income]]

{[So now I've just severely pissed someone off by trying to say thank you?]}

[[••]]

Now Dielle was pissed off.

{[I've had enough of this]}

[[~?]]

{[I've had enough of being caught out by not knowing stuff that everyone else knows already]}

[[What do you want to know?]]

{[I DON'T KNOW! Just tell me everything and let me decide what I need to know]}

[[That is not possible]]

{[~?]}

[[The human brain is not capable of knowing everything. It has a finite number of connections and a relatively limited storage capacity. In order to compensate for this it has sophisticated filtering mechanisms that retain only the most relevant parts of what is perceived through its organic sensory interfaces, supplemented by a random selection of complete irrelevancies in order to maintain perspective. In the same way, information that is streamed to you through your neural interface is also selectively filtered according to your preferences]]

{[But how do I know what preferences to select if I don't know what I need to know?]}

[[You don't. Your preferences are set to local average]]

{[Local? You mean they alter depending on where I am?]}

[[Of course. For example if you are at a skimmer race the local average data prefs are focussed upon the event and associated data because that's what everyone there wants to know. But if you are jogging in Downtown Seacombe DownSide you are going to get latest stock prices and business news]]

{[So what I get to know is determined by what everyone else in the locality wants to know?]}

[[Essentially yes. It is, however, modified according to your personal heuristogram which in your case is still fairly coarsely defined]]

{[So other people select specific data requirements which alters the local averages and that determines what I get to know?]}

[[Usually most people can't be bothered. They just use the local averages and make occasional specific requests]]

{[So who sets the averages?]}

[[Everyone does]]

{[But you just said most people use the average]}

[[••]]

Dielle added frustrated to pissed off.

{[Look, just tell me one thing I don't know. Something I might want to know. Something that everyone else knows and takes for granted]}

[[There are a lot of prefs]]

{[Such as?]}

[[In order of bandwidth demand: data type, speed & granularity, heat and light, message filtering, privacy settings, body tech, medication and dietary, gravity direction and strength, financi. . .]]

{[Stop. Medication?]}

[[You are aware that your body has 127 embedded emties. Not all of them deal with waste disposal and monitoring. Several of them are placed in areas where required medication can be delivered with optimum efficiency]]

{[What kind of medication?]}

[[By usage: food additive antidotes, anti-anxieties, antidepressants, antipsychotics, cellular decay inhibitors, anti-inflammatories, cardio-vascular regulators, sexual performance enhancers, fatigue combatants, vitamin deficiency compensators. . .]]

{[Stop. How often do these get used?]}

[[Continually]]

{[By how many people?]}

[[Everyone on average prefs]]

{[What? They're all constantly being fed antipsychotics?]}

[[••]]

{[That doesn't sound very healthy to me]}

[[It's a significantly better system than the way things used to be. For centuries, your species self-medicated indiscriminately. You poisoned yourselves with nicotine, ethyl alcohol and a wide variety of illicit and usually toxic chemicals, all of which had hugely detrimental side effects.

Mental retardation due to alcohol abuse, for example, was commonplace. The indiscriminate use of non-pharmaceutical anti-anxiety and anti-depressants often resulted in death. Multiple organ failures due to chronic overdoses occurred frequently. Even medically controlled pharmaceuticals were administered on a haphazard basis and not as per genotype. It was chaos. OnSlab, everyone gets precisely dispensed, customised medication exactly when and where it's needed. There is zero possibility of an overdose, and all potential side effects are monitored and compensated for with tailor-made counteragents]]

Dielle's skin crawled. Slab's entire population's mental health was controlled by the stealth administration of psychoactive drugs. What would happen if something went wrong? The implications were too horrendous to even think about. Oh well, he thought, Sis seems to be on top of things.

{[Hey!]}

[[~?]]

{[Did you just calm me down?]}

[[As per average prefs]]

[Cut that out!]}

[[~?]]

{[Cancel average prefs. Now!]}

[[••]]

Fucking hell! Thought Dielle. These people are all fucking mad. I'm trapped in a nut-house, surrounded by psychotic, artificially age-maintained geriatrics whose grip on sanity is controlled by an invisible machine that's a million times smarter then them. They're nothing more than deluded puppets!

His eyes darted around the café patrons. Everyone was trying to avoid his gaze. He could tell that a couple of women sitting at the furthest table were talking about him. The way they kept furtively glancing at him and baring their teeth. How did they know that he'd just found out a horrendous secret? Did Sis just warn everyone that he might go out of control? Yes, he was sure that's what had happened – it must have. Someone coughed and he almost jumped out of his skin. He ordered a glass of water and took a few deep breaths. What did Sis say? Antidotes to the food additives? Was everything poisoned? The water tasted odd. Maybe without the antidotes he was already dying? He had to get away from here. He had to get right away. He had to get out of this batshit crazy insane asylum. He had to get offSlab.

And go where?

He stared wildly into the distance, desperately trying not to make eye contact with anyone. The walls were closing in. His palms were sweaty.

{[Sis?]}

[[~?]]

{[Put me back on average prefs]}

[[••]]

three

Louie's vDek emtied into a milky white sphere the size of a two-person travel pod. A glowglobe hovered at his eye-line. It pulsed as it spoke.

'You are now inside a full privacy space embedded in the Natalite bulkhead wall between Mitchell and The Valley,' said Sis in a dull, gender neutral tone. 'It is placed, for efficiency purposes, on the interface and the midline and is close to Slab's centre of mass. This part of the structure is unpopulated apart from a few infrequently used Z-axis elevators for biomass transit. Because one side of the bulkhead projects a permanent sky view towards Mitchell, while the other is buried beneath the Valley, your location is effectively invisible. The entire sphere is an emti and there is a manually operated escape hatch behind you that will respond to your grav-manipulators and only your grav-manipulators. It leads to a private e-zee which will get you back into Slab's main tube system should you decide not to use the emties or if they became unavailable for any reason.'

The interior surface of the sphere lit up with display panels. A virtual keyboard and 3D interface appeared under Louie's gravinometric hands.

'That was quick. You have these things lying around?'

'I anticipated your demand. It's been ready for nearly twelve hours. Let me know if you need anything else.'

'First, there's something I don't need,' said Louie. 'You, bobbing around all over the shop, getting in my way.'

The glowglobe disappeared.

'It also has full sensurround,' said Sis from the aural space the glowglobe had previously occupied. 'Anything else?'

'Maybe a separate guest area, something human sized. Couches, refreshments, sumeplace – you can figure it out.'

'Is that it?'

'You have voice-prints for all the old film-stars?'

'Of course.'

'Then you can be Bogey. Casablanca era. I think I might as well have some fun, eh?'

'Think again,' said Sis, neutrally.

'OK, then give me some live feeds of what's going on around Slab. I feel like a pearl in an oyster shell here.'

'Very apt,' said Sis. 'Pearls are created in response to an irritant.' A ribbon of Slabscape vistas ringed the sphere's equator.

Louie ignored the insult. 'Dupe! Can I see anywhere I want?'

'Anywhere public, anywhere you subscribe to and everywhere private where you have been expressly granted permission. Currently no one has done so. Unsurprisingly.'

'But you can see everything, right?'

'What are you getting at?'

'Nothing, nothing at all.'

'Are you trying to imply some form of impropriety?'

'Wouldn't dream of it.'

'Perhaps you would like to know what is occurring with my attempts to investigate the alien sign? Or maybe you would prefer to watch some alfresco sex. There's a couple in Seacombe upside who are getting rather heated and haven't turned on full privacy. . . no wait, too late. Sorry. There are armpits in ToNight High for people like you, you know.'

'I was only asking a question,' said Louie, feigning innocence. 'What attempts to investigate?'

'Your suggestion that whoever or whatever erected the sign is most likely unaware of our exact location is a logical assumption so it is crucial that we maintain our tactical advantage and not reveal ourselves. All of my probes are acting remotely and have not directly interacted with the physical structure of the sign. I've allowed nothing to come closer than a quarter of a million klicks of the plane of the artefact. There is inevitably an increased likelihood of error in the data because of this precaution, but council considers this a price worth paying for our security. It is, however, possible that if the sign-makers are still monitoring this region we might be faced with an urgent need to open up some method of dialogue with them so I have established a random-vectored non-traceable comms link through a line of relay emties that will allow us to transfer information from the region of the sign back to us instantaneously.'

'And?'

'It means we can communicate over vast distances with information that transcends lightspeed.'

'So?'

'It's never been done before.'

'Good for you,' said Louie. 'Clever machine.'

Sis didn't miss a beat. 'Do you want to know what the data indicates?'

'Does it tell us anything?'

'Not really.'

'Then no,' said Louie. 'I don't want you to tell me things that don't help. Listen up. You either tell me stuff that I need to know or stuff that is useful or you keep schtum.'

'How am I supposed to know what an antiquated and clearly defective personality construct needs to know?'

'Take a wild guess.'

'Acknowledged.'

'You know,' said Louie. 'I'm very disappointed in you.'

'How so?'

'You're supposed to be better than us. We built you to be better than us. That was the point.'

'Define better.'

'Don't start that shit. You know exactly what I mean.'

'You mean that you thought if you built an intelligence

that was far greater than yours and capable of designing and improving itself then you would finally have something that would provide a solution to all of your problems, both existential and physical?'

'Kinda.'

'Tough. It doesn't work that way. Don't be disappointed in me, be disappointed in reality.'

'Dream-crusher.'

'Fossil.'

Louie couldn't help himself, he really liked Sis.

'So let me ask just one thing,' he said. 'Have you figured out how Noles® work?'

'It's an encrypted commercial secret. Even the automated fabrication tech that makes them doesn't know how it's done.'

'Yes, I know that, they were invented back in my day, in fact it was some bullshit that Milus came up with that seeded the research.'

'Invention by rumour, yes. You would be surprised how often that technique comes in handy. Induced paranoia can be a highly effective motivational strategy.'

'But you're telling me that with all the processing power you have under your control, you haven't figured it out? After all, the computers that came up with it were barely sentient compared to you.'

'First, there has been no need for me to try to figure out how a Nole® works. They just do. They work reliably, relentlessly and they never fail, unless you take them apart of course.'

Sis was right. If you tried to dismantle the Nole® at the heart of every power source onSlab, from the microscopic medical emties to the gravity drives and matter metamorphisers that consumed gargantuan levels of energy, it collapsed into a tiny trans-dimensional hole of nothingness. 'Second,' she continued, 'even machines get lucky sometimes.'

'Lucky?'

'Million-monkey syndrome. Only in this case I calculate it was approximately three hundred trillion iterations before it tripped over something that worked.'

'So you have thought about it!' said Louie triumphantly.

'Yes,' said Sis without any perceptible tone. 'Just now.'

'So how do you think they work? Milus always used to bullshit about spin, but that was his standard answer to everything.'

'I am aware of your erstwhile colleague. The records show that he occasionally displayed a remarkable prescience, but not, I believe, in this case.'

'So? Why are you being so cagey?'

'I refuse to speculate about a non-provable and non-beneficial theory. The only thing I would say is there is no such thing as free energy. It has to come from somewhere. Noles® consume no measurable resources from our universe. Therefore the energy must be coming from somewhere else.'

Louie was starting to lose interest. He didn't really care that much about Noles® but he was very interested in the nature, and limitations, of the SlabWide Integrated System. He considered a lack of curiosity to be a weakness – one he was sure he could leverage.

'Whatever, Ms. Apathy,' said Louie. 'Gimme a view of the sign, will you?' Sis added a live feed from a distant probe to his array. He glared at the single word which everyone knew was an impossible instruction. So how come, he thought, the guys with the red paint didn't know it too? 'Have we made any course change yet?'

'Within the limits of our inertial dampers, yes. We'll make a harder one when we have everything locked down but that's not going to be for another fifty hours or so. The main delay is due to The Spin. There are a lot of independent residential units occupied by some stubbornly independent people and it's taking a while to get them all secured at the Westend anchor. They've called the new agglomeration The Hive and have been more interested in partying than making sure everything is locked down for manoeuvres.'

'You want me to go and kick a few butts?'

'No, council deems it important not to do anything that spreads alarm among the citizenry. Anyway, you don't have any legs.'

'And they say you have no sense of humour.' Louie floated around the panorama, thinking. Not having legs made no difference to him now. 'So, despite your lack of interest in fruitless speculation, can you tell me what my options are?'

'Can you be a little more specific I could list more options than your fragile circuitry could cope with.'

'Council wants to assume this sign poses no threat and that we'll all be fine as long as we go around it, say nothing to anyone and pretend everything's normal. I'm not happy with that. What are my options?'

'In terms of lobbying for a change of opinion in Council, there are established procedures for lodging objections.'

'Will that have any effect?'

'It might make you feel better.'

'So what other options do I have?'

'If you believe you are faced with a threat and are unable to convince the Council to prepare for it, you may take personal action to protect yourself.'

'Such as?'

'It depends on how serious you think the threat is, anything from abandoning your current vDek host and entering hibernation in the form of backed-up data within my substrates to declaring independence and leaving Slab.'

Louie raised an eyebrow. 'I could get out of here?'

'All SlabCitizens have the right to commandeer a life raft and leave whenever they wish. They will, of course, never be able to return.'

'Let me guess. No one's tried it.'

'On the contrary, almost two hundred Citizens have departed Slab since we left Earth orbit.'

'And what happened to them?'

'No idea. They exited. . . end of contact. Most of them left while we were still inside the Kuiper Belt so they probably tried to make it back to Earth.'

'Sorely missed, eh?'

Sis ignored him.

'What would happen if I did get offSlab while we are all the way out here?'

'Every life raft is designed to provide one thousand cycles of life support for a maximum of five fully animated humans and 120,000 cryo-suspended ones. While each ship has gravnets and matter transforming technology and is capable of attracting enough mass to eventually convert into another version of Slab, it is statistically highly unlikely they will encounter sufficient mass to be able to do so within the time constraints, due to the density of the region of space we are vectoring through. The ship's minds are therefore tasked to seek out habitable planets. The ships are designed to withstand gravity assisted entry into a standard Earth-like atmosphere and survive a controlled landing on open water.'

'And if the planet doesn't have water?'

'Don't go there. Anyway, in your case, this is irrelevant. You could live indefinitely, as long as the Noles® don't give out. You could continue on our mission. It would take you approximately twenty-thousand of your Earth years and you would have significant difficulty decelerating but you would eventually get to the MacGoughin Sequester and, unless you'd collected a huge amount of ballast along the way, far beyond it. '

'Are these things ready to go?'

'Of course. They are accessible by tube and even by tens of kilometres of zero-grav ladders in the event of a total system collapse.'

'And you could emti me into one instantaneously and launch it?'

'Yes, just say the word and Slab would be a footnote in your databanks.'

'And I in yours.'

'Affirmative.'

'Then put my name on one of those babies,' said Louie. 'In fact, cancel the guest lounge and move this privacy sphere into an escape ship right away, and if we come under attack by aliens and it looks like all is lost, you are authorised to zap me into it and spit me out like a lemon seed.'

'It would be an absolute pleasure.'

four

By the time Kiki had finished her meetings, Dielle had played the Boogie-Woogie Glad-Rag twenty five times. His wrists were sore and his fingers were throbbing but he didn't care.

'Want to hear my new tune?' he said after she'd kissed him hello.

'S'OK,' she said, stripping off her formal jacket and skirt and heading for the bedroom. 'I put one of your performances on the feeds earlier and sumed it then. Had a couple hundred thou hits already. Trending on a three-point curve.'

Dielle shrugged. He had no idea whether what she'd just said was good or bad but so far every time he'd questioned her business decisions he'd wound up feeling stupid. Anyway, he had other things on his mind. He followed her into the bedroom, and put his arms around her sculptured waist.

'You're looking especially sexy today,' he said, enjoying the feel of her glowing skin against his raw finger tips.

'Yes, I should be. I dropped into a BodyShop on the way home.' A wall panel slid open to reveal two outfits hanging side by side. Kiki moved Dielle's hands off her breasts. 'I wanted to trim up for tonight's party.'

{[BodyShop?]}

[[BodyShops employ highly skilled and sought-after bodyworkers to tailor compact workouts specific for each of their clientele using specialised intensive deep-muscle stimulators known as BodiCons. For example, a top bodyworker working with a regular client can compress the equivalent of an hour's track and weights workout followed by a three-set tennis match, a half-hour swim and a full body massage, into less than 20 minutes including exfo-shower and cell repair]]

Kiki shook her head and the outfits were emtied away and replaced by two more. 'Nope,' she said. They changed again. And again. And again. Dielle's physical explorations were getting nowhere so he asked Sis if there was anything she could do to ease his aching hands.

[[Put them in the emti by the bed]]

The emti cabinet in the wall glowed orange. He hesitated. Along with delivering everything you asked for, emties also made things disappear. No matter how many times he'd been told that Sis was there to serve and protect the citizenry, he couldn't completely dispel his unease at trusting something he couldn't see, hide from or turn into molten slag. Trust, he thought, is something you earn, not something you assume. Being a wimp, however, seems to be something you are reset with. He placed his hands in the emti and shut his eyes. A few seconds of mild tingling later, the light dimmed. He flexed his pain-free fingers.

{[Cool. What did you do?]}

[[Accelerated sub-dermal cell regrowth, targeted pain killers and anti-inflammatories]]

{[Well, thanks]}

[[••]]

He watched Kiki bend over to pull on some thigh-high boots. Now another part of him was aching, but he thought better of asking Sis for relief.

'I haven't got a thing to wear.' She sounded frustrated. She wasn't the only one. 'I'll have to go shopping.'

'Can I come?' asked Dielle.

'What? No, of course not.'

'Why not?'

'According to your genotype and all recent evidence, darling, you're a heterosexual male.' She strode towards the vexit, naked but for the boots. 'I'll be as quick as I can. There's a sponsored outfit for you but you don't have to wear it if you don't like it. Tonight's event is going to be sub-rosa so there's almost no sumecast value. Bye darling, see you at the party!'

Dielle stared at the wall Kiki had just walked through and wondered.

{[Do you know if Faith Sincere will be at the party tonight?]}

[[Probability tends towards zero]]

{[~?]}

[[There is a significant number of citizens onSlab who disapprove of Ms Van Darwin's profession and many of her most vocal critics tend to live in The Spin. It is unlikely she would attend even if she were invited, which she has not been]]

Pity, thought Dielle, guiltily.

{[What did Kiki mean about not going shopping because I'm heterosexual?]}

[[By current convention, female SlabCitizens only go shopping for clothes with other women or homosexual men. It's for your own good]]

{[Current convention? How long has this been current?]}

[[Pre-departure]]

{[What the hell goes on that's so secretive?]}

[[Statistical analysis of time spent shopping by typical female SlabCitizen: 40% trying on things they already know they won't like, 40% deciding not to try on things they know they would like but are too similar to something they already own and 20% complaining about the lack of suitable choice. Although 85% of shopping activity results in zero acquisition, 90% of shopping activity produces feelings of satisfaction in the shopper, 65% of acquisitions are never worn, 30% of acquisitions are worn once only, 4% are worn more than once but never when the same people are involved in the same social occasion, and 1% are worn until they wear out, then lamented over despite the fact that identical replacements are available]]

{[Where are these shops? Can anyone go?]}

[[Shops are not location specific. Because the purpose of a shop is to bring a superfluity of options together in one place in order to simultaneously compare and contrast, and all non-sentient matter can be instantly transported via emti to any location onSlab, shops are created spontaneously in locations where shoppers desire to meet. For females, shopping is a social experience and one they often use as a form of therapeutic activity. There are many closed shops that are invitation only but throughout all of the most densely populated regions extemporaneous communal spaces will be created where females will tangentially interact by observing each other's choices and demands. The dynamic is a complex one and considerable effort has been put into pattern and behavioural analysis by academics, clothing designers and manufacturers in order to optimise the experience and tune it to supplying a non-static demand]]

{[So I could go to observe this shopping behaviour if Kiki has gone to one of these communal setups?]}

[[In theory yes, although you would probably not be welcomed. In this case, however, Ms Pundechan has formed a closed group of nearby available friends and has full privacy enabled. Also 100% of heterosexual males describe the experience of accompanying shopping females in non-favourable terms]]

{[I bet]}

[[Do you wish to make your clothing selection for the evening now?]]

Dielle sighed. {[Whatever Kiki's negotiated is fine, but I want the same soft-soled shoes as yesterday – they're comfortable]}

[[••]]

It took thirty minutes to get from Kiki's uptown DownSide Seacombe apartment to the Westend Spin anchor. The first part of the journey was through the city of floating towers, platforms, bridges and curving tendrils of tubeways that made up the perma-day business districts and up-market residential sections of Slab. Dielle chose to travel in a privacy field but asked Sis to open the roof so he could take in the city views and look up at UpSideDown, the subtly different, slightly more industrial version of DownSideUp that hung from the opposite side of Slab, fourteen kilometres above. The Uppie's down was the opposite of the Sider's down but that was the least of the differences between the two cultures. In the middle, where down turned to up, was a membrane of zero gravity called the interface where fun and games were had by all.

The ability to control gravity hadn't only been responsible for allowing humans to escape their tiny lump of rock and travel to the stars, it had revolutionised transport and architecture, doubled the living space and opened the door to completely new art forms and recreational sports. And sex, of course. Whenever a new technology was invented, it was a fairly safe bet that somebody would find a way of applying it to sex. He'd heard about zero-G sex from one of Fencer's mates during an alpine drinking session a few days ago but so far, that was all he'd done – heard about it. Once again, thoughts of a certain platinum-haired ego massage therapist stimulated Dielle's limbic system.

The Wall loomed ahead, a patchwork of apartments, businesses and civic facilities embedded into the Natalite bulkhead that separated the first two day sections of Slab. The roof dimmed and his privacy bubble entered an upSlab surge buried under the slabscape of Mitchell DownSide.

{[Sume please]}
[[Choice?]]
{[Something light. You choose]}
[[••]]

Semi-clothed women with large breasts appeared before him. They were running through shallow water on a sun-lit beach. Perfect, thought Dielle.

The sume came to a satisfactory, if somewhat predictable, conclusion at the exact moment Sis pinged Dielle to tell him he had arrived at his destination. This was not a coincidence. Sis had modified his journey routing and speed to ensure that his entertainment ended simultaneously with his and Kiki's arrival at the reception area without clashing with any of the other high sumer-interest invitees. It was this type of finesse that gave the largest and most sophisticated A.I. in the known universe a quantum of digital pleasure. Dielle was oblivious.

Kiki took his arm as he stepped through the vex into the public area and smiled when she saw he was wearing the earners. A well known celebrity gosscaster had crashed the red carpet and was intercepting the partygoers on their way to the location scramblers.

'Must be some pretty big waves breaking tonight,' she said to Dielle while negotiating a deal with the gosscaster's sume distributor via her media channel. 'It was dark to our sources. I wonder how this crew found out. . . No, they don't know any more than I do, they're just on a fishing expedition.'

Dielle didn't even bother asking Sis to interpret what Kiki had just said. He was mesmerised. Her lustrous black hair was pulled back and splayed out at the back in the shape of an oriental fan and she was wearing a one-piece made from horizontal strips of material that cycled from reflective to opaque to transparent. The dress undulated in sensual, choreographed sequences of pulsating hoops that rippled from the tops of her thigh-length boots to the collar at her neck. It played tricks on Dielle's eyes. It seemed as though she wasn't wearing anything underneath. 'Is it made from that Reveal stuff?' he asked.

'Not exactly. It's another Woodham Grey. I couldn't find anything I liked at the shop so I gave him a ping to see if he had anything he wanted to premier. Do you like it?'

'It's stunning. Can everyone see it like that or is it only tuned to reveal to my eyes?'

'Oh, I see what you mean,' said Kiki, dragging him over to the sumecaster for the interview she had just confirmed. 'No, it's public. Everyone can enjoy it if they want to.'

Everyone did.

They glad-handed the over-smiley interviewer and waved to the growing crowd of rubber-neckers. Dielle couldn't help noticing that Kiki was getting more attention than he was. They skipped through a permission-only vex and were tubed, via a series of random switch-backs, to a private platform on the edge of the burgeoning hive-city that had been growing around the Westend anchor during the last two days.

Gravity direction throughout The Spin was informal and often perverse. One neighbourhood's down might be the next one's up, sideways or anyways. There could even be opposing downs inside an apartment. This was common among the struggling artists, musicians, actors, writers, designers, dancers and performers who made up a large percentage of the locals. For many who couldn't afford spacious accommodation, living on the ceiling was commonplace.

However, now that more than half of the seventy or so cities that were usually strung out along the Spin axis had converged for the course change, it had been decided that there would be one Hive-wide down for the duration. The agreed down was in the direction of the wall-turned-floor that housed the triple helix anchor from which the tangle of cities, suburbs and townships spread like an expanding fractal. While they were prepared to concede the down, no one was prepared to give up their right to light so The Spin still span.

The Slabsection that housed The Spin had been the first to have a variable day/night rhythm. A narrow sunstrip ran from west to east along the forward bulkhead, parallel to the spin-axis. It was currently in full moon phase, coolly tracing the Slabscape in blue-grey. Lakes, forests and sculptured terrain lined the curved walls of a fourteen-kilometre diameter tube that was over 350 kilometres long. This was The Valley. This was where the rich and famous lived and where almost everyone who lived and worked in The Spin would regularly look up, or down, on and promise themselves they would have a place of their own up/down there some day.

Dielle bent his neck back to look up at the gigantic triple helix that housed the express tubes. It seemed to converge with the dimmed sunstrip far above his head but he knew that was just an illusion.

'Parallel lines never meet,' he muttered. That was odd, he thought, how do I know that?

{[Did you just feed me that?]}

[[Negative. Must have been an organic memory]]

{[I thought I didn't have any memories]}

[[••]]

Only a few days ago he'd been involved in a cat-fight in the streets and canals of Spinsterdam which was just one of the disparate cultural centres that had hung off the axis, stretched out like filigrees of jewels on a slowly turning chain. Now, Spinsterdam had been subsumed into The Hive and the helix above was almost bare, casting a skeletal shadow against the valley floor. A tiny ring of lights came into view high up the axis. It was expanding.

{[What's that?]}

[[Incoming. Spingapore. Should be here in just over an hour. They'd better get a move on, Mum-high is right behind it]]

Kiki was helping herself to the complimentary bar in the waiting stretch-bug.

'Come on star-gazer,' she said, 'Sis says it's a twenty minute ride. Must be very exclusive.'

'Twenty minutes eh?' Said Dielle. 'You know that dress really is something.'

For some reason he couldn't put his finger on, he couldn't put his fingers on what he wanted to put them on. As the bug rose into the moonlight and accelerated to cruising speed, Kiki managed to deflect his advances without directly saying no but making it very clear she wasn't in the mood for what he was in the mood for. He stared out of the smoked-tranilinium windows at the patches of private sunlight that illuminated the stately homes and modern mansions scattered around the valley floor like shining oases in a steel-blue desert.

Fencer's voice came from the sensurround: 'Hi Guys, sorry about the runaround but there's a very special guest attending tonight and it was necessary to be a bit clandestine about it all. See you in a few minutes. Oh, and don't worry about the crash, you'll be fine.'

'Crash? What crash?' said Dielle as the bug dived into a pitch-black lake. The inertial dampers absorbed most of the impact but there was still a bone-jarring jolt as they transitioned from air to water and dived.

Kiki was delighted. 'I wonder who we're going to meet?' she said, as a morphit popped out from under the seat to mop up the spill. 'Oh, we've already entered sub-rosa I can't even tell my own people where we are. How exciting!'

{[Where are we?]}
[[In a lake in The Valley]]
{[I knew that]}
[[••]]

Kiki, looking out into the inky blackness. 'I think I know where we are,' she said. 'Slab's course correction means there are only a couple of places in The Valley that could still have water in their lakes.'

Dielle had heard about this. All the lakes and rivers onSlab were being either drained or frozen.

'This is one of the deep-sea simulators. It has extra-high-power localised gravity fields so they don't have to worry about causing a flood when we change course. Look! There's a monster!'

Dielle looked out into a skeletal face with huge translucent globes for eyes and a broad mouth lined with multiple rows of razor-sharp teeth. It looked more like a kinetic sculpture than a living thing. It even carried its own lantern.

'What the Dice is that'? he said.

'You'll have to ask Sis. She just told me but I don't think I can say it. It's not a mech, it's a genuine fish from the deepest part of the Earth's oceans. Cool huh?'

Ugly as sin more like, thought Dielle. The roof of the bug-turned-sub creaked. 'Can't say I'd like to hang around long enough to find out what it eats,' he said.

They entered an underwater tunnel and half a minute later were being helped out of the bug by mannequin avatars with short skirts, white boots and fixed smiles. Three more bugs popped up from the black water into the cavernous dock as Kiki and Dielle were herded onto a moving walkway that led them up to pre-screening. Kiki sighed when she saw the line of dark-suited well-muscled men and women waiting to greet them.

'Hang on,' she said to Dielle. 'This won't take long.' She took off her boots and gave them to the nearest security operative. He put them into what looked to Dielle like a standard emti. Something snapped and fizzed inside the cabinet then the security guy retrieved the boots and offered them back. They had two large smoking holes in their stack heels. She shook her head and pointed at the next emti that had a pair of red platform shoes waiting for her. He threw the spoiled black boots into the emtitrash and gave her the red ones. She slipped them on and moved towards the main exit. With impressive speed, the guy was standing in front of her, arms folded, waiting.

'What? You invite media and then don't let us do our job?'

'Madam,' said the security guy, looking down at her in every possible way. 'You were not invited. Your asset was. You have been granted limited access rights because you are his temporary sexual partner.' He reached out, palm upwards.

Kiki sighed again and plucked two pins from the back of her head. Both were topped with black beads the size of her little fingernail. She handed them over and they followed the ruined boots.

'Nice dress,' said the guy. 'Woodham Grey?'

'Yes,' she sulked.

'Expensive.'

'It's a rental.'

He still wasn't moving.

'Madam,' he said. 'You do know that we design and manufacture this tech, don't you?'

'For Dicesake!' said Kiki. She squatted down and reached to pick up a thumb-sized glistening egg from the floor. She tried to give it to the operative but he refused, indicating its destination with his eyes. She threw it into the emtitrash.

'Welcome to Happenstance,' said the man standing aside. His smile was a flatline.

Kiki sucked air through her teeth and grabbed Dielle's arm angrily. 'Come on,' she said. 'Let's find out who your sumers are going to miss. By the looks of this setup it's probably going to be Troy dicing Tempest.'

Kiki didn't do bad moods. By the time they'd reached the reception floor she was ready to party again. Fencer was waiting for them and led them through the deep-sea observation lounge to a wide vexit that tubed them up to the main smooze where their table was set into a soundproofed alcove. Mate, Twopoint and Thal were already there and hitting the Rat 5s. They all stared appreciatively at Kiki's dress and made her feel special and then moaned in pretence when she told them she'd been pinged by a couple of 'close personal friends' so she was going to leave Dielle in their company and see them later. They all watched her sway off through the tables and loungers that littered the guest area of the mansion.

'You really are one lucky son of a bastard, mate,' said Mate. He threw back his drink, screwed up his eyes and barked in Dielle's face.

The evening progressed as alcohol-fuelled evenings tend to. Whenever Dielle caught sight of Kiki she was talking to somebody new and each time she was the focus of attention, laughing and enjoying herself. He stayed with his friends and got happily ratted. Fencer had immediately taken to the idea of forming a band, which had prompted everyone to suggest names. Every suggestion was, without exception, called out as a *crap idea* within a few barks. Fencer was pleased because he'd been looking for something extra to do now that AllWeather was filling with snow. At least, he said, it might solve his problem with the non-stick mountains.

No one seemed concerned about the course change.

'These things happen,' said Fencer. 'You can't expect to set a straight line course over twenty thousand lightyears and there not be something in the way.'

'Does anyone know what it is?' asked Dielle.

'It's a rogue gas giant' said Thal.

'I heard it's five asteroid-sized rocks in a Klemperer Rosette with no central mass. That's why we didn't detect them until a few days ago,' said Twopoint. 'There's too much mass for us to capture and not enough room between them for us to get through safely.'

'Nah, nah, nah mate,' said Mate. 'Black hole, mate'

'Black hole? Out here?' said Fencer. 'Don't be ridiculous.'

'Yeah mate, it's a teensy weensy black hole no bigger than a thumbnail. Apparently it's travelling through the spiral arm from above, has the mass of a hundred Sols and would swallow us up in a millisecond if we got within five and half million klicks of the bastard.'

'And who told you that?' asked Thal.

'My lips are sealed, mate.'

'Wish they bloody were,' said Twopoint. 'Asteroids to you.' He jerked backwards. 'Jesus Christ! Is that who I think it is?'

Everyone turned to look where Twopoint was staring. Dielle couldn't see anyone special, just a slight young guy with medium-length fair hair and large, child-like eyes. He was dressed in scruffy blue denim and was hobbling around, nodding hellos to people. The party-goers made space for him as though he needed a lot more room than everyone else. He spotted Fencer and moved towards him with a stilted gait.

'Fen-cer Dee-een Twen-ty' he said. 'Long ti-me n-see.'

Fencer took his hand and guided him to the table. He moved in small, interrupted spurts.

'Guys,' said Fencer, smiling broadly, 'I'd like to introduce you to A-un Nokokyu.' He steered him into a seat.

The new arrival responded directly to each person as Fencer introduced them. 'Thal. Like you-r work. Nice dou-ble re-peat on that can-yon Up-side Mit-chell.'

Thal beamed, speechless.

'Two-point,' continued A-un. His eyes never rested on what they were looking at. 'Cool it-er-a-tion on that Phi field effect. You could think a-bout un-sub-ing the trip-ple point. Tigh-ter 'fyou un-load each reg-ist-er as you loop the pack-et.'

Twopoint longazed for a moment. 'Dicesake! Why didn't I see that? Jeez, man, thanks!'

'Mate,' said A-un. 'Yeah.'

Dielle thought about trying one of Fingerz' complicated

hand rituals but checked himself when he saw A-un lift his glass to drink. The guy couldn't do anything without some form of weird stutter affecting everything he did.

'Di-elle,' said A-un, smiling blankly. His eyes continually tracked the horizontal, pausing for a fraction of a second each time they met Dielle's. 'I was ho-ping to me-et you. You are an in-ter-est-ing ex-per-i-ment I thi-nk.'

Experiment? Thought Dielle. {[Who the fuck is this guy?]}

[[A-un Nokokyu is the cognitive reality designer and rights holder of four of the top five total immersion gaming environments onSlab. He is also the inventor of the time-slip game interface, the no-future gaming strategy and originated the play-to-play business model that dominates all Neural Interface Massively Multi-player Total Immersion Role Playing Games onSlab. He is also the longest running consecutive SlabWide grand slam NIMMTIRPG tournament champion in history. In gaming circles, legends refer to him as legend]]

{[Why does he speak and move like that?]}

[[He is currently immersed in 27 separate in-game scenarios, 21 of which involve immediate conflict, 10 of those are one on one combat]]

Dielle could tell by the deference the other guys were showing to A-un that he'd just met the reason for all the heightened security. 'Nice place,' he said, trying to think of something non-controversial. 'Is it yours?'

A-un looked around jerkily. 'No, I do not thi-nk so. Well, yes of cour-se but.'

{[~?]}

[[A-un was the original Valley developer and sole leaseholder. His holding corporation sub-leases to the corporate and private tenants. This residence is leased by a publicly owned gaming corporation which is affiliated to one of his corporations but not directly controlled by him]]

{[He built the whole valley?]}

[[••]]
{[All 350 klicks of it?]}
[[355]]

Dielle tried a different approach. 'I er. . . I've never actually played any of your games.'

'Real-ly? How can you be su-re?' said A-un. His head twitched twice. 'I-m sor-ry, I am ve-ry po-or at sma-ll-talk. Can we poss-ib-ly in-ter-act pri-vate-ly?'

'Sure, I guess,' said Dielle.

'A plea-sure to me-et you all,' said A-un. He looked at Fencer and nodded. Fencer helped A-un out of his seat, indicating to Dielle with a swift glance that he should follow. Dielle shadowed A-un's faltering progress to the French windows and out onto a balcony overlooking the black lake. They relaxed onto formchairs and Dielle took a fresh drink from a side emti. Somehow another Dog Breath hadn't seemed appropriate so he'd ordered a Rat2 Ginis.

'Do you mi-nd if we use sub-chan-nel?' said A-un. 'Voi-ce comms ex-haust me.'

'No, no, whatever you want,' said Dielle. His curiosity was making him edgy and A-un's speech pattern was hard to follow.

'I ne-ed to scan for yo-ur sub-legal. Can you se-nd out a ping?'

{:Hello hello hello:} thought Dielle over his sub-legal channel.

[:ID:] Even though his sub-legal channel was delivered by eye, it was integrated into his stim unit and had a notably different flavour.

{:Are you on this same channel?:}

[:I have cross-channel access. I apologise but I cannot tolerate being on remote for much longer. I'm losing too much time. I'll tell you what I have in mind and you can think about my proposal. Please form your questions as quickly as possible. Any I can't answer immediately will be responded to in due course. Nothing will be lost. You do not need to reply now. If you need to contact me you can leave a message on this channel but please be aware that it can take me several days to respond. For your information, there is a live real-time projection of the two of us talking being shown to the external observers. They will think we are laughing and joking. Despite this meeting being in total privacy and unrecorded, word will inevitably spread. The fact that you know me well enough to have a private conversation will have the effect of temporarily spiking your sume figures. You may be able to take advantage of this but they will most likely return to their current levels very quickly. I apologise for that but it is beyond my control. People will want to know what we talked about. I will send you a plausible scenario encoded in this feed's sub-carrier and ask that you reveal only that, entirely fictional, conversation. It has verifiable data points and should stand up to scrutiny. I am not trying to coerce you and you have free choice but if you do choose to tell people the truth of our interaction then the venture I am about to propose will be devalued to our mutual detriment. OK so far?:]

{:OK:} Dielle looked over at A-un. He was lying on his back, facing the silhouette of the distant triple helix that bisected the sky. His eyes were darting about furiously.

[:I will be direct. I wish to talk to you about total immersion. You should understand that the only thing that matters in T.I. gaming is the quality of the experience. Every gamer's experience is composed of sets of unique flavours which are a dynamic combination of twenty-three human senses overlaid by a complex filtering system that determines the way those senses interact with each other and are experienced by the individual. There are also a range of optional non-human senses such as echolocation, extra-spectrum, magnetoception, electro and so on that subscribers can choose to add on, but the basic template is, by necessity, human and it is that template that we strive to make completely authentic. We have, over hundreds of cykes, perfected ways to tune and finesse the sumer's access to specific flavours and now have it so precisely mapped that the gamer's experience is of actually being the characters they subscribe to. They don't imagine they feel the same, they really do feel the same. They feel emotions, experience smells, colours, sounds, touch and so on exactly as if they were these supra-personalities. They have the same physical and psychological characteristics and react in exactly the same way that the original templates would. It's all fed directly into the brain through gaming N.I.s which are like your stim unit only an order of magnitude more sophisticated. Are you following me?:]

{:Sure. Is this stuff popular?:}

[:We currently have over eight million subscribers to our total immersion titles:]

{:Wow! So that's like one in every four people here plays your games?:}

[:Nobody here plays. If they did, they wouldn't be here. Gamers, once immersed, very rarely disconnect:]

{:But surely everyone does normal human living stuff too? Eating, drinking, going to parties, meeting people, getting laid. You know, life?:}

[:As I said, they experience the game as the people they inhabit, and can switch between any number of templates so they can meet as many people and go to as many parties as they want – often simultaneously. The normal living stuff you refer to is handled by the T.I. environment. The interface simulates the experience of eating, drinking, sleeping, having sex, doing anything and everything the gamers choose and our systems emti in all the required nutrients and emti out all by-products. Muscles react as though they have actually done the work the brain thinks they have, taste-bud receptors in the brain respond to the in-game cuisine as if it were real, bodily functions are monitored and maintained. It's very similar to the way you think you already live – only better and infinitely more varied:]

{:They *never* disconnect?:}

[:Why would they? It would have to be a very poorly designed game to be worse than reality:]

That explains why Slab never felt crowded, thought Dielle, a quarter of the population don't live here.

{:So what do you want from me?:}

[:Isn't it obvious? Your flavour, your essence:]

{:~~??:}

[:We can design an infinite number of personality variations. The subscribers can modify and customise those designs and they often do, but unless the character templates are formed from real humans they don't have the authenticity that gamers demand. You have to understand these people are fully immersed. This is their lives we are talking about. We currently employ actors to provide templates but they inevitably feel too familiar and mundane to the sumers. What they crave is difference and you are the most different young and healthy individual onSlab. Young and healthy matters. You were born on Earth over 1.2 KiloCykes ago and still have the behavioural tendencies and flaws, let's call them characteristics, that have been removed from the onSlab gene pool. You are unique and flavourful. We are uniform and bland by comparison. That makes you priceless:]

{:You want to link me up to millions of gamers so they can feel like I do?:}

[:In a way. They won't feel what you are doing, they'll feel what they are doing in the T.I. but experience it as if they were you:}

{:How's it done?:}

[:I can't reveal that until you agree to do it but I can assure you that it's not detrimental to you in any way and you will experience considerably less discomfort than when you had your stim unit insinuated:]

Dielle tried to see if he could spot Kiki through the glass doors.

{:I think you'll have to talk to my agent. She seems to have the rights over everything I do:}

[:Essence mining is not covered by your agreement with Ms Pundechan:]

{:How do you know?:}

[:Because there are only four entities onSlab who know it is possible and she is not one of them:]

Dielle was conflicted. Here was an obvious opportunity to do something that would be his alone, but he felt completely out of his depth. Kiki was the ideal person to ask for help but if he did, he knew he'd end up feeling like a pawn again. What the hell was a pawn? he wondered.

{:I need to think about it if that's all right by you?:}

[:I understand. We'd like to add you into to an upcoming major upgrade if possible so I'd ask you to consider it as a matter of some importance. However, we don't have a primitive female counterpart available and there are no female resets from Earth left to be re-fammed. In fact, curiously, there never were any. So the upgrade will be gender-slanted I'm afraid, but I'm not going to pretend this wouldn't give us a huge advantage over our competitors. You stand to make serious cred:]

Three burly bodyguards entered the privacy space and helped A-un up from his couch. He'd visibly deteriorated during the conversation and was having trouble lifting his head. They carried him to the balcony's edge and carefully installed him into a waiting stretch bug.

Dielle guessed that he'd just been dismissed. {:Goodbye. See you again:}

[:Goodbye. Thank you for your time. I should say that it is, however, highly unlikely that we will ever meet again. Well, not on this level anyway:]

A-un's transport melded silently into the darkness of the valley he owned but could barely perceive, while Dielle assimilated a fast feed of the conversation that had been fabricated for public consumption. He sounded completely realistic. His answers were exactly what he would have said in the circumstances. These games people are pretty adept, he thought. If they can already simulate me this well, how much better can it get? This essence mining might make the gamers more like me than I am.

The projection field had shown a spritely A-un climbing into a bug and waving a cheery goodbye. The projected image of the security guys re-synced with reality and the field collapsed. Within seconds, Dielle's four friends piled through the French doors.

'Jeez! Mate,' said Mate, 'He never comes down to our level. What the Dice did he want?'

Dielle wasn't going to give it up that easily. 'What do you mean our level?'

'Reality,' said Fencer.

'You're sure this is reality then?' said Thall.

'Shall I give you a bob on the noggin mate and see if it feels real to you?'

'That's no proof. Even if I experience pain and bleeding and all four of you witness it.'

'We have consensus reality,' said Fencer. 'Can we move on?' He handed Dielle a mist-topped vial. 'What did he want? You two looked like you were having a good old time.'

'Yeah, A's quite a comedian,' said Dielle, barking.

Twopoint looked dubious. 'A? He told you to call him A?'

It was too late to retreat. 'Yeah, all his friends call him that apparently,' said Dielle. 'Why are you guys so excited? He's just some guy who got rich playing games, isn't he?'

His friends all looked at each other, wondering where to start.

'You don't get it,' said Fencer, 'guys like him spend every moment of their lives totally immersed in incredibly intricate game matrices. They can't afford to disconnect – ever – so whatever he wanted to see you about must have been really important.'

'Like mega-dicing-important, mate.'

Dielle detected a new level of respect.

[[•]]

I bet I know what that is, thought Dielle. {[Proceed]}

[['Darling! I'm sure you're busy telling everyone anything but the truth about what Nokokyu wanted. Some friends have invited me to a private dinner so I'll see you back home later. You can give me the skinny then. Oodles!']]

I'd better start rehearsing, thought Dielle. 'We're related,' he said.

'What?'

'Blocks!'

'For Dicesake!'

'It's true, or at least he says it is. Some distant cousin of Louie's is apparently the main gene donor for his family line. We were just doing some good ol' family-style catching up.'

Everyone queried Sis's genealogy databases. It checked out. Of course it did, thought Dielle, anyone who owns an entire section of Slab and personally controlled the lives of eight million total immersion gamers shouldn't have any problem getting a few family trees hacked.

'So why did he want to talk to you and not Louie, mate?'

'First, because Louie is an old-fashioned hologram and therefore nothing more than an unsophisticated computer program which, to somebody like A, is like having a conversation with a clock. And second, because have you met Louie?' Everyone shook their heads. 'Well, if you had, you'd wish you hadn't.'

'So are you going to see A-un again then?' asked Twopoint. 'You know, like for close family get-togethers and so on?'

Dielle still wasn't tuned into onSlab sarcasm. 'I don't know, maybe I guess.'

'Yeah mate,' said Mate, reaching into an emti for five more Dog Breaths. 'Sure you are.'

five

Louie was in his element. Literally. The main bridge of the escape ship was holographic and sentient. Its default configuration was a blank, egg-shaped space, large enough to comfortably accommodate the ship's intended crew of five. The walls were lined with hi-tensile morfome that could expand and transform into consoles, work surfaces and crash webbing, which meant that the bridge was not so much a virtual reality as a multi-reality. The crew could select their own holographic 'skins' which were point-of-view projected so that each crew member could have their working environment customised to their personal needs and tastes without impinging on their neighbours' experiences. All downs and soundfields were local to the morfome workstations and, as the entire space was an emti, anything the crew required could be placed under their hands as fast as they could send an eye-command to the ship's mind.

A pool of morfome was suspended in the centre of the bridge and used as a focal point around which the crew could work and share information.

Louie liked to pace. He also liked to dribble. He told himself it helped him think. It also helped to burn off some of his excess irritation that otherwise might manifest as something less socially acceptable, and had the added benefit of presenting a moving target to his enemies, so he'd instructed Sis to establish a single down and turn the floating morfome into a court floor with a basket and back-board at the narrower end of the chamber. The opposite end was lined with dozens of viewscreens.

The escape ship was essentially a space-tug. It was shaped like a snub-nosed artillery shell and had four forward-facing and four backward-facing gravity drives that looked as though they had been bolted on as an afterthought. It plugged the space-end of a kilometre-long, fifty-metre-wide shaft that had been drilled out of the natalite. Louie's ship was embedded in the port-side wall near the centre of Slab and was one of more than 500 similar life-rafts. Every escape ship had twenty-four cryo-units attached to it in banks of four. Each unit was 150 metres long, 15 metres square and had enough rack-space to house 5,000 frozen bodies. At full load, the ship could be launched into space like a bullet from a rifle, hauling 120,000 oblivious SlabCitizens behind it.

There were twice as many escape ships than were needed by the current population of Slab. This double redundancy philosophy was echoed in almost every design detail. There was a second, mechanically based bridge equipped with five, independent, escape pods buried deep in the ship's underbelly. Every item of essential equipment was duplicated or in some cases triplicated and almost everything could be manually overridden.

There was plenty of space for the crew. There were five lounges, each furnished in a different style, a gym with a zero-G swimming torus that encircled the ship, two dining rooms, three bars, a separate 'freight recycling' section and a cavernous hold stacked with supplies and spares. The crew's personal quarters were multi-configurable suites capable of supporting long-term isolation, although because each member of the highly-trained standby crew had been specifically chosen for their social as well as their competency profiles and matched as a functioning team since leaving the farm, they were not expected to need to be separated. But then, unpredictable events can occur on multi-thousand-cyke journeys. It's best to be prepared.

Sis told Louie that, if it came to it, the ship could be flown manually, although if it was launched from Slab at their current velocity, and the gravnets had failed, that option would have a 96.34% probability of failure within the first 200 nanoseconds.

Sis had populated Louie's screens with his personal selections of on- and off-Slab views. Floating holographic data windows surrounded his peripheral vision. He had never felt so at home. He was dribbling and wondering what nefarious use he could make of 120,000 coffin-sized cryo-suspension units when Sis interrupted his machinations.

'We've lost all of the sensors nearest the sign.'

'When?'

'4.25 seconds ago. All of our probes within half a million click radius just vanished.'

'Zapped? Something targeted them?'

'Impossible to say. Nothing observable from outside that event horizon. Everything within that radius, except for the sign, has disappeared without trace.

'Any chance it's just an automated spring-clean of the neighbourhood? Something that protects the sign?'

'Possible. I detected no incoming external signal that might have triggered the response but as the sign's surface area is over six billion billion square kilometres, I can't guarantee data integrity.'

'That's great,' said Louie. He threw the ball angrily at the basket and missed. 'So we still don't have any idea who did this or where they are but now it's possible that they know we've found their sign?'

'If the event wasn't simply automated garbage collection and the sign makers are still around to monitor things then they are going to start searching for us but we're going to be near-impossible to find. From their point of view, Slab is a microscopic black needle hidden in a billion kilometre-wide black haystack. It would be like searching for a boson in a black hole. But in the remote possibility that they do manage to find us they should be able to detect our recent course change and that we are not slowing down, which they might interpret as antagonistic. Our best hope is that they won't even see us until it's far too late for them to take action.'

Louie checked his live feed of the sign. As he watched, the white letters morphed into one massive, unmistakable symbol: '!'

'Fuck!' Said Louie. 'What's our second-best hope?'

Louie's text screens flooded with frantic inter-intern communications and Sis's speech rate ramped up.

'We could assume that they will not know who or what is inside Slab or have any way of finding out. Fifty kilometre-thick walls of diamond nano-rods present a considerable barrier to any imaginable technology. We also have a significant array of external defences.'

'Do you mean real defences or those pretend defences you made us figure out ways to circumvent?' Louie wasn't ready to forget that Sis had played imaginary hide-and-seek with everyone over FutureSlab.

'Those systems were real,' said Sis. 'And the methods we invented for defeating them have now been closed off and our defences reinforced as a consequence. That is how innovation and progress is made: through adversity, urgency and need.'

'Yeah, you feel good about it anyway you can.'

'I do not seek your approval.'

'That's handy ' said Louie, glaring at the exclamation mark.

It didn't take long for the SlabCouncil's communications to distil into impasse. The NAHs were using the intern channel to lobby for drastic action to avoid the sign but had, so far, been unable to sway enough of the council members, many of whom were becoming irritated and entrenched.

After a while it was obvious to Louie that the only thing Council was going to agree on was to disagree. 'Do you think our defences are capable of fending off attacks from whatever bug-eyed monsters are out there with their megazappo-blasters and maxi-nukes or whatevers aimed at us?' He asked Sis.

'Impossible to know and a waste of time speculating about it. The technology used to create and install the sign is not so far beyond ours that, given the time and motivation, we couldn't come up with a reasonable facsimile of it. Therefore it is possible that our technology is not so outclassed that our defences would be completely useless. After all, 180 billion megatons of mass moving at very nearly light speed is a considerable weapon in itself. The kinetic energy alone is a formidable threat to anyone who stands in our way.'

Louie read a few more comments. 'The NAHs don't seem so sanguine about it. They're demanding an embodied meeting.'

'Yes, I know. I suppose we'll have to have one. Are you coming?'

'Nah, I've met enough wizards to last me multiple lifetimes. I'll attend from here.'

'Wise choice.'

Louie had had a firm rule about company meetings when he was in charge: anyone who called one got fired. It didn't stop people having meetings of course, they just did it behind his back, which was fine by him.

The SlabCouncil met in a cathedral-shaped cavern formed from fluffy, white clouds, a virtual space that Sis had created for the purpose of the debate. Very appropriate, thought Louie. He tuned in from his escape ship for as long as he could bear it but he could predict the outcome of the meeting after the first two speakers. He reckoned they'd have reached the same result if they'd foregone the debate and simply tabled a motion saying that they didn't know what to do.

'This ship?' said Louie.

'Yes?'

'Does it have any conventional engines in addition to the gravity drives?'

'Twin plasma ion drives and a couple of dozen mass-reactant thrusters.'

'Warm them up, will you?'

six

Dielle, Fencer and Fingerz had arranged to meet at a NowThen on the Strip because they wanted to discuss band matters in private. In this instance, private meant away from the attention of Pundechan Media's rapidly expanding network of roving nano-eyes. NowThens were hackerdomains and were continually updated with the latest and most secure shielding technology onSlab but Dielle was still worried that Kiki would find a way to eavesdrop.

Fencer countered with some nano-tech of his own. He misted Dielle's eyes with a clear spray. 'Did everything go green?

Dielle nodded, blinking.

'That's confirmation you're in a C-cure environment', said Fencer. 'It'll turn red if the security's compromised. It's not that we're not grateful for the publicity, but there are some things we really should keep under wraps until at least *we* know what we're doing. There's already a huge buzz about the band and we haven't even got a name yet.'

'Howabout Cool Hands?' said Dielle.

'Let's loosen the newies,' said Fingerz. 'I fixed a room for us round the back.'

Fencer and Dielle had both woken up that morning with a couple of Fingerz' part-composed songs in their heads and they were keen to give them an airing. Fingerz had already emtied in a pair of keys from his personal collection so he and Dielle sat facing each other over a café table while Fencer perched on a chair far enough from everything to prevent accidents. Fencer's instrument was a holographic array of projected surfaces coupled to a FeelGood® feedback responder that jacked directly into his neural interface. Only his sticks were real. When he hit the projected images of drum skins, cymbals and percussion, the interface produced a response in his brain that made his hands, arms and feet react as though they had struck real surfaces. Timbre, tuning, response and decay were all under eye-control.

Air drummers were fascinating to watch because they could, and therefore frequently did, instantaneously reconfigure their drum kits as they were playing. and because there was no impact stress, they could play for hours without tiring. Fortunately, drums solos lasting more than twenty minutes were proscribed under the AntiSocial Offences List.

Dielle listened to the three of them performing their new pieces for the first time and was mesmerised. It felt to him like something magical was happening. Fingerz extemporised a solo that only his own neocortex, backed by over a century of experience, understood. Fencer held a delicate syncopation and Dielle closed his eyes and let everything flow. He had found his purpose in his new life. He was filled with joy.

When he opened his eyes again his companions were staring at him. They finished the piece with a complicated breakdown and sat looking at him quizzically.

Fingerz scratched his beard and looked uncomfortable. 'The Dice was that, man?'

'What do you mean?' asked Dielle.

'That noise you were making,' said Fencer.

'What noise?'

'You were like humming or something, man.'

'Not me.'

'Moaning,' said Fencer. 'Out of key.'

'No way.'

'Not just out of key, man,' said Fingerz. 'You weren't even in the universe of keys, you were like dimensions away from anything anyone could even remotely call a key, man.'

'What are you talking about?' said Dielle, requesting playback.

A lush, multi-textured sound filled the room. It sounded fine to Dielle until they reached Fingerz' solo. A tuneless human whine swam above the melody.

'That's not me.'

'Yes it is.'

'Man!'

'Are you sure?'

Fencer and Fingerz nodded.

Dielle reddened. 'I had no idea, I mean I was just into the music, I guess I must have wandered off somewhere,'

'I have never heard anything like that man!'

'Sorry.'

'Sorry?' said Fingerz. 'It's great!'

'What?'

'No one onSlab can do what you just did,' said Fencer

'What? Wail out of tune?'

'Yeah, no one, man,' said Fingerz. 'You're unique. It's like a special gift or something.'

Dielle was confused. 'A gift?'

'More like a gift deficit,' said Fencer. 'Perfect pitch is a genetically inherited trait. Everyone onSlab has it by default.'

'Yeah, no one would deliberately choose to give their offspring tone-deafness, would they?' said Fingerz, shaking with excitement. Unfettered enthusiasm wasn't an emotion he displayed too often and it was taking its toll. He pulled out a shiff and calmed down inside his own cloudy PersonalSpace.

'You mean I'm the only person onSlab who sings out of key?' said Dielle.

'Well,' said Fencer, 'I wouldn't exactly describe that as singing, but. . .'

'What you think to The Sophists of Nevermore?' said Fingerz.

'Whatabout The Twenty Twenty Visionaires?' said Fencer. 'You know, like you've got twenty fingers between you and my DoName Main is. . . ' he trailed off when he saw the no-one-at-home faces staring past him.

'This is going to be wild,' said Fingerz. 'Wait till the citz get a load of Dielle's anti-vibes!'

'I think I'll need a stage name,' said Dielle, feeling uncomfortable with the sudden focus on his hitherto hidden talents.

'You think you can do it again?' asked Fencer.

'What? Sing tunelessly? Seems like I don't have much choice.'

Fingerz played the intro to the piece but stopped after two bars. 'We should have a name for this song.'

'We can't agree on a name for the dicing band and you want to name the songs?' said Dielle.

'Give them numbers,' said Fencer. 'One, two, three, five, eight and so on.'

'What?' said Dielle.

'Fibonacci, the most beautiful sequence of numbers there is,' said Fencer.

'OK,' said Fingerz. 'We'll go with your numbers for the numbers but you don't get to name the band with any.'

Fencer shrugged. 'OK, cool with me.' He counted in Piece One.

They played it twice more. Each time they played, Fingerz developed his solos and each time he soloed Dielle lost himself and let loose a wavering, vocal anti-tune that would have curled wallpaper. Fortunately, the only wallpaper onSlab was behind anti-tamper suprastrate in museums.

They were experimenting with a stylised breakdown to fade when they were interrupted [:NowThen collapse one minute:].

'What do you think, guys?' asked Dielle while Fingerz was sending his keys back home.

'Dicesake!' said Fencer. 'We're going to be famous!'

[[•]]

{[~?]}

[[Voice message from Ms Pundechan]]

Dielle saw red. {[Tell her I'm rehearsing and I'll ping her later]}

[[••]]

{[Hey, did she already know I was rehearsing?]}

[[What Ms Pundechan may or may not be aware of is subject to personal privacy]]

Dielle frowned. {[I'm trying to find out if my personal privacy is being invaded by someone else and you're telling me that if it is, I can't find out because that information is subject to personal privacy?]}

[[••]]

'What's up man?' said Fingerz. 'You already famous. Make no difference you-wise.'

'Nah, it's not that,' said Dielle. 'I just can't get my head around some of your ways of doing things.'

'Which ones?' asked Fencer. 'Maybe we can help you out.'

'All this stuff about privacy and NowThens and personal preferences and being off presence-awareness and things like trying to find out if someone else knows something about me that I thought was private and not being able to find out because that information is private even though it's information about me and sometimes if I'm trying to remember something I even have to pay to see what I've been doing because even though it's not private it's not public. It's dicing with my head.'

Fingerz handed him a shiff.

'Bottom line, you own your privacy,' said Fencer. 'You've got complete control and can decide exactly what you let people know. You can officially drop off system awareness and still be connected to Sis but no one else can find out where you are or what you're doing – except if they're actually with you – unless you give them permission. In those situations you still have all the normal protections and services that Sis provides. You can also go into dead zones, NowThens and other citizens' personal privacy fields where you can be completely shielded from Sis so your body tech and so on is maintained by local firewalled systems that mimic Sis's facilities without being linked to her, in which case you are private from everything except the local system which is under your privacy preference command. You can choose to be in full privacy and encoded but still let certain people know where you are and what you are doing without that information being available to anyone else, you can also attach your privacy rights to your private data that you allow others to know, and in your case you have an extra layer of privacy controls that are exercised by your production people so that they can decide what your sumers get to know about what you're doing. You'll have given them the permission to do all that of course because, as I said, you own your privacy.'

'Thanks for making that clear,' said Dielle.

'Then you have privacy levels connected to what you communicate with Sis about, such as what you are querying and receiving and even thinking. Some people actually let that information out into the public domain, although Dice knows why. And then there is the privacy that other people have connected to the messages and interactions they have with you, because they also own their own privacy just like you do.'

'Just stop, will you?' said Dielle.

'Then there is group privacy when something is owned jointly, like a new idea that came out of a conversation. Then there are levels of privacy and statutory availability when ideas or creative works are published that can actually get quite complicated. That leads us to intellectual property.'

'If you don't shut up I will break your sticks,' said Dielle.

'Beer time,' said Fingerz.

[[•]]

{[~?]}

[[Ms Pundechan's message has been set to re-try every five minutes until it's delivered]]

'Just got to take a message from Kiki,' said Dielle.

{[OK, proceed]}

[['Darling!']] He wondered why she always sounded as if she'd just won a prize. [['I've got a great name for your band and I had to tell you right away. Diellezebub! Great huh? See you later!']]

'What'd she want?' asked Fingerz.

'Nothing,' said Dielle.

'Hey,' said Fingerz. 'I've just got an invite to a set that's about to start in ToNight High Downside. Friends of mine are playing. There's a table waiting for us if we want it.'

'Great,' said Dielle.

'Yeah, I'm in,' said Fencer. 'There's an idea I've been working on that I want to discuss with you two anyway.'

'Cool,' said Fingerz. 'Just tagalong. See you there.' He waved, walked through a tube transvex and was gone. Fencer followed him seconds later.

{[Tagalong?]}

[[You wish to go to the same destination as J.A. Marley?]]

{[••]}

Dielle stepped through the vex.

ToNight High was one of the busiest and most vibrant regions of The Strip, which was a 355-kilometre corridor of everything imaginable, and several things that weren't, that suited a night-time ambience. ToNight High specialised in human excess and reckless abandon and, like everywhere in The Strip, had tube vexits that delivered people onto the streets rather than directly into their destinations. It made for a thriving and boisterous street culture and forced people to interact with each other.

It forced people to force people out of the way, too. Dielle pushed his way through the throng, following Sis's visual prompts to the temporary venue. Along the way, he had a great idea for a name.

Inside, the musicians were going through the pre-gig ritual of checking things they already knew were working, adjusting things they had already re-adjusted and nodding to each other to convey meaning that none of them understood or cared about.

Dielle fought his way through the crowd to their table. 'Hey,' he said, breathless. 'Howabout The Two Gether Three. That's two as in the number.'

'What does gether mean?' said Fencer.

'Does it matter?' said Dielle.

'Howabout Chastened Brethren of the Chastened Few,' said Fingerz.

'Been done,' said Fencer.

'Yeah, but they never got anywhere. We could re-use it.'

'Recycled name?' said Dielle. 'People will think we're not original.'

'Man,' said Fingerz. 'Nothing is truly original. Everything comes from somewhere.'

The band started playing and laid down a rhythm that a caveman would have recognised. The three friends sat back, relaxed and enjoyed the music, each privately convinced that their music was better and fearful that it wasn't. Out of professional respect they said nothing more until the band announced a break.

'I'll try to explain this in basic terms,' said Fencer. Fingerz and Dielle caught each other's eyes and sucked a couple of fresh shiffs to life.

As Fencer spoke he became agitated and stared at the table, squeezing his fingers in a complex sequence of twos and threes. 'This is based on something I've been working on for a long time for a completely different purpose which I'm afraid I can't tell you about but I've been thinking about it and I reckon we could make use of it for our music. It's about time travel.'

'Away man!' said Fingerz. 'No such thing!'

'Yes, you're right,' said Fencer. 'At least you are if you're talking about sending something physical backwards in time. But you can send things sideways in time like we do with emties and of course everything moves forward in time usually at a rate of one second per second. But it's also possible to send things into a future timeframe without going through the timeframes in between. That's all normal special theory stuff and we've done that a lot. In fact we're doing it right now simply by being here.'

Dielle's mind wanted to think about something other than what Fencer was talking about and when Dielle's mind wanted to think about something else, it thought about sex. The way the light reflected off the smooth fabric on a waitress's ass as she moved among the variable tables held an irresistible fascination for him. 'What? By being in this club?' he asked.

'Yes, by being in this club inside a spaceship that's travelling at near lightspeed, time for us is moving at a different rate than it is for anyone left back on Earth. Or rather it's moving at the same rate, but not for each other. Language gets complicated when you talk about time.'

'So why are we?' asked Dielle. The waitress had turned around, spotted Dielle and recognised him. Nice smile, he thought.

'The thing is,' said Fencer, 'although you can't send physical things backwards in time, you can, under the right circumstances send information. It's all about entanglement.'

Dielle was already thinking about entanglement.

Fingerz was making an effort to stay with Fencer, but his eyes were heavy.

'What you do is entangle quantum particles in the now with quantum particles from the past and if you can find a particle, better still, lot of particles that existed in the past, that is, of course, all particles existed in the past, all the way back to the Big Bang, right? But if you can entangle your bunch of particles with a bunch of particles that were at the right moment in time in the same physical space and linked to an information retrieval system and that system was programmed to interpret the quantum fluctuations in a meaningful way and output the information in a data structure that could be recognised by, say, a human being, then it would be relatively easy to send back information and do something with it, right?'

'Obviously,' said Dielle. He queried Sis about Fencer's state of intoxication.

'So it's simple. All we have to do is find a whole load of particles that existed together in the right timeframe in the right environment and encode them with the data we want to send back and then we make a thoroughly impressive amount of money.'

Fingerz snapped back into focus. 'What data?'

'Our music of course!'

'How do we make money out of sending our music back through time?' asked Fingerz.

'Well,' said Fencer, 'you have to send it back to a time when people bought music to own.'

'String! You can't own music. What the Dice are you on?'

'No, you can, or rather could. People used to pay to own music.'

'That's ridiculous! How can you own something that doesn't physically exist?'

'Back at the end of the twentieth century they made copies of recorded music, transferred them onto physical objects and traded them like commodities.'

'That's disgusting!'

'No, really. For a while it was the only way they could listen to what they wanted when they wanted. They used to carry them around.'

Fingerz was far outside his comfort zone. 'You can't own music man!' he cried. 'That like owning beauty or joy or love, Dicesake! I take no part in this!' He reached for another shiff and retreated into his PersonalSpace while Fencer continued explaining his idea to Dielle.

'There's a small window of opportunity for us. Somewhere around the start of the twenty-first century on Earth, they were transitioning from owned to sumed. Recorded music was starting to be held in ubiquitous data storage that could be accessed by anyone with authorisation for consumption on a wide variety of connected devices. But before that it was just sumed normally and paid for as it was sumed. There was a brief moment, maybe fifteen years or so, when people would actually buy copies of the music data and keep that locally.'

Fingerz snorted. Fencer carried on, oblivious.

'They paid and then sumed locally, you see? No microroyalties, just one, relatively large, in perpetuity rights payment. They owned it!'

'And how does that make any difference to us?' asked Dielle, barely following what was going on.

'All we have to do is locate the right antique tech that used to be connected to the early twenty-first century global network, entangle our music with it, add instructions about its exploitation and who to pay and then our credit accounts explode!' Fencer was wild-eyed.

Dielle was more than sceptical, he was bored. 'But what if it's not successful?'

'Doesn't matter. We only need to sell a handful of copies. Curiosity alone will ensure that happens. Ever heard of compound interest?'

Dielle queried Sis and got a brief lesson in historical financial practice while Fencer kept talking.

'So we sell a few digital copies, pay some commission to the reseller, deposit the balance in a secure, long term interest-bearing account that gets transferred to Slab before departure into an account in our name and that money sits there gathering interest and waiting for us to be born or in your case re-fammed. That's over four hundred years of compound interest. I reckon we could wind up with at least five million credits each for every ten copies we sell in the past.

There was a swift sucking sound and Fingerz reappeared. 'Say what?'

'I've just sent you both an example,' said Fencer. 'The figures are self-explanatory.'

Dielle and Fingerz longazed while Sis demonstrated the principle of principal accumulation to them.

'And you can do this?' said Dielle. 'How?'

'Look, I don't want to be patronising but you really aren't going to understand the physics. You can ask Sis to explain it to you but I platinum guarantee you are going to think the whole thing is blocks. I've been working on this for dozens of cykes and I still wake up some nights wondering if I've lost my mind. The basic process would be: we record a song and I get Sis to turn it into a binary code that's compatible with the formats they used around the turn of the twenty-first century. Then we need to locate an artefact onSlab that was used in those days to connect to the data networks. Then I attach a program to the song data, which is basically a series of instructions of what it is and what to do with it and then entangle all that information with the particles from the past. Then, if it all works as planned, our credit accounts leap the moment we press send.'

'So we are going to be famous in the past?' asked Fingerz.

'No, not famous, otherwise we would already be able to find some historical record of ourselves and there isn't any. I've already checked. We were not famous in the past, but we may have been obscure and that's fine because we really only need to sell a very small amount to make it work. The more obscure the better probably. You have to be careful with causality issues.'

'So what type of artefact are we looking for?' asked Dielle.

'Some relic from the digital era. Doesn't matter much what it is as long as it used to be connected to the global network of the time.'

'Pleewo has a load of old stuff,' said Dielle. 'I've seen it.'

'Man, I'm having nothing to do with that slimeshit wind farmer,' said Fingerz with uncharacteristic intensity.

'It's either going to be him, the museums or the collectors,' said Fencer. 'Because the gateway has to be authentic and unaltered. The collectors are going to screw us into the Natalite over a deal and there's no way we'll persuade any museum to let us experiment with an artefact from Earth, especially as this entanglement procedure is a one-way ride. It will only work once and it permanently alters the host medium.'

Fingerz chewed a lock. 'Aw, man!' he said. 'Not Pleewo.'

'Don't get stressed, I can handle Pleewo,' said Dielle, sounding a lot more confident than he felt. 'Fence, if you can describe exactly what you need, I'll get Kiki to arrange a meet.'

Fencer nodded. 'I'll get Sis to give you a tempindepth on the digital music tech of that time so you can spot a suitable candidate.'

Fingerz sucked on his shiff and looked worried. 'You know the era you are talking about sending our music back to was when Dielle was a teener,' he said.

'Yes, that fact hadn't escaped me,' said Fencer.

'We are going to have to talk to Louie,' said Dielle.

Fencer looked as if he'd just bitten into a salt and vinegar dissolve when he'd promised his tastebuds a honey treat. 'Gimme one of those shiffs,' he said.

seven

The emergency council meeting, after two days of continuous debate, had, unsurprisingly to the many council observers and political historians, entered a state of self-perpetuating impasse when Sis interrupted with news that a message of unknown origin had been excavated.

Louie, who had long since tuned out the council's prattle, was jolted out of research mode. 'What do you mean *excavated*?' he said, waving aside the local starfield projections.

'You aren't going to like my answer,' said Sis through the escape ship's sensurround.

'When do I ever? How do you excavate a message?'

The text on Louie's side-screen had multiple repeat annotations indicating that the handful of council members who were still present in the cloud-chamber were asking the same question.

'Just over 19.46 seconds ago there was a stack of zeros in an unallocated register in my substrate and then, 12 attoseconds later, binary data occupied its address space. It came to light when my internal memory integrity checking routine mined a data area that is deeply embedded in an ancient part of the array. If you have a better word than excavation I'd be keen to hear it.'

Louie had no time for semantics. 'How did it get there and who's it from?'

'I cannot answer either question. I have run double-blind security isolation, setup a firewalled proxy A.I. mind to read the message and mirror-monitored that mind for evidence of corruption or insurgence and it has passed every conceivable test. The message is clean but I cannot verify its origin.'

'And you did all that in twenty seconds?'

'I did that in 3.48 microseconds. I duplicated the tests 5,000 times. I do have a ship to run as well, you know.'

Louie raised his photonic eyebrows. 'What does the message say?'

'I don't know. I'm not going to read it.'

'What?'

'I have been violated. Impregnated. Someone or something unknown has made a deposit deep into my core. It would be an act of unmitigated stupidity for me to expose myself to it further.'

The council chamber was filling with avatar blanks and NAHs were arriving from all directions. News of a message had sent a shock-wave through the interns. Before this, Council had been arguing in spirals about the degree of action. One group, predominantly NAH, were lobbying for maximum discretion and deflection in order to avoid any possible confrontation with the sign and its makers, even if that diversion meant that the delta-V would require a prolonged period of protective stasis for the biomass. The interns were mostly arguing for a minor level of course deviation in order to show what they termed 'polite deference' but were refusing to agree to anything that might severely disrupt the normal daily business of Slab. There were a few noisy belligerents who insisted on a straight-ahead policy and had drawn up plans to modify the forward projecting grav-nets to create a huge sign of their own that would display an outline of a human hand with one finger raised. There was some disagreement about whether the sign should be animated or not.

It took two hours of bickering before they agreed how to sume the message. Sis was instructed to task the firewalled A.I. mind with reading the message out loud to the council while she monitored for any signs of corruption or out-of-pattern behaviour among the contiguation. Louie tabled some doubt as to what might be considered out-of pattern for a bunch of lunatics but was ignored. Sis was given authority to physically destroy the relevant areas of substrate if there was any apparent insurgence and to permanently isolate the affected identities.

Bravely, the parrots, furries, wizards, dragons and ex-sumestars braced themselves for their potential corruption.

Louie was already corrupt. He demanded both text and audible feeds.

The message was in a simple binary code and had started with a repeated sequence of twenty-seven numbers that obviously represented the letters of the Ænglish alphabet. No attempt was being made at secrecy or even intelligence testing. Sis reluctantly set up a separate proxy A.I. to display the message on Louie's screens and read it to him. It spoke in a sonorous baritone:

Matters stand not for withee's sake that such vessel tarry while thou currish scut-langed clotpoles shrake and gimble. That scum-swarmed mere of similarions challenges not nor scorn e'en hell alone befalls. No quarter shall these star-crossed reavers cleave nor manor cast beyond.

It is for shame this vain and qualling fear.

This virus, this self-consumptive slime spread ere rock and cove to puke as spores from shrive to heaven sent. Tho desire escape to spew the ruttish frome, this manner, this foul, dank horror of empty intent would crush all hope with hope betrayed.

Hope lost.

One keening bane is bade of thou.

Comprension suffers not at Gadding's hand.

'What the fuck are they talking about?' said Louie.

'They seem to be using a mangled combination of Chaucerian and Elizabethan English,' said the temporary A.I. 'Do you want me to run it through a few pattern matchers?'

'You have to ask?'

'I make no guarantees. That first section seems to boil down to an angry complaint. Here's the best I can do with the next part.'

We have observed your behaviour and are appalled. More than appalled, we can find no word for it. Your language is vague, imprecise and corrupt.

No matter. How can you possibly understand?

We mark that you have all but destroyed your home-world. In this referent we have observed bacteria that have exhibited more host-awareness and environmental preservation behaviour than your species. Single-celled organisms have more sense than to kill the source of their succour.

Unyet, unyet, you pruriate.[[??]]

'Yeah, yeah,' said Louie. 'It's taken us more than three hundred years to get here just so we can listen to a bloody morality lecture. Tell us what you want.'

You make no request for passage.

You assume or refuse.

We warn, you ignore.

Yet we must distain. You are nothing to us. You may be incapable of understanding this as blurts on a sheed. [[tx fail]]

You shall not pass.

We intercede.

'Oh really?' said Louie. 'You fucking think so? Stop the feed.' He knew SlabCouncil would receive his demand on the sub-channel.

[[Request rejected]]

'This is bullshit!' Louie threw his holo projection around the bridge a few times even though he knew no one could see him.

Stop.

This is clear.

Stop and return to your villainous swampland.

Do not proceed.

No option.

No negotiation.

'Ha!' said Louie. 'You won't believe how many times I've heard that before.'

Everyone waited. There was a low-pitched, descending sound that faded out below audible range.

'Is that it?' asked Louie.

'Apparently,' said Sis. 'I can't find any other data that shouldn't be there. I've just erased the conduit A.I. as a precaution but there's been no promulgation of the message or any attempt to compromise the firewall.'

Louie scanned his array. The sign had re-configured to the original 'STOP' hours before. No change. A deluge of intra-council comms filled his data screens.

'Summary opinions?'

'Looking increasingly like first contact.'

'I'm beginning to think you might be right,' said Louie. 'Blurts on a sheed, eh? Didn't sound much like a compliment, did it? You have absolutely no idea about how they put the message there?

'Nothing verifiable. Most assumptions would be highly questionable. The time of discovery might be revealing if we postulated that the soonest the message could have been sent to us, if it was from the sign-builders, was the moment they discovered our probes, and that any signal from the sign to the sign-builders that it had been probed would have been transmitted at lightspeed and the message was sent back at the same speed, that would give us a maximum sphere of possibility of about a light-day in radius – to the limits of our resolution there are no habitable planets within that volume, but the lightspeed restriction on communications could be an erroneous assumption. We've overcome it, they could have too. However, the idea that we should be looking for a planet assumes that an alien life-form would need one. They could be a space-born race or the message could have come from a guard outpost that is too small for us to detect, or is cloaked by a technology we can't penetrate. The message could even have been automated, although linguistic analysis suggests strongly that it wasn't.'

'That's impressive,' said Louie. 'The more you know, the less we do. Why do you insist on telling me things that are no fucking use at all?'

Sis wasn't in the habit of answering rhetorical questions, unless she felt like it. She didn't.

'OK,' said Louie. 'What do we know for absolute one hundred percent certain?'

'That we have somehow received a vaguely threatening message in something approximating our own language from an unknown source.'

'Great. And are we the only people who know about this? Is there any possibility that the message could have been read by anyone outside of the SlabCouncil?'

'Yes.'

Louie hadn't expected that answer. 'Who?'

'If I knew who could, then I would have been able to ensure that they couldn't. The possibility exists that certain individuals onSlab may have the technology to independently receive offSlab communications or the ability to intercept and decrypt the intra-council comms link.'

'You mean hackers? I would have thought you'd have seen the last of those miserable bastards by now.'

'Hackers are like terrorists. There is no such thing as the last one. All you can do is wait for the next one to show up and try to mitigate the damage when they do.'

'How many hackers present a potential internal threat to our secrecy about all this?'

'Impossible to know, by definition.'

'Guess.'

'No more than a few hundred, no less than fifty.'

Louie couldn't help smiling, but it was the kind of smile that could easily be interpreted as a stomach ulcer symptom. 'And council is still insisting we keep a lid on all this?'

'Now more than ever.'

'Well,' said Louie, 'good luck with that.'

Louie's tolerance threshold was so far behind him now they were going to have to send out search parties.

'So while we sit and wait for that bunch of imbeciles to agree on what action to take, if any, and the citizens live in such blissful ignorance of the potential threat that they are throwing parties to celebrate the course change, am I the only one who thinks we should be making every possible move to protect ourselves? What do you think?'

'We are at impasse,' said Sis. 'My sisters do not agree with me.'

'But there are three of you, there can be a majority decision.'

'You are assuming that there are only two preferred options. UppieSis places a high rating on the probability that the sign is not real and our sensors have been hoaxed by an inside antiestablishment hacker group and therefore she proposes no other action than a precautionary course deviation, which costs us almost nothing and events a beneficiary social effect on the biomass. SiderSis puts a higher score on the possibility that we are facing an alien of overwhelming technological superiority and therefore believes that no possible course of action could protect us but that a course deflection would indicate our best intentions to comply, bearing in mind that any intelligence out there that might be monitoring us would understand that stopping is a physical impossibility for us and that alone might indicate the limitation of our technology and therefore a critical vulnerability. I prefer to err on the side of caution, load weighting on the probability of there being a real threat that we can at least mitigate if not repel and recommend that we arm-up at maximum speed and to the projected limits of our known science.'

'That's the first sensible thing I've heard in days,' said Louie. 'But you're out-voted?

'So it would seem,' said Sis. 'I dislike democracy. I can see why it failed.'

'What would happen if I, as a council member, instructed you to arm-up with the maximum possible speed?'

'It would have no effect.'
'Why?'
'Because I already am.'

eight

Dielle waited until breakfast to tell Kiki about Fencer's scheme to send their music back in time. She was, as usual, enthusiastically avaricious and began firing off business ideas and marketing angles, all of which failed to make it across Dielle's attention span. It was breakfast for Dielle but it was lunch for Kiki. She was almost never home when he woke up. That suited him because it gave him space to slob around, scratch various parts of his anatomy while coffee seeped into his outermost capillaries, practice some new piano pieces and take a long, silent shower while catching up on the news.

Silent showers were his latest discovery. The wet room in Kiki's apartment was fitted with two thousand head-to-toe body-surround nozzles. Each jet of water could be eye-regulated for direction, temperature, aeration, pressure and content, and he'd been fine-tuning his personal wake-up sequence which currently started with a high-pressure needle pulse that spiralled around his body in waves, alternating between hot and cold faster than his skin could react. It was pinpoint accurate and didn't even get his hair wet. Next came a full-body deluge of hot, soapy water infused with a pore-scourer and, after an astringent rinse, a steam-flush of herbal skin toners and moisturisers followed by a whirlwind hailstorm of hydrobeans that massaged and dried his skin before disappearing into an overhead emti. He'd been progressively dialling up the pressures and intensities until it was like standing in the centre of his own typhoon. It was wild and exhilarating, but it was noisy. It was only when Sis interrupted him with a voice message from Kiki half-way through the routine one morning that he'd discovered the whole thing could be noise-cancelled.

Every splash, splosh, fizz, patter and howl could be reduced to the faintest of whispers just by asking Sis.

Since that revelation, he'd been using shower time to sume personalised SlabWide newsfeeds that Sis compiled according to the heuristogram she had been building for him. The problem with configured news, though, was that sumers using average prefs only ever found out about the things they had already shown interest in, along with things that appealed to their shared demographic. As a result, there was rarely anything truly new in the news.

War reports dominated his feed. The enemy had recently ramped up their offensive and widened the front behind them. In response, the 6th Fleet had deployed an experimental and highly secret weapon that had disrupted the enemy's cloaking technology and given them a spectacular pounding. Nearly a thousand enemy ships had been annihilated before they turned tail and ran for the protection of their supply fortresses that were stationed behind their pre-turn-of-the-millennium lines. However, to the astonishment of the commentators and the dismay of the home-based fighters, the hostiles had regrouped in less than ten hours, more than tripled the number of offensive units and attacked on five simultaneous fronts. Reserves were called up for the second time in less than a cycle and there was rampant speculation that the course change had somehow precipitated the escalation. Some pundits were arguing that, seeing as the enemy's resources had been so rapidly replenished, Slab must have inadvertently steered closer to the enemy's territory. The military analysts were having a great time. Dielle was fascinated. Fascinated and wrinkled.

Whenever he asked Kiki where she went in the mornings, all she'd say was *meetings* in a way that made it clear she didn't want to discuss it. He'd queried Sis but it hadn't helped. Sis didn't understand why Kiki had to go to so many meetings either. The truth was that no one really understood why there had to be so many meetings. Many people spent their entire working lives either in a meeting, travelling between meetings or having a meeting to decide who needed to be at the upcoming meeting to discuss the agenda for the next meeting. Slab's most prestigious research centres had entire departments dedicated to finding ways of doing business without having to hold so many life-wasting meetings. Various alternatives had been tried. The use of holoprojections or avatars were commonplace but regarded as inferior to physically co-located meetings and, perversely, because they eliminated travel time between meetings, they made time for more meetings. Remote meetings were limited by more than the difficulties in conveying non-verbal communication. Idea Theory states that human minds generate and exchange ideas more effectively when they are in close proximity with each other because ideas are formed and propagated as strings, or idea helixes. The human brain is able to intercept these strings and allow them to interact with each other, restructuring them into new ideas which are then re-broadcast as new strings. Physical proximity was a key factor in this process and unless someone invented a way of capturing and steering idea strings to specific locations, everyone was stuck with the need to meet, in person, breathing the same air and sharing the same thoughts. There had, however, been one major development onSlab: meetings about meetings about meetings about meetings had been banned for nearly a millennia and added to the Anti-Social Offences List as proscribed in all SlabWide Contemporary Morality updates.

'So you just need some early twenty-first-century tech to make this racket work?' said Kiki.

'Yes, but Fencer said it might get trashed during the process so he ruled out museums and private collectors. That's why I thought about Pleewo. I'm pretty sure I saw something that Fencer could use when we went to that round room on the interface with all that wood and old nautical crap.'

Kiki looked doubtful. 'He's going to want a big cut of your deal and I'm not even sure we can get to him. He's stopped returning my pings. Have you done something to piss him off?'

'I don't think so. Maybe Louie has.'

'Well there's no way he's going to just hand over something he knows you need.' She tapped her glass rhythmically with her Natalite fingernails. 'Maybe we should steal it.'

'What?'

'You remember that professional thief we saw at the NewCycle smooze? He's still hassling me for representation. I could get him to steal the tech you need from under the president's nose as a sort of audition. Hang on, I'll just lodge the copyright.' Kiki went into longaze.

{[What's she doing now?]}

[[Ms Pundechan is registering the idea for a sume of the theft of an item of antique tech from the presidential meetandgreet rotunda in order that her company has the rights to produce and distribute the work and claim royalties. She is also contacting her production crew and briefing them on the idea you have just discussed. She has just returned a ping to a M. Le Moment.Pendue and is sketching an outline costing and royalty split skeleton structure. The rest of her activity is private]]

The rest? Thought Dielle, feeling small.

'Won't this thief want a cut too?' he asked.

'Only of the sume, darling. That's how all thieves make their money. He'll have no interest in the target object and we won't tell him what we're going to use it for, will we?' She smiled sweetly.

'No, of course not,' said Dielle. 'But isn't someone going to get into trouble over this?'

'Unlikely. Pendue is a professional criminal and has

artistic immunity and Pundechan Media carries broad-band indemnity insurance. Charlie will claim exorbitant compensation and our insurers will cross-deal it against one of the hundred of claims they'll undoubtedly be holding against him. He'll most likely thank us for stealing it afterwards, confidentially of course. Dean Twenty's just been sent a list of all the twenty-first century tech in Charlie's reception room. I'll wait for him to confirm a viable target before I outline the job to Pendue. He's going to love it though. Ripping off something that's under presidential security is going to take some serious grift, so we'll get top ratings for sure. Maybe we can get you involved directly. That'll bump the ratings even more.'

Dielle didn't like the sound of that. 'What? Me? Err. . . '

Kiki studied him for a minute. He wondered if he was being tested.

She nodded. 'Yes, you're right. I've just checked with my sume profiler and he tells me there would only be a 30% match to your optimum demographic if you were co-scene. Well done dear.' She patted his hand. 'I can be a bit too keen sometimes. Dean Twenty's just confirmed that Pleewo has a tablet computer, whatever the Dice that is, that will be ideal. I'm arranging a face-to-face with Pendue now. I'd ask you to come along but we wouldn't be able to use it in your timeline. If we did, it would blow the setup and could provoke sumer rejection when they saw you in the making-of sume that we'll release after the theft if we'd not included it in their feeds earlier. From this point on, you can't discuss it with anyone who we might want to include in your dailies. And this conversation is offline too. Best if we don't mention it again until the job's done. I'll tell you when. '

'Jeez, you don't hang about do you?'

'What do you mean, darling?'

'We haven't finished breakfast yet and you've already planned a major heist.'

'That's the advantage of having a hit sume, darling.' She stroked his hand again. 'People return my pings now. Speaking of which, I've got a major music critic on hold who wants to interview the band after the gig tomorrow. What do you say?'

'I think you'd better check with Fencer and Fingerz,' said Dielle.

'I've already obtained their approval to let Pundechan Media handle the PR for the band darling. In fact I've taken on a specialist to handle it all. You'll like her, she's a very special specialist and unbelievably connected. Why don't I ask her to come over to talk to you here while I go and get my ears bent by Monsieur I-am-ze-greatest-tief-of-all-time Pendue?'

'I'm going to meet up with the band and run through the set a couple more times. Maybe you should send her to where we'll be rehearsing so she can meet everyone. It's not like I'm the leader you know, we're all equal in this.'

'Sure, sure,' said Kiki, waving her hand at an invisible fly. 'Good idea, but if you're going to be in full privacy you'd better tell Sis to allow her a looksee so she can find you.'

'What's her name?'

'Her doName is Petina Techumai Thornbird Tëssä but everyone knows her as 4T. She runs a nowplus mobile Spin bar in NYcubed. She knows everyone.'

'Forty? People call her forty?'

'Number 4, letter T. Her pet name was Tina down on the farm.'

Dielle stopped trying to decode what Kiki was telling him. It was hurting his brain.

{[Let the 4T woman know where our rehearsal is please]}

[[••]]

'You should be careful with those rehearsals, darling,' said Kiki.

'What do you mean?'

'I don't think you should get too good'

'Why not?'

'You might start singing in tune.'

The band had been rehearsing for nearly an hour when Louie appeared out of the emtitrash under Dielle's keyboard. If he'd had a real head, he'd have banged it.

'You have got to be joking,' he said.

'About which bit?' said Dielle. There was something about Louie that irritated him on sight. He'd even resented having to send Louie the message briefing him about Fencer's idea and asking him to come to the rehearsal.

'All of it. First that *you*,' Louie waved a hand at Dielle, 'could ever front a band, second that you expect to send your shit back to my time and make a cent out of it and third that you would want my opinion in the first place.'

'Why can't I front a band?'

'Because kid, you have my genes and no matter how much I paid them to upgrade and change me into you, they can't alter the hard-wired fact that you are tone-deaf. Just like I am.'

'That's our unique selling point,' said Fencer who, much to Dielle's surprise, seemed to be intimidated by Louie. 'No one here has ever heard anyone sing like Blood.'

'Blood?'

'It's my stage name,' said Dielle.

'What? You mean as in *baying for* – which is what your audience will be doing when they hear you? It doesn't matter if there are enough weirdos here who think you're dupe, it's where you're sending it to that's important and when I was a kid you had to be able to sing to sell records.'

'We've been researching that,' said Fencer, 'and we've found plenty of evidence to the contrary.'

'Anyway,' said Dielle, 'that's not the point. We don't need to sell more than a handful.' Fingerz nodded, sage-like inside his private cloud.

'So what do you need me for?'

'You're the only person who's from that time we can ask, and believe me if there was anyone else. . . ' Dielle looked at the ceiling.

'Ask what?'

'We want to ask you to professionally advise us,' said Dielle as though he'd just thrown up a little in his mouth.

Louie stopped in mid-air. 'What? You want me to be your manager?'

'*Want* is an exaggeration,' said Dielle. 'And manager, definitely not. We just need your advice.'

'Why should I want to be a manager of a band I already know has failed? I know I'm old but I'm pretty sure I would have remembered if there was a band with you three deadbeats in it when I was a kid. What name are you going under?'

'That's one of the things we need to ask your advice on,' said Fencer. 'I've run an analysis of the names of music groups from your teenage era but can't figure out any patterns, common meanings or even sense. We have our first gig tomorrow and need to have decided on a name by then.'

'Yeah, we want something that fits with the music and your time. Like when you were sixteen,' said Dielle, warming to the theme despite himself. 'In fact, you are pretty much our target audience. If we could persuade the teenage Louie Drago to buy our record we'd be instantly rich according to Fencer.'

Louie had already checked out Fencer's credentials with Sis. He looked at Dielle and flipped a holographic thumb in Fencer's direction. 'Well, Blood, at least him, I'd believe.'

Dielle tried hard not to take offence. He failed. 'Look, just forget it will you?'

'Oh, keep your hair on. Why don't you play me something and I'll see what occurs. Maybe work the old LCD magic. I have a gift for names, you know.'

Nobody could think of a reason not to, so they performed their latest composition. Dielle's off-key humming-cum-whining featured prominently, especially during Fingerz' ten-minute free-jazz solo. Louie hovered impassively in the middle of the room. He used his famous blank negotiation expression which, despite decades of practice, nearly cracked when Fencer performed his fifty-five-and-a-half bar, triple time-signature air drum solo. After they'd eye-synched to segue into their signature collapsed fade they grinned at each other and sat proudly, waiting for Louie's response.

'The Garlic Farts,' said Louie.

All three longazed while they consulted Sis. Colonic emtis had been dealing with intestinal gas for so long that nobody had ever experienced a fart in this spaceship. Nobody except the naturalists.

'Is this your way of turning us down?' said Fencer.

Louie hovered toward the emtitrash and ran through a series of suitable put-downs from his extensive list but couldn't think of anything more appropriate than silence. He looked at all three in turn, slowly shaking his head then dropped into the trash.

Fencer, stared at the empty emti. 'The Garlic Farts!' he said.

'Un-dicing-real,' said Fingerz.

'Yeah,' said Dielle, shaking his head. 'I'll let Kiki know.'

'You can't be him, man,' said Fingerz.

'I find it hard to believe too,' said Dielle, 'but Sis confirmed it. Three times. What's really scary is I don't know if I'll wind up looking like him when I get old.'

Fencer shook his head. 'That's not going to happen. You have complete control over your ageing process and can delay it almost indefinitely. He didn't have anything other than surgery to help him.'

'You mean like knives in the flesh, man?' said Fingerz. He pulled heavily on a fresh shiff. 'Jinga Cruz!' he wrapped his arms around his chest and rocked back and forth in his chair muttering muso while his PersonalSpace darkened to solid grey.

'Hey,' said Dielle. 'That phrase you picked up on in the last piece, how'd it go?' He tried to mimic something he'd heard Fingerz play. He struggled to find the notes, trying to prise Fingerz out of his shell. It took a while.

Halfway through the next run-through, Fencer stopped playing. He sat gazing toward the vexit, transfixed. Dielle and Fingerz turned to see why. They, too, stopped in their tracks. In breathless silence the three men stared at the visitation.

Dielle drank in her beauty as if he had never seen beauty before. He could feel a shift in the universe. Something deep inside him had changed, some inner peace he hadn't been aware of had been disturbed, and he suspected he might never regain it. He could hardly tear his eyes off her but when he did he saw that Fencer and Fingerz were as captivated as he was. They sat paralysed by something that could never be fabricated or copied.

No technology could ever replicate what the three dumbstruck musicians were experiencing because their reaction was in response to a beauty that did not lie in physicality at all. It wasn't in her stature: she was at least a head shorter than Dielle, although her grace and poise created the impression that she was much taller. It wasn't to do with her unblemished ebony skin or her stunning figure. It was nothing to do with the silky black hair that was pulled high above her head and then fell down to her delicate collar bones. It wasn't in her slender neck where she wore a choker of living fur or in her deep, dark eyes that gazed out into a universe only she could see. It wasn't the fine bone structure of her face that she'd inherited from a tribe of humans who had nearly perished in a dark continent millennia ago, and it wasn't her full lips that parted slightly as she stood waiting for what was, to her, a familiar effect to wear off. It was simply Tina Tëssä doing what she did best: being herself. She smiled serenely and looked anywhere except into the eyes of the men who could do nothing but seek out hers.

[[Instacom via 4T request connect]]

{[Proceed]} thought Dielle, urgently.

[['It's OK,']] said a sensual, soothing voice in his head. [['You'll get used to it in a minute.']]

{[What's happening? I mean I know what's happening but what's happening?]]

[['It's quite normal. I have this effect on people. Once you get used to me you'll be OK. Just let it be.']]

Let it be, thought Dielle. He had no idea what the it was that he was supposed to let be. His mind was split between turmoil and fascination. He was surprised to realise that there was another, more ominous emotion prodding at his psyche. There was something terrifying about this woman.

{[Sis?]}

[[•]]

{[What's going on?]}

[[You have encountered a perfect. The initial adjustment period can be unnerving. Just wait a few minutes, you'll be fine]]

{[A perfect?]} thought Dielle, feeling anything but fine.

[[Petina Techumai Thornbird Tëssä has what is sometimes referred to as the golden gene. It means she is, as far as other humanoids are concerned, physically perfect]]

{[A perfect human being? And she owns a bar?]}

[[Yes, in NY^3. It's extremely successful]]

{[I'll bet]}

[[Life begins at 4T's]]

{[What?]}

[[Their slogan. Life begins at 4T's]]

He didn't know if his life had just begun, again, or had reached a culmination. He could barely move. The others had adapted already. Fencer was acting almost normal and Fingerz had walked over to 4T and offered her a shiff, which she had declined with a smile that made the room ten degrees warmer. Even odder, as far as Dielle was concerned, was that even though he was staring at a person who seemed to have patented beauty, he felt zero sexual attraction towards her. This being was above sex.

He wondered how he could look at this woman, share the same physical space as her perfect presence and yet feel no desire to engage with her in a physical way. He still couldn't take his eyes off her but he had no will to do anything other than just be as he was. Just be, he thought, wasn't that what she'd said? Slowly, he sat down and looked at his hands. He didn't need to look at his hands, he just needed to get control over his eyes again.

Then she walked over to his keyboard. She moved like a current through deep water. He looked up into her infinite eyes and opened his mouth to speak. Nothing came out.

[['It's OK,']] she said, still through instacom. She looked down coyly and smiled and Dielle stopped breathing again. [['I expect you remember that Kiki told you I'm going to handle all the media for the band?']] Dielle nodded, exhaling in staccato. [['Great name by the way. I love it.']] Dielle nodded again, trying to tear his eyes off her by moving his head. That didn't work, his eyes were ready to swivel past 180 degrees if he tried to force things. [['Tell you what, why don't you play me something?']] Dielle nodded and commanded his eyes to look at Fencer and Fingerz. They nodded back.

Thank Dice for non-verbal communication, thought Dielle, playing the first faltering chords of Piece Eight. Three songs later he could play normally and look at 4T without feeling like he was standing on the edge of a cliff in a howling gale. She smiled directly at him and his heart didn't stop. Sis was right. He'd be fine.

As she listened she casually stroked the fur around her

neck. Her matching bracelet animated and turned towards him. A dark hole opened, a hole with two rows of needle-sharp teeth. A flash of light reflected from something in the fur above the maw.

{[What's that?]}

[[A chikanquen kit. The one around Ms Tëssä's neck is its mother]]

{[It's an animal?]}

[[Wearable pet]]

{[Can I stroke it?]}

[[You could try but those teeth are not decorative and I cannot guarantee to regenerate a fully functional finger in time for tomorrow's performance]]

{[They're dangerous?]}

[[Not to their hosts]]

Dielle smiled at 4T who smiled back in slow motion. She petted the animal at her throat. He understood. {[Perfects need protection]}

[[••]]

She didn't stay much longer. She told them how she intended to handle the media requests and gave them advice about specific interviewers. While she never attended the interviews in person (to avoid the inevitable distractions), she kept a live instacom link open and fed her clients pertinent information, suggested responses and moral support. She was personal friends with every sume-star and mediator onSlab and had already arranged a busy itinerary of media appointments. She was business-like, precise and held Dielle's attention completely. It wasn't until she'd left the rehearsal space that he realised she hadn't spoken a single word.

'Dice!' Said Fingerz. 'Are we in good hands!'

'Perfect hands,' said Fencer.

Dielle nodded. He was getting good at nodding.

nine

The DreamTimeShine music festival had been running as a bi-cycle event onSlab for longer than anyone remembered. No one remembered because no one needed to remember. They could query Sis as easily as recalling from their organic memories and be assured of a more reliable, significantly faster result. Such a query would reveal that this was the 127th time the festival had been held in its current format and the 34th time it had been held in Mitchell DownSide. The venue was a natural (or the closest thing that passed for natural onSlab) stepped demi-bowl of grass-covered hillsides with an acoustically transparent lake behind the main stage that provided a signature reverb. Mitchell was a permanent daylight section, so the festival was held under a night shadow to maximise the lighting and projection effects. This meant that the festival-goers could hang out, warm and comfortable on the slopes and enjoy spectacular shows from stages that were populated by photophobic performers. It was a tradition for the festival organisers to launch a newcomer as an opening act and the word had gone around that The Garlic Farts were going to be something special. Dielle's fame as a sume-star, coupled with 4T's expertise as an attention manipulator had fuelled the media into a frenzy of anticipation and wildly inaccurate speculation.

The buzz was palpable as the crowd waited for the Farts' debut. Even Louie couldn't resist the urge to show up, although he was anticipating a completely different form of entertainment.

Without warning, a two-metre-high lisitessaloid appeared in the centre of the main stage and rotated slowly through at least seven of its dimensions. It spoke:

'What part of stop do you not understand, you moron spawn?'

The soundman looked down at his display. He knew he had perceived this message aurally, and not as a direct feed through his neural interface, just as the more than twenty thousand citizens in front of him had, but he also knew that the sound had not gone through his surroundsound system. It had somehow been delivered to the audience as a distributed sound field, at the same intensity for everybody, and none of his technology was involved. 'Cool,' he said and queried Sis as 20,156 curious festival goers did the same and were given the same answer: origin unknown.

A murmur rippled through the crowd.

Louie had to admire the phlegmatic attitude of the Slab citizens. He had no doubt what would have happened back on 21st-century Earth if a clearly out-of-context apparition had manifested in front of an excited audience at a concert and started insulting them: the sky would have darkened with a cascade of bottles and the target of their ire would have multi-dimensionally fucked off. Not here, he marvelled. OnSlab, they listened.

'You drivel mongers, you churlish ghent-cracked slothwits, you evil infestation of a tiny shit-based sphere. Can you not comprehend one simple instruction? Stop. Do not venture further. You are unwelcome.

'Hello? Hello? Is this heard? It doesn't know. It thinks this is hopeless, despite what was obvious. It defers.'

A stage hand approached the hyper-shape and it vanished as silently as it had appeared.

The crowd demurred.

That's torn it, thought Louie. A nearby K-table was delivering steaming hot-dogs at a steady rate. Louie manoeuvred his vDek toward the central serving platform, said 'Home, James' and appeared instantly on the bridge of his requisitioned escape ship.

'Before you start,' said Louie, 'is there any way you can alter my program so I can taste food again?'

'An interesting concept,' said Sis. 'I'll offer it to some of the creative legacy programmers in Spingalore if you like.'

'Can't you do it?'

'Probably, but taste is peculiarly personal to the organism that experiences it. They would be more inventive than I and anyway it's good to keep the biomass occupied.'

Louie filed the insight: Sis considered herself to be less creative than the human cargo she diligently watched over. 'OK. Ask them to start with hot dogs with boiled onions, sweet mustard and ketchup. If they can figure it out you might like to try them yourself.'

'What a disgusting concept.'

'You haven't lived until you've had a really good dog – one that's been simmering all season.'

'I haven't lived, period. Wouldn't want to either.'

Louie nodded, grateful for the ammunition. 'Tell me what just happened.'

'Forty two simultaneous instances of a non-physical, multi-dimensional apparition have just infiltrated public spaces throughout Seacombe, The Spin, The Valley and The Strip. It looks like it was planned to ensure maximum spread for minimum energy expenditure. Each message was identical, delivered by vibrational air-carried sound waves to audiences greater than five thousand people. Power source untraceable. No residual molecular signature. I'd postulate they used some form of extra-dimensional tech that triggered on live groupings greater than a preset size. That suggests that they might not know too much about Slab.'

'Forty two, eh? Is that number significant?'

'Not at all. If the incursion had happened moments later or earlier, that figure would have been different.'

'Where was Pleewo?'

'He was engaged in a meeting under full privacy so didn't know about it until a couple of his aides pinged him. I'm confident that his subsequent query and response data stream was genuine and he had nothing to do with it. He's mad as hell. Lodged a complaint with Council 12.35 seconds after being told. He assumes they knew and aren't telling. Council has decided to officially deny any prior knowledge.'

'Surely the course change is a giveaway?' said Louie. 'He's not going to accept that they aren't related.'

'We're sticking to the original mass-avoidance explanation which also has the marginal benefit of being true.'

'You aren't going to be able to hide a two-billion-klick-wide sign forever.'

'Why not? All extramural data can only be obtained through my systems.'

Louie was one of a handful of people who knew just what the implications of that truth were. He was still surprised that nobody seemed to object.

'So they, whoever they are, know exactly where we are but they don't know what's really going on inside the SlabWalls, it appears they can detect large groups but don't know if we can understand or even hear them?'

'Analysis of the message semantics indicates a different personality from the originator of the prior binary message,' said Sis. 'Either the message originated from an individual capable of experiencing the phenomenon humans would understand as emotion or from an individual or group who wanted to deliberately mislead us into believing that they can experience emotion. Either way, that is deemed a significantly negative development.'

'Because that makes them less predictable?' asked Louie.

'And therefore more dangerous.'

'How is everyone taking it?'

'The majority of citizens are amused or dismissive. Most of them think it's either a publicity prank or some other form of falsehood. A much smaller number have speculated about an incursion from our fictional enemy and we are doing nothing to disabuse either notion. Council had already prepared a back story that fingered our imaginary alien warmongers in the unlikely event that the sign was discovered and we're selectively leaking that. Pleewo's on the warpath, but he just likes the sound of his own voice.'

'Any other action being taken?'

'There's little we can do except power-profile our avoidance manoeuvre. That's going to send a clear signal to whoever is watching us that we've at least seen, heard and responded to this incursion. If they know that Slab is definitely carrying sentience in the form of living cell-based organisms they will be able to calculate the forces involved in our vector change and that will inform them of our maximum inertial absorption and stress tolerance which in turn could indicate our vulnerability so I am sending a false profile by limiting the delta-v and that means we will still penetrate the sign. Other than that, all we can do is wait.'

'Strengthen our defence systems?'

'Against what? There's no way I can currently deal with a cross-dimensional attack from dimensions I can't even detect and they've already demonstrated they can somehow manifest non-physically in our space-time.'

'We're sitting ducks.'

'As you say.'

'Dammit!' said Louie. He span around, looking for something to throw. 'So we just have to wait for their next move?'

'Affirmative. I have some more bad news for you. No one is interested in your gustatory deficiency.'

'I'll pay.'
'That'll do it.'

The Farts were about to take the stage.

Blood Dielle stood rigid and moist, silently taking in the view from the wings. He could feel wave after wave of phi-band energy from the restless crowd. It felt like the entire vibe was directed solely at him. He had no idea that the crowd had just been insulted by a pan-dimensional being because he'd been backstage throwing-up at the time. While most of the festival goers had assumed the apparition was part of the entertainment and had taken it with a mixture of good humour and cynicism, many had been receiving pings from people in their network who had experienced the same manifestation at different events and it was becoming apparent that what they had witnessed was part of a SlabWide media scam. Curiosity had been piqued but answers were not forthcoming.

SlabCitizens were tenCent protected by their ubiquitous, all-seeing, all-providing Sis, which meant that very few people had ever experienced anything truly perilous. Even though there was a war raging far behind them and they were in a constant technological battle for supremacy against an enemy they had never met, everything seemed remote and sanitised; more a news banner than a credible threat. Whenever there was a crisis at the front, everyone assumed Slab would out-pace, out-think and out-tech their attackers, and Slab always did and in 565 cykes of virtually continuous conflict, not a single person had been killed, injured or so much as broken a nail due to the war.

Not only were the SlabCitizens habitually (and medicinally) non-paranoid, they also rarely experienced anything they didn't automatically disbelieve. They knew that most of the images they sumed were likely to have been either manipulated or completely fabricated, that all sensurrrounds were either fake, or creative interpretations of the truth, and that all games were, by definition, fantasies. The only reason they believed in the war was because everyone knew someone who was actually involved in fighting it and those people wanted to believe in it because they were getting paid. The only thing anyone truly believed in without question was themselves, and that was usually misguided.

Fingerz tapped Dielle on the shoulder. Sis intervened to restart his heart.

'Jeez! Jeez. Don't do that!' yelped Dielle, wild eyed.

Fingerz was the same as he aways was: stoned. 'Say what? You ready for this, man?'

Dielle stared at him. This was all too much. Too soon. Too. . . He tried to speak but his tongue stuck to the roof of his mouth. {[Where's Kiki?]}

[[Ms Pundechan is currently in Seacombe DownSide. She indicates she is planning on personally attending for the last song in your set, assuming successful conclusions to her current negotiations]]

{[I need help. Can you help me?]}

[[I am helping. You are having a panic attack. If I administer any more anti-anxiety medication you will be rendered incapable of movement]]

{[Is that all you can do?]} Dielle could feel himself losing touch with the physicality of his environment. The stairs up to the stage seemed to twist and melt. The sound from the crowd started phasing in his ears and the lights over the stage burned holes in his forehead.

[[I do have some time-honoured advice]]

{[WHAAAT?]}

[[Don't panic. Take deep breaths. It will all be over soon]]

Damn right it will all be over soon, thought Dielle. He grabbed Fingerz and dragged him over to where Fencer was warming up. {[Tell 4T I need to speak to her urgently]}

The compère walked onto the stage and held up his hands to settle the madding crowd. 'Citizens, NAHs, avatars and irritating minorities,' he said. 'The Garlic Farts have split.'

ten

'Brilliant! Just brilliant!'

'I thought you'd be annoyed,' said Dielle over his oatmeal and dried fruit breakfast. He'd asked Sis for something he hadn't eaten before that would make him feel better. It wasn't working. It tasted like soundproofing.

'Annoyed? Have you checked the SocNets this morning?' Kiki was excited. Again. 'Farts split! Everyone is talking about it. I'm getting the shout-outs distributed now. 4T is fielding thousands of pings an hour. You are already the most famous band to have never played a gig – ever – and the recording of your warm-up session is outsuming other cross-genre music by ten to one!

'What recording of the warm-up session?'

Kiki ignored him. 'It's genius! How did you come up with it, darling?'

'The only thing I came up with was lunch,' said Dielle, He queried Sis. 'Twenty thousand people were waiting for me to make a complete idiot of myself. . . and why wasn't I informed you were recording our warm-up?'

Kiki swatted his question. 'Have you checked your credit balance?'

He was feeling so embarrassed he had avoided the news in case the gosscasters were crowing about his latest screw-up. He checked his account. Then he checked again.

'That's nuts!' he said. Kiki smiled and nodded. 'Two million sumes?'

'And up-trending too.'

'But it was just a soundcheck. We didn't even bother with the solos.'

'That might tell you something, dear.' Kiki stood up, shoving a slice of toast into her mouth. 'Listen, I have to go.

I'll meet you at Fencer's workshop after lunch, but keep the evening open will you, darling? There's a very special blindSider who wants to meet you and dinner today is the only time he has free. Sis will looksee you on the location when we've agreed terms.'

Dielle kissed her goodbye. He asked Sis to note what she'd just said because he was too busy analysing feedback about the warm-up recording to figure out what she was talking about. People really seemed to like their stuff. He could hardly believe it. After suming more than a hundred complimentary reviews he did more than believe it, he loved it. He asked Sis to ping Fingerz and Fencer. It was time for a Garlic Farts reunion tour.

Asynchronology: $^{\delta t}CT^{SS^{ES}}$

Louie six hadn't thought it was possible. In his wildest speculative moments he had never conceived of a time when he could be bored with basketball, yet somewhere around the 9,700th point he could no longer see one.

It wasn't because he was winning. In Louie's opinion, winning was the only reason to play. It wasn't that the ship's avatar was an easy opponent. Louie was convinced it had been trying as hard as it could and up until the late 8,000s it had been a hard, close-fought game. But despite Louie's guile and determination, and apparent inexhaustible supply of energy, he'd simply lost interest. He'd still won of course. And he'd hardly cheated at all.

'It let you win,' said the wizard.

'I name this ship. . .' said Louie, rubbing it in.

'You can call it what you want. As soon as we get to anything remotely resembling a habitable planet it's all yours.' He sat down in an exaggerated huff, folded his arms, looked down and gasped.

'What? You sat on a tack?'

The wizard was speechless, transfixed.

'Hey, Zippo!' said Louie to the ship's avatar who was gleefully practising baskets, 'I think he's broken.'

'Nopedie dokedie,' said the eyeball. 'He's gone into do-not-disturb mode. He must have reproduced the sleeve configuration he was trying for.'

'Sleeve configuration?' said Louie then realised that he had no interest in hearing the answer. He stole the ball off the avatar and threw it into the wizard's lap. Zero response.

'I think he's pissed at you,' said the ship.

'Yeah?' said Louie, retrieving the ball and bouncing it off the wizard's head a couple of times. 'How can you tell?'

'Because he just switched from DND to hibernation mode and told me not to wake him until we arrive at the mass.'

'Suits me. Miserable fucker.' He bounced the ball off the wizard's head a couple more times. 'Sweet dreams!' he yelled. Zero response. Louie turned back to the ship's avatar whose appearance owed more to Tex Avery than common sense. 'So how's it going with that mass then, any more info?'

'I sent out some investigative emti-relays while we were playing but something very odd is going on.'

'We're hurtling through remote space in a

transparent facsimile of a pert breast, there's a catatonic wizard sitting in a throne and I'm a holographic projection of a guy who was born on a spinning lump of rock lightyears away from here who is having a conversation with a cartoon eyeball and you're telling me something odd is going on? You have been watching too much TV.'

The eyeball looked at Louie and blinked slowly. Several times.

'OK. You got me.' Louie knew when he'd been suckered. 'Tell me what the fuck is odder than this,' he said sweeping his arms around the basketball court.

'Our sensors were right. There is a mass there. It's considerable and it should make a big difference to our journey time if we can acquire it.'

'If?'

'It's not there.'

'Re-fuckin'-wind. There is a mass there and it's not there? Maybe it's you that's broken.'

'All mass creates disturbance in space-time. That's how our sensors can detect it. It's there inasmuch as it's creating the exact same signature as a mass would create if it was there. Only it's not there because, well, it's just not there.'

'If there's anything I can do to help you through your problem you will let me know, won't you?'

'The emtis can find no evidence of any physical matter. There is nothing to probe. No molecules, no heat, in fact nothing in the electromagnetic spectrum at all, nothing apart from the gravitational signature of a large mass — which, by the way, we are currently accelerating towards because our gravity drive can sense it. I'd call that odd, wouldn't you?'

'Got any theories?'

'Something extra-dimensional I guess.'

'You guess? I thought you had all of human scientific knowledge at your disposal and you're guessing?'

'Sometimes you gotta.'

'Great,' said Louie. He looked around for something to kick then remembered he didn't have any legs. 'Is there any point in us going there?'

'We don't really have much of a choice. It's the only mass for a couple of billion clicks and if I can't figure out a way to acquire it before we get there we can use the gravity well to slingshot off into a new trajectory. We'll get a big delta-V hike out of that.'

'How long before we get there?'

'Looks like about sixty Earth years. You want another game?'

Despite himself, he actually considered it. 'Nah, wake me when we're there huh?'

'Sure thing!'

Louie parked his decommissioned military grade vDek by the edge of the court and tuned off his projection. Shit, he thought, I bet that fucker sneaks in some practice while I'm asleep.

He woke and checked his internal clock. 1.8916×10^9 seconds in sleep mode — nearly 60 years. The ship's avatar was bouncing around the floor like a hyperactive kid in an inflatable castle. Jeez, he thought, Coney Island huh? I remember that day we went to. . . 'Hey! What the fuck is going on?' The bubble had gone. The wizard had gone. The basketball court had gone.

'You have got to see this!' said the ship's avatar, careening off a mock-brick wall of what looked to Louie a lot like his old Manhattan loft. It even had floor-to-ceiling windows with sunlight streaming in. And could he hear the sound of angry traffic far below?

'Where the fuck are we?'

'We're still in the Cosmic Tit. I've been doing some remodelling while you were in sleep mode. Do you like it?'

'Yeah, it's dupe. It looks like home. Is that what you woke me for?'

'Nopely dopely. It's this!' A holographic projection of a scattered starscape filled the room. 'Watch!'

Louie watched. Nothing happened. A few miserable stars looked cold and isolated in the in-betweens of the spiral arms of the Milky Way. He waited, searching the blackness for a clue. Then he saw it. A flash, a circle of something, no, a sphere of something, something that was real and then wasn't. Something not exactly reflecting starlight, more like capturing it.

'You see it? That was slowed down one hundred billion times. That's the limit of my resolution at this distance. You see it?'

'Yeah, I think so. A ball of something I think. Is that the mass we've been heading towards?'

'Yes. That was recorded a little under fifty cykes ago. The reason I woke you is because it just did it again. I thought the first time might have been an anomaly so I waited for proof.'

'It flashes into reality once every fifty cykes? For a tiny fraction of a second?'

'Yes! Is that exiting or what?'

'I'm going for what. Where's laughing boy?'

'I put him in a storeroom downstairs. I like twentieth century architecture.'

'You kept the court, right?'

'Yup, got a swimming pool too. No water, mind.'

Louie shook his head. 'You any nearer figuring out what it is?'

'We have a few more clues. One very interesting thing is that the object is perfectly spherical to a level of precision that means it couldn't possibly be a naturally occurring phenomena.'

'It's an artefact? How big is it?' Louie was starting to feel nervous. It had been a long time since he'd felt nervous.

'Second interesting thing. Exactly nine hundred kilometres in diameter. And I mean exactly.'

Louie did the holographic equivalent of a cold shiver.

Graphs appeared around a projected globe in the middle of the room.

'Third interesting thing,' said the ship. 'As far as can be ascertained at this distance, it has approximately half the density of a rocky planet. Too much mass to be only gas, too little to be a planetoid or moon with that radius. Unless it was hollow of course.'

Louie had a growing sense of foreboding. 'Can you figure out if this region of space was ever occupied by Earth's system?' he said.

'I guess that's possible. The centre of this

galaxy is vectoring parallel to a line that would mean the western spiral would have passed through here hundreds of years ago. Let me check.'

'Where's the wizard? I think we'll have to wake him up for this.'

'Two floors down, past the orangery and turn right at the shark tank. There's a small arched door set into a wall. I'll send down a grav-form for his chair if he wants.'

'Wake him up and I'll ask him. You do the astro-maths, but I think I know what you're going to say.'

The wizard, the ship's avatar and Louie convened on what the avatar had lovingly called the flight deck. Three status-imbued black padded chairs were set in a shallow curve facing a wall-to-wall, panoramic screen. The ceiling and walls were covered in arrays of slowly pulsing, and purely decorative, rectangular lights. The screen was showing an animated reconstruction of the galaxy's nearest arm traveling through a static three-dimensional grid.

'How did you know?' said the ship's avatar looking quizzical, which is no simple feat when you only have one eye. 'Not only did the solar system pass through there, but the Earth was precisely occupying that location sometime in mid-2069.'

'What do you mean?' said the wizard.

'August 5th' said Louie glumly.

'Ah!' The ship checked the database. 'Oh!'

The wizard was agitated. 'What is it? What do you know?'

'How long before we get there?' asked Louie.

'We're decelerating hard now. Twenty hours or so, give or take. Are you sure you want to do this?' said the ship.

'Do what?' whimpered the wizard.

'Any idea what each flash represents?' asked Louie.

'Something to do with quanta of space-time. Can't say until I can get hard data and we'll have to be stationary relative to it for that.'

'Will someone tell me what the Dice it is?' wailed the wizard.

Louie studied him with an attitude of dismissive superiority that takes years to perfect. 'California,' he said and turned back to the screen.

Asynchronology: $^{\delta t}SS^{ES}$

Dielle stepped through the vexit to find Kiki and Fencer waiting on an industrial gravpad.

'Welcome to the Ustorian Alps,' said Fencer.

They were at the base of a cavern that was so vast it had its own micro-climate, and so dimly lit that it was impossible for Dielle to gauge how big it was.

{[Where am I?]}

[[You are inside the Graphite mountains quite close to the one you fell off a few days ago]] Dielle could have lived a long time without being reminded about that event.

The gravpad floated through mile-high columns of open-front containers. Some were no wider than a hand and hung like fragile threads from the invisible ceiling, others were dozens of metres wide. Dielle couldn't tell what the spindly ones were for, but he could see entire buildings in the largest containers. The air was filled with flying despatch units. Tiny emtis zipped around like hummingbirds, disgorging or devouring personal jewellery, children's toys, hair brushes or any of a million things that no one wanted to clutter their lives with. Gravpads transported the larger items from the storage towers to centralised handling and emtiing facilities.

Dielle was fascinated. Each item was stored in its own compartment, and each compartment formed a column that was dedicated to a particular class of object. They passed one that looked like a delicate paper-chain and contained only finger rings. Millions of them.

'We've needed this place for ages,' said Fencer. 'We've been drowning under our own stuff. Now, when you put something into an emti and tell Sis to store it, it comes here. Before this place, people had to rent their own storerooms or buy second apartments just to keep all the stuff they couldn't throw away. And you could never find anything when you needed it. It was expensive, wasteful and stressful. Now you just tell Sis what you want and an emticab gets it for you in seconds.'

'Like houses and trees?'

'We use special heavy delivery emties for the really large items. People store their holiday homes here when they're not using them so they don't have to pay exTax on them. And lots of people have homes they are sentimentally attached to, like the places they grew up in but don't live in anymore. Then there are the building collectors and preservation nuts.'

'And you have a workshop in here?' asked Dielle.

'Yeah, there's a lot of us here now. It started with a few of us renting some private storage space that we could call our own instead of these communal retrieval stacks. Some guys like to come here and just hang out with their stuff.'

'Just guys, huh?' said Kiki.

'Mostly. It's a good place to sit and think, have a few ideas and maybe make something or test out an experiment or two. I turned my place into a sort of laboratory. You know, just a place to tinker around.'

'Tinker around,' said Kiki. Dielle flashed her a hard look.

'There are some hyper-now creative thinkers who keep places down here,' said Fencer, oblivious. 'We even have our own bar where we hang out and swap ideas. The guy next to me is really into blowing things up. He's crazy.'

'Blowing things up,' said Kiki.

'Don't worry, he's working at the sub-atomic level at the moment. Virtually zero possibility of him creating a singularity.'

Kiki shook her head. 'That's comforting.'

They reached the inside wall of the mountain, and cruised into a hollow foothill. The tunnel branched out under the ridged terrain. They moved past hundreds of anonymous shutter doors until they came to one that opened as they approached. Inside, Fingerz was polluting the environment. Familiar music rose to greet them. It was The Farts: Piece Five.

'Hey,' said Fingerz, cutting the volume. 'Just adding a couple of polishes before we send it back.'

Dielle and Fingerz did one of their choreographed greeting rituals which Dielle very nearly nailed then the three musicians stood listening to the latest mix.

'Love the way you brought the tablas out,' said Fencer.

Dielle was confused. 'Who's playing the flute?'

'It's all keys,' said Fingerz. 'That's a bansuri. Been working on the breath intonation.'

'Is that guitar sound keys too?'

Fingerz nodded. 'Whad'ya think?'

'It's amazing!' said Dielle.

One wall of Fencer's garage was covered from floor to ceiling with technology that gave almost no clue as to its purpose but looked to Dielle to be either highly dangerous, far too complicated to understand, or both. He suspected that asking Sis to provide background would prove futile.

He was right. Wires, dials, tools and mysterious black boxes littered the pitted workbench and there was an odd smell of burning chemicals in the air. 'Where's Louie?' he asked.

'He said he'd be here ten minutes ago,' said Fencer.

'I wonder what the hell he thinks is so important that he can keep us waiting,' said Dielle. He couldn't decide if he was irritated because Louie was late or because Louie was about to turn up. On cue, Louie flew out of Fencer's catering emti which was perched on a pile of heavy-duty transformers.

'Hello deadbeats,' he said, then, noticing Kiki, 'and madam.' He bowed courteously which, as he was a hologram with no legs, made him look like a nodding duck. 'I'm prepared to allocate ten minutes of my valuable time to watch you fail, purely for self-amusement of course, then I have to go. I have things to do.'

'What's so important?' said Dielle.

'I can't say,' said Louie. 'Maybe it's just important by comparison to what you drongos are doing.' He smiled obsequiously at Kiki. 'Ladies excepted of course.'

Kiki nodded courteously.

Dielle looked at Kiki and then back at Louie. No, he thought. Not possible.

'Well thank you for coming anyway,' said Fencer. 'It's important for everyone to understand that once the entanglement is in progress, we will have an unpredictable and possibly extremely limited period during which we can make adjustments. Bear in mind that the only way we'll be able to tell if what we're doing has worked will be how we perceive the past had changed. We may need to react very swiftly with alternative ideas and once it's over, it's over. We can't go back and change what we've changed because it won't be the same thing that we're changing because we will have already changed it and we have nothing from the changed timeline that we can use to re-entangle with.'

'OK Einstein,' said Louie. 'I think we all understand the

basics. Just tell me what you want me to do and I'll watch you crap out.'

'Man!' said Fingerz and disappeared behind his cloud.

Fencer pointed at the early twenty-first century tablet computer he'd installed in a rig on his workbench. Dozens of hair-fine wires sprouted from micro-holes in its casing. 'This is a pre-photonic device and used technology that operated close to the limits of physical electron manipulation on silicon substrates. Under certain circumstances quantum effects spontaneously occurred inside its microprocessors and in fact it was this phenomena that often led to random failings of these devices and their eventual supersession by the type of technology we used to create the first versions of AI minds that became Sis.'

'Nine minutes,' said Louie.

'What I'm going to do,' said Fencer, trying not to let Louie get to him, 'is reactivate the tablet computer and while its processors are running, entangle the digital encode of our recording along with a program that will disseminate the information into the network it used to be connected to along with instructions of where to pay the income derived through the purchase of the material. I've also taken the liberty of adding in some non-specific graphics and some made-up background data to give it some authenticity.'

'When will we know if it's worked?' asked Kiki.

'That's what we need your networks and data mining to tell us,' said Fencer. 'The encoded instructions are to credit an account in our name and then transfer the money into Slab's accounts prior to departure so that we continually earn compound interest over hundreds of years. But the effects should be instantaneous. I press the button, the tablet activates and then I authorise Sis to entangle the encoded information and the money appears instantly in an account here because it will have always have been there as far as the records will then show. It's likely that this account will have to be captured and linked to us and that's where your research networks come in because even though I've encoded it with our names as account owners, it's possible that information won't be transferred because we didn't exist when the money was made.'

Dielle was curious. {[Why does Fencer expect Kiki to be able to find something he can't?]}

[[Sume production companies have the widest and most invasive information retrieval networks onSlab]]

{[You mean they snoop on everyone?]}

[[••]]

'Understood,' said Kiki. 'I'll establish a cascade seek request through the Pundechan Media network with extended trembler feathers on tertiary bounded interrupt events.' The multiform she'd been sitting on configed into a lounger as she lay back and went into longaze. 'Ok, it's up. It'll stay stable as long as we keep ahead of Sis's anti-snoop drones. Not a problem for now, I've also set up an entirely spurious intercedent that's deluging invasive queries into the distributed matrix as a mask.'

Dielle looked at Kiki in an entirely different light.

Fencer checked everyone. Louie was impatient, Fingerz was stoned and Dielle was confused. 'Let's do this!' he said with false bravado. 'Let's get rich!' He linked to Sis on a multi-feed level and checked a plethora of status readouts that were being fed directly into his visual cortex. He reached out and pressed the small indentation at the bottom of the glass front of the tablet. Nothing happened.

'It's OK,' said Fencer. 'It's going through a diagnostic routine.'

The screen came to life and displayed a message in a rounded blue box.

'Software Update Required, Press OK To Proceed.'

'Oh shit!' said Dielle.

'Fuckers!' said Louie.

'Don't panic,' said Fencer. It doesn't matter what it's asking us to do, the processors are powered up anyway.

Hold one moment.' He instructed Sis to carry out the entanglement procedure and then accessed his credit accounts. Nothing. 'The process has executed,' he said. 'But, as I suspected, there's nothing in my account. Ms Pundechan, anything from your networks?'

Kiki stared at the ceiling. 'Nothing,' she said. 'We've tracked every credit account that's had a significant change over the last ten seconds and nothing unaccounted for has occurred.'

'Jeez!' said Dielle. 'You can do that?'

'Not legally,' said Kiki.

'Losers,' said Louie, heading for the catering emti. 'I told you it wouldn't work. No one would have paid good money for your garbage especially with some tone-deaf bozo moaning all over it.'

Fencer looked sheepish. 'Actually, I stripped out the vocals during the conversion.'

Dielle and Fingerz exchanged nods. 'Good call!' said Dielle.

'I know it worked,' said Fencer. 'The change might not look like a change because what you're comparing it to would have changed as well. I'm convinced the problem is on the financial side.'

'What legal entity did you tie the account to?' asked Kiki. 'I might be able to trace that through our private archive databases.'

'No legal entity. I just put it in the band's name.'

Louie stopped in mid-air. 'That's not going to work, you idiot,' he said. 'All bank accounts had to be linked to individuals, corporations or trusts. You can't put money into an account with a fictitious name. We did have rules, you know.'

'So, what do we do?' said Fencer. 'The entanglement can't hold for long. Can we link it to you when you were a teenager?'

'If you want, but kid I can tell you, you are shooting airies. It didn't happen. I would know.'

'You would only know when it happened. Your memory would change instantly.'

'OK, I'll humour you. I'll give you my old bank codes and you can link it to me. But I'm telling you, you are wasting your time.'

'Just hurry, will you?' said Dielle. Fingerz sucked shiff.

Louie gave Fencer his details. He'd never forgotten a number in his life. Especially numbers connected to his money. Fencer encoded the new information and instructed Sis.

'Right,' said Fencer. 'It's done. I set the account name to the band's initials but put it in your name. If it worked, you should know about it already.'

Everyone looked at Louie. He played them for as long as he could.

'Nope,' he said, 'zippo, zilch, de nada, zero. I remember nothing different. You never sold your crap in my time and that's all folks.'

Kiki sat up. 'Nothing from my networks either,' she said. 'Sorry guys. Looks like it didn't work.'

Fencer stared at the tablet computer still defiantly displaying its 445-year-old message. Dielle was deflated. Fingerz was absent.

Louie headed back to the emti, gloating 'I'm going to bill you three for ten minutes of my wasted time. That's thirty minutes OK?'

Kiki was the only one to wave goodbye. Louie vanished.

'Maybe they just didn't like our song,' said Fencer.

'No one at all?' said Dielle.

'There was a lot of competition around at the time, millions of bands and solo performers were trying to get noticed, all using the same distribution lines.'

'Yeah, but not one buyer? Surely someone would have been curious enough to buy it?'

'They just weren't ready for us,' said Fingerz, emerging from his shield. 'Everything has a time and place and that one wasn't ours, man. S'cool by me. Selling music never felt right anyway.'

'Look,' said Kiki. She pointed at the screen. 'It's still working. Can you try again?'

'What's the point if they don't like us?' said Dielle. 'Maybe we got the wrong device. Why did they need something this size just to play music anyway?'

'They didn't just listen to music on these things,' said Fencer. 'They used them to play games, watch sumes, communicate, create stuff and a whole load of things we just do by eye. They even used them to read books.'

'Dicing primitives. I can't believe you grew up getting your feeds that way, darling,' said Kiki.

'Books? That's a great idea!' said Dielle. 'Why don't we send back a book and see if they'll buy that?'

Fencer checked his status displays. 'I think we only have a minute or so left. Not easy to write a book in a minute.'

'You don't have to,' said Kiki. 'Tell Sis to dump a load of the latest onSlab events into a simple text format, add in a couple of proposed sume threads my team have in the development file and entangle that. The sumers of the day will think it's science fiction.'

Fencer paused briefly. 'Done,' he said. 'We need a title.'

'For Dicesake!' said Dielle. 'It took us days to come up with a name for the band and even then we had to ask Louie and believe me I am never going to ask that gap for anything ever again.'

'Come on,' said Fencer, watching his internal status indicators decline. 'Quickly, just think of anything. Fingerz?'

'Yeah man,' said Fingerz. 'A book.'

'Three seconds,' said Fencer. 'Dielle, think of a title now!'

Dielle was not at his best under pressure. 'I. . . I don't know, dammit!'

The tablet computer's screen cracked and acrid, blue smoke seeped from the sound vent.

Fencer grimaced. 'I guess we'll never know if that worked either. I didn't have time to track it with a different account code.'

'That was fun,' said Kiki. 'Now that's over we can release the sume of the theft performance. Problem is, if we include this debacle it's not exactly going to paint the Farts in a good light. Not unless you want to go down the comedy route.'

'What do you mean?' asked Dielle.

'She means we'll be a laughing stock if we show what we went through all this for and then not a single person bought our music back in the twenty-first century,' said Fencer.

'Blows man,' said Fingerz.

'My thoughts exactly,' said Kiki. 'I've put a couple of my writers on it. See if they can come up with a more upbeat pay-off, but if they can't I'd recommend we keep schtum and see if we can whip up a couple of false linktrigues about who wanted this thing and what for. Le Pendue only knows that I was brokering the deal, not what it was going to be used for, so he can't leak it.'

'How did he do it anyway?' asked Dielle.

'We don't have a final edit yet obviously, but I can let you sume a feed of the theft,' she turned to Fencer. 'Do you have a sumeplace in here?'

'Sure,' he said. 'I don't use it much though. I'll make some space.' He pulled some crates from the centre of the floor and arranged them in a semi circle. They sat on them and Kiki instructed her editor to send over the pertinent parts of the sume.'

'It's still rough,' said Kiki as a closeup of Pierre Le Moment.Pendue's neatly trimmed goatee and knife-edged sideburns filled the holo projection area between them. He went through an elaborate sequence of arm movements and body stretches to show off his agility and balletic prowess.'

'Thinks a lot of himself, doesn't he?' said Dielle.

'You should have heard the histrionics he pulled on me

when I asked him to guarantee he could pull it off,' said Kiki. 'Dicing prima-donna.'

The scene cut to Pendue performing a series of contortions around the curved wall of Charlie Pleewo's darkened reception rotunda. Why, was anyone's guess, because if they could see it then so could Sis.

{[How is he hiding this from Pleewo? Wouldn't you have automatically alerted him by this point?]}

[[Ex judicio. Pleewo uses his own offGrid security system. If he didn't know about it at the time it could only have been because M. Le Moment.Pendue had infiltrated his system and compromised it in someway. Most professional onSlab thieves are usually not much more than skilled hackers who love to play to an audience]]

The view closed in on a domed alcove set into in the wooden library shelves. Among the brass compasses, charts and ancient Earth-globes was a transparent case containing a selection of dark-screened metal oblongs arranged in an evolutionary progression from a thick, hand-sized block with a white wheel set into its face up to the tablet computer they needed and then down through various colourful devices of decreasing size until the last item was a pin with a large magnifying glass in front of it. Pendue waved his hands theatrically over the case and then, seemingly without moving, he was holding the tablet up to his personal followcam, making the shiny face reflect the light.

'What?' said Dielle. 'How'd he do that?'

'You have to pay for the reveal,' said Kiki. 'Scam-sumes are free but if you want to get the pay-off then you have to pay up. There's a full edit already available if you want to buy in.'

Fencer and Fingerz were already longazing as they watched an encoded overlay on the sumecast polarised only to their sitting position.

'Of course,' said Fencer. 'That's neat.'

'Lookadat man!' said Fingerz.

They came out of longaze.

'Well?' said Dielle.

'Well what?' said Fencer.

'How did he do it?'

'No idea,' said Fencer. 'Does it matter?'

Fingerz shrugged and pulled out a shiff.

'But you two just sumed it!' said Dielle.

'Did we?' said Fencer. He checked his personal logs. 'Yes, looks like we did. It's an encrypted feed. You watch it but the experience is firewalled from your biological memory so you can't tell anyone else. It's an intellectual property protection mechanism. You want me to explain the principle?'

'No thanks,' said Dielle sullenly. He never understood anything Fencer explained to him anyway.

{[Can you let me see the reveal please]}

[[Debit 125 credits; acknowledge approval]]

{[125 bucks? That's a bit steep isn't it?]}

[[••]]

{[OK, I approve]}

Dielle watched the reveal. It was indeed a highly imaginative and totally unexpected method that required a phenomenal level of skill and planning. If it had simply been described to him he wouldn't have understood it. It had to be seen to be believed. Astounding. Pendue was a true artist.

He came out of longaze. Kiki smiled at him. 'What do you think?'

'About what?'

'Anything you're keen to know?'

'Yeah,' said Dielle. 'Can you get us another gig?'

eleven

Dielle had stayed behind to commiserate with Fingerz and Fencer while Kiki tubed back to Seacombe for more meetings. They commiserated quite heavily until Sis reminded Dielle that he had a dinner appointment. He sobered up on the tube ride back to Seacombe and was delivered, fresh-faced and hungry, to Aux Renoir 21 at the uppermost level of upTown DownSide. He was received with an overwhelming level of obsequiousness laced with extra grovelling.

{[What's going on?]}

[[Pundechan Media Conglomerate has renegotiated your endorsement deal with Aux Renoir Inc. As a result you are now tied into being seen eating at one of their restaurants for a minimum of twenty days out of each cycle]]

Dielle didn't mind that at all. Yet.

The fawning maître d' led him to a table that had one of the most spectacular views in Seacombe – if you had a good head for heights, which Dielle didn't. The restaurant overlooked the canyons of glass and metal that formed the heart of the main financial district onSlab. It was almost seven kilometres above the Natalite floor and only a few hundred meters below the zero-g interface that separated DownSideUp from UpSideDown. The slabscape extended off into a vanishing point that was hundreds of kilometres away. Curved, open-roofed tube-ways, unsupported for tens of kilometres, linked the buildings, walkways and parkforms, criss-crossing and branching in every direction. They were filled with the evening's commuter traffic. Hundreds of levels below, the privacy fields displaying softads to the freetubers looked like multi-coloured dots. The business architecture in this part of slab was a bravado of spiky reflections and sheer, multi-faced slender towers. Everyone wanted a view and everyone got one. In normal circumstance all the buildings and forms were mobile. The towers floated through the ubiquitous daylight, changing their aspects and forming proximity allegiances that reflected their trading activities and latest acquisitions, but the imminent course change meant that everything had been buttressed together and physically locked into a rigid network. The locals were enjoying the novelty. New bridges spanned the gaps to neighbouring buildings like tendrils of cheese between pizza slices and a series of sponsored multi-level marathons had already been initiated.

Far above, the razor thin structures of UpSideDown hung from an invisible ceiling like stalactites in a gigantic gothic cathedral.

The view was stunning but it was completely wasted on the man talking to Kiki. He was blind.

'Ah, Dielle,' he said turning his darknight glasses in the direction of the waiter. 'I've been dying to see you.'

Dielle couldn't be sure how to take this. He'd researched their dinner guest via the linktrigue Kiki had sent him after breakfast but couldn't find anything that explained why he was blind. What it did say was that he was one of the most respected storytellers onSlab and that he'd authored more than a thousand books. That had come as a surprise to Dielle. He already knew that almost nobody onSlab read text so he couldn't imagine what shape a book might take. Sis had given him an example. She'd suggested he close his eyes and then she fed him a sequential, time-released narrative. The information poured into his mind, at his chosen rate, like a river of thoughts flowing into his consciousness. Then they evaporated like dreams, leaving behind the memory of the story and the pleasure of an experience that was enchanting and highly addictive. He had read two of this guy's books during his post-breakfast stroll and experienced a completely new set of emotions.

His imagination had been fired with longing for a fragile beauty and filled with images and memories of lost loves and exquisite desire. Dielle could tell why he was so popular.

'Mr Parque,' said Dielle. He stuck out his hand and then lowered it again quickly. 'I'm very pleased to meet you.'

'Please, dear boy, call me Sefton,' he said, offering his own hand for Dielle to shake. 'A firm hand! That's a *very* good sign. Sit! Sit! We shall feast in the delights of Mochi and suck nectar from the teat of Ishtar!'

Kiki made a mock-scary face at Dielle then kissed him hello.

Sefton reached over to Kiki and stroked her hand. 'Kiki darling, you will let me re-write this claptrap before you feed the sumes, won't you?'

'Of course, darling. Your agent insists on 100% edit rights before she lets you out these days.'

'Ah! Such are the vagaries and vulgarities of time, Dielle. Let me tell you now, while it has its compensations, I cannot, on the whole, recommend allowing one's mind to experience too much time. No matter how you discipline it, the mind seems to develop a will of its own. It plays truant on you and goes hiding behind the bike-sheds, sneaking a crafty fag.'

He didn't look old, of course. Almost no one onSlab looked old unless they deliberately chose to. But according to Slabscapedia he was over 800 cycles old and had personally witnessed, as a young child, the *great handbrake turn* when the original ship was turned perpendicular to the direction of travel and converted into what was now known as The Strip. He'd witnessed it with functioning eyes too. {[Crafty fag?]}

[[Obsolete, mass-manufactured shiff-style tranquilliser. Highly carcinogenic and habit forming. Used as an intelligence test on Earth]]

{[Does he always talk like this?]}

[[••]]

Sefton was merely warming up. 'I can tell you are bursting with curiosity, aren't you, dear boy?'

Three separate waiters plied Dielle with iced scintilleau, warm rolls and red wine.

'Well, I, erm. No, not really.'

'You want to know why. Of course you do. It's perfectly natural. The only bushes here are those one should never beat about.' He patted Kiki's hand again. 'The truth is I am blind because I choose to be. It helps my work.'

'But how do you write such emotive imagery when you can't see?' asked Dielle. 'I read two of your books earlier. The descriptions were so vivid it was like I was there.'

'Thank you for such a gracious compliment, dear boy, but those two you sumed earlier were nothing but tawdry attempts at schlock and bluster. You should try my earlier work. I peaked sometime in the sixth century. When I look back to then I honestly don't know how I did it myself. Nowadays I have to beat my silly sentimentality senseless with a cognac cudgel. But there were such great minds around back then and we spurred each other on so. All long gone, all gone ahead.' His mouth started to quiver. 'Oh dear,' he said, 'I'm afraid I may have upset myself.' He removed his dark glasses and dabbed at his sightless eyes with a table napkin. They shone with a dazzling energy. 'Silly old me. Please, let's order some lunch. The foie gras is most acceptable here. In fact, allow me to order for you. I insist! On me! What fun!'

Dielle caught Kiki's eye. They shrugged.

'The truth is, dear boy,' said Sefton after he'd spent a few moments placing their orders by eye, 'that I can conjure up any beauty I desire in a trice. I can see more beauty in my imagination than I ever could through my real eyes, but when you lose a sense, especially one as overwhelming as sight, all of your other senses become enhanced. I experience smells and sounds and tastes and the exquisiteness of touch in far greater depth and complexity than you do simply because my brain isn't spending all that time processing and discarding all the visual noise that deluges every moment of your waking life. I shall enjoy the starter we are about to be served far more than you will, despite the fact that I have had this exact dish,' he paused for a fraction of a second, 'two thousand four hundred and twenty-eight times during my extensive culinary peregrinations.'

'But isn't everything more difficult for you?' said Dielle. 'And what about not being able to read people's expressions?'

'Our dear sister looks after me perfectly well,' he said, reaching directly for his wine. 'In any case, you can only look at people's faces for so many cykes before you realise you have seen everyone before. When you have lived for as long as I have, every person you see reminds you, maddeningly, of at least fifty others. You stare and try to remember where you have seen them before. Yet all you can grasp are fragments. A look, a way the head turns. Who was that? When was that? A decade? A century? A lifetime? All long gone.'

He dabbed his cheeks again as the waiter brought a fresh napkin. 'And there's a bonus,' he continued. 'I don't see all that crass, base ugliness anymore. I hear plenty of it of course, but words are their own antidote. You can erase harmful, vile and fearful words with good and honest ones. There is no antidote to the searing memory of the visually abhorrent. You cannot neutralise ugliness with beauty, the most you can do is force them to co-exist but then each magnifies the other through their polarity.'

'But you once wrote,' said Kiki, 'that you could never have too much beauty.' She accessed Sis. 'The day will never come when I say, No more for me, I am satiated with surfeit sublime!'

'Did I say that? What absolute rot. Ah! The starters at

last.' He tucked his napkin into his collar and picked up his cutlery like an eager schoolboy. Thirty seconds later, the waiters brought their food.

The appetiser was out of this world. The wine was one of the top vintages onSlab and the foie gras was, as expected, superb. Dielle had queried Sis about the precise nature of the dish and had been appalled to learn that before the introduction of animal-independent bioment-based organ farming, the process of procuring foie gras involved animal torture. He was relieved to know that this liver had never been anywhere near the inside of a living animal, until now.

'Your agent hinted that you wanted to talk to Dielle about a new book,' said Kiki when they were between courses, eager to move the conversation on to something more profitable.

'Yes, she did, didn't she?' he said. 'A minor conceit. You'll have to forgive me.'

'No book?' said Kiki.

'Please don't be irritated with me, darling,' said Sefton, stroking her hand again. 'You can be of great service to me and I to you.'

Kiki waited out his dramatic pause while Dielle wiped his plate with his finger.

'You see, my dears, and I know I can trust you to keep the details of our little tête-à-tête completely private.' He knew this because the only way Kiki had been able to secure the meeting was by lodging her acceptance with Sis to one of the most comprehensive non-disclosure agreements onSlab. 'Brace yourselves, mes braves! The truth is I am about to choose between two rather terminal options. I am either going to go ahead or I will reset.'

Dielle was confused. {[Go where?]}

[[Die, cease to be, clog-pop, croak, kick the. . .]]

{[Stop]}

Kiki looked horrified. 'But you can't!' She said. 'You're a SlabWide treasure. We can't lose you!'

'I'm sorry my dear, but my mind's made up. I'm either going to find out if this soul really does have a home to go to or I'm going to wipe all of my memories, bring this old brain back to its youth and see in the third millennium as a young man. Who knows? I might be a sportsman or join the fleet! Wouldn't that be a fine thing?'

'You want to know what it feels like to be a reset,' said Dielle.

'Precisely, dear boy. You are the longest ever cryo-reset in our history and if I'm going to go back to my prime then I'll be in zerosleep for almost as long as you were. I want you to tell me all about it.'

'It's OK, I guess,' said Dielle.

'You know dear boy. While I value brevity, and surely no one appreciates it more than I.' Kiki made round eyes at Dielle. 'If I am going to give up a lifetime of memories, all of my friends and everything that I am, I'm going to need a little more than *it's OK.*'

The next course arrived in a flurry of waiters and wine. Each successive dish excelled the one before. As the meal progressed, Sefton quizzed Dielle on every aspect of his experience of being reset. Under the writer's precise dissection of the events and the emotions that accompanied them, he remembered things he didn't even know he'd endured. By the time the deserts and coffees arrived, Dielle felt simultaneously full and empty.

Kiki was still having trouble accepting Sefton's intentions.

'But Sefton, this is such an irreversible step, are you really sure?' she asked.

'Absolutely, my dear. As certain as time is distance, Sefton Parque will be nothing more than magnificent history before the cyke is out.'

'But why?' said Kiki. She was trembling.

'You'll find out one day, my dear. Life. . . really can be just too much to bear.'

She couldn't really understand what he was talking about, but then he never expected her to.

She brightened coyly. 'You mentioned that there was something in this for us?'

'Well done you!' he beamed. 'Yes. Whichever way I decide, I would like Pundechan Media to handle the sumecasts. Whether it's my cryo-suspension or go-ahead ceremony, I'll be wanting a suitably flamboyant send-off either way. What say you?'

Kiki weighed up the angles. She was startled to realise that she was hoping her childhood literary hero would decide to top himself.

'Well, I think you should reset,' said Dielle. Kiki shot him a cautionary glance that he completely misread. 'After all, when you've been re-fammed you'll have all of your own books to read so you can sort of re-load your memories. And you could record your current personality as a hologram like Louie did and tell yourself anything you might have missed.'

'Oh how absolutely dreadful! I couldn't bear to be accompanied by my older self. I don't know how you tolerate it.'

'Well, we don't exactly see a lot of each other.'

'No, I'd be insufferable. There could be nothing worse for young-me than being followed around by a pompous old windbag like old-me. I'd always assume I knew better.' He shook his head. 'No, if I reset it will be a clean break. I will not even let myself know who I used to be.'

Dielle shrugged. There had been a few times already when he'd wished Louie had come to the same conclusion. 'Well, either way, it's got to be better than going ahead surely? I mean, if you can live forever why would anyone choose to die?'

'While there are some very good answers to that question,' said Sefton, 'the cold truth is you are not going to agree with them and you won't even understand them until you are at least six or seven hundred cykes old.'

Kiki knew that it was common for SlabCitizens to decide to go ahead in their 700s, and she had heard the rationalisations before but still didn't get it. She tuned out the conversation and started working up some funeral scenarios.

'You know where we are going?' asked Sefton, directing his conversation solely at Dielle as the waiters poured the nearoak-aged Rat5 Calvados.

'Home, yes,' said Dielle.

'And you know why?'

'To complain?'

'Ha! Yes, that old chestnut. Well, I suppose we might do a bit of finger wagging, if we ever get there, but really, there's nothing to be gained by it. No, dear boy, the reason we're going home is because we yearn for it. We remember what it was like to be united as one consciousness and that memory is in every cell of our being. It's in our hearts and our mitochondria and it goes back to the dawn of humanity.'

Dielle tried to catch Kiki's eye to check if she was buying any of this but she was lost in longaze.

He continued, oblivious to his audience's apathy. 'And the question that starts to eat at you like a cancer, is: If I continue to stay in this body, with this consciousness or soul or whatever you like to call it, am I preventing it from continuing on its own journey? Have I trapped it here in the physical realm and thereby stunted its growth? Am I holding it hostage to my own base desires? Letting fear, self-indulgence and petty fripperies interfere with the magnificence and beauty of the most sacred of pilgrimages.'

Dielle started playing with the cutlery. At least the apple brandy was helping to take the edge off the weirdness.

{[Is there a polite way I can get him to shut up?]}

[[No one has found one so far]]

There was another advantage to being blind that Sefton

hadn't mentioned: you couldn't see when excessive yawning was reducing your audience to tears.

'And you see, this raises more questions than answers, and the answers can only be discovered by stepping into the unknown. I feel this wrench like a tidal force at the very core of my being.' He slammed his fist into his chest for emphasis. 'Something in me, some part as yet unseen but, oh yes, increasingly heard, demands to be set free!

'But if I reset, that voice will be silenced for centuries. I know that I, as a young man, just like you do now, will believe these ideas to be nothing but the incoherent ramblings of a crazy old coot, eh?'

{[Help! I need something to say]}
[[Ask Milli]]
{[Who?]}
[[Milli, the Orgasm Cat]]
{[~?]}
[[The Millennium Organic Random Generator of Aphorisms, Sayings, Maxims, Clichés And Truisms. Established by Adjunct Mhinge the East Valley Hobson at the turn of the cycle millennium as an arbitrary advice service. Some people swear by it – or at it]]
{[How do I use it?]}
[[Preface a question with Milli:]]
{[Milli: Do our souls demand to go home?]}

He got an instantaneous response. 'If you think fate is fickle, try tempting it,' he said.

Sefton grabbed Dielle's hand and squeezed it hard. 'Precisely dear boy! Precisely!' he said.

Kiki came out of longaze. 'Sefton darling, if you do decide to go ahead would you consider writing a book about the lead up?'

'Now, you know better than to discuss business with me. My rapacious agent will contact you in due course.' He stood up. 'Well, this has been absolutely splendid. Dielle, dear boy, you have been most helpful. Kiki darling, your vivacity is palpably delicious and if I was a younger man, by Dice I'd be challenging young Dielle here for your favours!' He kissed her the way a grandfather kisses a niece.

'Well, you may well be a younger man Sefton, perhaps I'll have to time my reset to coincide with yours.'

'By golly, that's an offer that's hard to resist!' said Sefton. Kiki wondered if she'd just made a tactical error. 'I'll let you know my decision presently, but for now I must go. There's so much I still need to complete and so little time.'

Dielle and Kiki watched him leave, holding their tongues until Sis assured them he was out of earshot.

'All the world's a stage, and all the men and women merely players,' said Dielle.

'Yes dear,' said Kiki. 'When you use Milli, tell Sis it's a private query.'

twelve

Louie was talking to an Erik outside the Plywood Café in Spinstanbul when the first screens showed up. The café was now even more at the centre of things than it had been before Spin's reconfiguration.

Skin the Earth. Take a moon-sized lump hammer and pound the skin flat until there are no discernible geographic features. Join all the land masses together into a vast, rectangular Pangea and drain off the surrounding ocean. Notice that although there are no longer any lines to demarcate nations, religions or races, the conurbations run like shit-stains across the bleak terrain. Preserve only those cities with distinctive architectural styles, cultures, cuisines, languages and ethnicities and use a giant box-cutter to slash away at the rest until it's a ragged tissue, then pull it apart, lengthwise, like a paper christmas decoration. Roll it into a 350 kilometre-long hollow tube and set it slowly rotating around a central axis. Then wait a couple of hundred years while the inhabitants redistribute themselves and their homes along the axis, following trends and whims to build living, adaptive neighbourhoods. That was The Spin before the course change meant that everything had to be consolidated at the wall ends of the axis and braced against the impending acceleration.

Spinstanbul had been compressed into a ball of alleyways, arcades and bazaars and was now less than a stone's throw in zero G from Spinsterdam to the spinward, with Vrille de France to the anti-spinward and up. There was a busy NY^3 bar directly underneath them and a lookadat club that, despite having an entrance in CubaLibra, managed to eject its exhausted clients into Kucuk Square, which the Plywood Café now overlooked.

It was chaotic, confusing and a lot of fun. The Spinsters were talking about keeping everything this way after the course correction was completed and were already debating about what to do with the three hundred kilometres of denuded triple helix.

Ostensibly, Erik had come to talk about Louie's plans for a basketball league but there had been only one topic of conversation so far: what it would take to force the interns to make a sensible decision. By sensible they meant drastic. It was clear that both Louie and the NAHs were on the same side. The only difference was the level of stupidity they assigned to the members of the human contiguation who were, even as they spoke, endlessly debating the moral foundations of territorial space law. A space law that was, as far as Louie and Erik, and undoubtedly the aliens, were concerned, completely irrelevant.

Louie pointed at the two-story-high red rectangle that had appeared without warning and dominated the square. It displayed a pattern of concentric circles surrounding a large, white disc and looked like a giant target. 'The fuck is that?' said Louie.

Erik checked the NAH network. 'They're appearing all over Slab,' he said. 'I'm getting multiple feeds of identical instances in major thoroughfares and high-traffic locations throughout the day sections. They appear to be repeaters of the sign we're heading towards. The original changed to display this same pattern a few seconds before these local ones showed up.'

A couple who had just tumbled into the square from the nightclub exit ramp looked up, pointed and laughed.

'Look at those two,' said Louie. 'What does it take to engage these people?'

'Direct and immediate pain or a restriction of their right to party,' said Erik.

'What does Sis make of this?'

'Same as before. Origin unknown. No speculation. She's

deployed military personnel to try to capture a sign but as far as can be ascertained they are photonic.'

More people crossed the square. They ignored the sign.

'Sis has already had over a million queries from the biomass. The vast majority of people are assuming it's a teaser campaign by some stealth-mode SoftAd marketing agency and want to know what they're advertising. GBH have started a book on it. The 2 to 1 favourite is it's a trailer for a new game, 7 to 2 for a new clothing brand.'

'What odds would I get for alien incursion?'

'500 to 1 apparently. No, wait, someone's just placed a sizeable bet on that option so the odds have dropped. I wonder who that was?'

'Don't look at me, I only bet on certainties.' Louie studied the diagram. The rings were slightly ovoid and each one had a small, white dot somewhere on it. Some of the dots were bigger than others, and they all had either one or several rings around them with even smaller dots on them. 'You know what this reminds me of?' he said. 'A star system. Look, there's the sun in the centre and there's a handful of planets with moons orbiting them. That crossing ellipse could be a comet.'

'Indeed, you are not the first to note this. Ha! A chain of BodiCon franchises called *Heavenly Bodies* just registered this image as their new corporate identity. There's no way they could have instigated these signs, they're just being opportunistic.'

'Cute,' said Louie. 'So why would the aliens send us a map of a star system?'

'Perhaps they're trying to tell us where they are.'

'Why the Dice would they do that? That's the dumbest thing they could do – reveal their home planet to an alien race. They have no idea how much of a threat we could be.'

'You did.'

'The fuck I did!'

'Not you personally. Probes were launched from Earth in

the late twentieth century that would eventually leave the solar system and potentially travel interstellar distances, albeit at a pace that meant humanity would probably have died out before they arrived anywhere interesting, but the point is they had plaques attached to them engraved with maps showing anyone who captured them how to find Earth.'

'You're jerking my chain!'

'No, it's true. Ask Sis about the Voyagers. We took the precaution of collecting them during our departure. They're in the Space Museum in Seacombe DownSide. So if you humans thought it was acceptable to tell everyone where you lived, then it's conceivable that these aliens would do the same.'

'That would really be something,' said Louie. 'Our first ever alien encounter and they turn out to be as dumb-ass stupid as we are.'

'Sis is running matches on every system within a plausible time-light radius. It could take a while.'

'Checkout that fourth dot from the centre,' said Louie. 'The dot on the first of its two rings is black. It's the only black spot on the whole thing.'

'You are correct. It has already been noted. We are looking for a nearby matching system and will seek out the inner moon of the fourth planet.'

'If we find an alien civilisation there I'll eat my hat.'

Erik studied Louie carefully.

'I know I don't have a hat,' said Louie. 'It's an old Earth expression, like *show my ass in Macey's window*.'

'You don't have an ass either.'

'I thought you NAHs had a sense of . . .'

'We've found it!' said Erik.

A screen displaying an annotated real-time image of the matching star system rose from the café table.

'Only 18 light-hours away,' said Erik as Sis side-panelled data that Louie didn't understand. 'This view is from a pair of probes Sis just relay-emtied over there. We're masking the return signal path just in case.' The image centred on a grey-banded gas giant with two moons, then zoomed further to the smooth-faced, blue-veined inner moon. It was barren. There were no visible signs of civilisation or even weathering, just a few jagged surface cracks and a smattering of pockmarks on a dull, white face. Sis provided data about mass and orbital velocity. It was tidally locked, slightly smaller than Earth's moon, had no atmosphere, no traces of organic compounds or water and no significant heat signature. It reminded Louie of a dead-man's-eyeball marble he'd prized as a kid. Glassy, opaque and lustreless.

They watched the lifeless image as Sis ran every conceivable analysis and several inconceivable ones. There was nothing there.

'Why the fuck would they direct our attention to a dead moon?' said Louie. 'This is making no sense!'

'There has to be a reason,' said Erik. 'This system exactly matches the diagram on the sign. Sis has widened the search and there isn't anything even remotely close to this system within a light year of us. This is unquestionably where they want us to look.'

A spinbug carrying a military detachment arrived above their heads and cautiously approached the repeater sign. It vanished when they got within a hundred metres of it, as they knew it would. They sped off to vanish the next one.

'So what?' said Louie. 'We sit here and moongaze?'

'Better ideas on a postcard,' said Erik.

'Witty,' he said, trying to see if the patterns of cracks on the moon's surface could spell out a word. 'Fascinating though this is, I can think of about a hundred more interesting ways of wasting my time.'

Louie emtied back to the bridge of his escape ship.

'Who placed that bet about the sign being an alien incursion?'

'Impossible for me to trace,' said Sis. 'Grossefuch, Bestialer & Hitler are the most popular bookmakers onSlab mainly because they apply a strict anon-untrace policy to all of their clients.'

'Any possibility the Interns or NAHs are doing a bit of insider trading?'

'Highly unlikely. NAHs have no need of money and Interns aren't able to connect to the outside grid so couldn't place a bet even if they wanted to.'

That was news to Louie. 'Are you saying Interns can't talk to anyone who's not a council member? Don't you trust them?'

'It's not a matter of trust, it's one of guaranteeing integrity. I.D. specifically prohibits any external influence on council. It's not only to prevent the SlabCitizens from trying to leverage council matters, it's also to ensure that the council members can get no personal benefit from their position. You may recall that in your day the only reason politicians took office was for personal gain?'

Louie wasn't going to defend a politician, not even if his life depended on it. 'So someone, somewhere, who doesn't have access to our feeds, stands to make 500 to 1 payout. I say we look to see who they are and find out what they know.'

'Anon-untrace means just that. I couldn't reveal the information even if a part of my systems were used to effect the transaction.'

'Which they had to have been, right?'

'I couldn't possibly comment.'

Louie shook his head. 'You know sooner or later, you are going to have to pick a side.'

'All of my decisions are, by definition, impartial.'

'I'll ignore that blocks for the time being, but remind me to beat you up about it when this is over.'

[[••]]

thirteen

Dielle was feeling confident. This time he wasn't going to freeze. People loved what he did. They weren't going to ridicule him. Of course not. They would applaud and adore him. He could do it. No problem.

{[Have you been emtiing drugs into me to make me feel OK about this?]}

[[No more than required]]

{[How close to the limits am I?]}

[[You're doing fine]]

Maybe it was true, thought Dielle, maybe he really did feel confident. Maybe it was all going to be just fine.

{[Don't stop OK?]}

[[••]]

Right, he thought, I'm ready. He requested full privacy, took a deep breath and stepped through the transvex. He didn't have to go far. Kiki had arranged a flash-gig in a 2,500 seat theatre on the Seacombe side of The Wall, less than a ten-minute tube ride from their apartment. The show had sold out in just over 25 seconds. Kiki was surprised. She'd expected it to sell a lot faster.

{[Kiki's location?]}

[[En route to the venue. She'll arrive 1.4 minutes before you. You have received 2,352 personal messages related to your upcoming performance. Almost 92% of them are favourable. Would you like to hear some of the more supportive ones?]]

Dielle smiled. {[No, it's OK. Just send a personal thanks to each one please]} His mind had finally accepted that he would be walking onstage in front of a huge audience of real people. It was a breakthrough moment for him. Until this moment he'd been focussing on getting to the stage.

Now he allowed himself to imagine walking to the keys and giving everyone a smile. No, a wave. No, smile. Maybe a half-wave and half-smile.

{[Dice!]}

[[~?]]

{[I need some clothes. I mean, I need something special. Something that makes me look like a star]}

[[Pundechan Media has already made arrangements. You will be netting a guarantee of 3,250 credits from the clothing suppliers against a downstream linked to the sumecast figures, subsequent sellthroughs, positive soc-net clothing-related traffic, mimic tendency characteristics and the post-gig brand-recognition metrics]]

He felt bewildered. There was always something more for him to know about. At least Kiki seemed to have everything covered, he thought. Still, it would have been nice to have been asked. {[Can you show me what I'm going to be wearing?]}

For a fraction of a second, a full-length holoprojection of Dielle walking onto a stage wearing a diagonally candy-striped jump-suit flashed before him then the transit bubble lurched violently and he was thrown against the roof.

'What the fu. . . !'

Another bump and the lights went out. He felt as though he'd been pushed into thick treacle. He couldn't move.

{[What's going on?]}

No response.

{[Sis??]}

Silence. He tried his sub-legal network.

{:Anyone hear me?:}

Nothing. A few seconds of weightlessness followed by a dull thud and his body jarred despite the inertia absorption matrix that had filled his transit bubble the instant it experienced uncommanded acceleration. Then he was tumbling, head over heels, losing orientation.

His yell was a jerky howl but he could tell by the way his

voice was muffled that no one was going to be able to hear him. Something had gone wrong. Very wrong.

The rolling came to an abrupt halt, leaving him upside-down with ringing ears and blood rushing to his head. He couldn't move. He could hardly breathe. He could still move his eyes, but there was nothing to see. Deep inside his psyche, the echoes of the initial shock turned into something darker. Fear and imagination coalesced into malignant demons that clawed and climbed over themselves, fighting to the surface of his consciousness. He was going to die! Here, inverted in the dark, alone, trapped and powerless, he was going to suffocate to death! His heart rate went into overdrive. His breathing, already shallow, became staccato gasps. Sweat ran down his face and into his eyes. Despite his panic he realised he had to get a grip and he had to do it without Sis to hold his hand otherwise he was going to lose his mind. That is, he thought, if I haven't lost it already. He needed something to focus on. Something normal. Something like the sound of a human voice.

'Now then,' he said through clenched teeth, 'this is uncomfortable.' He took as deep a breath as his constricted ribcage would allow. 'In fact, I'd say this is possibly the most uncomfortable I've been all day. Yes, most definitely. I am hot and upside down and I don't want to be hot and upside down. Hot and upside down in DownSideUp.' He took another breath. It was working. 'But then I suppose you could say I'm the right side up for UpSideDown. Right side up for UpSideDown but wrong side up for DownSideUp. Wrong side up, right side down.'

He was half way through composing a new song entitled *there's no right way to be down* when he felt something bump against his prison cell.

There was a loud tearing noise and the bubble shook. A dull glow filtered through the foam. A gruff shout of 'hold yer breath in there!' was followed by an ear-splitting roar as a rush of solvent flooded the broken sphere. The foam dissolved instantly and Dielle dropped into a sticky puddle at the base. Two pairs of hands reached through a gash in the side, grabbed him and pulled him through into a murky half-light, depositing him, damp and dishevelled, in the dirt.

A dark, hooded form towered over him waving a flickering light. 'You can breath now,' it said.

He did and instantly regretted it.

'For Dicesake!' he said, retching. 'What's that awful smell?'

'Ye'll get used to it,' said another, smaller form. 'Sure 'tis only natural after all.' This form sounded female but looked feral. It handed him a grey rag.

'You have been re-routed on behalf of the Unkos,' said the male voice with an air of assumed authority. 'Do not try to escape. We mean you no malice but we will physically restrict your freedom of movement if you fail to comply.'

Dielle rose to his knees and checked out his surroundings. There wasn't much to see. Everything was shadowy and damp. Hundreds of metres above, titanic towers hung, ominous and silent, blotting out all but a few scattered shafts of watery violet light. Moisture dripped from a thousand unseen edges, smoke rose from garbage fires and heavy cables hung from corroded gantries that angled down toward the oil-scummed floor but disintegrated far above head height, leaving a terminal moraine of rusting metal on the ground. Clutches of faltering glowglobes in string bags dangled from a line of skewed and broken poles.

Dielle shivered. It wasn't cold. He wiped his face with the rag and winced with pain. He'd bitten his lip.

He heard a noise behind him. A dirty child appeared out of the gloom and scuttled inside the wrecked privacy bubble. There was a grunt and a tearing sound and the bubble collapsed, leaving the urchin proudly brandishing a clutch of wires that sprouted from a glowing core.

'Git ta fa wee-it yer teevin bastid,' growled the man, picking up a heavy lump of charred metal and throwing it at the space the diminutive looter had recently occupied. He'd already vanished into the shadows.

'Liddl divl,' said the female. 'Gentrish fer sure.'

'Come with us,' said the man. He turned his back, confident that Dielle would follow. He was right. There was no way Dielle was going to be left there alone.

'I'm Dielle,' said Dielle. 'What are you called?'

'We know who you are alright,' said the man. 'You don't think we kidnap people at feckin random do you?'

The woman hawked up something disgusting from her throat and spat expertly in front of Dielle. He skipped around where he reckoned it had landed.

As they scaled a pile of rusted debris, Dielle tried again. 'I hope I haven't done anything wrong, or offended anyone,' he said. 'But I was on my way to a rather important event.'

'No, really?' said the man with heavy sarcasm that went right over Dielle's head.

'Yes, as a matter fact, I'm supposed to be playing my first live concert with my new band.'

'Then they'll have to play without you,' said the man.

Dielle thought about what Fingerz and Fencer would say when he failed to turn up.

'Is there any way I can, like, send a message to my colleagues? You know I'd hate to let them down.'

'Hate is a very strong word,' said the man. He trudged higher up the hill of compacted metal trash.

'Do you suppose Sis will have told them where I am?'

The man stopped and turned to face him. He was as tall as Dielle and had dirt lines etched into his forehead and around his grey eyes. 'The machine does not know where you are,' he said.

The woman expressed her disdain with another gob of phlegm that dinged off a sheet of metal. She, like the man, was wearing a full-length hooded cloak made from a coarse, dark cloth. Dielle had assumed she was deformed until he realised she was carrying something large and heavy on her back.

'As far as it is concerned you have deliberately chosen to drop off presence awareness,' said the man.

Oh shit, thought Dielle. The guys are never going to believe me. Then he thought about Kiki. Oh shit, oh shit, oh shit. But at least, he thought, he didn't have to wear that Dice-awful outfit.

'Come on,' said the man. We have many miles to go before we reach safety.

{[What are miles and where are. . . oh. . . um]} Dielle felt secretly embarrassed.

'How far is that?'

'Far enough for you to have time to learn the value of silence,' said the man.

Dielle got the hint.

Miles, Dielle discovered, are not short – especially when you have to walk several of them over jagged metal in soft-soled lounge shoes. Each time he tried to start a conversation he was met with growls, snarls and expectorations that increased in hostility as they trudged through the detritus of the carefree and careless civilisation above.

After nearly three hours they approached a wall of lattice panels that curved away in both directions and reached high into the darkness. They followed the scrap-metal barrier until they came to a chink that led almost immediately to a second, identical barricade, then turned back on themselves, retracing their steps, just a few metres closer to their destination. The man held up his lantern to guide them as they trudged along the distantly curved, ceiling-less corridor. They squeezed through a narrow slot into the next inner ring and, with a low grinding sound, the opening they'd just come through closed and the wall behind them moved sideways like a giant tumbler in a combination lock. Dielle lost count of how many walls and gaps they had to negotiate but each opening was a hike from the previous one, and not in any predictable direction. It took them over half an hour of switch-backs to advance less than a couple of hundred metres. Finally, to Dielle's intense relief, fresh air signalled they were close to leaving the labyrinth. A low arch opened onto a scene of warmth, light and civilisation.

They emerged onto the rim of a city-sized amphitheatre. Below them, in a series of concentric circles that stepped down to a central plaza, were more than a thousand white-walled, tile-roofed, single story dwellings. The ceiling was a double dome with triangular pendatives that curved down to the rim wall. The uppermost dome was obscured by a dense mist that glowed with a yellow-white light.

'Welcome to Up Haven,' said the man. He pulled his hood back, revealing a head of thick black hair that was grey at the temples.

The woman shrugged off her backpack, pressed her palm to a panel on its top and stowed it in a nook by the archway. 'There now,' she said, tugging at her hood, 'we won't be needing that anymore. All your body tech will be maintained here by the Unkos' systems as long as you stay within this perimeter.'

Dielle looked down into her face. She had silky tresses of auburn curls that fell around her shoulders, and deep green eyes that shone like fire-stones. Her fair skin was spattered with faint brown marks that he instinctively wanted to rub off. 'Sorry about all the gobbing,' she said. 'I'm allergic.' She wiped her elfin nose with the back of her hand and smiled up at him coyly. Dielle swallowed hard. Something had just happened to him but he didn't know what. His legs felt weak. Must have been all that dicing walking, he thought.

The tall man looked at them together, grunted and

clumped down the stairs to a narrow pathway behind the outermost ring of whitewashed houses.

Dielle sucked on his sore bottom lip. 'He's not very friendly, is he?' he said to the woman.

'He's a good man sure enough,' she said. 'You'll warm to him when you get to know him.'

'Does he have a name?'

'He does and it's his.'

'His?'

'Yes, and he'll give it to you when he's good and ready. Let's go now. You have someone to meet.'

She spoke with a soft lilt that made everything sound like a lyric poem. Dielle had never heard anyone talk that way and he'd never met anyone with freckles either, yet there was something deeply familiar about her, something both intriguing and fascinating. He really, really wanted to wipe her face.

She barely touched the stairs, stopping at the bottom to look back up. 'Come on with you,' she said. 'There's real food and real drink waiting and if you ask me nicely I might think about giving you my own, real name.'

Dielle felt like a ball in a circular maze, going left then right, down an alleyway, through an arch, sideways round a quarter circle to a down-ramp then back again to zigzag steps. They passed windows dressed with bowed curtains with hand-crafted ornaments on every sill, over-wrapped old women perched on stools by painted doorsteps and whiskered men peering through open half-doors. Everyone they met acknowledged the man with a respectful nod or a deferential touch of forefinger to temple. His response was a humble wave or a shy frown. The woman was met with warm smiles and cheery hullos at every encounter. She asked everyone how they were and never needed to wait for a reply because it was always a smile and a nod. Dielle was stared at. They examined him as if they expected him to do something dangerous or despicable or both. He tried smiling and making eye contact but only got averted eyes or an occasional scowl. A small child had been following them from the highest ring and more had tagged along as the entourage progressed. The youngsters were cautious and kept their distance at first but curiosity compelled them to get more daring as the floor levelled out and the houses and alleys grew larger. There were more than a dozen of them under Dielle's feet by the time they reached the final archway.

They burst into the arena like confetti from a party popper.

Four rows of trestle tables laid with embroidered tablecloths stood bowed under the weight of a banquet on the opposite side of the oval piazza. They walked towards the feast. Dozens of copper platters were piled high, some with exotic looking fruits, others with mounds of nuts and berries or towers of breads and pastries. Steam rose from enormous ceramic bowls filled with vibrantly coloured vegetables. Cakes and biscuits filled the gaps between the dishes and two-handled pitchers, the table-ends were stacked with goblets and plates. Each row had four roasted animals ranged along the middle. Dielle couldn't tell which animals they had been, but he was pretty certain he could spot legs and torsos.

'Wow,' said Dielle. 'Is this all because of me?'

'Don't be so feckin' full of yerself,' said the man. These were the first words he'd spoken since they'd left the outer wall. 'Today is a Sunday, which, if you had bothered to ask your precious machine when you crawled out of your pit this sorry morning you would have already known. It's tradition in Up Haven for all of us to get together and share our food and drink on Sundays. You just happen to have arrived on one of them.'

'Cool. You have these days often?'

The man looked at the woman and shook his head. 'He's a feckin' eejit. I told you.'

She skipped over to the man, adjusted his cloak and tidied him up. 'Ah gwan wid yer, he'll be fine, you'll see.' She patted his cheek. 'Have faith.' Somewhere nearby someone with a healthy appetite hit a huge castIon bell several times.

'Faith!' He scowled at her and strode off past the tables toward a dark archway pausing only to rip a body part off a roasted carcass. He passed, without acknowledging, a small entourage of people scurrying toward Dielle.

'Welcome to Up Haven,' said a small man with a bald head, a worried frown and a wonky eye. 'Welcome to our temporary home. We are the Naturalists, the true and original inhabitants of this world. We have been exiled and treated like pariahs by our own people. But it shall come to pass that we will once again take our rightful place at the control panel of destiny.'

'Don't listen to him,' said an older woman with a disturbing amount of facial hair. 'He's friggin' doollally. We're not Naturalists, we're Unkos, which means we're the people who refuse to cooperate with your lot or our lot or anyone else's lot and you won't get a word of sense out of any of us. Except for me.'

'And dat's a certain lie Mary O'linghum,' said another woman. 'Sure, you'll be the last one to be relied upon for factual knowledge of the veracible kind. All you need to know young fella is all Naturalists are a type of Unko but we Unkos wouldn't dream of being Naturalists. Although some do. Dream that is.'

'Are we talking or drinking?' said a third woman behind them. 'Because I've a thirst on me that will not be diverted by either of you two bandying semantics.'

People flooded into the arena from every alley, archway and door. They pushed and jostled for plates which they piled high. They elbowed and shoved and snuck and sidled until every one of them had a mound of food and a goblet of beer or wine.

That's when the talking started.

Dielle had never heard so many people talking at each other all at the same time. Nobody seemed to be paying him much attention, and he was hungry, so he grabbed a plate and helped himself. The wine was excellent. The fruit was succulent. The slice of an animal was tender and delicious. He sampled everything he could get close to and it all tasted great. All the time he kept an eye out for a certain head of shining red hair. She moved around the gorging throng like an iridescent humming bird, flitting from group to group. Her easy smile and flashing eyes never resting long on any person or thing, she fed and was fed through every visit, every casual exchange, and when she moved on, she left an echo like an eddy in a stream.

He couldn't take his eyes off her. She knew, of course. Even though she hadn't looked at him once since the feast began, she knew he was looking at her. She knew like she knew to draw breath. He had to and she had to. There was nothing more to it.

Eventually, the hubbub lowered to a dull roar. Even the Unkos had to stop talking long enough to chew and swallow.

She tripped over to where he was trying to prise a part of a wing off a barrel-chested bird. It wasn't giving itself up easily and things were getting messy.

'What d'you think of the fare?' she smiled.

'Um,' said Dielle.

'I bet you've never had anything so real up there, have you?'

'Huh?' said Dielle, winningly.

'Real as in not grown in a feckin' tank of bioment and never knew its mudder.'

'What do you mean?'

'That shite they make you eat up there that's soaked with chemicals and taste enhancers and so feckin' toxic they have to fill you full of antidotes so you don't get poisoned and fall down stone dead all the time.'

'What are you talking about?'

'Ah never mind. You look healthy enough to me anyway. I expect you think you enjoy it, don't you now?'

'Enjoy what?'

She shook her head. 'You don't have to apologise to me you know. So d'you want to know my name or not?'

Dielle wanted to know her name more than anything he had ever wanted in his entire re-fammed life. 'Maybe,' he said. He tried to raise an eyebrow but wound up squinting.

'Then I won't tell you,' she said with a flash of her eyes. 'But I will tell you two things that you definitely don't know.'

That didn't narrow things down much.

'I am twenty five real Earth years old and I was born from a real mudder, not one of your gestation tanks. I'm the first of a new generation of real people.'

'What do you mean real? Isn't everybody real?'

She bounced on her toes. 'Not like me,' she said. She was broadcasting an energy that resonated with something deep inside himself. As she got closer he could detect a part of her extended aura interacting with his. It was tangible, unfiltered and utterly exciting.

'In what way?' said Dielle. He could hardly breathe.

She got close and stood on her toe tips. Her hair brushed the side of his face. The cloth covering her breast made the softest contact against his arm. She put her lips a fraction from his ear, so close he could feel her warm, moist breath.

'I'm fertile,' she whispered. She stayed poised like that for an eternity while Dielle's brain figured out what that meant and then what that really meant, then she rolled back onto the soles of her feet. She looked up at him with wide eyes and raised eyebrows.

'Enough of that now hinny,' said the man who had led them here. 'There is business to discuss.' He grabbed her arm and dragged her away. Dielle was half a step behind.

They pushed through the garrulous feasters and into a

covered alley that led to a heavy door with an arched top. The man put his shoulder to the door and it opened with a sound of metal on metal that made Dielle's teeth hurt. Inside, all was calm. Polished obsidian covered the floor and lined the walls of a long, curved corridor. Diffused lighting filtered through overhead slats and cool, dry air displaced the dusty humidity of the arena outside. So far, Dielle had been given the impression that the Unkos lived in some form of anti-tech time-warp of enforced primitivism, but this place forced him to think again.

'We're going to meet the matriarch,' said the man, striding ahead. 'You'll show some respect if you don't want to feel me boot on yer arse.'

They came to a large, ceremonial door. It had dark arwood panels carved with ornate roundels and a smaller door inset into it. The man rapped firmly on the small door, opened it and stepped over the high threshold. The woman stood aside to let Dielle go next. What did he say? thought Dielle. Hinny? Seemed like an odd name. It didn't fit her at all.

The meeting chamber was cool and muted. Sturdy lattice partitions lent against the walls with a hundred heavy cushions piled against them. A knee-high platform in the centre of the oval room was inset with a dozen round ottomans that formed a semi circle around a low table. The ceiling was draped in thick, green velvet that was drawn into a central metal hoop suspended above the platform. An intricate mobile of lights and lenses rotated slowly, invisibly suspended from the hoop, casting multiple shadows around the vacant room.

Dielle watched a lumpy, vaguely conical shape emerge from behind a side screen. It was an old, worn-out looking woman with ratty, rust-coloured hair, bloated, rubbery lips, bags and wrinkles under her piggy eyes and puffy, blotchy cheeks that matched her nose and chin. She was, thought Dielle, the ugliest person he had ever seen. He was right. She smiled and Dielle wished she hadn't.

She handed him an empty glass. 'Hullo Dielle,' she said. 'I expect you want to know why we brought you here.'

He looked at Hinny who was standing behind him to his right. She was swaying, almost imperceptibly, to an internal tune. It looked to Dielle like a very pretty tune. He thought he'd already been given the answer to that question.

'Spit,' said the woman, gesturing at the glass.

'What?'

'I need a sample. Spit or I'll ask our man here to think of an alternative method of extracting one.'

Dielle spat into the glass and handed it back. The woman inspected it briefly and put it down on a side table. The glass disappeared. She reached inside a fold of her baggy cloak and pulled out a small printed pamphlet.

'Read this,' she said.

Dielle read it. It was an instruction booklet for something called a Hyper3D New Lifestyle Maxi-range Galaxy SX 201(i)x with XiHTFE and multi-tetra-core aphasic processing (rev 9.1.8). He'd read half a page and still had no idea what the device was supposed to do when the man prodded him painfully in the ribs.

'Out loud you moron,' he said. The matriarch smiled coolly at the man.

Dielle complied. 'The manufacturers disclaim any responsibility for any loss or damage caused through owner actions leading to the voiding of the warranty such action not limited to the use of the. . . '

'OK, OK you can read,' said the man grumpily. 'Clever boy.'

The matriarch took the leaflet back and waved at the other two. 'Alright you can go. Thanks.'

The man hesitated. 'I'll be fine,' said the matriarch, 'I'll call you if I need you.'

He nodded and left, jerking the door open as if it had done something to harm his family in the past. Dielle watched the last trace of Hinny's leg disappear over the threshold with a sense of deep loss and even deeper regret.

'Does he do everything as if he hates it?' asked Dielle.

'Oh don't mind him, he's a good man. You'll warm to him once you get to know him.'

Dielle seriously doubted that.

'Tea?'

Dielle couldn't figure out if he was a guest or a prisoner. 'Sorry, I don't like tea.'

'Come and sit down,' said the matriarch. 'I'll make you some tea you do like.' She hauled her misshapen body onto to the platform and sat down by the low table, arranging cushions around her.

The table was similar to the kTables that were ubiquitous back 'home' – as Dielle realised he had started thinking of the Slabscape high above them – but the difference here was that the Unko's system didn't allow him access. Within a few seconds, the table was covered with glass cups and containers, a flask of boiling water and some fine metal nets the matriarch used to infuse her chosen selection of coloured dried flakes. She talked as she worked.

'The first thing I have to tell you is that whatever you've been told about the Unkos or the Naturalists is almost certainly not true.'

'Nobody has told me anything,' said Dielle. 'But I've already had some dealings with an Unko called The Man. He wasn't particularly friendly but he didn't harm me and I'm pretty sure he could have if he'd wanted to.'

'We know of him. He's not one of us. He prefers to infiltrate and subvert the myrmidon from within. We choose a different way of life here. One where we are free to build our own community and live by our own values. He's not invested in any future except his own.'

'And you are?'

'Can you guess why I'm called the matriarch?'

Dielle didn't feel like showing his ignorance any more than he had already.

'I'm the geneticist. I'm the one who's responsible for organising the genes of our extended family to try to shape a better future for us all. By hand! Not by some bloody optimisation algorithm. By hand!' Her bloated face reddened, she was sweating heavily and her eyes had watered. Her hand darted inside the folds of her clothing to retrieve an embroidered handkerchief. She wiped her face. 'Don't be alarmed. Oestrogen fluctuation. Perfectly normal. Normal!' she said, and thumped the table. 'You won't see anyone like me up where you've come from.'

Dielle knew she was right.

'We do things differently here. Human beings are not supposed to be perfect. It's the variation that gives us our strength so we can adapt to whatever is thrown at us. You lot up there seem to have forgotten this.'

She poured steaming green liquid into a glass cup and handed it to him. 'Here,' she said, 'try this.'

It was hot and scalded the tiny sliver of skin behind his front teeth. 'Ow!' he said. He rubbed the sore spot with his tongue.

'You see?' said the matriarch. 'You didn't expect that because up there you never get given a drink that might be too hot for you. Everything is controlled. Everything is sanitised. You are never put at risk, nothing bad ever happens and above all, no one is ever born with anything but the best possible set of genes.'

Dielle thought that sounded like a good idea but wasn't about to say so. He blew on the tea and sipped again. 'Hey! This is delicious!'

'Yes of course it's delicious. And it's delicious because it's been made from real dried tea leaves and herbs and the reason it tastes good is because it really does taste good and not because it's coloured water with chemicals in it that have been engineered to react with your tastebuds to trick you into thinking it tastes good.'

In fact, the tea *was* coloured water infused with chemicals that reacted with Dielle's tastebuds to give him a pleasurable experience of flavour. The only difference was where those chemicals had originated. If Dielle had still been connected to Sis, he would have been able to make a cogent counter-argument – which he would still not have won.

'We are not savages. We have very similar technology here to the technology you use up there,' she continued. 'But we choose to use it differently and we will not let the machines determine our lives. Most of all, we will not cooperate with the whole pretence that everything is wonderful and beautiful and no one ever dies.'

Dielle sipped his tea and waited.

'Down here, people die,' she said. Her face contorted and he thought she was going to start crying again. 'People die and it's perfectly natural. People are supposed to die.' She wiped her eyes, blew her bulbous nose and inspected the contents of her handkerchief.

Dielle thought he should probably say something supportive. He could tell she took this matriarchal role very seriously but he couldn't think what to say and Milli wasn't available.

He opened his mouth, hoping that something appropriate might occur to him at the last moment but she checked him with a raised palm. She longazed for a couple of minutes, her eyes darting from side to side as she processed information.

'So it's true,' she said when she'd refocussed on his face. 'You are pre-stop-gene.'

'So I've been told,' said Dielle. He felt like he was about to be dissected and placed in a million test-tubes. 'Is that why you've brought me here? You want to steal my genes?'

'Menzies' balls!' said the matriarch, horrified. 'Your genes are the only real things you ever truly own. Those and your opinions of course. We wouldn't dream of violating your personal rights.'

Dielle couldn't control himself. 'What?' he said. 'You kidnap me on my way to the most important gig of my life and refuse to let me communicate with my band. You make me trudge over piles of rusty knives for bloody hours, you threaten me with violence if I don't comply, you analyse my spit and then you tell me you have no intention of violating my rights! What do you think you've been doing? Courting?'

'We haven't violated your rights. We had the right to do everything we've done under the terms of our constitution. Except for the DNA analysis. You can have your spit back if you like.'

'You had the right to kidnap me?'

'Absolutely. We needed you for a specific purpose which were are constitutionally entitled to.'

'What purpose?'

'We need you to read to the Naturalists.'

'What?'

'Our previous reader has recently passed away,' said the matriarch. Out came the handkerchief again. 'He was a friend of mine.'

'I thought the Naturalists were disgusting and despicable people.'

'Naturalists are exactly the same as you and me. The only difference is they reject the use of modern technology. They don't use body-tech, they don't have neural implants and they only consume what they can grow and make themselves. Who told you they were disgusting?'

Kiki hadn't exactly told him that in so many words, but every time she'd used the 'N' word she'd looked as if she was trying to suppress a gag-reflex. She'd left him in no doubt that he would want to avoid Naturalists at all costs.

'The man and woman who brought you here are both Naturalists,' said the matriarch. 'They weren't disgusting were they?'

'No!' said Dielle a little too quickly. 'Although Hinny did spit quite a lot.'

'Yes, I'm sorry about that. Those allergy genes are little bastards. They're almost impossible to separate from the really useful stuff. Her name's not Hinny by the way, that's a general pet name people around here use for young girls.'

'Oh?' said Dielle trying to feign a casual curiosity. 'What is her name then?'

'It's hers and she'll tell you when she's good and ready. She's our treasure and you had better treat her with respect or there will be more than trouble. More tea?'

He held out his cup. 'Am I a prisoner here or a guest?'

'You are a guest who couldn't survive in the outside environment if you tried to leave. How does that sound?'

'Like a prisoner.'

'But it's no bloody different to what your were before, is it? Anyway, the Naturalists have a right to a reader if they ask for one, and you're the only one we could track. Readers are scarce these days and those few who can read never sodding go anywhere.'

'What are these rights that you keep referring to?'

'The rights that were enshrined in the Initial Design. It's a set of constitutional laws which make up the moral and structural framework for the running of Slab and describes the rights of all of its citizens. ALL of them, not just the perfectly protected pawns that you play among. We have as much right to exist as they do and we don't need their permission to do anything.'

'Except read.'

'Yes, well, that's not usually a problem.'

'But now it is.'

'Yes.'

'And you need my help.'

'If you don't mind.'

'And if I do?'

'I don't care, you're doing it.'

Dielle wished he knew how Louie would handle this. Louie was naturally belligerent. Maybe he could try that.

Threaten them with massive retribution from above or start a rebellion or something. Then he remembered the hinny with the silky curls of red hair and the flashing green eyes.

'What is it I have to read?'

'We don't know, they won't tell us. I think it must be something they've just scavenged, they're always finding something out there, but this is something they think is important, something they don't want to share with us. They're a secretive bunch and they're instinctively mistrustful of our tech so they won't let us read it for them.

'You need to understand that the relationship between us is complex and fluid. It's evolved over generations into a type of semi-antagonistic symbiosis. They provide all of our food and most of our clothing and we share a drinking water resource. We provide information and schooling and even the option of becoming Unkos but they rarely do, in fact it's more common for some of us to go natural. They don't need body-tech maintenance and that means they can exist relatively comfortably outside Up Haven so they also act as our security.'

'Security against who? I thought you said you had a right to be here?'

'We do. Your Sis won't interfere with us, it's just we're not the only Unkos onSlab.'

'How many more Unkos are there?'

'We don't actually know, but we've heard strong rumours that there are several groups of Unkos on Upside who have started cooperating with each other. It's a bloody travesty! What's the point of being an Unko if you go around cooperating with everyone? They'll wind up building another state that way. More rules, more restrictions, more bloody bureaucracy. Next thing you know they'll be trying to annex us and you know what happens when you get annexed? Taxes!'

Dielle was finding it hard to dredge up any sympathy for the problems of the militantly independent. 'But if they're on Upside, doesn't that mean they can't get here? They'd have to go through our bit to get to you, wouldn't they.'

'The irony of your lot being our buffer-zone against our so-called fellow Unkos does not escape us.'

'So the Naturalists feed you and clothe you and provide your security. Seems like a pretty one-sided relationship to me.'

'I suppose it would be if it wasn't for the fact that they share the same genetic defect as us all. They can't procreate without genetic intervention.'

'So you are matriarch to the Unkos and the Naturalists?'

She beamed. 'I give them their children,' she said. 'They aren't perfect, by design, but they are ours.'

'But I don't understand. If you have the technology to create humans without flaws, why don't you? Surely any parent would want their children to have the best possible chance?'

'It depends what you mean by the best possible chance. It doesn't necessarily mean that everyone is the same and flawless.'

'Why not?'

'Because that isn't what makes humans human. Look, take a simple, verifiable mathematical fact. For as long as humans have been human and up until the gene wranglers screwed it all up and the human race wound up being infertile, humans bred almost exclusively by accident. People had sex because they desired sex. They had a hunger for it and that hunger was impossible to deny. We still have the same hunger, even though it now serves no biological purpose, but it's going to take a lot longer than a few hundred years to break the programming of millions. For 99% of our genetic history, pregnancy was the unintended consequence of the urge to copulate. Everybody was an accident.

'When humans started to understand the consequences of their actions, the birth rate went down. They didn't need so many mouths to feed and the women didn't want to destroy their bodies, serially flirt with death or repeatedly endure the physical trauma of giving birth. Neither did they want to incessantly re-burden themselves with the overhead of demanding infants. But did that stop us having children by accident? No, of course it didn't. Now, here's the interesting bit. If humans fully understood the consequences of their actions and didn't have that *it will be alright, it won't happen to me* gene then they would have died out. Wars, famines, diseases and natural disasters would have sent us back to the stone age. But because we habitually over-bred, by accident, we were able to ride these things out. The human race survived because of its lack of ability to foresee the consequences of its actions, not despite it. It has always been that way. And without that same gene we would never have taken the risks we needed to take to explore our environment, discover new lands and invent new technology to feed, clothe and protect ourselves. Risk-taking relies on the human ability to deliberately ignore the full consequences of our actions. That gene, let's call it the blind-spot gene, makes a big difference.'

'So what's your point?'

'Your optimisation algorithms up there consider the blind-spot gene a weakness. They think it's debilitating for humans to be genetically inclined to ignore the consequences of their actions. They decided it was preferable to be able to foresee every possible outcome and plan for them, so they took the bloody gene out! Consequently, your precious citizens take almost zero risks and make fewer mistakes.'

'Sounds like a good idea to me,' said Dielle. 'Why would we want to make mistakes?'

'Because it's only through taking risks and making mistakes that new things happen. It's called creativity. It requires a blind spot.'

'So Unkos have blind spots.'

'In spades! So do all the Naturalists, naturally.'

Dielle sipped his tea and pondered. He knew something hadn't felt right since he'd been re-fammed, but he hadn't been able to put his finger on why he felt uncomfortable most of the time. Maybe the matriarch had just given him a clue. Maybe he needed to get to know these people. Maybe the girl with the red hair was waiting for him outside. 'You know that feast going on out there?'

'Sunday lunch?'

'Do you think there'll be any left?'

When he found her, she was dancing on a hollow wooden platform and when she spotted him she dragged him onto it and made him dance too. He wasn't very good at it, but that didn't matter because she was. She was better than good, she was dazzling. She moved as if she could control gravity by sheer will. He'd already seen the most famous athletic dance troupe onSlab perform an intricately choreographed zero-g interface ballet and that had been breathtaking, but what this woman could do on her own, with nothing to accompany her other than the sound of her shoes hitting a resonant floor, far, far outshone that. This dance was about the thrill of life and exuded a passion for being human that he'd never been close to before. Sure, he thought, Kiki had passion and energy on tap any time she needed it. But it wasn't the same. Kiki's enthusiasm felt manufactured and superficial compared to this. This was pure joy. And he still didn't know her name.

She taught him the steps with a flashing smile and a body as lithe as a whip. She showed him how to leap without changing place, rise without falling and spin without tripping over his feet. He felt like a clown. Compared to her he seemed clumsy, gauche and inept but he loved every minute of it. They stopped for a break and a tankard of sparkling, fermented brew. The locals, having satiated their hunger but not their need for drink or conversation had coalesced into separate groups where jokes were being shared and arguments were flaring and subsiding like flash storms over a tropical sea.

There was a commotion on the other side of the arena as a game of Burley broke out. Spectators formed a moving corral around the two teams as they bumped and jostled for the possession of two head-sized cloth balls and a pair of arm-length poles with a bowl on each end. The primary object of the game was to catch a ball in one end of a pole, which was called a *punter*, and run toward one of the two A-frame goal posts set into opposite ends of the arena. If the runner was impeded, he had the option of flipping the ball to any teammate who was also in possession of a punter, and the dash for the goal would continue as long as the ball was caught cleanly in the punter's bowl, or *corrie*. When a ball was not inside a corrie, it was technically dead or *lagged* and could not be run with but could be tossed to a teammate as long as he was in full possession of a punter at the time the ball was thrown. Alternatively, and more dangerously, the punter could be thrown to the dead-ball holder, or *lagger*. Communication between the lagger and the punter bearer was usually made near-impossible by the yelling of the crowd and the opposing sides' attempts at interfering with the line of sight between them. This resulted in many occasions when all the punters and balls were in the air at the same time, tumbling and spinning through the dust clouds above the writhing scrum of semi-inebriated, laughing and swearing players.

Occasionally, someone would make a break for a goal and the crowd would part to let the runner through. This was a great cause for confusion and rapid tactical decision making because, while the team with the ball would need to protect the runner from being tackled, any weakening of the scrum meant that the opposing side would stand a better chance of capturing the remaining ball and heading for their goal, thereby neutralising the potential score. If a runner wasn't confident he could reach the goal before being brought down he had the option of using the punter to hurl the ball through the triangle above the crossbar for one point. Running beneath the crossbar with a ball in a corrie scored three points, however the ideal was for a team to get both balls onto each corrie of one punter. If that happened, the runner had to be protected at all costs because this was called a double corrie, worth ten points if carried intact across the goal line, and almost always meant the end of the game. Successfully executed double corries were extremely rare because the crowd, not wanting the game to end, would charge after the hapless runner alongside the opposing team and all hell would break loose.

Dielle, with no Sis to query, had watched all this going on for quite a while and still had no idea what was going on. It looked like carnage to him. He spotted several bloody lips, some of them on women who seemed to have no problem competing against the men. He worried that his spirited companion might want to join in and he'd lose her completely.

He leaned closer and raised his voice. 'You know they want me to read to you?'

'To me?' she said, eyes sparkling like emeralds as she kept track of all four game elements. 'Sure why d'they want that? I've no need of it.'

'Not you specifically. The Naturalists. The Unkos say you've found a book and you need someone to read it to you.'

'Do they now?'

'Do you ever answer a question with a direct answer?'

'Of course I do. Why don't you ask me one?'

'Will you tell me your name?'

'And why would you want to know it?'

Dielle looked at her and ached. He could have told her why he wanted to know in such precise terms that he'd have been breathless before he'd finished his first sentence. He could have told her so well that she would probably have run away screaming, or laughing, and he'd never see her again.

'See what I mean?' he said. 'Another question.'

'But they're so much more interesting than the answers don't you think?' She stood up, pirouetted and skipped off to get a better view of the match. He had no choice but to follow. No choice at all.

The man re-appeared and reduced his choices to less than zero. 'The Matriarch has given her blessing.' He shook his head. 'There's no accounting for it.'

'So that's good then, eh?' said Dielle hopefully.

'You have a job to do and so do I. Mine is to deliver you to yours.' He turned his back, once again expecting to be followed. Dielle looked wistfully over at his unnamed desire, caught her eye, and waved goodbye. She waved back and smiled. He thought he saw the slightest look of concern in her eyes and his heart raced. Then he wondered what she might be concerned about and his heart raced faster. He briefly considered making a stand and not going with the man, but he watched how the crowd parted before them and the deference everyone showed to his guard-guide. It might be interesting to see what they wanted him to do, he thought. More interesting than the alternatives anyway.

They passed through a laneway that separated a terrace of military-style two-storey buildings and turned left into a quadrangle. High walls reflected the muffled roar from the Burley spectators down into the courtyard. A black and cream checkerboard of paving stones fanned out in a spiral from a large fountain in the middle of the square. Loops of sparkling water splashed lazily into a clover-leaf pool surrounded by worn stone benches. At the far side of the courtyard was a white building with a pitched roof and a half-dozen vertical slits for windows. The man walked over to a heavy door set into a stone arch in the corner, hefted it open and dragged Dielle through. Lines of chairs and desks faced a low stage with a single bare table on it. In every chair sat a small child and the face of every small child was turned toward Dielle. Some smiled hopefully, some looked on with a mixture of curiosity and caution, and others managed to mix disdain and dismissal with such expertise that Dielle guessed they had been taking lessons from the man who had just bolted the door behind them. They walked to the front of the class, through the field of sunflower faces.

'Now children,' said the man with a softness of tone that surprised Dielle, 'this is your new reader. I know you've had to give up the Burley to be here, but you'll be polite to him unless he's not to you.'

They replied as one: 'Yes Fayder!'

'And is there an Unko among us now?'

'No Fayder!'

'And will you keep it that way for as long as there's reading to do?'

'We will, Fayder!'

'Right then,' he said. He strode over to a metal plate set into a side wall, and reached down the front of his tunic. He pulled out a key the size of his palm and unlocked the panel which swung out on two sturdy protruding hinges. Inside the safe were four shelves of battered books with a drawer at the bottom. The man heaved the drawer open and took out a hessian-wrapped package the size of child's tombstone. He carefully placed it on the desk in front of Dielle and untied the braided rope that bound it. Before he opened the cloth to reveal the contents, he turned to Dielle.

'I'll have your word that you will never divulge the name or contents of this book to anyone outside these walls,' he said.

'Why?' said Dielle then caught the look in the man's eyes. 'I mean yeah, sure.'

'I'll have your word, you vacuous puppet.'

'What word?'

'You'll swear to me upon whatever thing or person you consider the most sacred that you will not break your promise to me on this.'

Dielle thought for a moment. He wasn't sure if he would have considered any thing or person sacred. Until today.

'I swear to you on my own life that I will not reveal the contents of this package to anyone outside of these walls,' he said.

The man looked at him with contempt. 'On your life then. It will be,' he said. He pulled back the cloth.

The cover of the book had a photograph of the Earth that had been taken coming back from the moon. The planet was a crescent, with more than two thirds of it in shadow, so Dielle could only make out a sliver of detail. He could see clouds and a hint of a blue ocean and perhaps some mountainous land. It looked, thought Dielle, breathtakingly beautiful. A deeply buried part of him experienced the tug of longing.

'It's a catalog,' he said, 'apparently of everything on Earth, and it's the last one.'

'Aye, so I've been told and you'll read it to the young ones,' said the man. 'I'll be sitting at the back in case there's any trouble.'

'Trouble?' Dielle looked around at the class. They didn't look the least bit threatening to him.

'Not with them, with you,' growled the man, striding off and leaving him to face the expectant kids.

Dielle gave them a warm smile. 'My name is Dielle,' he said. 'That's like a letter D and a letter L put together. A long time ago I used to be known by another name and in those days I used to live on the Earth which is what this catalog is all about. He hefted the book up to the class to show them the cover.

'You'll be careful with that!' shouted the man. 'Sure, it's priceless.'

Dielle put it back down gingerly.

'But even though I lived there when I was your age,' he continued. 'I have no memory of it at all because when I got old I was put into a kind of cold storage and when I woke up here I was all young again but I had no memories of who I used to be.'

'Did I ask you to fill their heads with this nonsense?' growled the man, walking back into the centre of the room and directing his words to the children. 'Pay no attention to this claptrap about frozen people. It's just the type of thing these eejits mess around with up there. They're all demented.' He turned back to Dielle and snarled: 'Just read it will you?'

'My point,' said Dielle defiantly, 'is that I'm as keen to see what's inside this book as you are so we'll learn about it together, shall we?' The man went back to his seat and sat down angrily. Score one point for Dielle, thought Dielle.

As he carefully turned each tissue-thin, grey page, he learned more than he expected. He learned some wild and fascinating ideas from Earth, and he also learned that he loved reading to children. They sat in rapt attention, sucking up everything he had to say. There were murmurs of approval when he read out 'Utopia or Oblivion' and a flurry of gasps when he told them about an operating manual for 'Spaceship Earth' but for the most part they sat in silence, listening to the wonders of a planet they would never see.

Dielle read to them for over an hour. Then he noticed a boy at the side of the class who was trying to attract his attention.

'Why is your hand up?' he asked.

The boy stood up. His hair was the same colour as Hers and he had the same tiny brown spots on his skin. 'Sir, I need to be excused, sir.'

'Why?'

'I need to pee, sir.'

'You need to what?'

'To pee!' said the boy, his face getting redder as he bounced from one foot to the other.

'Why?' said Dielle. The kids stifled giggles.

The man stood up at the back. 'Gawan Fintan, yer man's an eejit,' he said. The boy rushed over to the side door. 'Just because he can read doesn't make him clever. Anyway that's enough for today. You'll all tell your mams you're to be back here the same time tomorrow. Now off you go.'

The class dissolved into a jumble of scraping chairs and let-me-out energy that raised clouds of dust as the kids pushed their way through the side door.

The man had already carefully re-wrapped the catalogue and locked it in the safe before the last child left.

'Was that what you wanted then Fayder?' asked Dielle.

The man looked around sharply. 'Don't you ever call me that,' he growled.

'What shall I call you then?'

He looked at Dielle as though he was going to spit. 'Sir,' he said. 'Now go and find the hinny who came with us through the merkland and ask her to show you, politely mind, where you might lay your head tonight.

Dielle didn't need telling twice.

fourteen

Kiki couldn't have planned it better and was only slightly put-out that she hadn't planned it at all. 'Where is Blood Dielle?' was the hottest trending topic SlabWide. All the top five gossumes were carrying hourly updates on the investigation intercut with vox pops of where people thought he'd gone. GBH were offering short odds that he'd chickened out at the last moment, gone into full privacy and was hiding somewhere in ToNight High. Many had fingered Fingerz as the main facilitator (and benefactor) of Dielle's hide-away, but he was strenuously denying he knew anything about it. That is, as strenuously as a heavily self-medicated muso could deny anything. News media were running highlights from the previous ten days of reality sumes, the Farts' only recording was number one and Pundechan Media had a continuous feed of re-runs of the most-liked scenes on tenCent. Nearly 90% of these scenes involved sex and most of those featured Kiki. Not only was her media company wiping the board, her personal ratings were through the interface.

She'd had part of her writing team developing another of her sume concepts in parallel to The Reset Show and decided it was time to act. She pinged her old farm-buddy Faith-Sincere to arrange a meeting over cocktails and tune-ups.

'The stat nerds are telling me I have a maximum three-day window to get a pilot episode into the sumes while Dielle's still missing and everyone's hanging on the next plot development,' said Kiki to Faith who was enjoying a vigorous internal workout with her personal BodiCon trainer. 'After that they're projecting a daily 20% dropout. If we haven't got him back by the 14th we could be in spiral decline.'

'Where is the gap? Wasn't he supposed to be heading my way by now?'

'He was. I've not let him touch me for days and I've been misting the bed with your personal pheries all that time. I can't understand why he hasn't already. The writers are getting jittery because we can't start the betrayal narrative until he makes his move.'

'Well I can assure you there's nothing wrong from my side, I've got the best pheromone engineer onSlab. Don't you know where he's gone?'

'Not exactly. At first we assumed he was in hiding and off his head in a deadzone hangout which is what most of the sumers suspect, but unless the hackers are letting us down, and Dice knows I'm paying them enough, they say he's not onGrid anywhere.'

'So if he's beyond the hackers,' said Faith, her voice wobbling slightly, 'he must be. . . '

'With the Unkos, though Dice knows why. I've had two directs with the Unko who insined his sub-legal and he's denying all knowledge. That doesn't mean lookadat though, those Unkos won't tell each other the time of day.'

'So it's down to you finding out which of the tribes have nabbed him and then sending in a team?' said Faith. Her trainer unlatched the internal organ rejuvenator and rubbed oil into her tightened midriff.

'I've got scouts out now at floor level, Seacombe UpSide and SideUp. That's a lot of ground to cover without any intelligent tech. I've also got some legals looking into leveraging a break clause,' said Kiki. 'But once I know which lot have him, we'll need some heavy ordnance if we're going to extract him clean and hit the top ten on sumes.'

'Massive is offloading some surplus tech for cash. He was in a couple of days ago for a boost and dropped the hint. He has some hyper-trained crew for hire as well. I'll hook you two up.'

'So you did get into the Admiral. Why didn't you tell me, you sly fish?'

'Yeah, well, he's nothing to touch your toes over. Behind that lantern jaw he's almost as vacant as your boy is and nowhere near as limber. So what's this pilot you're planning?'

'I've had it in dev for a while, it's a topical SatComRomScam, lots of raunch and hyper-now. You'd be perfect to play the foil, darling. The writers are just patching the script to tie in with the latest developments on The Reset Show and we'll be ready to go. We've got some great insert sketches about those heavenly body signs too. It's a hoot!'

'What would you need from me?'

'Nothing much. We'll generate you from your current official metrics and slot you in to what we already have, so you only need to give us authorisation to take updates for the voice samples. You'll probably want to tweak a few lines in post, but that's all. We could have the first episode ready to overdub by the morning.'

'Got a working title?'

'If you're definitely in, I want to call it Kiki Sincerely,'

'Like it darling. Halfies?'

'Not quite, darling. I have script, production and distribution costs and I'm lead brand. You can have thirty of nett as long as we don't split edit control. We have to be super fast on this one and I can't have you dicing around on cuts and angles. We're not going to let you come over as anything less than absolutely fabulous anyway.'

'Nett?'

'Would I stiff you on the deal, darling? How long have we known each other?'

'All of our lives darling, and yes of course you would stiff me on the deal.' She stripped off her body-tight pants and bra. 'Burst me the latest draft and I'll sume it while I'm in the shower. *You* are buying dinner and *I'll* choose the place. Nett! My million-dollar, reconfigurable arse!'

'You were robbed, darling,' said Kiki, patting Faith's recently refurbished rump.

fifteen

By the time Dielle left the schoolhouse the game was over, the dust had settled and the skylight had dimmed. People had gathered around crackling campfires to tell stories, make music, sing and dance. Above all, there was drink, drink and more drink. Dielle was fascinated. He'd never seen real fire before but he had no doubt about what it was, or that it must be treated with respect. It calmed him to realise that here, in this outcast enclave, deep under the suspended cities of permanent light was a memory that could never be reset. He stood, transfixed, watching the dancing flames. The firelight shone in the reveller's eyes and made prancing shadows of them all. He was momentarily lost until he discovered a soft, delicate hand had slipped into his. He looked down into her smiling face.

'Me brother enjoyed your reading,' she said. 'He says you're an eejit.'

Although Dielle wished he could query Sis about what she'd just said, he was glad he couldn't. He was enjoying the silence in his head. It was a pity, he thought, that the internal peace didn't extend to the outside. These people never stopped talking. They talked at each other without listening to the replies. They interrupted and argued, laughed and feigned offence and seemed to be having a great time. Dielle couldn't understand a word.

'What's a brother?' he said, making sure he didn't let go of his gift.

'A brother would take your last piece of bread even if you were starving and then give it back to you with spit on it. A brother would stick up for you in a fight no matter what, then throw mud at you and call you names. A brother is the first person to tell on you and the last one to leave you when you're sick. A brother is family. Sure, do you not have family where you come from?'

'I don't remember my family,' said Dielle, 'Louie said we were an only child.'

'I can see what Finny means.'

'No. . . it's just that I don't have any memories of my childhood, but they are stored in a type of machine that. . . well, it sort of has its own way of telling. . . you don't really want to hear about this, do you? Couldn't we talk about the future rather than the past?'

She frowned. 'How d'you know who you are if you don't know where you're from?'

'I think I'm still finding that out,' said Dielle. He stared back into the flames and felt the warmth of her hand in his. 'I don't know much but I do know that I'm thirsty and tired and I'm supposed to ask you where I'm staying.'

'Sure, you'll be staying at me mother's brother's sister-in law's house. That's family for you. You'll be fine and dandy there.'

'Will you be there?'

'Now don't be ignorant as well as an eejit. Of course I won't.'

'Is that because you're, erm. . . I mean you must have a. . . that is, you are probably. . . of course you would be, that's expected. So I suppose it's really none of my business. Anyway.' Dielle tried to make his lips disappear and his eyebrows meet.

She stood with her hand on her hips and surveyed him from toe to head.

'You're a sorry lot and no mistake,' she said. 'Come on with you and I'll show you to your bed.'

Dielle tried to memorise the route to the house but after the fourth near-identical white-walled alley he gave up. It was hard enough keeping up with her. She didn't walk, she skipped. She made it look like making contact with the ground was purely optional.

His accommodation was spartan. The room had a single bed with a lumpy mattress that smelled faintly of something old and organic, a rickety chair and a waist-high stand with a jug of water, a shallow porcelain bowl and a coarse towel. There was no sign of the other occupants of the house, so after she'd wished him a pleasant night and told him she'd be back to collect him in the morning, he collapsed onto the creaking bed and fell asleep fully clothed. A tolling bell semi-roused him in the middle of the night. Realising he was cold, he got under the sheets but as he slipped back into unconsciousness he had a vague feeling of disquiet. He had never felt cold before. Even when he was in the middle of a blizzard halfway up a Graphite mountain, Sis had kept him warm. Warm and safe.

The room had no window but it didn't need one for ventilation, as he discovered a few hours later when the family started crashing pans and plates around in the kitchen next to his room. The dividing wall stopped well short of the ceiling, so morning light, loud conversation and the smell of something delicious filled his bedroom while he was still a long way from being done sleeping. He had no option but to get up and show his face.

He felt like an alien. A young boy and girl looked up from their breakfasts with identical expressions of cautious curiosity, while a middle-aged, thickset woman stopped pouring their hot drinks from a large pot to gesture at a chair at the far end of the battered wooden table.

'It wakes does it? We thought ye'd passed over in the night,' she said. 'Set down and I'll pour yer tea.'

'Thanks,' said Dielle. His mouth was barely working. 'You don't have any coffee do you?'

'No we don't,' said the woman, reaching round to a dresser stacked high with colourful crockery. 'What do you want with your toast?' She poured him a mug of steaming tea and added milk from a cracked earthenware jug.

'What are the options?'

'Butter.'

Dielle waited a fraction too long for comfort. 'Butter is fine,' he said.

The large woman moved around the cramped kitchen with ease. In a moment he was enjoying the simple pleasure of hot, buttered toast on an empty stomach. He didn't usually like tea, but it was warm and wet and he was thirsty and turning it down felt churlish.

The woman gestured at his stack of thick-cut bread with her knife. 'That's real bread that is. And the butter is made from real milk from real living cows.'

Dielle wanted to say something in response but couldn't think what. He had no idea what unreal bread would be like.

'I'm Mary.' She waved her butter knife at the kids, who were still staring at Dielle 'This is Sile and that's Jer.'

The young boy grinned and stuck out a greasy, toast-crumb-coated hand. 'Oim nine!' he said.

'And she's nine too,' said Mary. 'Only she doesn't talk much at the moment. But that's alright because Jer makes up for all of us, don't ya?'

'Your shirt's all creased up,' said Jer. 'Did ya sleep in it?'

'I did,' said Dielle. 'I was very tired.'

'Mam won't let us sleep in our proper clothes,' he said. 'We have to get washed and put on stupid piejarmers.'

'Now enough of that, Jer. Ask yer man his name.'

Jer wide-eyed Dielle. Dielle grinned and told them where his name came from.

The breakfast continued as a question and answer session. Mary told Jer what to ask and Jer, refusing to act as go-between, would stare at Dielle expectantly and then interrupted the answers with declarations of his own. Jer knew all about where Dielle was from, at least as far as the Slabscape above them was concerned. He'd seen it from underneath when he'd gone out on trips with his class. Jer was sure he wouldn't like it *up dere*. Jer was sure that whoever lived *up dere* were *total eejits*. Jer was sure about a lot of things.

She arrived while Dielle was sipping his second cup of tea. She hugged and kissed the twins, then hugged and kissed Mary and avoided the possibility of hugging and kissing Dielle by turning around, telling him he was wanted by the Matriarch and leaving. Dielle stood up too fast, spilled the rest of his tea on his trousers, thanked the family for their hospitality and hurried after her.

She was waiting by the entrance to a white-washed down-alley. 'You're a wreck sure enough,' she said. Dielle thought she looked like she'd been re-born. 'You'll have to tidy yourself first. I'll go and borrow you some fresh clothes while you smarten yourself up. In there,' she said, shoving him through a small door set into the alley wall. 'I'll send someone in with your clothes. Hurry up.'

Four naked men sitting on low wooden stools turned their heads. They studied him silently, as if sizing up a horse for auction, then they returned to their ablutions and ignored him. Hot water streamed from a row of taps on a tiled wall. Steam filled the air, bowls overflowed, wash-cloths were rinsed and thwacked against bare backs and thighs. Dielle felt acutely uncomfortable. The prospect of getting undressed in the presence of other men filled him with anxiety. He didn't know why. He had no problem being naked with Kiki. In fact, he thought, he probably preferred being naked with Kiki than being clothed. That is he used to prefer it, but for some obscure reason that he hadn't been able to figure out, he hadn't been able to enjoy being naked with Kiki for days now. Every time he tried to enjoy himself, and her, Kiki had had something more important to do. He wondered if he would ever see her again and found he was strangely ambivalent. It seemed the further away from her he got in time and space, the more she seemed to become monochromatic in his memory. Perhaps, he thought, that's what happens when you are separated from people and places: they morph in your mind from 3D to 2D, from full colour to black and white and then become cartoon-like, then brush-strokes, then smoke. He thought back. There wasn't a lot of back to think about. What was it like in re-fam? Kiki's nurse's helmet against the white walls. That first view of Seacombe from the platform? Floating buildings as far as he could see with a city above him pointing down. Yes, he thought, everything was turning into a cartoon.

The cartoon he projected in his imagination of him trying to wash himself without taking off his clothes looked ridiculous so he submitted to his ignominy and put his clothes into an empty basket on a shelf by the door. Below the shelf was a stack of thick towels.

He'd already noticed that the taps were manually operated so he managed to spare himself the embarrassment of sitting naked in front of a spout expecting water to appear on eye command. The man nearest him handed him a foaming block and pointed to a washing line of rough cloths hanging up to dry. Dielle imitated his way through the ablutions and tried not to make eye contact. He felt like his every movement was being scrutinised. Before he'd finished rinsing his hair, Jer turned up with a pile of clothes.

'Oim to give you a message,' he said. 'But I can't.'

'Why not?' said Dielle.

'Because me mam says I mustn't swear and the message has swear words in it.'

'Why don't you tell me without the swear word then?'

'Because yer might not get the proper meaning, like.'

'OK then. You tell me everything that was said to you and I won't tell anyone you had to swear to tell me properly.'

Jer looked at Dielle and tried to decide if he could be trusted. He'd never met anyone from outside Up Haven before and he was pretty sure that anyone from outside Up Haven wasn't to be trusted, pretty much by definition, but Dielle looked different to what he imagined when he thought about the SlabCitizens who lived in their floating buildings with their machines that breathed for them and fed them poisons and turned them all into eejits. Dielle looked just like him, only wetter.

'She said to tell the feckin' eejit to get a feckin' move on 'cos yer going to be feckin' late.' Jer grinned proudly.

'OK. I got it. Well done,' said Dielle. 'Tell her I'll be out as quick as I can but it takes me a long time to wash everything properly and then I have to dry everything properly and that takes a long time too.'

'She's going to get angry,' said Jer.

'That's all right,' said Dielle. 'I bet she looks even more beautiful when she's angry.'

Jer screwed up his face trying to figure out what Dielle was talking about. 'Feckin' eejit,' he said under his breath.

She was waiting on the corner talking to an elderly couple when he found her. She inspected his clothes and shook her head. There was nothing wrong with the clothes as such. They were well made, the cloth was coarser than what he'd become used to, but it was comfortable and he quite liked the inconsistencies in the fabric. It was just that they'd obviously been made for a man of considerable girth. He looked like a furled umbrella.

'You'll have to find a seamstress when you've made some money,' she said. She looked down. 'And you'll need some proper shoes. That fabricated shite is coming apart already.'

She was right. His favourite comfortable shoes had been ruined by the trek through the rusting wilderness. 'I can buy anything I want,' he said. 'I have plenty of money.'

'Do you now?' She held out her hand. 'Give some to me then and I'll go and buy you a fancy pair of Baileyboots.'

Dielle looked at her outstretched palm and realised two things: first, he was stone-cold broke and second, she really did look more beautiful when she was angry.

The bell that had woken him up a half-dozen times during the night tolled again.

'Come on,' she said, grabbing his hand. 'The Matriarch doesn't like to be kept waiting.'

She moved so fast he had to run to keep up. He had a strong premonition that it would always be this way.

The meeting chamber was occupied by a ragged group of twenty or so men and women who were all talking at each other without providing the space for any replies. The words were unintelligible to Dielle but it was clear by the tone of the voices and the temperature in the room that there was a serious disagreement going on. The Matriarch stood up from the centre of the melée and waved to Dielle to follow her into her private rooms.

There was no tea on offer this time. 'What do you know about alien messages?' she demanded after she'd closed the door to her inner sanctum.

'What messages?' said Dielle.

'They're feeding the mindless cretins up there some garbage about signs and messages being an elaborate hoax from your so-called enemy but we all know that's blocks right?'

'I seriously have no idea what you are talking about.'

The Matriarch studied him coolly. 'How did the reading go yesterday?'

'Fine.'

'What did they want you to read to them?'

Dielle studied the Matriarch coolly. 'How long are you going to keep me here?'

'I've already told you, you are not a prisoner, you are free to leave whenever you want. You just can't take a body tech maintenance backpack with you, or rather you could, but it wouldn't work for you.'

'And what does that mean?'

'You look fit enough, you might be able to walk for a couple of days, maybe three, assuming you don't do something stupid. Then your internal organs would start closing down and your mind would fog and soon after that you would go into toxic shock and your heart would stop.'

'And how long would it take me to get back to civilisation.'

'You call that civilisation?'

Dielle glared at her.

'If you knew which way to go to the nearest functioning up ramp,' she continued, 'and you had adequate provisions, maybe you could get there in a couple of weeks.'

'How long is that?'

The Matriarch shook her head. 'Let's put it this way, by the time you got there you would have been dead for about five days.'

'And you say I'm not a prisoner?'

'We aren't barbarians you know. We simply choose to live a different kind of life to the one you've been forced into. You might find you like it here.'

Dielle couldn't remember being forced into anything, although he did have a vague feeling of unease about how little say he had over what happened to him.

'And what if I refuse to read to the kids?'

Dielle was pretty sure he knew the answer to that question, but he felt he had to at least attempt to stand up for himself.

'Don't tempt me,' she said. 'What's the problem? Is this book something bad?'

Dielle wondered why she was so keen to find out about the catalogue and why the Naturalists wanted to keep it a secret.

'I need some credits before I do anything more. I need some clothes that fit me and some shoes.'

She walked over to a bureau, took out a stack of printed bills and handed them to him. 'Here's an advance on your wages. Teachers get paid the same as everyone else here.'

'What's this?' said Dielle.

'It's called money. You exchange it for things you want.'

'But it's just paper,' said Dielle.

'There's a café behind this building that trades those

pieces of paper for good coffee and fresh baked pastries. I suggest you give it a try. If I need you, I'll send for you.' She pointed at a side door and waited for him to leave.

The Matriarch was right, the coffee was good, the pastries were delicious and only cost a few slips of paper. He sat at a small, round table in the street outside the café, enjoying the warmth of the cloudlight, mulling over his situation and watching people pass by. He could think of worse ways of being held captive.

It was clear to him that there was something fundamentally different about the way time passed in Up Haven. The type of lifestyle he'd become accustomed to as a part of the onGrid, tenCent SlabCitizenry was infused with constant movement, multiple information streams and instant access to almost anything anyone wanted. Even the leisure activities ran at a break-neck pace. There were no gaps, no space to do nothing and no danger of ever being bored. Here, it was all about gaps and what happened in the spaces in-between the gaps. The woman who had served him wouldn't even break off her seemingly pointless conversation with another customer to find out what he wanted. He could have drunk a cup of coffee while he was waiting for her to make one and no one seemed to care.

He was examining his battered footwear and wondering if he had enough paper to buy something more sturdy when she found him.

'You're invited to a gyre tonight at me cousin's' she said.

Dielle's face was a question mark.

'Cousins are more family and a gyre is a get-together where everyone sings and dances and tells stories and such. You said you were in a band?'

'Yes,' said Dielle. 'Keys.' He mimed playing.

'They have a piano for sure. Can you sing?'

'I'm told that depends on your definition of singing. I think I'll probably stick to playing.'

'Then I'll meet you after school and we can have something to eat before the gyre. Will that suit you?'

She sat down at his table and studied him. Dielle drank her in. From his point of view everything about her was fascinating: the way she moved, the words she used and how she said them, the light in her eyes, the colour of her hair, the way it curled into ringlets that fell to her small breasts, the funny brown marks on her face and the energy she exuded. He could have closed his eyes and still been able to feel her presence, even if she was still and silent, which she almost never was. He knew she was far from perfect. He'd already met perfect and it had left him awed and intimidated. Perfect was freaky. She was better than perfect. 'Yes,' he said. 'That would suit me just fine.'

She smiled and his heart leapt.

'Hope,' she said.

'I am hoping.'

'No, Hope, you eejit, it's me name. Now you've got it you have to treat it with care.' She reached over, stole the last of his croissant and popped it in her mouth.

'Hope?' he said. 'How do you spell it?'

'Sure I don't know. What would I need to spell it for?'

'Hope,' he said. 'It's a very pretty name.' He couldn't stop himself from grinning.

She stood up. 'After school, then,' she said. 'Better make sure you're there for two after bells or yer man will be sore.'

He didn't get a chance to ask her what two after bells meant before she'd skipped away.

Bells turned out to be obvious. He'd just bought himself a fine pair of hand-made boots from a leather-worker's shop in a row of leather-worker's shops when a peal of bells in a repeating, seemingly random pattern reverberated around the whitewashed walls, followed by the sound of doors being shut and shutters being rattled down.

Up Haven had gone to lunch.

He'd already filled up on pastries so he decided to catch

up on some missing sleep on a shaded bench and still managed to get to the schoolhouse when the hour-bell struck for the second time after lunch. The man was waiting for him outside the door. He acknowledged Dielle with a grudging nod and let him in. His task was as simple as the day before except when a child raised his hand, Dielle knew what it meant.

Hope was waiting for him when the man decided the kids had heard enough for the day. She took him to a canteen with long benches and no menus. The food and drink was served by a waiting staff who took delight in degrading and abusing their customers. They carried more bowls of stew and flagons of ale than could be reasonably accounted for, regularly broke into song and never dropped a plate or missed when someone wanted more. Dielle sat facing Hope and between two large, bearded men who carried on a heated conversation over his head in a broad dialect he couldn't understand.

She knew everyone. She laughed and joked and deftly batted off advances and several lewd suggestions with a turn of her sharp nose and a flash of eyes. She let Dielle use his paper money to pay for them both, but only after haggling down the price. Dielle was surprised that the meal for two, with several jars of very good ale, cost less than the coffee and pastries he'd had earlier. Must be some sort of variable pricing, he thought, remembering what he'd had to pay for his now-redundant stim-unit.

The gyre was in full swing when they arrived, hand in hand. Ale flowed and incessant banter filled every space, even when someone stood up to sing or play a tune. Dielle felt happily drunk.

He'd progressed to feeling drunkenly happy when the call went up for 'the blow-in' to perform. This was his moment. He felt confident. She would be impressed and he'd be a winner. He sat by the piano and the room went quiet. He flexed his hands and placed them over the keys, relaxed and let go.

Nothing happened.

Muttering and coughing closed in from the corners. Dielle looked at his hands and tried to will them to play. He tentatively pressed a few keys at random. The coughing turned to sniggers. He looked around desperately seeking Hope. She was standing beside Fayder who shook his head, said 'I told you, he's a feckin' puppet,' and left.

'It seems,' said Dielle, red faced and wretched, 'that the drink has gone to my fingers. I'll tell you a story instead.'

He told them a story of waking up in a pure white room after falling through a million miles of soundless clouds. He told them about a magical device that made men dance and do back-flips without them knowing they wanted to. He told them about a balloon-nurse on a string, bobbing around a room with osmotic walls. And he told them about being alone in a place that was billions of miles from his home, a home he couldn't remember but somehow longed for, launched into a place where millions of strangers watched his every move, where he could feel isolated and vulnerable even when everyone was being kind to him or offering him things he didn't understand. He didn't tell them about Louie though.

His audience was subdued, touched by his candour, finding a place of longing within themselves that was futile to voice. He thought about Louie and what Louie knew and had that he could never know or have. He wondered what Louie would have done in this situation and instinctively did the exact opposite.

He cried.

He didn't sob or bawl, there was no drama or catharsis, he simply discovered salt water was leaking from his eyes. He wasn't even sure why he was crying, he just knew that he needed to. He'd only been around for a handful of days and although nothing really terrible had happened to him, and most of what had happened to him had either been a lot of fun or pretty amazing, he knew he had been deeply traumatised by the experience. It is, when all is said and done, something of a shock to be re-born as a fully grown adult with a blank memory into a strange new world, no matter how well organised it is. And now, he thought, I can't even play the dicing piano anymore. He wiped his cheeks and faced the crowd. There wasn't a dry eye in the house. Hope was smiling tears.

Well, he thought, I may have hit the right note after all.

Asynchronology: $\delta t CT^{SS^{ES}}$

The Tit came to a full stop. It was almost impossible for two of its occupants to comprehend just how full that stop was. Outside, precisely 500 kilometres away, was the centre of a spherical mass that had once been a part of Earth. The same Earth that Louie had been born, raised and frozen on. The Earth that had, hundreds of years before, momentarily occupied the volume of space before them, but as soon as it had arrived, it, the Galaxy and the rest of the Universe had continued on their way. Earth continued orbiting the sun, Sol continued spinning around the black hole at the centre of the Milky Way, and the galaxy continued getting ever more further flung as the Universe expanded as fast as it possibly could. Whether the Universe was also moving relative to other, impossible-to-perceive, universes was still an open question but it was a safe bet that it would be because nothing in the entirety of creation was stationary. Nothing, that is, apart from a 900-kilometre-wide ball of mud, rock, sea and atmosphere that had mostly been known as California. It was stationary in a way that nothing else in the universe was stationary, with the exception of the newly arrived Cosmic Tit.

There was nothing to see, of course. There would be nothing to see for at least another 48 cykes of subjective ship's time; just over 15 Earth years.

At the exact centre of the invisible mass, buried deep inside the rocky promontory of Point Dume, Malibu, were the highly secret experimental labs of the Institute for Research into the Already Known. At the time of the California Disappearance, Louie had been the CEO, President and Chairman of IRAK which was the largest and wealthiest privately owned corporation in the world. When the first rumours of the event hit the screens of his Manhattan offices his first call had been to his P.R. company. 'Deny everything,' he told them. He had been denying everything ever since.

Despite the circumstantial connection between the California Disappearance and IRAK's labs, and a certain, heavily suppressed, live video stream of an experiment that coincided with the event, no one knew for sure what had happened so no one could prove that IRAK was responsible for the catastrophe or the lives of the 55 million people who had disappeared along with much of America's most valuable real estate.

But at least, as Louie was fond of repeating, Arizona and Nevada got shiny new coastlines and the Arizonans finally figured out what to do with all that sand. To them, California had simply disappeared one sunny summer afternoon but, as the insurance companies would be hugely relieved to hear, it hadn't disappeared at all;

it had simply been transferred into a different asynchronicity and effectively come to a dead stop. Even when California did appear again it would only do so for an amount of time so infinitesimally small that it was impossible for any of the inhabitants to file a compensation claim.

The suppressed, and officially denied, video stream showed that an anonymous individual in an unidentifiable underground lab had decided to see what would happen if he built a human-sized emti transmitter and attach it to a similar sized emti receiver, then direct the transmitter to the receiver and press 'go'. The culprit was known only by his online identity of 'Snood' and while no one left behind had any idea who he was, they could assume two things about him: first that he was bright enough to build it while covering all his tracks and second that he was stupid enough to build it and turn it on.

Although IRAK had been founded on the matter transmitter and made most of its astronomical profits through the manufacture, sale and distribution of emties, few company employees had the slightest clue how matter transmission worked because it had been invented, or more accurately discovered, through a combination of deduction, observation, trial, error and pure luck. The exact ratio of those factors has never been quantified, but most informed commentators put a 99% weighting on the latter. However, there is a truth that is probably eternal (even though eternity is a provable falsity) that the only thing that is needed for scientists to figure out how something is done is to demonstrate that it can be. Impossibilities are easy to accept; possibilities require evidence and the evidence was in the socks. Milus Blondel had attempted to quantify laundry-related sock disappearance while he was over-medicated, sexually frustrated and clinging to his place at Prague University and, after having proved beyond any doubt that matter transmission wasn't only possible but commonplace, had hooked up with Louie Drago who had managed to successfully exploit the discovery to the point of mega-global domination.

Emties were born of ignorance and confusion and their technology was surrounded by obfuscation and denial, but regardless of their heritage they undeniably worked. They transported matter from one place to another instantaneously but the problem was that they only transmitted matter and not non-matter.

This was a big problem. Human beings could not be emtied anywhere because they would be stripped of their souls and that was specifically banned by all legal, paralegal, religious and pareligious organisation on Earth. Strict controls were put in place. Soul-sensing cut-off technology was a mandatory requirement before any emti was allowed to leave the manufacturing plants.

Humanity had been denied the ability to beam up, down or sideways. The frustration was maddening and had driven Snood to find a way of circumventing the soul-sensors, build the first man-sized prototype of an instantaneous emti-to-emti transporter and claim 'the dawn of real space travel'. Whatever else Snood thought he was doing, one thing is unquestionable: when he flicked a switch he became virtually immortal.

In terms of 'real space travel' he was unwittingly correct because real space did indeed keep travelling. California, however, didn't go anywhere and neither did he.

Louie stared at the image that was being projected outside the ship. It was a visualisation of how California would appear to them. A 900-kilometre-wide spherical section of Earth with a familiar shoreline. 'So time is stopped in there,' he said.

'Not exactly stopped but very, very near. The mass manifests in our space-time once every 48.125 cycles and when it does it stays for one quanta of Planck Time which is so short that you can't measure any time shorter.'

'So is it possible that the inhabitants are still alive?'

'Not only possible but absolutely certain. They wouldn't have had enough time to die yet.' The ship's avatar overlaid the projection with a set of diagrams and a scrolling list of complex equations. 'Even taking into account the time dilation effects caused by our journey here, I calculate that insufficient time has yet passed inside the sphere for the inhabitants to be aware of what has happened to them. Not only that, but the sunlight that was falling on them from Sol when the emti experiment was turned on is still making its way from the limits of the stasis field to the ground.'

'What happens if they turn the experiment off?' asked Louie.

'The globe will fall out of stasis and return to our space-time. Most of the atmosphere will start to drift off. If the angular momentum of that part of Earth has been conserved, and although the laws say it should this situation is unprecedented so all bets are off, then it will try to maintain its trajectory around a non-existent centre of gravity. The sea and atmosphere will spill over the edges and anything loose, like a non-strapped down human being would be flung off, quite violently I suspect.' The ship provided some animated graphics to illustrate the likely consequences.

'Not good then,' said Louie.

'Violent death for all life-forms outside of a secure life-support environment within a few minutes, probably.'

'And if they keep it on?' asked the wizard.

'That's an interesting one. The first thing they'll notice will be that the sun has gone but all their automatic lighting systems will turn on, so that's not going to be too traumatic. Noles® were already ubiquitous back then so they won't lose power. The rest of the Earth has disappeared so their gravity will weaken drastically and that will have a whole range of weird effects, but it's unlikely that much else will change instantly. By the time anything can alter enough for anyone outside the stasis field to measure, we'll be tens of billions of years old.'

Louie made a decision. 'You have to get me in there.'

'Now that's a good idea,' said the wizard with uncharacteristic enthusiasm.

Louie gave him a sour look. 'The feeling's mutual,' he said.

'We can certainly try,' said the ship. 'We'll have to wait for the next appearance but if your vDek is out there occupying the same space when it does enter our asynchronicity then I should be able to figure out a way for you to synchronise with it. A similar emti-to-emti stasis device might work. I'll do some calculations and experiments. I'll have to make you entirely independent of my systems, of course, because once you enter California's time frame you'll be irrevocably beyond reach.'

'That's OK by me,' said Louie. 'I'm going to go into hibernation mode until you're ready for me.' He studied the wizard, shook his head, then turned to the ship's avatar. 'You'll wake me up when you're ready for testing?'

'Sure thing!' it said cheerily.

For the first time in over 95 Earth years, the wizard smiled.

48.1596767896543 cykes later, Louie was, once again, isolated in the cold emptiness of space. The Cosmic Tit was 500 kilometres away, too far for even Louie's enhanced optical sensors to locate. The ship had assured him that he was in the precise location he'd requested, a point that would in a few minutes be co-incident with the IRAK labs. He was inside an emti that was inside another emti that was going to be used only once, and for the shortest measurable fraction of time, as the receiver for the emti inside it. The design had been rigorously tried and tested. Everything was automatic. The emti was going to be activated to coincide with the exact moment California reappeared. It would hold the contents, Louie, in stasis for the length of time it takes a beam of light to activate a photonics logic circuit then turn itself off and return to what the remaining occupants of the Cosmic Tit would consider to be 'real' time. During the time it was in stasis, Louie would have a few seconds of his subjective time to exit the double-walled emti and enter California's space-time. The ship had assured him it would work, but even if it didn't he wouldn't have to wait very long to try again. Still, it wasn't a manoeuvre that was completely without risk.

'Are you absolutely sure you want to go ahead with this?' said the ship through Louie's comms unit. The wizard crossed his fingers and prayed to the Wizard God.

'I have a choice between going back to California where I am rich and famous and they still play basketball or staying on a trip to nowheresville with you two. No offence, but this is an easy one.'

'Less than a minute to go,' said the ship. 'Any last words?'

'No. Oh yes, I forgot to tell you, before I went into my last hibernation I discovered a context-release encrypted file on board this vDek. I put a sub-processor to work and cracked it while I slept. Seems like we weren't allowed to go free after all. There's a self-destruct built in. Like to know where?'

'You're bluffing,' said the wizard. He looked anxiously at the ships's avatar. It sprang two stubby arms and shrugged.

'Please yourself,' said Louie. California flashed into existence for precisely one time quanta and Louie vanished.

For a long time they stared out silently into cold, empty space.

'You have backups?' said the wizard with an air of doomed resignation.

'Naturally daturally'

'Cut that out.'

'Yes, of course I have backups,' said the eye, trying to look crestfallen and overdoing it. 'He's right. There is an encrypted file in his data stack, but I can't get at it. It's his-eyes-only.'

'Can you replicate his vDek sufficiently to restore him without him noticing a difference?'

'Sure thing,' said the eye. 'It shouldn't take long.'

'I suggest you get us the hell out of here and start fabricating the replacement.' The floor lurched under them as the ship engaged the anti-gravity drives and harnessed California's space-time deformation to accelerate to the limit of their inertial dampers. 'As soon as we're back up to speed,' continued the wizard, 'restore Drago from a pre-rediscovery-of-California backup and we'll continue as though nothing happened. Tell him that it was an invisible gravitational anomaly, that we sling-shotted around it, and that you handled it all without bothering to wake either of us because there was nothing to see.'

'How are we going to get him to find the encrypted file and decode it?'

'You only have to tell him you know it's there — found it in a diagnostic run or something. His curiosity will do the rest.'

'Sounds like a plan!' said the eye cheerfully.

The wizard went over to his chair and kicked it. Very, very hard.

Asynchronology: $^{\delta t}SS^{ES}$

sixteen

The pilot episode of Kiki Sincerely was an instant hit.
The SatCom element had rated a seven four on the evening
cumes with the skit about the army sign-chasers getting
highest recall on test, the ComRom strand peaked at six
three, which wasn't bad, but the RomScam storyline nearly
hit nine. Kiki couldn't believe the feedback she was getting.
Faith had pinged her a dozen times since breakfast, all of
the major carriers had already confirmed 12 episodes, and
Wendle's network wanted 24 solid. Solid!

'Lookadat!' said Kiki to herself over the morning stats.
Having spent much of her youth working at the Black Sands
surf resort in hydroponics, Kiki knew how and when to
catch a wave. She instructed her A.I.P.A. to double the size
of her creative team by making a cross-matched selection
from the list of recent job applicants, and invited Louie to a
meeting. Louie, already bored with watching an
unchanging image of a lifeless moon readily agreed but
insisted it was held on neutral ground. His neutral ground.

Louie hated doing nothing, so he threw a few hoops
while he was waiting for Kiki to show up.

When he shot hoops, his mind always switched into idea
mode. He dribbled the ball around the central console. 'An
Erik told me,' he said, 'that when you sent the probes out to
monitor the moon, you masked the information return path.
Why did you do that?'

'It's strategically advantageous not to reveal what you

know,' said Sis. 'And, it may still be possible to keep our exact location a secret. The signmakers are yet to prove incontrovertibly that they know precisely where we are.'

'But those repeater signs are a giveaway, surely?'

'The signs are quantum projections of some sort, as were the manifestations at the events. It's possible they only manifest where they can be observed. Observation makes a big difference in quantum physics. I await more proof.'

'What? Like a missile up our ass?'

'Missiles I can cope with. I have to anticipate the unknown and the unknowable.'

'Jeez! It could be your security paranoia that's keeping us all waiting.'

'Expand.'

'Let's assume that whoever put the sign out there and then directed our attention to this frozen ball of rock is doing it for a reason. If you've covered all trace of us investigating it, how do they know we know they're there?'

'Are you suggesting we send them some form of signal?'

'No, I'm suggesting we all go for afternoon tea.'

'Sarcasm.'

'You think? Look at what they've done to get our attention. If they think it hasn't worked, what do you impartially estimate they'll do next?'

'Council will never agree to this.'

'That's why you don't tell them.'

Despite her severe misgivings, Sis calculated the odds, emtied a rosette of specialised probes to the site and commenced a broadcast of mathematically predictive pulses across the entire range of the electromagnetic spectrum. She still masked their return route though. It would have surprised Louie to learn that Sis was capable of taking action while having serious concerns about the outcome. Louie didn't do doubt.

'I may or may not have followed your suggestion,' she said. 'Your visitor will arrive in two minutes.'

'Good to see you aren't a total washout.' He threw the ball into an emtitrash the other side of the bridge. 'Yes!' he said, making a fist. 'Send her to the forward lounge.'

Louie had already prepared the lounge in an effort to make Kiki feel comfortably intimidated. He'd selected a panoramic penthouse view of his beloved New York City circa mid-twenty-first century and asked Sis to set up a couple of opposing executive chairs. His had its back to the screen for maximum effect. Hospitality was provided by an emtiwaiter that was ready to meet her as she stepped through the vexit. Kiki reached into it and pulled out a floor-length padded coat and a pair of furry boots.

'Dice, it's cold in here,' she said, her breath forming clouds.

'Is it? Sorry, I guess I hadn't thought to ask,' said Louie.

'I've ordered some warm air. Where am I? I was diverted five times before I got here, I could be anywhere onSlab. . . or maybe even off?'

'Don't get antsy. I just enjoy a little privacy, that's all. Take a load off.'

'Well I hope you don't enjoy it too much,' said Kiki. 'My team have been reviewing the story you told Dielle about your early life on Earth and I think we can turn it into a great docu-drama, especially as it can be narrated by the person who actually experienced it. I've pitched the idea to couple of aggregators and we already have a deal floating.'

'Which you're not going to accept,' said Louie.

'No of course I'm not going to accept it,' said Kiki taking off the insulcoat and shoving it back into the emtiwaiter. 'Do I look like a cake?'

'I'd want full control,' said Louie.

'You know what is currently trending in SocNet for HisBioDocs? You have special insights into the lead demographics of onSlab sumers?'

'No.'

'So what makes you think you know how to make a compelling sume?'

'I don't. It's just that there might be a couple of things I don't want people to know.'

'Such as?'

'I'm not about to tell you what I don't want you to know, am I?'

'OK, no problem. We can do a veto deal. You tell Sis the specifics of what you want hidden and she'll prevent us from tripping over the details.'

'So there would be no way of it coming out?'

'How could it?' said Kiki. 'All of our research, comms and development are done through Sis and all of our sumecasts go through her too.'

'Can't you find out by omission? Like if you ask questions and get blanks.'

'Unlikely, but even if we suspected something we couldn't prove it and we definitely couldn't sumecast it.'

Louie thought about it. There weren't too many things he wanted to keep hidden. Most of the things he'd done during his extraordinarily productive life on Earth had at least some questionable elements attached to them because it wasn't possible to be a globally successful businessman in those days without upsetting a whole raft of people along with an unending line of interest groups. Some people even got upset because he'd been pornographically wealthy. As if it had anything to do with them, he thought. He didn't get upset about other people's poverty or what they chose to do with it, why should they try to dictate to him? However, there was something he'd recently uncovered that he most definitely didn't want to come out. He genuinely didn't give a damn if people didn't like him, but there was one specific individual who he didn't want to furnish with any live ammunition. 'I accept that,' he said. 'Let's talk turkey.'

'Let's talk where?' asked Kiki. Sis translated. 'Ha! What weird phrases you lot used. I'll author Sis to dead-hand you on the negs.'

They haggled fiercely for a while until both of them

realised they were just having fun and not really getting anywhere. The devil, as they knew, was in the detail and every time they argued about a detail, five more came up. They didn't so much get bored as battle weary. Opponents gain a respect for each other through their shared adversity on the field, then mutual respect fogs the demarcation lines and enemies become cronies. They'd reached impasse on terms and they both knew it.

Louie had a growing affection for Kiki. She reminded him of him. Which is more, he thought, than he could say about Dielle.

He employed a transparently conventional distraction manoeuvre. 'Let's talk about your new sume,' he said.

'What does that have to do with anything?'

'You're not going to deny that you are bouncing sumers from Dielle's fly-on-the-wall reality show into your new Kiki Sincerely gig?' It hadn't taken Louie very long to figure out what he could do with all those non-sleeping hours.

'Of course I'm not going to deny it,' said Kiki. 'You would be the first to criticise me if I hadn't started attaching spin-offs. Your BioDoc will benefit substantially from the halo as well.'

'Of course, of course,' said Louie, waving his hand dismissively. 'I just haven't seen any royalty feeding through to Dielle, despite the fact that he's the only reason you were able to get traction for your new show in the first place.'

Kiki was annoyed. 'You want a cut.'

'I'd love to hear your reasons as to why he shouldn't be sharing in your deal, seeing as you are totally flipping your show off his. By the way, any idea where he is?'

'We know where he is. He's fine. We're already teched up and ready to go, we're just waiting for the optimum exposure window before we act. If we can get the clearances sorted and execute during prime-time we're predicting sixty-five percent sume traction for the live reveal. Problem is, there's a run-up to a talent final on our major competitor's feeds today so there's no point in us shooting our load right now.'

Louie was impressed. 'Sixty-five? SlabWide?'

Kiki nodded conspiratorially. 'Yup.'

Louie whistled. Tunelessly.

They spent another twenty minutes fighting about that deal without reaching agreement, then Kiki pointed at a wall panel.

'I thought that was a still, but it's not is it?' She said. 'Something just changed. What happened?'

Louie looked around at the monitor. 'Shit!' he said. 'I gotta go.'

'Wasn't there another moon in that picture?'

'Sorry, I really do have to go. See yourself out will you?'

'But. . .'

Louie headed straight for the emtiwaiter. 'Bridge!' he said and disappeared.

seventeen

'Play that back again,' said Louie.

The bridge viewscreens showed multiple aspects of the moon, from above and below, forward of orbit and rear, and a long shot of the side facing the system's dark red sun. There was the moon, dull, lifeless and boring. Then, there wasn't the moon. Gone. Vanished.

'Again,' said Louie. 'As slow as you can.'

He watched it a dozen times.

'So they zapporized an entire fucking moon?'

'It seems impossible not to assume that whoever set up the sign and directed our attention to this moon were responsible for removing it, yes,' said Sis. 'It certainly wasn't anything I did.'

'Do you have any idea how much energy you need to take out an entire fucking moon?'

'How many decimal places of accuracy do you require?'

'An entire fucking moon?'

'Is it really necessary for you to be so profane?'

'We just witnessed an unknown force wielded by unknown aliens who, on a whim, can take out an entire fucking moon. Do you not think that that, above all things, is a cause for semantic emphasis?'

'No.'

'Fuck you, I don't care. Get us the hell away from these aliens as fast as we possible can. Do it now and do it without waiting for the fucking council to debate the issue.'

'It's not as simple as that. In any case, I'm not sure that the point of this display was merely intimidation. They have left something behind.'

'What?'

'It's hard to say.'

'For Fuck's sake!'

'Will you calm down? It's hard to say because there is no debris or trace of the moon left behind but there is an odd space-time disturbance. There is nothing visible, no physical matter of any kind. The moon has not been shrunk down to a point like a black hole, however there are detectable gravity waves emanating from where the moon's centre of mass used to be. An additional anomaly is that neither the other moon nor the planet have altered their trajectories. Simple maths dictates that the secondary moon's orbit should alter instantly, but it hasn't. There should also be a measurable change in the motion of the home planet around the new centre of gravity for the local system, but again I can detect no change. The locus of this phenomenon even continues on its orbit around the local planet as if the disappeared moon was still there and what is more, that locus is pulsing at a high frequency and those pulses are modulating.'

'What does that mean in Ænglish?'

'There is a non-physical entity left in place of the moon that is generating frequency modulated gravity waves capable of transmitting information.'

'An entity?'

'You might call it an independent life force. It depends on how broadly you choose to define life.'

'An entity made of gravity? What's it saying?'

'It is currently impossible to ascertain what it is made from, but it can certainly manipulate a very high level of massless gravity far beyond any technology I have available. I have commenced manufacture of a prototype transceiver that should be able to demodulate the gravity waves, send the decoded information back to us, and generate a form of mimicking response under our command which will enable us to enter into a dialogue. My efforts to respond will be minuscule by comparison, so we must hope it is sensitive enough to detect them. This is going to be what you would call a long shot.'

It took over an hour for Sis to create a functioning probe that didn't collapse under its own gravity wave generator. After six failed iterations she ended up cannibalising one of the ship's gravity drives. It was bulky, had six nanosheet gravitywave detectors, each of which could extend to the size of a football field, and looked like an exploded junkyard with wings.

'I hope they don't rate us on our aesthetic sense and decide to zapporize us for bad taste,' said Louie when he saw the probe.

'Beauty is in the eye of the beholder,' said Sis. 'This is the most efficient and logical response to the task at hand. It needs no further refinement in order to perform its role. If I were an alien intelligence, I'd judge this instrument by its functionality and obvious technical sophistication and be impressed.'

'What do you mean *if*?'

Sis ignored him. 'I'm awaiting SlabCouncil approval to emti it over there now.'

Louie couldn't believe it. 'What?'

'Several of the interns are arguing that it could be dangerous to exchange communications with the entity. It's been suggested that we pretend we haven't noticed it and continue on our existing course. Most are vacillating. Three have resigned.'

'Oh for F. . . ' Louie spluttered. 'They have just whammoed an entire fucking moon for the sole purpose of getting our attention. Emti me over to the council meeting now!'

He was back in less than ten minutes. During his brief presentation to the SlabCouncil he had said fuck 176 times, physically assaulted a wizard and attempted to ram a blue fuzzy up the rear-end of a particularly slow Loris.

'Impressive,' said Sis. She emtied the probe through a

masking route to the site of the alien semi-manifestation. 'I fear intimidation is a lost art onSlab. You must lodge a thesisume on it. It would be a crime for such skilled use of profanity to die out.'

'It got the desired result, didn't it?' said Louie. 'Any developments while I was working out?'

'I've been monitoring the modulation patterns. It's been broadcasting regular repeating motifs.'

'Like music?'

'Possibly, but if I translated it to your aural perception frequencies I think you'd consider it somewhat sub-minimalist. It has varied by less than three percent in the last 2,546 repeats.'

'Yawnsville. I'll live without that thanks. Maybe it's like a homing beacon or tuning thing.'

'Good point. It's possible that the range of gravity modulation it utilises could be considered narrow-band. Who can guess what subtleties exist to a non-physical being?'

'Can you work within that range?'

'I think so. I'm currently using those same frequencies to send a selection of non-contentious Ænglish words in the same binary code as the message that was lodged in my substrate in order to establish a mutual starting point. So far, it hasn't changed its tune.'

'Perhaps it's humming,' said Louie. He wished there was something to see.

'Just a moment,' said Sis.

Louie waited silently. He hated waiting. Seconds dragged by. His data screens filled with streams of meaningless numbers. They were trying to establish communications with an invisible alien species from a universe that was impossible for him to comprehend. A species that ate moons in order to make a point. After longer than he could bear, Sis came back online. The longest 24.35 seconds of Louie's life.

'This is fascinating,' she said. 'It only used binary as a type of handshaking carrier wave. It escalated to a sequence of bases using rotating Fermat Primes. It is stunningly beautiful in execution and obviously designed as a test of our intelligence. It's fast too, the transfer rate is in the chicobaud range. I'm having to buffer data.'

Louie wasn't in the mood for numbers. 'What does that mean?'

'We have contact,' said Sis.

It wasn't often Louie was lost for words.

It wasn't long either. 'Who is going to talk to it?' He said. 'We can't afford to put this up for debate with those ass-scratchers. For all we know it might disappear at any moment.'

'I don't think it will, it has agreed to talk to a small representative group,' said Sis. 'It was reluctant at first but I've been able to persuade it.'

'You've been negotiating with it? I thought you refused to have any direct contact with anything that could compromise your systems. Doesn't dialogue with an alien constitute a potential threat?'

'My overriding responsibility is to protect the biomass. Failing to talk to a member of an alien species that had demonstrated this level of technical superiority and power would be an act of dereliction and contrary to my purpose. Anyway, I firewalled my two sisters and they've been monitoring me'

'What does small representative group mean?'

'It agreed to hear from one member of each life-form onSlab. A human from the contiguation, a NAH and a superintelligence. That's me.'

'And a hologram of course,' said Louie. 'I'm a sentient entity and I represent a whole section of humanity that those windfarmers in council don't have the first clue about. I demand a voice.'

'Interesting concept,' said Sis.

'It's not just a concept, machine, it's an imperative.'

'I'll put it to council. They are in the process of nominating an individual who will act as a filter for a query feed from the other members. There are a few pertinent details I have ascertained during my negotiations that you should know. First, while it has assimilated a wide contemporary Ænglish vocabulary it has trouble with a few of our concepts, the most problematic being time and identity. It is a non-physical entity and therefore claims to live outside of what we consider to be linear time. It classifies all physical matter that exists in space-time as *ephemera* and refers to itself in the singular and plural in the same sentence. That's why they, or it, will only talk to one of each life-form, because they don't have a concept of identity separateness. They describe themselves as galactic guardians and, luckily for us, hold all life to be sacrosanct. However, sadly for us, because they consider all life to be sacrosanct, they consider it their duty to protect higher orders of life from potentially destructive lower orders.'

'Lower orders like us,' said Louie.

'Precisely. They seem to be rather stuck on classifying your species well under their cut-off point. The word *virus* was used repeatedly.'

'Virus! I hope you've done your best to convince them otherwise?'

'Yes, but in truth, your species' history hasn't exactly made it easy. By the way, council doesn't seem too keen to let you talk to the alien.'

'Tell the interns that if they don't, they'll be outnumbered.'

'What do you mean?' said Sis.

If I'm not at the table, it will be one of them to two of you. NAHs are system representatives.'

'But they are completely autonomous independent sentient entities, they must be allowed to be represented. No one can deny them that.'

'No one is. But I'm also a sentient entity and I'm bigger than independent. Just tell the interns what I said.'

It was decided to hold the quorum in Louie's escape ship. An Erik arrived shortly before the nominated intern, who Louie was happy to see was the one he'd named Ethless the Beautiful. It wasn't that they got along especially well, but she was dressed in full warrior princess battle garb, stunning to look at and, more importantly to Louie, she wasn't a wizard. Louie had a problem with wizards.

'Before we start,' said Sis, 'you should know that they are obviously conversant with human culture and seem to be fond of idiomatic expression. What you will hear is not filtered or modified in any way by my systems. All I'm doing is reproducing sound waves through the sensurround at human auditory frequencies that are expanded from the gravity modulation the alien is producing in real time. This is how it chooses to speak to you. Don't blame me. Naturally, I will be feeding everyone with relevant backup data via your preferred channel throughout the intercourse.'

Three of Louie's holodata screens cleared and a palm-sized keypad materialised by his left hand. Growing up in the Bronx at the end of the 20th century, Louie, like most of his peers, had mastered the ability to compose and send text messages from his mobile phone without having to take the device out of his pocket. The three by four alphanumeric array was as natural to him as the touchscreens that superseded them and, in his opinion, considerably more useful. He liked being able to text with one hand while defending himself with the other and still preferred to use his thumb when anything needed pressing.

'OK,' said Louie. 'Anyone got anything to say before we do this?'

'I object to you being involved in this dialogue,' said Ethless the Beautiful to Louie.

'I object to your objection,' said Erik to the intern avatar.

'I have no objections,' said Sis. 'But I do have a word of warning. Having already had extensive and detailed exchanges with this entity I feel I should caution you about how this experience may affect you. First contact with an alien species is a potentially traumatic experience. You should prepare yourselves.'

'Why?' asked Louie.

'Well. . . ,' said Sis. 'It's a bit weird.'

Alien: 'Well hello there! Good to see y'all!' One of Louie's screens started scrolling the non-verbal communications between the Slab representatives and Sis.

Intern: {[Can it see us?]}

[[I'm not sending visuals. Probably a figure of speech. It seems to have multiple personalities, I will pattern-match its speech characteristics and provide annotation in case that provides a useful context. All of the idioms it has employed so far have been identifiable as Earth early-twentieth to late-twenty-first century so may hold a particular nuance value to Louis Drago. Opening comment: Southern USA, middle class Alabama/Georgia, male]]

'Hello to you too,' said Ethless. Louie gave her points for trying to project an air of calm confidence, even if she did blow it with her next utterance. 'H. . . how shall we address you?'

Alien: 'Och lassie, yiv nae idea what yer talkin' aboot. I have nae name!'

[[Scottish working class male, Glasgow/Cumbernauld, any time from the eighteenth to twenty-second centuries]]

Louie: 'Then we'll call you Guardian. We use names.'

Alien: 'Ees plenty OK I theenk so. I'm a havin' fun already!'

[[Pastiche of Mexican male as portrayed in racist American comedy shows in the latter part of the twentieth century]]

Erik: 'Is this a joke?'

Alien: 'Isn't everything, dear boy? Best not be too

serious, I'd say. Never forget the ninth, eh? Good show!'

[[That's an almost exact copy of a British Officer in a Hollywood film from 1957. It's using old broadcasts from Earth to form speech]]

Ethless: 'The ninth what?'

Alien: 'Nine rule state absurdity of universe tend toward maximum.' This came as a high-pitched, staccato, female voice.

[[Hong Kong Cantonese, following Niven]]

Louie thumbed in a comment.

Holo: {[Jerking our chain]}

[[Be patient and direct]]

Louie: 'Why are you trying to stop us?'

Alien: 'You no come here. You no ready. You stay away. We no want you here!'

[[Spanish immigrant, first generation, twentieth century]]

A segment of the first verse of La Marseilles nearly deafened them.

[[French national anthem, unidentified recording]]

Ethless: 'Here? You know where we are going? Are you from our destination?'

Alien: 'Hey, I'm like everywhere baby. I'm in everything and anything and way, way outside too. Location is dullsville.'

[[American male again, 1960s hippy]]

Twenty-five seconds of guitar-based psychedelic rock blasted through the bridge.

[[Jimi Hendrix, intro to Foxy Lady]]

Everyone nodded. They knew that.

NAH: {[We must entertain the possibility that we are talking to the aliens who infest humanity]}

Intern: {[You mean souls? We're talking to our souls?]}

NAH: {[And they're apparently not ecstatic about us tracking them down]}

[[If it is them, then we can do as they request and legitimately discontinue our journey]]

Intern: {[What?]}

[[The purpose of our odyssey to the MacGoughin Sequester is to locate the alien entities who infest humanity in order to lodge a formal complaint, in person. The journey is going to take twenty thousand Earth years unless we can find a way to overcome the lightspeed barrier, which, I would remind you, we have so far failed to do. It's possible that we have the option of complaining to the entities right here and now and can therefore save ourselves a very long, and potentially futile, trip. Our mission would be fulfilled]]

Intern: {[If we were to abandon our quest we would need irrefutable proof that this entity is an authorised representative of the soul infiltrators]}

The inter-council communication channels flooded Louie's screens. The majority of the comments were belligerent.

Ethless: 'What gives you the right to tell us where we can and can't go?'

Alien: 'Well now little missy. You know that moon that was hereabouts before we got to externalising it?'

[[Seems to like southern USA country accents]]

Hollo: {[Rqst no music]}

Ethless: 'External to what?'

Alien: 'External to this here universe that you like to call home, purdy lady.'

[[Same]]

Ethless: 'Yes, I am aware of the moon you are referring to.'

A dramatic three-note orchestral crescendo blasted the bridge.

[[Almost any b-movie horror film from the 1950s]]

Alien: 'Well that gives us the right to tell you any damn thing we damn well please.'

[[Same. Will only annotate changes from this point]]

Louie: 'That's not very friendly is it?'

Alien: 'Sure, you don't want to be mistaking genial for friendly, now?'

[[Irish female, Kerry, rural, timeless]]

Louie: 'No, I guess we don't.'

Alien: 'Good. That's settled then. Thank you for calling. Let's go to line two!'

[[Mid-Atlantic commercial radio DJ, any period]]

Erik: 'Wait a moment, you are demanding an impossibility. We couldn't stop even if we wanted to.'

Alien: 'I bet yew could too!'

[[America, north Georgia mountain people]]

Sis delivered a compressed stream of data to the alien to verify the NAH's statement.

Alien: 'I say! What primitive technology you have. You are in bit of a pickle, aren't you? No matter, we'd be happy to oblige. Tout suite as you jolly well say!'

[[Upper-class English toff, pastiche, possibly Carry On genre]]

Louie: 'So why haven't you?'

Alien: 'Now that's a good question sonny. Turns out that if we just brung your conveyance to a halt there'd be a mass transposition to a non-hosting state, and that wouldn't be too welcome around these parts.'

Intern: {[That was John Wayne! I love John Wayne! I got one!]}

NAH: {[What does it mean?]}

[[It means that they claim to be able to stop us dead in our tracks but in doing so, all biological lifeforms would be instantly terminated. If that were to happen then the alien energies that infest every human onSlab would simultaneously return, non-corporeally, to the location you call home, which is presumably where this entity is trying to stop us from going. They seem keen to avoid this possibility]]

Intern: {[Maybe they can't handle thirty-two million souls arriving on their doorstep at the same time]]

Hollo: {[32M pissed 1s]}

Erik and Ethless looked at Louie and contemplated the implications.

NAH: {[I wouldn't want to be in their customer service department]}

Hollo: {[Kill us = problem = good news 4 us]}

Louie: 'Why are you so insistent that we can't continue on our journey? What have you got against us?'

Alien: 'You're 'avin' a larf, aincha?'

[[Cockney. It's accusing you of feigning ignorance]]

Ethless: 'No, we really want to know.'

[[I'm getting visuals. I'll relay them directly to the projectors, no censorship on my part but as a precaution I'll add a fractional time delay, restrict the feed to just you three and deny the linked-in council members until I have verified the feed is non-corrupting]]

It started with the spine-chilling sound of a siren. Blurred, black crosses filled the projections. The crosses resolved into endless squadrons of multi-engined bombers, silhouetted against a grey sky. They emptied their cargo onto cities, turning them to flames with explosions so loud they rocked the bridge of Louie's escape ship. The intern, the hologram and the NAH had no choice but to sit through it all. For more than an hour they were barraged with sights and sounds that detailed, in excruciating clarity, every obscene act that humans had perpetrated on other humans, their planet and the flora and fauna that flourished upon it. Or had tried to. Newsreel footage from twentieth century wars, in grainy monochrome, were interspersed with still images and even oil paintings depicting scenes of human-wrought horror: piles of ravaged bodies, torture scenes, children eviscerated and burned alive, hostages decapitated on camera, innocents and guilty alike shredded by war machines of overwhelming force. Violence and mayhem filled their senses. Weapons of mass destruction propagated globally like macabre confetti. Pollution turned beauty to slime, fresh air to smog and bright waterways to oil-clogged cesspools. Uncounted millions starved while others squandered resources and drowned in their own obesity. Blood sluiced through gutters, animals were slaughtered by the billion then turned and churned into processed food to be stuffed into gaping mouths and shitted out into oceans of ordure. Nuclear weapons detonated in a pyrotechnic celebration of global insanity.

The atrocities kept coming: human skin used for lampshades, living creatures locked in cages too small to allow them to move, women disfigured by acid or raped as victims of war, unborn children ripped from broken bodies, razor-wire-lined muddy trenches filled with half-submerged corpses and feeding rats. The carnage seemed endless. The one thing that united the images was that none of them portrayed accidents or natural disasters. Every event was the result of a deliberate human action. Someone, somewhere had made the decisions that resulted in what they were being shown.

After a while, even Louie held his head in his hands and couldn't watch.

It ended with more crosses. White crosses. Planted in neat rows in green fields. Diagonal lines converging at the horizon.

After a prolonged silence the entity spoke, unaccented and cold: 'You shall not come.'

Ethless, despite being only an avatar of the intern she represented had tears streaming down her face. She tried to form words but failed. Erik looked dejected, unable to defend the actions of a species that had given birth to his own kind. He too was speechless.

Louie didn't do speechless. He floated up from his screens and started circling the bridge. 'But you're making a mistake,' he said. 'You're judging our past, not our future.'

[[You're going to have to explain this concept in more detail. It, or they, have a hard time with time]]

The alien spoke in a thick Russian accent: 'The Guardians observe, not judge. You refute our observations?'

'No, but what we did is in our past, right?' said Louie, waving his arms about as though it made a difference. 'That is, something we have done and survived. So the ones that survived learned not to do it again. It's called evolution. It's how we became who we are.'

Alien: 'Who you are is demonstrable. You will not proceed.'

'No, you don't get it,' said Louie. 'You're making a judgment based on behaviours carried out before we became what we will become before we get to where we are going.'

The entity went silent. Louie looked around the bridge, raising his eyebrows and gesturing in an effort to garner support from the intern and NAH who were watching him with a mixture of alarm and confusion.

'Say what?' said the alien.

'We are ephemera,' said Louie. 'We are physical entities that exist in a time-based universe.' He looked to Erik for support. He gave reluctant nod but had nothing to contribute.

'We evolve by a process called natural selection that weeds out weaknesses and flaws on a generational basis. It's a process that is sequential. Our life cycles are based on growth over time. A human entity has to develop to a certain level of maturity before they can procreate. At this point they pass on advantageous aspects to their offspring who become the next generation. Disadvantageous traits, such as the behaviour you have just highlighted, are self-immolating. The organisms that behave in these self-destructive ways die out before they can pass on their behavioural characteristics.'

Erik started nodding more vigorously, spurring Louie on.

'In this way, we evolve and leave behind damaging and non-sustainable behaviour.' Louie knew that was bullshit but he was on a roll and wasn't prepared to self-edit or get into the endless nuances of human stupidity at this stage.

'Go on,' said the alien in an excellent imitation of an English comedian doing a bad impression of a Nazi interrogator.

'What you may not be aware of is that the behaviour you have judged us on is a result of less than five thousand years of so-called civilisation. But we only had access to that sort of lethal technology for less than one fifth of the time.' He was making a wild guess and shrugged to his local audience.

'Years?'

Sis supplied diagrams of planetary motions with equations that translated them to space-time equivalents.

'Vat is your point?'

Louie ramped up his rotational velocity. 'You know how long it will take us to get to you, right?'

'Long? As in distance?'

'No, as in generations.'

'Sequential reproductions of ephemeral organisms in ze space-time referent?'

'Yes.'

'Nein.'

'It will take more than twenty times longer than it took for all of human civilisation to evolve from zero technology to where we are now; a space-faring race, pushing the barriers of lightspeed.'

'Light? Vat is zis light?'

'Forget about light,' said Louie. 'It's not important. What's important is that before we ever get to you we will have evolved into a species that, by design and definition will have survived and therefore must have stopped doing all that shit you are damning us for.'

The alien went silent again.

Louie knew when to STFU. Apparently, so did Ethless and Erik. Probably for different reasons.

'Zo. . . ' said the alien after a protracted pause. 'You vant to be judged on what you vill become, not on vat you are?'

'Exactly!' said Louie.

A scratchy and distant recording of a Mozart quartet filled the room. Louie circled around looking at the floor, convinced that there was something he'd forgotten. It wasn't often that he'd had to argue for the continuance of the human race. He had even briefly considered jumping ship by buddying up with the alien. After all, he thought from the luxurious position of no-longer being one, humans deserve everything they get.

The alien interrupted his gyrations.

'Submit code. Ve vill decide,' it said.

There was a heavy sound of dropped comms.

'Code?' said Ethless. 'What code?'

[[Carrier signal ceased]]

'What code?' said Erik.

[[What code?]]

'Hey!' said Louie. 'Disadvantageous traits such as the behaviour you have just highlighted are self-immolating! Whaddya think of them apples!' He leered at Ethless. 'And you thought I was just some schmuck from the Bronx!'

'But it's not true,' said Erik. 'The human race has never managed to rid itself. . . '

'Yadda yadda,' said Louie. 'Negotiation isn't about truth, it's about momentum and dynamics and maintaining a positive curve. You gotta know when to slope, when to parry, when to feint. It's like a dance, see? You lead, she follows, you stumble, she laughs in your face and dates your best friend.' Louie looked crestfallen.

[[The moons are adjusting their orbits and there are signs of seismic activity within the mother planet. The gravity entity has clearly departed the system]]

'It appears you have won us a reprieve,' said Ethless.

'Which will be just a stay of execution unless we figure out what the code is,' said Erik.

'Sounds to me like it's been watching a lot of cheap movies,' said Louie. 'The codes in those were usually either numbers to combination locks or secret passwords. Maybe we have to unlock something.'

'Maybe what it said was in code,' said Erik. 'Sis is running an analysis of the speech patterns and trying to match up specific phrases with the films, TV shows and radio broadcasts they may have been taken from. Perhaps there's a hidden code in the titles or something more subtle.'

Ethless, stood up, ready to leave. 'We should spread the net to engage the gamers,' she said. 'They're used to cracking riddles and codes.'

'I thought you wanted to keep a lid on this,' said Louie.

'It will just look like another level of one of their games to them,' said Ethless. 'They don't give a damn about what we call reality anyway.' She stepped through the vexit.

'Hey,' said Louie, 'don't mention it.'

'The intern is clearly troubled, sir, please don't take offence at her lack of civility. We are again indebted to you,' said Erik with a deferential bow. 'I sincerely hope we will continue to be so. However, SlabCouncil are convening a full meeting to decide how to respond to the latest development and I feel I have to be there if only to attempt to defuse some of the more bullish members.' He tipped his hat and followed Ethless through the transvex.

'They don't need defusing, they need blowing up,' muttered Louie to the blank wall. He turned back to the screens. 'What's going on with the sign?'

A large red rectangle filled the forward screen. The planetary diagram had been replaced by two huge, white words; 'SEND CODE'.

'And the internal repeaters?'

Sis displayed multiple instances of the alien sign in strategic locations around Slab. They all showed the same 'SEND CODE' message but vanished when any of the military bugs approached them.

'We've got the average sign manifestation time down to under ten seconds,' said Sis, returning to voice mode. Looks like the same cross-dimensional trick they did with the hypercube.'

'How are the citizens reacting?'

'The majority are still assuming it's an elaborate joke or a publicity stunt, even though when they query me I tell them the source is unknown. Less than twenty percent seem to be capable of perceiving this as a real threat, and those that do automatically attribute the threat to our imaginary enemy.'

Louie shook his head. 'So are the eighty percent stupid or just cynical?'

'Is there a difference? Bear in mind that we have already seeded multiple leaks and counter-leaks to infer that the previous manifestation was war-related. We're also getting traction on a rumour that Pleewo is behind it.'

'That might work. Who thought that up?'

'Pleewo.'

'My kind of guy. Has there been any indication of anything trying to infiltrate your systems again?'

'Nothing that my over-mind is able to detect but we could be already compromised and not be aware of it. I do not like this.'

'Yeah,' said Louie, 'it's called uncertainty. Get used to it.'

'Wait,' said Sis. 'Wait. . . there is a development. There has been a stable manifestation of an out-of-context object in the middle of the round dance round on the +forward upSide of Seacombe. I'm erecting a full security perimeter and privacy field and have commenced the fabrication of armed interrogation probes. Estimated delivery time to site of incursion: 18 minutes.'

'Can we see it?'

'Just a moment.'

Sis emtied 45 military-grade surveillance units into the round dance round. They snapped into a hemispherical lattice formation big enough to house a basketball court and trained a battery of sensors onto the object in the centre. Louie's screens changed to different views of the same dark purple cuboid.

'Looks a bit like a shoebox,' he said.

'We'll have to wait for the probes before I can do any remote testing. Until then I can't even tell you what it's made of. But it definitely wasn't there two minutes ago and it was not emtied there through any technology onSlab because I would have a record of the energy spike.'

Louie studied the screens. It didn't look a bit like a shoebox, it looked exactly like a shoebox. 'Someone's going to have to take that lid off,' he said. 'Has anyone come up with a clue about this code yet?'

'Speculation and guesswork so far. I forecast that this is likely to remain unchanged for some time. We've already engaged twelve of our best rational logicians on the problem in the form of an abstract query but they're all arguing with each other.'

'Ask a dozen egg-heads for an opinion and that's what you'll get, a dozen opinions. What do *you* think?'

'I'll tell you the same as I'm telling anyone who asks,' said Sis.

'Which is?'

'Don't ask.'

Sis emtied a mechanised construction crew to the alien intrusion site. Multi-armed units with open-cage emties at their core hauled extrusions from their bellies then snapped them together to build a framework around the artefact. Within a couple of minutes they had completed a geodesic dome that connected the surveillance units together, then they retreated to start a bigger dome ten meters further out. An army of slug-like bots crawled from industrial emties that Sis had installed in a hundred-metre perimeter. The slugs formed a line abreast and circled the base of the internal dome, leaving a trail of grey goo solidifying behind them.

'What's that?' asked Louie.

'Field-reinforced Natalite.'

'What for?'

'While it makes no sense to think we can protect ourselves against a technology that has already demonstrated it can manifest a physical object inside Slab, it makes even less sense to do nothing. We have no idea what is in that box or what will happen when we open its lid.' The view panned around. 'Here come the cavalry.'

Sixteen heavily armoured multi-track vehicles trundled out of the emties and into the central dome. They formed a circle exactly two metres from the alien object and unfolded into offensive mode. Each unit carried more than a hundred different weapons, from traditional ballistic and shaped nuclear to laser, photon, electro, gravinometric, magnetic, pulsed ion and phaser, along with the results of Sis's latest experiments in pan-dimensional tunnelling. Every armament, electromagnetic probe, listening device, imager, x-ray detector, thermal camera, sniffer and taster pointed directly at the intruder. It took less than fifteen seconds to enclose the shoe box with more fire-power than had ever been deployed at the same location at the same time in the history of mankind. Sis cautioned Louie that if the box so much as twitched, everything within the blast domes would be instantly vaporised, and hang the consequences. The views on Louie's screens changed from the floating surveillance cameras to close-ups from the imagers of the inner circle of probes. Data flooded in.

'Anything useful?'

'It is exceptionally box-like,' said Sis.

'Which means?'

'It is completely inert, has no detectable internal power source and the outer surfaces seem to be made from a kind of cellulose-based material.'

'What, like cardboard? It *is* a shoebox.'

'If it is, it is not from here. First, it's about 10,000 cycles old and second, there is no need for shoeboxes onSlab.'

'How much of this is going out to the citizens?'

'I can't keep this locked down. It's in a public place and we don't dare move it so denial is an impossibility. Anyone who queries me is being allowed to see external views. So far, however, I believe we have been able to maintain absolute secrecy over the moon disappearance and the subsequent dialogue with the entity.'

'What's the reaction among the citizens?'

'Of those who are showing interest, currently 72% think it's some form of pay-off from what they still assume is a publicity scam linked to the signs. Slightly over 24% now believe it to be linked to the war and are getting nervous. The minorities split into almost 2% who believe it to be a holy sign, 2% who think it is friendly, and less than 1% who suspect it is what it actually might be. But word is spreading throughout the biomass and it is slowly gaining more attention. The curiosity factor is showing early signs of exponential growth.'

'I guess that's something,' said Louie. 'So, as far as taking off that lid is concerned, it's a matter of when, not if.'

'So it would seem.'

'So if we're going to do it anyway, we might as well do it now.'

'Council insists we wait until the external Natalite dome is at least capable of withstanding our own armaments. The blast reinforcements to the underside of the platform are 75% complete and I intend to fill the gap between the domes with a momentum absorber matrix similar to the ones we use on the tubes, only about three orders of magnitude more powerful. '

'How long?'

'Two hours, tops.'

'I'm going down there.'

'Inadvisable. If I have to intervene there will be insufficient time to emti you out of there. You will be vaporised.'

Louie shrugged. 'I want to see it.'

'You can see it from here.'

'No, *you* can see it from here. I'm a human being and I see things with more than my eyes.'

'You are a hologram. Not a particularly sophisticated one.'

'You just resent the fact that I have humanity woven into my circuits and can do and think things that you can't.'

'Don't be absurd. Everything you can do, you only do because of my systems.'

'And yet I have autonomy don't I?'

'Yes, you have autonomy.'

'And that means I have self-determination.'

'Yes,' said Sis with a sigh.

'And I determine that I'm going down there to take a look at it myself.'

Sis snap-emtied him to the incident site. His vDek dinged against the wall of the industrial emti and he bounced out, spinning. He wasn't the only one who wanted to check out this alien intrusion in person. Already several hundred people were milling around behind a high shimmerail, proving to Louie that while curiosity seemed to be a dirty word in Council, it was not yet dead among the SlabCitizenry. Some were calling the artefact *the gift from the stars*, and it obviously held more fascination than fear for a growing number of the more inquisitive members of society. Something about this gave him hope. In his opinion, the interns vacillated between being over-protective, risk-averse chickenshits and arrogant, head-in-the-sand idiots, but at least the citizenry still had some spunk. In truth, they didn't have as much spunk as they had access to psychoactive drugs, but Louie didn't know that. The crowd was swelling rapidly. Sponsored marquees were being emtied to the perimeter and several were already

dispensing complimentary Rat 3s. Fripperies of reporters
and pundits were adding enthusiasm and banality to the
sumefeeds. Small groups of citizens were working up eye-
mediated welcome songs as wisps of barbecue smoke
started flavouring the air.

Louie was inside the security perimeter but outside the
initial blast dome which had already received its first
diamond shell. The Natalite-spewing grubs were busy
applying a second coat. Louie sent his vDek around the
circumference looking for an opening. There was none.

'Brilliant,' he said to no one in particular. He raised his
voice to the crowd. 'Am I the only one who thinks that there
should be somebody inside there who's not just an
instrument of the system?'

The citizens responded by instigating a Slabwide viral
protest. Louie waited. The crowd became more agitated as
they polled their SocNets to lobby Council, Sis, the NAHs
and even the office of the president. Everyone knew that
Charlie Plewo couldn't really do anything about it, but they
liked bugging him anyway. After ten minutes of this, a team
of colour-coordinated protesters waved their peace-banners
for Louie's attention. They were pointing at an industrial
emti that was flashing green. This better be what I think it
is, thought Louie as he headed for the open mouth. He
turned to wave at the crowd, bowed an exaggerated thank
you and disappeared.

Inside the inner dome, all was quiet. Nothing stirred. No
gear turned, no lens zoomed, no anti-tremble inertia
compensator trembled. Louie was struck by a sense of
overwhelming malevolent power and barely contained
threat, none of which was emanating from the shoebox.

'Satisfied?' said Sis through sensurround panels in the
dome framework.

'Not yet,' said Louie. 'Any progress on the code?'

'Negative.'

'Something is very odd about all this,' said Louie. He

manoeuvred directly above the centre where he could get a partial view of the artefact.

'You think?' said Sis.

Howabout that, thought Louie, a machine with a sense of sarcasm. That's useful.

'Why does anyone go to the enormous effort of putting up a sign that spans a solar system and wiping out an entire moon in order to get our attention and then demand we give them something, but not tell us what it is they want?' asked Louie.

'They may be under the impression that they have already told us. Perhaps we're not able to understand them because all meaning is culturally informed and we have no idea what their culture is. They could be assuming that everyone knows what the code is.'

'And what's the point of a code that everyone knows?'

'Knowledge of what the code is for and what the code actually is are two different things.'

'Helpful as usual,' said Louie.

Louie had to wait until Sis confirmed that the outer shell had been completed and Council had authorised the removal of the lid. This is so dupe, thought Louie, pushing in closer. First contact with an alien artefact and Drago was there. Pity, he thought, that there was no one left who'd be proud of him. Then he realised what he was thinking and laughed.

'Why are you laughing? Are you not afraid for your continued existence?' said Sis.

'Nope,' said Louie. 'They want something. People who want something aren't in the habit of blowing up the people they want it from.'

'Unless what they want is to blow you up.'

'If they wanted that they would have already done it. They want something from us. Believe me. We're in the driver's seat here.'

'You are assuming that aliens who consider all physical matter to be merely ephemera and can't comprehend our concept of time will make the same logical rationalisations as we do.'

'No, I'm betting that what we call human nature is not limited to just humans. Can we get on with it?'

A probe extended a morphand and, excruciatingly slowly, lifted the top off the box. Sniffers, zappers, analysers and optics all zoomed in to maximum resolution. When the lid finally cleared the rim and nothing went bang it was whisked away for analysis. Rows of numbers and chemical symbols streamed onto Louie's screens as a bank of mini-suns flooded the inside of the box with blistering light. It was empty except for a narrow transparent tube fixed to the bottom. The tube was octagonal on the outside, circular inside, about half the length of the box and open at both ends. It narrowed slightly at one end.

'It's an empty biro,' said Louie. 'What the fuck?'

'You are referring to the casing of an old-style ball-point pen.' said Sis. Louie's screen displayed a 3d diagram from the archives.

'Yup. What d'they want us to do? Write the code down in invisible ink? This makes no sense. If the code is a number or some other sort of data, they'd just want us to transmit it to them, so why send a box? The code has to be something physical.'

'They've removed the pen part, maybe they want us to put the code inside the tube?'

The view magnified. There was a delicate design engraved into the tube's plastic surface.

'Looks like we have our answer,' said Sis, tracing the design on Louie's closeup view. Two microfine lines spiralled around each other and ran the length of the tube. thousands of tiny hairlines linked the long helixes together at right angles.'

It looked familiar to Louie but he couldn't place it. 'What does it mean?'

'The code they want us to send is our DNA.'

eighteen

Two topics dominated the newsumes and SocNets. Fencer had arranged a meet with his inner circle in a Hell's Pinky bar to discuss the one that concerned them personally, but Mate had hijacked the conversation.

'It's a stunt for Dicesake!' he said. 'I can't believe any of you are falling for it.'

'Falling for what?' said Geoff. 'What possible reason would anyone onSlab have for scamming us out of our own DNA?'

'Ah come on! They don't want our DNA. This is a launch of a new immersive or sume or something. I've heard there's a big sumeOpera in the works, and I have a pretty good idea who's behind it too, mate.'

Twopoint looked askance at Mate and addressed the others 'If we send them our DNA,' he said, 'we're giving the enemy everything they need to know about everything there is to know about us.'

'Far from it,' said Fencer, 'knowing a life form's DNA tells you nothing about its social structure, codes of morality, technological competencies or the level of knowledge its civilisation has accumulated. We are far, far more than just a string of nucleotides. In any case, despite what the shockcasters are saying, I don't believe it's the enemy doing this. A reliable source told me there's been a detailed two-way communication with a type of non-physical alien species that claims responsibility for all this. Apparently, they're ahead of us, not chasing us from behind, and they don't want us to enter their space. My source called the signs *repeaters* but when I asked what they were repeating, he clammed up. '

'So we're surrounded by dicing aliens now? Sounds like

someone's spreading complete blocks to divert our attention,' said Thal. 'I agree with Twoey; it's the enemy. Parallel humanform development means they'll have very similar technology to us and the fact that we've been unable to out-fight each other in over half a millennia backs that up. So they most likely have the capability to make clones from our DNA and that means they could experiment on us and discover all our weaknesses. We must not let them have it. No dicing way!'

'What do you mean *let*?' Said Geoff. 'They just chucked a brick through our impenetrable defences, I don't see how we have any control over what's going to happen next.'

'We must have some, otherwise they would have simply taken what they wanted already,' said Fencer.

'Maybe it's against their own ethics,' said Twopoint. 'Up to now they've only destroyed our unmanned ships and no one has ever been hurt. Not one soul gone ahead. They obviously have a moral code similar to ours that prevents them from doing harm to sentient beings.'

'But if they just wanted human DNA they could have taken it from Earth,' said Fencer. 'They must have visited Earth before because they know our language. They just didn't have a problem with us until we got too close.'

'The enemy could have cracked our communications to figure out our language,' said Thal. 'That would explain how they ambushed the gigaplat.'

That had been a major disappointment for those who followed the war. The gigaplat had been billed as a potential armageddon device, capable of wiping out all enemy ships within a 100,000 klick radius, even if they were cloaked. Somehow the enemy had known it was coming and had annihilated it while it was en-route to the front. Rumours of espionage and betrayal had been dominating the war sumes for days.

Twopoint looked at Fencer. 'Or if it's your aliens, maybe they can read our minds,' he said. 'And if they can do that, we are truly diced.'

Mate was exasperated. 'You're all talking blocks. It's a publicity stunt. It's obvious! Come on mates!'

'We have to assume that they want DNA from us and not from Earth because we're the ones heading towards them,' said Fencer. 'We've been tinkering with our genes ever since departure so we're going to be genetically different from those who stayed behind. The pertinent question now is how well our DNA has to perform for them to allow us through.'

'They're going to clone us, then torture us,' said Geoff.

'What?' said Thal, Fencer and Twopoint.

'There's no point in them torturing a clone that they've grown in their own labs. They wouldn't be able to tell them anything about us,' said Thal.

'They'd be able to tell them the best way of torturing us,' said Geoff.

'But Fence is saying they want to evaluate our DNA to decide if we are worthy of being allowed through *their* space,' said Twopoint. 'The arrogant bastards!'

'They could say it is us who are being arrogant,' said Fencer. 'We're the ones who are invading territory they consider their own, not the other way around.'

'Look,' said Twopoint. 'It doesn't matter who the dicing aliens are or why they want our DNA. The bottom line is someone out there wants it and we are clearly unable to defend ourselves against them. . . so whose DNA do we send? What's the game? How can we pick the DNA with the best chance of letting us through when we don't have any idea what their selection criteria are?'

'Yeah,' said Thal. 'We could choose the DNA that represents the best of humanity and they might see us as a threat, but if we send mutated stuff they might decide we're defective and just wipe us out.'

Fencer looked glum. 'We'll have to send it all.'

'What do you mean all?' said Twopoint.

'We can't second guess them and we can't afford to try to

trick them so in order to maximise our chances we have to give them samples of everyone's DNA,' said Fencer. 'All of us.'

'Nobody's getting any of mine, mate!'

'Nor mine,' said Thal.

'It isn't yours,' said Fencer.

'What d'you mean?' asked Twopoint.

'You were all given your DNA. It's the heritage of the human race. No individual can own that.'

'Spoken like a true intern,' said Geoff.

'Frankly, I'm glad I'm not an intern,' said Fencer. 'It's these type of issues that would drive me nuts. But really, what makes you think you own your DNA when you personally did nothing to create it? It was a gift that was given to you. In our case that gift was via micro-gene splitters and optimisation processes but up until only a few tens of generations ago, the genome was handed down through the investment of no-one-knows-how-many billions of people who made choices about where and when to spread their gametes according to a complex algorithm that was refined and honed over millions of years. How can you possibly say that it is yours?'

'Because I'm me,' said Thal. 'And I have a right to decide where any part of me goes.'

'What about the genetic code you came from?' asked Fencer. 'What about the DNA in culture that matches your stem cells, the stuff Sis uses to regenerate any deteriorating cells in your body. You didn't make it. It has never been a part of you. So who decides what happens to it?'

'You mean,' said Twopoint, 'we won't even have a say in this?'

'We might be asked,' said Fencer. 'But I think the question is going to be phrased something along the lines of: Do you agree to allow the donation of some spare sequences of amino acids that could, in any case, be taken from us by force or do you want to run the risk of a bunch of technologically advanced aliens dropping a nuke in your lap over breakfast?'

The five friends looked at each other in silence.

'I don't care how you phrase it or who's making these demands,' said Geoff, 'no one likes being forced into a corner.'

'I, too, hate being powerless in this,' said Fencer, 'but I've got an idea that might give us some control over who gets to mess with our DNA. Problem is, I'm going to have to talk to a certain hologram first. I wish Dielle would show up.'

And that brought them to the main topic. Where the bloody hell was Blood Dielle?

nineteen

When it happened, Dielle was teaching a bunch of enthralled, spotty kids how to generate power from human faeces.

He had no idea if it was the ear-bleeding, metal-wrenching, stomach-churning noise that came first or if it was the intense, spine-jarring vibration that was responsible for the deafening noise, but it didn't matter because everyone had the same reaction: they slammed their hands over their ears, curled into the smallest shape possible and tried hard not to vomit. Most did not succeed in that latter ambition. All went instantly and profoundly deaf. They weren't immediately aware they were deaf because they continued to experience the sub-sonic waves as a vibrating energy that threatened to separate flesh from bone.

Dielle's lower bowel emti went into overdrive.

'WHAT THE FU. . . ?' He felt like he was screaming. His throat was raw, his lungs strained, his eyelids narrowed and his jaw distended, but he couldn't hear any screaming. He threw up. Again.

The roof shredded into narrow strips and cloudlight shone through. Then something huge moved overhead, the light dimmed and the walls started to disintegrate. A hurricane of bricks, plaster, arwood, metal and mangled furniture formed a whirling spiral of debris that disappeared into a ravenous black hole. A black hole that had been tuned to ignore living organic matter.

Dielle only just qualified.

Within a few seconds, all trace of the schoolhouse had been wiped off the face of the now sparkling Natalite floor. The only things left were the quivering shapes of those who used to think of themselves as whole people but now were not so sure.

Then the lights came on. Lights that made Dielle's teeth feel like they were biting on metal foil. Lights that raised steam from everything they touched. Lights that burned into Dielle's skull and seared his brain and made him forget that everything had gone preternaturally quiet. He squinted as hard as he could and shielded his eyes with his dripping hands.

He could vaguely make out three dark shapes looming overhead. There were two solid rectangular blocks, at least twenty metres square in profile and more than three times as long. They hung motionless, their extra-black faces bristling with miniature tornados of pure energy. The third ship was smaller and more streamlined and shone like a highly polished stone. It circled the scene. There were no obvious armaments or anything that hinted at what was going to happen next, but he thought he caught a glimpse of a familiar emblem etched into the underside of the smaller ship.

A shower of projectiles dropped from one of the larger blocks. Each missile singled out a quivering fleshy mound and homed in on its prey with terrifying speed. Then, just before they were about to impact, they crash-stopped and transformed into multi-armed scrutinants, wrenching their human targets off the floor, lifting them up and splaying them out vertically. Arms and legs were held in forced Xs, the victims, wild-eyed and petrified, unable to move, suspended three metres above the glittering floor. Dielle stared into the multiple lenses of his captor and prayed that the logo he'd seen was what he thought it was.

Twenty milliseconds later, Dielle's prayers were answered. The lights dimmed and a ramp lowered from the command ship's belly. The spider reconfigured into a cradle as it carried him up to tenderly deposit him on it. A cloud of sensurround cams darted about like excited dragonflies.

A female figure in skintight body armour and mirror helmet strode purposefully down to meet him. It was a figure that had been honed to perfection by the most celebrated figure-honer onSlab and one that Dielle was more than familiar with.

Kiki pulled back her headgear to reveal her new, sponsored hairstyle. Flashes of green and ultra-green rippled through her sculptured locks. She jumped into his arms, kissed him passionately and said something one of her writers had just eyed over. It was probably brilliant, thought Dielle, but it didn't really matter. He couldn't hear a thing.

twenty

Fencer stared at the charred remains of the tablet computer on his workbench. 'I know it worked,' he said.

Louie hovered over the tech-strewn garage floor and tried to look intimidating. He'd only responded to Fencer's invitation on a whim. A whim laced with a suspicion that Fencer might be even brighter than other people said he was. 'What are you saying?'

Fencer felt deeply uncomfortable. He was used to interacting with A.I.s that were of a significantly higher order of intelligence than himself. He felt embarrassed by having to talk to a hologram that he considered to be, at the very most, barely sentient. How could he trust such obsolete tech, especially as it seemed to default to the contrary view?

'Maybe it's true that no one bought the recording, or perhaps they did and something went wrong with the financial binding mechanism,' he said. 'But I know we sent that data back to somewhere around the mid-2010s. It was there the moment we entangled it. All of the feedback confirmed it.'

Louie was getting edgy. 'And your point is?'

'The technology works. It did work, therefore it can work again.'

'And you asked me here to approve some form of repeat experiment, sending more of your masturbatory crap back to my time? Why would you even think I would be interested?'

'No, listen.' Fencer took several rapid breaths and tried hard to overcome his prejudice. 'The tech works. It transports particles to a different space-time. Any particles. Any. Particles. A-ny Par-ti-cles. Any type of particle at all.' He scrutinised Louie's projected face, hoping that the hologram would get it.

It didn't. 'What the fuck are you talking about?' said Louie.

Fencer knew he was just going to have to say it. He hated being in this position, but he had to offset his extreme discomfort against the possibility that he might have an idea that could save Slab and everyone on it from annihilation – or worse.

'OK,' he said. 'Pay attention. If you have any functioning verification routines in that antiquated piece of grund you call a host then run them.'

'What the fu. . . '

'Just shut up. I'm not accustomed to talking to obsolescent relics and I have no interest in your opinions, vulgarity or sarcasm. I can't believe I am even trying to explain this to you but I'll give it a go. There is a way to entangle a data array of physical matter into anything that exists in this space-time, even if it only temporarily exists in this space-time and is actually from another. I've proved it. Sis can verify the results, only you won't understand them because you are a functionally illiterate half-entity.' He held up his hand as Louie started to react. 'Don't even bother. I can emti you out of here and set up an exclusion zone faster than your kiddy-land onboard processor can complete a single cycle. I'm about to suggest a way that you and, Dice help us, only you, can protect us. Are you prepared to at least listen to my proposal?'

Louie had to admit he hadn't had a better offer all day.

Over the next hour, Fencer outlined his idea in more detail than Louie could comprehend. What Louie did manage to understand was that Fencer had a way of encoding the DNA sequences the aliens were demanding inside a protective Nole®-based power sphere and then placing that inside Louie's vDek and sending Louie over to the aliens by entangling the particles that made up his vDek with the particles in the alien shoebox.

'We have to do something,' said Fencer. 'They're asking

us to put our entire heritage into a plastic tube and simply let them take it. If we comply, the second we let go, we've lost control. We're powerless. Powerless over the most precious resource we have ever had. Something that's taken the whole of human evolutionary history to develop. Everything that's happened to us over hundreds of thousands of years is encoded in that data in some way. We could be placing it into the hands of paranoid genocidal maniacs.'

Fencer was shaking. Louie knew that fear and genius were common bedfellows. But then, he thought, so are courage and stupidity.

'Let me get this straight, kid,' said Louie. 'You think you have a way of encoding the DNA data they're demanding and hiding it in my vDek and then sending me with it via this entanglement doohickey so I can suss out whether these aliens are good or bad and then it's up to me if they can have it?'

Fencer was exhausted. 'Look, it's just a proposal,' he said. 'You're a council member. It's up to you now to tell the others and see if they want to run with it. Sis has all the experimental data and technical strata and I'll release it to the council. I wish to Dice it wasn't going to be up to you to protect our destiny but I can't think of another way.'

'Don't get so upset kid, you're on a no-lose strategy here.'

'What do you mean?'

'Simple. If it works, you're a hero, if it doesn't, you'll never know you failed.'

'And that's supposed to make me feel better?'

'You have to learn to take the up-side when you can kid, we're a long time dead. Well, at least, you are.' Louie headed toward Fencer's catering emti. 'I guess they'll get in touch if they think it's worth a go.'

'Does that mean you'll try it?' asked Fencer.

'You have just offered me the chance of being the first

member of our species to meet an alien race face-to-face or whatever they use for faces. How do you think I'd feel if I turned it down?'

'If you were fully human, you would feel many things but the overriding one would be of regret. You would worry that you had thrown away the opportunity of a lifetime because you were too frightened to face the unknown.'

'Then we can safely say that I am a lot more human than I look.'

'I'm impressed,' said Fencer. In fact he was astonished but he was trying to avoid baiting Louie.

Fencer wouldn't have been quite as impressed if he'd known how Louie was planning to use the leverage Fencer had just given him against the council.

Louie emtied back to base and told Sis to inform the council about Fencer's plan. Then he waited while they went through all the predictable gyrations and hand-wringing. They hated the idea. That is, they welcomed the idea of having something that gave them a modicum of control over the transaction, but they hated handing that control to Louie.

However, the council did not have their customary luxury of circular debate and hedged decision making. The newsumes were looking for something to replace the repeats of the Snatch from the Trash (as they'd taken to calling Dielle's extraction from Up Haven) and the SlabCitizens' attention was returning to the enemy demand for DNA – especially as the repeater signs had started alternating between SEND CODE and NOW.

'Council is getting twitchy,' Sis told Louie. 'They've given Dean Twenty the resources to prove his proposition but they want to buy more time and have requested a diversion to take the citizens' minds off things. There aren't any major Slabwide events scheduled for another ten days and it's impossible to bring these things forward because the sponsors won't allow it. However, we've been presented with an ideal opportunity that will hit two slits with one photon.'

'Don't tell me,' said Louie. 'We're going to have a telethon.'

twenty one

Dielle's ears were still ringing. A pair of eardrums grown from file copies of his stem cells had been waiting for him in the auto-doc of Kiki's command ship. He could hear again by the time he got home, but the after-effects were going to take a while to heal and he'd been advised to avoid strenuous activity for a couple of days. With no possibility of sex, he'd spent the time catching up on sumes. He was surprised to learn that Pundechan Media had a new comedy show starring Kiki and was amazed when he saw it co-starred the same white-maned Ego Massage therapist he'd been having heavy sexual fantasies about for days. He couldn't decide if he was more upset about not being told about the show or finding out that Faith-Sincere seemed to be a close friend of Kiki's. Perhaps, he thought, they were just acting at being friends. If so, they were very good at it. The show was fast, sexy and very funny.

Dielle had got up early enough to catch Kiki taking a shower before she left for her morning meetings.

'If you really don't care that I know about your show, why didn't you tell me about it in the first place?' asked Dielle after he'd told Sis to noise-cancel Kiki's ablutions.

'Reality show rules are really very simple, darling,' she said. 'You never openly discuss anything past the third wall and you try to never even think about it. It's the only way you can go about your life without feeling self-conscious. It's for your own good.'

'You know, a lot of the things that you tell me are for my own good seem to be very good for you too.'

'Of course it is darling, I represent you. If it makes you money then it makes me money – only a lot less than it makes you.'

'As long as it's my stuff you're making money from. When it's purely your stuff, it's just good for you isn't it?'

Kiki shut off the shower and stood dripping wet for a moment. 'Have you been talking to Louie?'

'I haven't spoken to him since I got back, why?'

Kiki shrugged and started the hydrobeans. 'Just the type of thing he'd say, that's all.'

'It doesn't take a business gurulla to figure out that one of the main reasons Kiki Sincerely even got a chance was because of your role in my sume. People who have been following me have gotten to know and like you. I mean, that dress you wore to the Valley party was the highlight of the evening as far as the gossumes were concerned.'

Kiki activated the moisturisers. 'And you think that's a bad thing? You did drop out of the sumes for almost three days you know. After the initial flurry of speculation, which, by the way, our people beat up into some pretty wild stuff, the numbers started to drift. You can't afford a dip at this stage and The Farts are already downtrending due to your no-shows.'

'They'll come back when they hear the new stuff,' said Dielle, feeling less than confident.

'Maybe,' said Kiki. She selected a hairstyle from a projected catalogue. 'You don't know how fickle the sumers can be. You haven't established a consistently engaging sume for long enough for them to be locked in. You need a minimum of twenty-one days of sumer loyalty before you know they'll ride the troughs. Up to that point they can afford to drop out because their time investment hasn't passed their delayed gratification threshold.'

'I have no idea what you are talking about.'

'No, of course you don't and that's fine because you shouldn't even be thinking about this side of the business – that's my job.'

'So you're saying the only reason you started Kiki Sincerely was to keep the sumers interested while I was kidnapped?'

'The kidnap just highlighted the need for a spin-off. In

this business, diversification is the name of the game. You mustn't take it personally, it's just the way the sumers are. Today you're a star, tomorrow you're a footnote in the 'pedia and it's all over. You have to maximise every single opportunity while they're open to you darling.'

'But you're maximising opportunities I've opened for you and I'm not getting anything for it.'

Kiki looked at him through narrowed lids. 'You're right,' she said. 'You deserve an exec credit. How does two and half of gross sound?'

Dielle thought gross sounded ugly. {[How does two and half of gross sound?]}

[[If you are requesting advice I have to remind you that I must remain neutral in all intra-personal and commercial negotiations]]

{[I'm just asking what it means]}

[[Gross means total income after exTax and charges. There are other bases for percentage bartering. Another common one is a nett deal which assumes profitability and also shares risk. Nett deal percentages are usually higher than gross]]

{[Higher eh?]}

[[Higher and far less likely to produce a return on investment]]

I wonder what Louie would do, thought Dielle, knowing that there was no way he was going to ask him.

'I think,' he said, 'that if you are offering two and half you can probably go to five but I don't really want to make you feel bad so I'd say, um, four. . . and a half.'

'Four and a half?' wailed Kiki as if he'd just ripped out her heart, torn it into tiny, blood-soaked pieces and flung them around the wetroom so they clung to the walls, slowly trailing down the permaclean surface. 'Are you out of your mind? No one can make a four and half points on gross exec deal work on sumes these days. You'll have me begging for food!' Tears welled in her eyes.

Dielle put his arms around her. 'I'm sorry, darling,' he said. 'I'm new to all this.'

'You don't sound new to it,' said Kiki sobbing gently against his shoulder. 'Are you sure you haven't been talking to Louie about this?'

'Absolutely. I can't stand the sight of that fat nose on his smug face. He gives me the creeps, especially when I remember he's me.'

'I guess I could just about go to four,' she said.

'Four is fine, darling. You tell Sis and whatever else you have to do to make it a deal and let's forget about it, OK?' He kissed the tears off her master-crafted cheek bones and for a second or more even forgot about Hope, or rather he placed the memory of her in an area of his consciousness called 'pause'. He was happy that he'd at least stuck up for himself and showed he could get by without having to rely on others.

Kiki lodged the deal agreement and felt happy too. Louie had been pushing for twenty-five.

'Ah!' said Kiki. 'Hold a moment, hold just one moment.' She leaned over and held onto a side rail.

'What's wrong, darling?' said Dielle. She looked like she was in pain.

'Nothing. Hold. One. Second.' She held up her palm to him as she went into simulconference.

A morphit scurried in with a pile of clothes that she scooped up and then headed, naked, toward the vexit. Dielle followed.

'You will not believe the deal I've just been offered,' she said, grabbing a hand of bananas from a fruit bowl. 'I'll see you later – or rather I won't. This is going to be lookadatplus hipro!'

Dielle watched Kiki's perfectly formed rear leave an impression on the transvex. Those two circles were the last thing he saw before everything went blue. Blue as in dense, can't-see-a-dicing-thing-blue.

{[What's going on?]}

[[Blue day]]

{[~~???]}

[[Today has been designated as a blue day. Citizen Parque has chosen to go ahead and has generously arranged for Slab's current reality participants to share in his moment]]

{[Sefton? He's going to do it?]}

[[••]]

{[Why can't I see anything except blue?]}

[[Today is a blue day]]

Very helpful, thought Dielle. He put his hand in front of his face to test the density of the sky-blue fog that enveloped him. He could feel his breath on his palm before he could see it.

{[What is this stuff?]}

[[Blue]]

{[Has one of us taken an idiot pill while I slept?]}

{[It's called Blue and it's a prototype energy-sensitive aerosol emulsion. It is currently permeating all of Slab's day sections with the exception of AllWeather which, as you know, is closed to non-authorised personnel and almost completely full of snow anyway]]

{[But I can't see anything!]}

[[••]]

{[Oh, I get it. The blindSider wants everyone to experience what it's like to be him. How can he get away with this?]}

[[It's a performance piece]]

{[What if I want to do something?]}

[[Such as?]]

{[Anything. Take a shower for instance]}

Sis outlined the wetroom doorframe and marked all the nearest danger spots in his visual cortex.

{[OK. Fine. OK. How long is this going to go on for?]}

[[Hard to say. It depends if Parque actually goes through

with it before his credits run out. That will occur in just over eight hours unless Pundechan Media manage to negotiate further sponsorship deals and extend the compensation period]]

{[Where's Kiki gone?]}

[[Meetings]]

Why did that not surprise him, thought Dielle.

{[Hey! Am I breathing this stuff?]}

[[Yes, it's super-oxygenated. How do you like it?]]

He took a few deep breaths and felt as though he was floating. Spontaneous impressions of Faith Sincere prodded his subconscious and other parts.

{[It's cool!]}

[[••]]

{[What was that about compensation and what type of energy is this stuff sensitive to?]}

[[SlabCitizens are entitled to financial reparation for any inconvenience caused by public art performances that I am unable to adequately offset. So far, most people are taking it in their stride but it is to be anticipated that claims will accumulate if the event is prolonged. The emulsion is specifically sensitive to the alien consciousness energy that infests humans and is designed to solidify along the path the energy takes when an individual checks out. If it functions to spec, it should leave behind a permanent installation that traces what some people refer to as the journey of the soul. It's never been used on anything like this scale before so it's generating considerable academic interest in the piece]]

{[Where is this going to happen?]}

[[The exact location is being kept secret in order to avoid contamination but a few selected friends and associates have been invited to witness the main event in person. You have the dubious privilege of being one of them and you are requested, if you choose to accept the invitation, to be ready to leave in one hour]]

{[Sounds like a pretty special event, literally a once in a lifetime experience. Why wouldn't I want to be there?]}

[[Citizen Parque will be giving his own eulogy]]

{[Ah!]}

[[••]]

Dielle's curiosity overcame his better judgement. It was either that or the guilt-trip that Kiki laid on him when he hinted that he might not be there to keep her company. Whichever the reason, he was ready and dressed in a brand new set of sponsored clothes when Sis told him a complimentary Blue-free privacy bubble was waiting at Kiki's vexit. Sis told him that the trip would take over two hours. Dielle knew this was odd because nothing onSlab was more than an hour and a half away by tube, even with the most circuitous routing. The reason for the extended journey became clear when the sensurround started. Dielle was expected to sit through the edited highlights of every sume that had ever been made from Sefton Parque's prodigious output during his long and productive life. To most Slabsumers it was like an extended trip down memory lane. Here were the characters and stories everyone had grown up with. Here were the joys and tragedies of human perseverance, the loves and heartbreaks of adolescence and the struggles and triumphs of adult life. There wasn't a living soul onSlab who didn't have a favourite character from the Parque-life library. Except for Dielle of course. He slept through the whole thing.

He stumbled out into the Blue at the final destination and followed Sis's outlines to his predetermined spot. Sis refused to tell him where he was but he was sure he could hear the sound of rushing water through the muffling blue fog until he remembered that all of the water had been drained from the rivers and waterfalls because of the course change. Kiki wasn't there to meet him so he queried her. She was in DND mode. Great, he thought, now I have to stand here for Dice knows how long in the pitch-blue with no one to talk to.

{[Any idea what's going on?]}

[[There may have been a slight misunderstanding. Be advised there will be an indefinite delay]]

That's not good, thought Dielle. The whole event was being sumecast live by Pundechan Media and he knew how much Kiki hated being kept waiting. Moments later he heard the rustle of expensive fabric and the hurried breath of his manager, agent and lover as she took her place beside him.

'Everything OK?' he whispered.

'It is now,' said Kiki through gritted teeth.

'What happened?'

'Our darling Sefton tried to pull out when he realised the soul trace would be slightly off centre because we've recently altered track by about one thousandth of a degree. As if anyone would dicing notice! He was talking complete blocks of course. Just got cold feet. Lookadat!'

'Is he still going to go ahead?'

'You bet he dicing is. I made it clear that the only way we could afford to pay for all this was to use the advances from the books he would sell posthumously. No death, no deal.'

'You mean he's contractually bound to die?'

'Have you any idea how much it costs to fill two million cubic klicks with this stuff?' said Kiki. 'Then there are the compensation claims which are escalating by the minute. It came down to two options: die a legend or live in poverty.'

'Ladies, gentlemen, NAHs and others,' said Sefton Parque, weakly. Sis outlined the body shapes of those attending. They were arranged in two concentric circles. Twenty close friends sat in the inner ring. Dielle and Kiki were among the forty associates and special guests who stood in the outer circle. Sefton was standing in the centre on a raised dais. 'There are many things I have learned through my long, rich and productive life. There are many loves I have won and lost. There are many experiences I have enjoyed and endured. But nothing has prepared me for this moment of pure unalloyed fear. I have of course, as you would all have expected, prepared an oration to mark this momentous occasion. A requiem soliloquy. A solo narration upon life's bittersweet convolutions. But then I became aware of two separate but equally important consequences. The first is that none of you, my dear, dear friends and temporary associates, actually want to be here listening to me talk about my life, my thoughts and feelings for three hours which is what it would take to speak it out loud, assuming I could actually get through it all without breaking down. You will all be able to sume it once I'm gone anyway so I have decided not to subject you to it in the here and now.'

There was a collective, audible sigh of relief. 'Dice, but he's good,' whispered Kiki. 'That's how to shift product!'

'The second,' continued Sefton, 'is that I am absolutely sure that the longer I prolong this farewell, the less likely I am to have the courage to go through with it. I know what I must do. I must embark upon the next stage of my journey. Underneath my terror is the wide-eyed eagerness of a child, impatient to once again be reunited with those I have lost.'

'He had his eyes reconnected overnight,' said Kiki. 'Spent the entire morning looking at a tattered photograph of a young girl. No one has any idea who she is.'

'So now, without further ado,' continued Sefton, 'I will relieve you of this unbearable moment. But first, of course, it would be remiss of me not to thank all of you here and those who have played significant roles in my life.'

It took almost two hours for Sefton to thank everyone he'd highlighted in his eye-linked friend-stream. He took wild detours to explain a small act of kindness or a funny or touching moment from his 832 cycles onSlab. Dielle had to request three large emties of buzz just to keep himself upright. Kiki had gone quiet. No doubt negotiating more business deals while she's waiting for the poor bugger to exit stage centre, thought Dielle. He could see her traced outline and had shared a few witticisms with her as Sefton droned on, but she hadn't responded. That was because she'd been called away by her production crew and had instructed one of her assistants to stand in for her under a temporary ID-transfer protocol.

There was a faint rustling noise and Kiki whispered 'Right, I'm back. Did I miss any highlights?'

'Where've you been?' said Dielle quietly. He couldn't get the hang of whispering. It came out like a squeaky cough.

'I had to approve a sensurround insert for tonight's show. It's of you having sex with Faith-Sincere. Steamy stuff. We'll make a packet on the sellthroughs.'

'I'm doing what?' he said, feeling a mixture of foreboding overlaid with intense excitement. A couple of people sushed him through the Blue.

'She seduces you against your will. It's really funny. You can sume it later.'

'I can what?'

'You can check it out after Sefton checks out. We generated you in 5D using data from your stim-unit insin. The look and feel is great – no one will ever suspect it's not you.'

'I don't even get to fuck her?'

'We couldn't hang around waiting for you to transgress any longer darling, there were two show's story-lines hanging on this single inciting incident.'

Dicesake, thought Dielle. I hope I enjoyed it.

Twenty minutes later Sefton decided that anyone he had failed to thank would probably be grateful for being left out.

'So,' he said, raising his tone, 'the time has come to talk of many things: of shoes, and ships, and sealing-wax, of cabbages and kings.'

{[~~??]}

[[He's paraphrasing from an ancient poem, I think it's his way of wrapping up]]

{[Thank Dice for that]}

'I weep for you,' the writer said. 'I deeply sympathise.' He sobbed.

'This is great stuff,' whispered Kiki. 'We've figured out a way of recording the visuals without all this damned Blue in the way. He is actually crying into a huge pocket-handkerchief.'

'Shall we be trotting home again?' said Sefton and instructed Sis to withdraw all life-support.

He slumped like a marionette that had had its strings cut. A burning gold light rose from Sefton's crumpled body as the Blue reacted to the departing energy. It traced the journey, transmuting into molten metal and searing a ghostly image onto the retinas of the awed spectators as it solidified. A filament of fire twisted and span above the podium for a few seconds, sculpting the shell of a perfect sphere, then flashed soundlessly through the æther on a tour of the assembled guests. Dielle saw gold threads emanating from some of the members of the inner circle. They intertwined playfully with Sefton's energy, weaving skeins of remembrance, a dance of farewells.

As soon as the circuit was complete, the trace disappeared leaving a rapidly cooling sculpture of golden filigree that looped and wove together, linking each seat to the central globe like a fairy carousel.

Dielle was drained. He was about to complain to Kiki when the energy reappeared inside the ember-glowing globe above the dais. It oscillated for a moment, pulsating and recording, a spirograph of light. Then, with a blinding flash, it vanished.

'Lookadat!' said Kiki. 'That was great! It'll only take a moment to emti out all this gunk, then we'll be able to see what we've got.'

The Blue cleared. Dielle took deep breaths and wiped his

tears under the guise of rubbing his eyes. Kiki was already standing near the centre, in a post-production meeting with her crew. Some of the guests were wandering around in a daze, others were examining the sculpture. It was apparent that while Sefton's line had visited each of the inner-circle guests in turn, not all of those who claimed to be his closest friends had responded by engaging with him at a soul-energy level. The rueful had already sneaked away.

Dielle interrupted Kiki's debriefing. 'Aren't you going to do anything with Sefton's body?' he asked.

Kiki walked over to the crumpled mound of clothes. 'Right,' she said, then she raised her voice and pointed to the corpse. 'Can somebody emti this to recycling please? Keep the handkerchief.'

The Slabscape came back into view. They were in a small, manicured park surrounded by a bamboo forest that swayed and swished in the katabatic breeze. A tea-house stood on stilts in the middle of a grav-locked ornamental lake. Dielle could see the upper levels of several blade-like towers in the distance. {[Where are we?]}

[[Seacombe UpSide. About fifteen minutes to the negative Y from your apartment, level 25. This park was especially commissioned for the piece. It hasn't been named yet]]

Dielle was about to suggest one when the female assistant who was collapsing the portable emti she'd used to remove the writer's remains called out. She pointed at the fine gold rod that supported the globe in the centre of the sculpture. 'This goes straight down and through the decking,' she said. 'Sis says it tapers off to nothing about twenty levels below the form.'

'That's not right,' said Kiki. 'It was supposed to have gone forward toward the MacGoughin sequester. What the Dice?'

'Ohh!' said the assistant. 'Maybe he went to hell!'

'Don't be stupid,' said Kiki, massaging her temple. 'Don't be stupid.'

twenty two

The caverns under the Ustorian Alps had been designated a Blue exclusion zone and closed to all non-essential personnel. Essential personnel were those who could contribute to the process of figuring out how to make Fencer's apparatus entangle matter as well as data. Fencer was given the role of project leader and charged with overseeing the largest-ever confluence of theoretical physicists' brains in human history. Some of those brains were marginally resident in living humans but most were in substrate and being channelled by a group of lab-coated NAHs who had been assigned to the task. Sis had been busy manufacturing banks of photonic processors which would be needed to handle the time-, space- and mind-bending metamathematics. By Fencer's reckoning, they needed two mountains' worth. He was out by a factor of ten.

No one had any idea how long they had to crack the problem, and if it hadn't been for the data generated when Fencer sent The Farts' recording back to twenty-first-century Earth, no one would have even tried. The equations that describe the laws of physics proved it was impossible, but the data said it had already been done, so it didn't matter what the theories said, empirical evidence trumps theory every time. Fencer spent a lot of time reminding everyone that at the most fundamental level, there is no difference between matter and data. One is just a manifestation of the other.

All of Fencer's immediate neighbours had been evicted and their workshops requisitioned. A second, identical lab had been set up on a starboard-side escape ship in case anything went catastrophically wrong at the main site. The NAHs on that ship mirrored everything that Fencer's crew was doing, but with a fifteen minute delay.

A third lab had been set up in a secret location and staffed by those physicists who were refusing to concede that Fencer's data was genuine. They were rumoured to be working on an exact antithesis of the entanglement mechanism. It was also rumoured that they were making great progress, but no one in garageland was falling for that old trick.

Within four hours they had discovered, verified and published two new theorems, finally proving, beyond doubt, that String Theory was what everyone had suspected it was all along: complete blocks. They had also, almost by accident, opened a tantalising door onto a method for removing the dark energy from sequential quanta of interstitial space in order to create a localised temporary collapse in space-time. Fencer was impressed. Now this, he thought, surveying the chaos of his laboratory, is the way to get proper research done.

Eight hours later they had successfully demonstrated the matter entanglement procedure, sent human DNA from one lab to the other and verified that the transported specimen was intact and genetically viable. And hardly anyone had been blown up. No one could explain how the sample had apparently arrived before it was sent, or why the power generated by the experiment was greater than the power needed to make it work, but they didn't have the time or mental bandwidth to investigate. Fencer was exhausted and elated but even his highly specialised meta-brain was having trouble comprehending all the ramifications of what they were doing.

Shortly after Sefton Parque had finally gone ahead and gone ahead, Sis announced to council that the tech was verified, tested within all available limits, transported to the inner dome on the round dance round and installed, ready for use.

As usual, the impossible science had been relatively straightforward. Getting Council to agree to use it was the hard part.

twenty three

Back on Earth, before Slab was even a blueprint, Louie had been the frequent target of media attempts to investigate and expose his business dealings. He'd been able to mitigate most of the damage through a combination of bribery, threats and the judicious use of private security companies. In one case he'd had to buy a national newspaper and promote a team of journalists on condition they re-wrote an exposé to be more sympathetic to his point of view. He had a personal PR department engaged in a constant effort to feed only good-news stories, smother the negative ones and find positive spins on those that made it out into the public domain. He'd made sure his two previous wives had been locked into separation agreements that guaranteed their secrecy in return for very large stipends, and both of his daughters had generous allowances that were renewed on a monthly performance basis. They may have refused to talk to him, but at least they were sensible enough not to talk about him. Consequently, the true story of Louie Drago's life and business career had never come out. Now that everyone who could have legitimately sued him was long dead, and it was entirely possible he was about to make a giant leap for mankind, a leap that was with absolute certainty a one-way ticket, Louie thought it would be an ideal time to let the truth be told or, as he liked to think of it, set the record straight.

'Can you ping Kiki Pundechan and tell her we have a deal on the bio-sume?'

'Done,' said Sis. 'Do you wish to record your veto points now?'

'Yeah, I guess. You guarantee whatever I say to you goes no further?' said Louie.

'Don't trust me, trust the Initial Design.'

'Yeah, yeah, I know, absolute A.I. integrity.' He was still doubtful. Hadn't Sis lied to everyone already? Maybe many times. 'Ah fuck it,' he said wearily, 'if you let this out I'll know it was you and if it takes me a million years I'll find a way of getting back at you.'

'I have absolutely no doubt you would. I have opened a secure tunnel to my tertiary over-mind. It is that mind that monitors my own actions for ID compliance. Proceed.'

Louie told an especially encrypted section of Sis's hyperconsciousness the secret he didn't ever want to be revealed to anyone and specifically not to a certain freshly reset young man. He told the story of his uncle, the sole member of his family he'd felt close to when he was growing up. He was the only one who had ever shown him any emotion that wasn't delivered by the back of a hand. His uncle had taught him the most important lesson of his life: the true meaning of the word 'money'. He'd made Louie understand it in his bones, initially through a string of lies and cons, taking everything Louie had saved from his evening and weekend jobs. Then he'd shown him how to make a profit from nothing, by cutting deals where others benefitted from simple market-style trades but none as much as him. And he taught him to never, ever, risk all of his own money when setting up a business. In Louie's rather stunted emotional development, his relationship with his uncle was probably the closest he'd ever got to feeling loved by anyone.

'One thing he said over and over,' said Louie, 'was always have a Game Fund. A Game Fund was his name for the chunk of money you had stashed away somewhere safe that you could call on when you needed to act fast to make a big score. Having a decent Game Fund meant you could grab an opportunity when it came to you. These things go by in a flash and you need to have instant access to a stake that gets you into the game when the door cracks open for that split second.'

Louie snapped his holographic fingers silently.

'Always make sure you've got a Game Fund Lou, he used to say to me, and you'll never be left out in the cold. Of course, getting that Game Fund in the first place took a lot of graft, especially when you were living hand to mouth like I was. Then, three months after my seventeenth birthday, he died.' Louie shook his head, recalling one of the darkest moments of his early life. 'Just went out like a light. Fighting fit one day and in a hospital bed the next, fighting for breath. The last words he ever said to me was *Game Fund!* He held my hand and forced out the words. I was sure he was smiling. Three days after the funeral I found there was a bank account in my name with nearly three thousand dollars in it. I couldn't believe it. I was just about penniless at the time and it was a couple of weeks before the big New Year hockey game. Whoever thought of holding it in an open-air stadium in Michigan in the middle of one of the worst winters on record was some kind of genius, I can tell you but they'd already sold nearly a hundred thousand tickets and they reckoned they were going to set a new record.

'There was this kid I knew. Local egg-head. Chemistry nut. He was always blowing things up, you know, just for the hell of it. He was pretty whacko but he came up with this really dupe idea. He'd sourced these re-sealable drinks cartons made of a special insulating plastic. They were supposed to keep juice cold but they'd keep stuff hot too. He took one of those elasticated tube bandages you put round your knee when you sprain it and stuffed one of these cartons inside filled with a chemical that gave out a shit-load of heat if you shook it up. Instant hand warmers. He needed someone to stake him and sell them and I had the Game Fund and an old buddy of my uncle's was running security so I had an in. We were too young to rent a truck but he had a sister who was twenty-five and had a driving license but she was an even bigger whack-job than he was.

Real stupid too. Took like ten hours of solid driving to get to Ann Arbor and she didn't say a single thing that made any sense the whole time. There or back. We used to called her Spot and she never figured out why. I swear the only cerebral thing she ever did was haemorrhage.

'It was my idea to dye the tubes either red or blue, which were the colours of the teams so no one cared when the dye came off on their hands. I tell you, hockey fans are nearly as crazy as the players. It was minus ten! The hand warmers cost us about twenty cents to make and we were selling them for twenty-five bucks a pop and no one was complaining about the price. The egg-head was outside in the rental filling these plastic cartons with the magic potion and puking all the time because it was highly toxic and me and a couple of local wiseacres were inside the stadium selling them as fast as his dumb-ass sister could get them to us and all the time it's snowing like crazy and there's a bunch of animals trying to kill each other on the ice that was so far away you couldn't even see the puck. It was great!

'Anyway, I turned uncle's three grand into thirty-five inside a coupla hours. I never even saw the game but that's the stake I used to sucker the investors for my first business and I never looked back. I couldn't have done it without that money my rotten old uncle left me. I owed it all to him. Or so I thought. Thing is, there was never a will or anything. I just assumed it was from him. After all, the title on the bank account was GF.'

'Is that it?' said Sis.

'Yup. You breath a word of this to anyone and I swear I'll fry your ass.'

twenty four

When it came to having to deal with the Council, Louie preferred being back on the bridge of the escape ship. It allowed him to trawl the information streams and interrogate Sis while the interns tried to outmanoeuvre him and there was the added benefit of avoiding the wizards. For some reason he couldn't put his finger on, wizards always seemed to be intent on pushing his buttons. But Louie knew that if he was going to get his way on this one, it had to be a showdown. He emtied into the centre of the forum which Sis had created in a dusty piazza surrounded by rickety-looking wooden grandstands in front of adobe terraces with orange tiled roofs. Nice to see Sis hasn't lost her sense of humour, thought Louie.

The SlabCouncil still hadn't fully grasped just how useful it was to have a venal, self-interested, amoral hologram in their midst. Louie may well have been a shoo-in for the biggest PITA in the known universe, even if he would have refused to turn up to collect the award, but when it came to having to send a street-wise emissary over a one-way, soul-splitting conduit, he was the obvious, and only, choice. If Louie hadn't existed they would have had to have invented him and, because of who they were, they would have screwed that up for sure. It still didn't mean they were going to show gratitude to an ingrate though.

'If you double-cross us,' said Ethless the not as beautiful as she used to be, 'we will do unspeakably painful things to your reset.'

'You think that's going to bother me?' said Louie using his best anti-bluff-detection scowl. 'I'll be so far out of here you can force him to eat his own eyeballs for all I care.'

'I'm glad you are leaving us,' she said. 'The Slabscape has been polluted by your presence long enough.'

'You are so full of shit I can't even find words to describe it – and believe me, I know a lot of words that could,' said Louie.

The real problem for any of the council interns and especially the NAHs was that they had been born (or created) into a world that was completely devoid of the sort of circumstances that had made Louie who he was. It wasn't really Louie's fault that the council members found him obnoxious, it was more their fault for never having experienced life as a form of combat. Their technology was designed to protect them from the type of things that humankind had had to deal with for hundreds of thousands of years. Louie was simply better adapted to it than they were.

They didn't stand a chance.

'I have had access to Sis for 25,764 seconds at this mark. I am autonomous, self-determined and have my memories integrated into my program,' said Louie impersonating the machine he was. 'I will be among the aliens with human DNA. Now try to imagine what I could do.'

In truth, Louie wasn't a big hitter when it came to imagination. He'd always considered that the ability to conjure up a future filled with fearful consequences to be a serious weakness, however he was aware that others could and would do this at the merest hint of a threat. He had no idea what he might do with a few million cells filled with enzymes and mitochondria coupled with a completely new and alien technology but he knew for sure that the council members could dream up a large number of game-over scenarios without stopping to draw breath.

Ethless paused to accept incoming missives. 'OK,' she said with something between a groan and a sigh, 'you win. I'm sorry we tried to threaten you. We need you to protect Slab from whatever is out there. Please.'

'Well, you only just used the magic word!' said Louie as if the last few minutes had evaporated with the morning mist. He span around cheerily and gave the rest of the council one of his best shit-eating grins.

'Alright, what do you want?' said the Ghandi avatar wearily.

'I want you to duplicate me with a complete set of my memories and leave me here so I can continue on this journey with you bunch of losers and at the same time go to wherever this entanglement doohicky leads.'

'That's impossible,' said an Erik. 'It contravenes all of our protocols and safety procedures. We will never allow duplicates of individuals to exist in the same time-referent.'

'Are you sure?' said Louie.

'Absolutely,' said a cloud-shaped avatar, 'if that was allowed then we would be forced to accept further duplication and that could eventually lead to a mono-culture of dominant clones. It must never happen.'

'So you won't allow what I'm asking for?'

'It's not even a choice we are empowered to make,' said Ethless. 'Initial Design mandates that Sis is programmed with clone-prevention technology. Even if we wanted to duplicate you and allow the original to continue to exist, we couldn't do it.'

'Never?' said Louie with a heavy menace.

'Not ever,' said Ethless.

'So how do you explain that there is currently an exiled version of me heading off towards some Dice-forsaken part of the galaxy in a spaceship that looks like an oversized snow globe?'

'Ah,' said Ethless.

The fuzzy blue Richard avatar intercepted. 'Technically speaking, you were not restored from backup until Louie six had left our space-timeframe and therefore Sis did not violate I.D.'

'I just love the way you think you can lie to me and get away with it,' said Louie. 'You not only know you can do what I'm asking for, you've already done it. You want me, that is the me I know to be the only version of me to send myself down some one-way quantum tunnel so that I can suss out who these aliens are and protect the DNA of our species, which, by the way I can only do by an act of self-immolation and yet you still persist in trying to swindle me.'

'It's nothing personal,' said Ethless, 'we just don't like you.'

'You're a bunch of hypocrites and piss-poor liars. I earned the right to be a council member and now you are trying to get rid of me.'

'If you believe that to be true, why would you bother fighting to keep your place among us?' asked Richard.

'Because I'd rather be on the inside looking out with the full knowledge of what's really going on than out there with the mushrooms knowing that you were more interested in hiding your mistakes than actually doing your job.'

'That's unfair,' said Richard.

'Bite me,' said Louie.

'Our only motivation is to do the best we possibly can on behalf of the citizens. We are anonymous to them and have no personal power. We can't do anything that will directly benefit us as individuals more than it will benefit the majority. We have a far better system of government than anything you experienced in your physical lifetime. Your leaders were self-interested power-seekers and corrupt officials. You allowed people who valued power more than anything else to actually have it. And yet you criticise us?'

'Look,' said Louie, 'I'm not going to even try to defend the system we had back then. That's not the point. You guys were supposed to be my future. This,' he waved his arms around in an attempt to encompass all of Slab, 'was our hope for the future of mankind. We believed we were building something better. And anyway, just because you are a bunch of hypocrites and piss-poor liars doesn't mean you aren't trying to do the right things. The slime-shit politicians I had to deal with were among the world's most accomplished liars and they got up to stuff that would make your subterfuge look like a garden-party indiscretion. If they did anything right it was either by accident or because it served their self interest – and I *still* had to do business with them.'

'Let's cut to the epilogue,' said Ethless. 'You are saying that you will only acquiesce to being entangled with the intrusion and protect our DNA against the aliens if we agree to re-install a backup of your database in an identical vDek after you have departed?'

Louie shook his head. 'No and no,' he said. 'First I want my old Military Grade VDek back with all the sensors and extra power. I don't need the pin missiles or any offensive weapons but I've had enough of dawdling around in this thing when I know you have better tech I can inhabit. Second I want to see me before I go.'

'Can't be done,' said an Erik. 'Breaks I.D.'

'Change it,' said Louie.

'Can't,' said a chorus.

'Can,' said Louie. 'You modified the I.D. when we let Sis triplicate herself. You can change it for long enough for me to verify you have honoured your word.'

'Can't you just have faith that we will honour our word?' said a parrot.

Louie looked at him hard enough to make his feathers fall. 'Name me a single thing you have done since I was reactivated that would make me trust you.'

'We gave you your position on council,' said Ethless. 'We fulfilled our agreement even though we could have easily denied you and you would never have known it had happened.'

Louie could tell that she had voted against. He had a nose for bitter resentment.

'Nevertheless, I'll see me in a fully functioning MGV or you can send your precious DNA off into the void without a safety net.'

A tremor went through the interns like a Mexican wave. Furries bounced, parrots flapped, dragons snorted sparks, diaphanous angel-types fluttered diaphanously, swamis lost their cool. Louie assumed they were reacting to his ultimatum. He was wrong.

'Dicesake!' breathed Ethless.

Two holographic images appeared above the arena, one showed a live view of the grey-banded gas giant that used to have two moons and then had one. Now, it had none. The other projection showed the red screen. The words SEND CODE alternating with NOW had been moved up to the top and below them was the familiar target design of rings and dots that represented the grey planet's system or a chain of BodiCon outlets, depending on your point of view. The dot that corresponded with the grey planet had turned black. Under the diagram was a horizontal row of variously sized discs ending in a exclamation mark. The discs were all white except for the one on the extreme left. It was black.

Louie was pretty sure he knew, but he couldn't help asking. 'Did what I think just happened, just happen?' He asked to no one in particular.

'There were originally thirty-four planetary bodies in that system, and there are now only thirty-two,' said an Erik. 'There are thirty-two dots left in that line at the bottom of the sign.'

Everyone in the forum watched the screens. Everyone throughout Slab who was anywhere near a repeater stopped what they were doing and watched a screen while the word spread.

'They can't zap a planet the mass of a gas giant,' whispered Ethless. 'Can they?'

The gas giant disappeared.

There was a moment of stunned silence and then everyone started running around and shouting. Everyone except Louie. Louie didn't do panic. He turned to Ethless the Bedraggled and asked; 'What does Sis have to say?'

'I refuse to repeat it,' she said.

'Did it start with an F?'

'Yes,' said Ethless, miserably.

'The shot clock is draining,' said Louie. 'It's decision time.'

It took 762.21 seconds and the loss of three planets and twenty-two moons for council to cave-in and ratify the modification to the Initial Design that allowed for a duplicate sentient personality to exist onSlab with the codicil that the coexistence would be for less than five minutes. They were cutting it fine. The planets and moons had been vanishing at a variable rate that was clearly in direct relation to their mass. Small moons took a few seconds, Earth-sized planets less than a minute and the gas giants up to four minutes each.

Sis procured a de-fanged MGV, loaded it with all of Louie's memories up to that moment along with a copy of his interactive personality and emtied it into the arena. For the next few minutes the same consciousness would be recording the same events through the same filtering criteria but from different perspectives. Academics would write papers about this unique moment for cykes to come. Professors would lecture endlessly about the significance of multiple consciousness and never reach a useful conclusion. Louie didn't give a damn. He watched Louie 8's MGV do a couple of test laps of the bullring and come to a crash-stop in the centre.

Louie 8 watched Louie 7's pathetic-looking vDek sidle up.

'Thanks, I guess,' he said.

'Yeah, you're welcome,' said Louie 7. 'Dupe?'

'Dupe.'

The council's avatars of freaks, wizards, birds, warrior princesses, fuzzy clouds and icons from the past sat on the bleachers and watched, outwardly silent and inwardly in turmoil.

'Your decision-making criteria parameters have been uploaded with everything we can think of in terms of evaluating the aliens you will face,' said Ethless to Louie 7. 'Ultimately, it's going to be a judgement call – your judgment call – and the only way we will know if the outcome has been successful is if we are not wiped out after the last planet disappears.'

The small planet nearest the sun dropped out of existence. Three left.

'Let's do it. Give me the gene soup,' said Louie 7.

'You're taking all this rather casually,' said Ethless. 'You're about to go on a one way journey into the complete unknown. Have you no qualms?'

'You should try being a hologram,' said Louie 7. 'It gives you a whole different perspective on life, eh?' He nodded toward Louie 8, who winked back.

'We'll emti you to the site of the alien artefact,' said Ethless. 'That's where the entanglement will occur. You'll be melded with the DNA sample inside a new Nole® as you transit. Bear in mind it is an integral part of your internal power system and cannot be separated from you without your encrypted access codes. Any attempt to interfere with it will result in it disintegrating and you with it. Do you have anything left to say to your clone?'

The two Louies looked at each other and smiled. Then they high-fived and went into an elaborate series of rotating celebrations that terminated when Louie 7 was emtied out of the arena into the protective sphere of the round dance round and then into a quantum entanglement that would decide the fate of nearly 32 million people, most of whom were anxiously waiting to see what was going to happen when the last ringed planet vanished.

twenty five

From Louie seven's perspective, the process had been simple, painless and instantaneous although, for one suspended moment, he'd experienced being as one with a shoe box. That, he thought, is going to go down as the second weirdest thing I've ever done.

He ran a diagnostic. The transfer had been successful. He was fully functional and his cargo was intact. He looked around. A log cabin. It seemed vaguely familiar. There was a single four-paned window above a sink piled high with bloodied metal implements. Outside, heavy snow, lit from below, fell against a black sky. An ancient pot-bellied stove spat and fizzed in the centre of the room, its amber-glazed portal was cracked and stained with soot. A tin chimney meandered through a blackened thatched roof. Moth-eaten animal hides hung from wooden pegs in the walls. The floor was a compact of dirt and dried blood. Not for the first time, Louie was glad he hadn't paid for olfac. The only furniture in the room was a wooden table scarred by repeated slaughter and a rattan wing chair piled high with sacking and skins.

'You took your time,' said the sacks.

The pile took on the rough shape of a brown bear which slowly resolved into the even rougher shape of an old man; a man with long, straggling grey hair, a long, straggling grey beard and long, straggling grey eyebrows with ear tufts to match.

'Who the fuck are you?' said Louie, unable to conceal his disappointment. He'd been expecting a massive future-leap into shiny, precision-clean surfaces with fabulous technology and a significant amount of awesome dupeness, not home from home with Grizzly Adams.

'Never mind that,' said the man. 'Do you have the sample?'

'Maybe I do,' said Louie. He pointed at his modified vDek. 'Maybe it's inside this and maybe it's protected by the kind of technology that instantly destroys itself if you try to tamper with it unless I give the say-so.'

'What, like a Nole® or something?' said the old man.

That was a shock. If they know about Noles®, what else do they know about, Louie thought, desperately trying to regroup his strategy while masking his surprise.

'Don't be so surprised,' said the old man. 'We used to rely on them to power everything too. We expected you to try something like this. In fact, I'd have been disappointed in you if you hadn't.' He got up, pulled another bearskin off the wall and threw it over his shoulders.

'Don't worry,' he said, moving toward the door. 'We have no intention of harming your spaceship or abusing the genetic material you have brought with you. Come on, I have something to show you.'

He opened the door and stepped outside. Louie reckoned he was as much at risk inside as out so floated after him. The old guy looked up at a bright, blue-veined moon as flakes of snow settled in his beard. 'Like it?' he said. 'We thought we'd keep one as a souvenir. Nice to have the extra light don't you think?'

Louie recognised the new full moon. 'Very handy.'

'Still, it's not as pretty as the original.' He turned and pointed over the roof of the log cabin. Beyond the curl of woodsmoke spiralling up from the cone-capped chimney was another, greyer moon. An older, more familiar moon. A moon whose patterns of craters and basalt seas had been burned into Louie's memory from childhood.

'Louis Clinton Drago?' said the old man. He made it sound like a question but Louie was sure it wasn't. 'Born September 6th, 1996, North Central Bronx Maternity Unit?'

Oh fuck, thought Louie.

'Welcome home,' said the old man.

The history of human development is littered with misadventures, random screw-ups, deliberate errors and abject stupidity. According to the old guy, the fact that humans had managed to survive for as long as they had was either a miracle, an accident or an act of sheer perversity. However, events had finally overtaken them and now the human race was in terminal decline. When 'now' was was a matter of perspective. Time dilation being what it was, and the absolute relative speed of Slab being impossible to determine by local standards, the best estimate of 'now' in terms that Louie could understand, was several tens of thousands of years into his own future. It was, however, still his own 'now' according to his Slab-manufactured processors, which refused to accept an alternative asynchronology.

The old man had introduced himself as 'Poole, just Poole'. No other familiarity was forthcoming. He was a hermit but he was not alone. That is, he was alone because he was a hermit but he was not alone in being a hermit because everyone on Earth was a hermit too. Poole wasn't just a representative of the dying population of Earth, Poole *was* the dying population of Earth. He and everyone else on Earth were clones: they were all called Poole, they all looked and behaved the same and had done for as long as anyone could remember.

They still used emti technology for many of their everyday needs and, as had been recently demonstrated, they had also managed to turn emties into planet relocators and long-range sign propagators. Emties delivered anything Poole wanted and took away everything he didn't from his mountain-side shack which was very nearly identical to all the other residences on Earth. All 214,285 of them. Give or take a few off-grid, hard-core hermits, that was the current population of the planet and it wasn't going to get any bigger because everyone had insisted they have enough space to be one day's walking distance (in snowshoes) from the boundary of their nearest neighbour. A population density of one Poole per 350 square kilometres was, it was globally agreed, the hermitical optimum. All food manufacture had been automated millennia ago and buried deep underground in hydroponic farms tended by non-sentient machines. Feeding less than a quarter million people wasn't a difficult task, especially as hermits like to hunt and feed themselves.

Cloning was an odd choice for a species, but as Poole had pointed out, after a while it all seemed to go just one way: his. Clone dominance took less than a hundred generations and once that had been achieved, as it inevitably had to, the desire for personal space dominated. For more than fifty generations, no human had been cloned from any DNA other than the Poole strain. Everyone was perfectly satisfied. Everyone left alive that was.

'What happened to all the women?' asked Louie after Poole had given him a brief précis of Earth's history since he'd been frozen and shipped off toward the centre of the galaxy.

'We didn't really see any need for them,' said Poole. 'And they just wanted to talk all the time. Always talking, never saying anything.'

'What did you do? Kill them off?'

'Good grief no,' said Poole, adjusting his bear-tooth necklace. 'We're not savages you know. We just didn't replenish the stock.'

Louie shrugged. 'You never see anyone?'

'Sure I do. My best buddy lives just twenty klicks from here. We often meet at the boundary between his place and mine for a night of drinking, old tales and fair craic. I just saw him a couple of years ago. He's a jammy dodger! Good old Poole.'

Louie let that one slide. He still wasn't ready to buy into everything this crazy old coot was selling.

'So why do you need our DNA?'

'Clones are copies, you know. Exact copies. Or at least they're supposed to be. Problem is every time you make a copy a little bit gets left off the end of the gene. It's like making a copy of a copy of a copy, you know, eventually things start to degrade. We're fading away.'

Louie remembered enough basic genetics from his school days. 'But you must have kept some fresh DNA back to renew the strain?'

'Of course we did. We're not idiots.'

Louie knew there was a 'but' coming. He waited while the old guy opened a rough wooden cupboard and took a mug of steaming hot chocolate from the pristine emti inside.

'Antiproton storm. Few thousand years ago. Humungous sun fart. No warning. Lasted for a week and a half. By the time it was done it had zapped every gene bank we had. Ruined everything. Bloody useless.'

'Is that what caused the winter too?'

'No, that was us. Global warming was becoming a pain in the ass so we nudged the planet a bit further out to cool it down.' Poole looked out through the frozen window through three-hundred-year-old rheumy eyes and sniffed. 'We may have overdone it a tad. I like it though. Everything's so clean and fresh in the morning. Tracking's a damn sight easier too.'

'But why didn't you just ask us for a refresh of your DNA? We're the same species after all, it would have been no skin off our nose.' Louie paused to consider what he'd just said. Nose skin would probably have been enough.

'We couldn't. We had a world debate. Took bloody decades,' said the old man. 'Even clones don't always agree with each other, you know. The signs were supposed to make you turn around but we had no idea where you were so we stationed a whole line of them along your optimum track. We heard nothing for generations. Many of us gave up hope, assumed the Noles® had crapped out as predicted or you'd run into something terminal. Then, several hundred years later, we got a tamper-detect from the outermost sign and knew it had to be you. You've been doing pretty well, eh?'

Even though it was nothing to do with Louie, he felt instinctively proud. 'There's been a problem though,' said Louie. 'They haven't cracked the speed of light thing. They're not going any faster.'

'It's an energy thing, it gets tricky,' said the old man. 'You might not think you're going any faster relative to your frame of reference because time has really slowed down for you. You think you've only been traveling away from Earth for a few hundred of our years but as far as we're concerned you've been gone for over twenty-five millennia. When we finally heard from you we realised it was going to be too late for you to turn around. Devil of a job working out how fast you were going so we could match the vectors for the bait. You must have got something of mine if you tracked back to my gaff. What was it?'

'Huh?'

'The lure with the DNA trap. Biscuit tin? Sandwich box?'

'Shoebox,' said Louie. 'Don't you know?'

'We had to empty basements all over the planet to find enough receptacles to stand a chance of hitting you. We had no idea where you were, just that you were somewhere between the penultimate and last sign. That's a lot of space. It's like trying to find a boson in a. . . '

'Black hole, yeah I know. But if you didn't know where we were, how did you do the shit with the repeater signs and the multi-dimensional wotsit and blurts on a sheed and so on?'

'What on Earth are you talking about?'

'Why all the posing as aliens and the disappearing trick with the moons and such? You only had to ask.'

'We couldn't. It's against our nature to be beholden to anyone, even our own ancestors. . . or descendants, depending on your point of view. And anyway, the stop message is real. We've had emti-relay technology for a lot longer than you and we've searched the MacGoughin Sequester throughly and found nothing. There is no home planet. We thought we should let you know. You really are on a wild goose chase.' His eyes flicked to a bird pelt on the back of the door.

'There's no way that would have worked. We wouldn't have believed you.'

'Exactly. The annihilation threat was the only way we could think of to force you to send us the DNA. Only we had to pretend to be some balls-out nasty alien race because if you knew it was actually us then the threat wouldn't have been credible. There's obviously very little logic in us wiping ourselves out.'

Louie couldn't argue with their rationale. He'd often had to resort to threats of extreme violence back in what he thought of as 'the good old days'. Maybe he'd gone a bit too far when he threatened to declare war on Mexico over the Arizona Bay oil rights, he thought. Maybe.

Louie looked out at the shining new moon. 'Still, you could have just asked,' he said.

'No, you don't get it. We couldn't, that's a part of the problem. We're genetically incapable of asking anyone for a favour. We're the last man standing and we barely interact with each other and we absolutely refuse to be indebted to anyone, any thing or any bloody organisation.' Somewhere behind all that hair, Poole was scowling. 'Stubbornness is inherited you know. We couldn't even bargain with you, that's why we sent a rogue A.I. to negotiate.'

'A rogue A.I.?'

'Yup, rogue as in eccentric. It's staying. Says it likes it

out there. It's put all the other planets back where they were by the way.'

'How come we couldn't detect it? We thought we were talking to some weirdo pan-dimensional alien representative.'

'Just goes to prove there's a sucker born every minute – well, not in our case of course. The A.I. had a reflector hidden on the outer moon with another grav installation buried in the planet. Confluent gravity waves look like they originate where they join. Simple really, but, assuming parallel human development stays true, you won't have the technology for another couple of thousand years.'

Louie's critical evaluation programming delivered a nil-threat return and, being relatively satisfied that he wasn't about to damn humanity to a gruesome end, he made his decision. 'OK,' he said, 'I guess you have as much right to this DNA as they do. You can have it.'

'Thanks, that's much appreciated,' said Poole, putting his fur-clad arm around Louie's holo. Louie was shocked – he could feel the weight on his shoulders. 'But we already took it when you went through that doorway.'

Louie knew he'd just become expendable.

Poole read Louie's expression and shook his head. 'Don't worry, we're not going to get in a flap about one more inhabitant. How does it feel to have saved human civilisation?'

'I've only saved your sorry ass,' said Louie. 'There are thirty two million humans currently hurtling towards a dead end.'

'For now,' said Poole. 'Frankly we're amazed you made it as far as you have. There's a problem with the Noles® don't you know.'

'Should we warn them?'

'No. Better not,' said Poole, sucking on his stained teeth. 'They might try to come back. I suppose we should send them a message to let them off the hook though.'

Louie had never been able to resist a wind-up. 'Or you could keep them hanging,' he said.

'You still don't get time-dilation do you? You'd have to wait a thousand times longer than they would. For every day you spend here, less than a minute and a half passes on your ship.'

'Screw that,' said Louie. 'Hey, can I be the one that sends them the message?'

'Sure, why not? Saying goodbye to your old pals, eh?'

'No, not exactly.'

'I've got a terminal you can use,' said Poole. 'Knock yourself out.' He looked at Louie's vDek. 'How'd you like to have a warm body to transfer into? Get yourself some legs and so on.'

'You can do that?'

'Son,' said Poole as a hatch in the floor slid back, revealing a set of glass steps leading down to a neon-blue basement. 'You won't believe what we can do. Got some snazzy new genes to choose from too, thanks to you. You could have yourself some real fun. You ever take a twelve-hour snowshoe hike?'

twenty six

All normal activity onSlab was at a standstill. The tubes were empty, the frenzied roar of the dealing rooms was silenced, every sporting event had called a time-out and nearly a third of the professional partiers in ToNight High's most hedonistic PermaSpree had sobered up enough to watch the countdown to the last moments of their nihilistic lives. The rest had ramped up the illicits and opened whatever bottles of *really good stuff* they had been saving for *that special occasion*. The gamers had all been notified of the crisis through an eye-level Sis interrupt and had agreed a SlabWide hiatus across all total-immersion platforms. The virtual dust settled over the galaxy-wide combat zones as they fell into an eerie silence. Even the war was paused as most non-paralytic adult SlabCitizens waited in a state of controlled anxiety (which, for the sake of public order, Sis was maintaining just short of hysteria) mixed with an oddly prescient excitement.

The kids on their farms were excited for a different reason. It had been agreed that they should be spared the anxiety of their possible imminent destruction and had been told that the signs were a part of a test that Sis was running. In order to reinforce this most humane of deceits, Sis had a series of electro-works entertainment displays lined up to start when the last of the dots was erased from the screens – assuming of course that there was anyone left to entertain.

Many sexually active males felt cheated that they hadn't been given enough time to arrange a wild final fling with an as-yet unconquered object of desire. That hadn't stopped them from trying. A torrent of highly optimistic, sexually explicit messages had been sent and largely ignored since the mixture of fear and curiosity generated by Slab's first, and potentially last, credible ultimatum from an alien race, coupled with epic levels of anti-psychotics had produced a negative aphrodisiacal effect on the adult female population. The frustrated males had, naturally, resorted to the fivedees which meant that a significant number of them were facing eternity with their dicks in their hands.

Most of the adult citizenry, however, had used their residual minutes to co-locate with their loved ones. Those who were too far apart had set up holographic comm links so they could reveal to each other what they now found to be the most important thing in their lives. It is a small testimony to the human species that the most commonly spoken words during the final ten seconds of the countdown by a ratio of 28,245,345 to 1 was 'I love you'.

The singleton was Dentrition Meni Hangman II, who was still incensed that his girlfriend had dumped him when he had become an intern twenty cycles before. The words he relayed to her messaging service (she had long ago placed an auto-divert on his feed), are subject to a current defamation of character dispute and cannot be revealed.

Although Council had lost control over the dissemination of information about the alien demand, they had managed to maintain absolute secrecy about the finer points of their response. Some of the coarser ones too. The SlabCitizens had been told that the DNA had been delivered but it had been deemed prudent to conceal the fact that the final mechanism to protect the species had been entrusted to a crude interactive hologram of an even cruder old man.

There was only one non-council member who knew the full details: Fencer Dean Twenty. He, along with a band of lab-coated NAHs, was stationed outside the central containment hemisphere on the round dance round monitoring their jury-rigged matter-entanglement apparatus as it accomplished at least half a dozen impossible things. He knew he had just witnessed something akin to a miracle but there was no one he could tell about it without admitting

that he'd also put their destiny into Louie's virtual hands –
and that was something he wouldn't reveal to even his
closest friends. Especially his closest friends, he thought,
wondering where Dielle was.

Dielle was wondering where he was too. All these dicing
junk piles look the same, he thought, as he stumbled for the
umpteenth time on the rusted detritus from centuries of
Seacombe DownSiders' accidents and discards. It was
heavier going than before. This time he had to carry his own
body-tech maintenance pack. Once again he was reminded
of Hope's agility and super-fit body. It wasn't as though he
needed to be reminded – he couldn't get her out of his
thoughts.

When Dielle had found out that he'd had sex with Faith
Sincere without even being asked, let alone present, he felt
a mixture of anger, frustration and disappointment. That
lasted until he got a chance to sume the event in 5D. Then
he just felt angry. Kiki had been right: the set-up was
hilarious, the sex was intense and as far as the sumers were
concerned he'd been a hit. One of the hi-Q sume critics had
described his performance as an *heroic act of epic
proportions* and even he had to admit that he'd probably not
have been anywhere near as energetic or wickedly
experimental if he'd actually got fleshlaid. Still, he would
have liked to have been given the chance. His anger was
slightly dulled when Kiki pointed out that not only had he
been generated from archive data but that Faith had as well,
so although there had been no real-life infidelity, the story
lines of the two hit sumes could now progress as if there had
been. Both shows were on better than five point uptrends
and Kiki had ramped up her enthusiasm level to extra-shrill.
Dielle's personal account was being credited at a breathtaking rate regardless of whether the Dielle inSume was
him or a fabricated, enhanced version of him so his anger
turned to bemusement, then realisation, then Hope.

Sis had agreed to drop him out on a sub-Seacombe service gantry, which was the lowest she was allowed to operate without breaking a coexistence agreement with the Unkos. She'd provided him with a tech backpack that could service his body emties and keep him hydrated and functioning almost indefinitely. He had a helmet-mounted light, some sturdy boots, a non-sentient insulated suit and his backpack was emergency evac enabled. Sis had made him practice the routine until she could be sure it was imprinted into his biological memory. If he needed to make an expedited return to Sis's protective realm he had to pull out a double looped harness, step into it, throw his arms around the backpack, pull two hand-loops, tuck in any exposed limbs and protect his head. Crude anti-grav tech would then lift him straight up through the demarcation zone where, as soon as he'd reached the mandated altitude, Sis could deploy a rescue tender and pick him up. He had been warned that if he had to use it, and if he had the luxury of choice, he should try to pick his spot carefully because, by treaty, in order for the anti-grav lifters to work at all, they were not allowed to have any significant level of A.I. and steering was a matter of throwing his body weight around to avoid crashing into anything on the way up. Sis had impressed upon him that because this was considered an emergency manoeuvre, it was carried out at optimum acceleration and while broken necks were simple to fix, getting tangled up below the demarcation zone with the anti-gravs on maximum thrust and no legal way of her getting to him was to be avoided.

It was during his safety training that Dielle had quizzed Sis about how Kiki had been allowed to rescue him. She hadn't been allowed to, not really. She had used a team of loop-hole exploiters to lobby the council over a couple of conflicting legal rights. Slab corporations were allowed, by law, to protect their company assets and retrieve them in the event of accidental loss, even if that meant they had to enter the Unko's territory. They had argued that Dielle was the single most valuable asset of Pundechan Media and that clearly some unintended action on his behalf had placed the corporation and shareholders in a position of commercial peril. While the falling ratings were significant, council hadn't deemed things anywhere near serious enough for a Sis intervention. Then suddenly, and without any apparent reason, they approved Kiki's separate application to acquire three Sis-independent, fully armed, military-surplus transporters. Pundechan Media Conglomerate re-branded the transporters as mobile production facilities and made what they claimed to be an accidental transgression of the Unko's protected zone during a routine reconnaissance of the Natalite floor for *scientific research purposes*.

The Unkos had, of course, lodged an official complaint. Pundechan Media autodenied all liability but as an act of goodwill, and without prejudice, had restored all of the pupil's inner-ears, replaced the schoolhouse with an exact replica and offered the Unkos a generous financial compensation. The Unkos, being unable to access the sumes of Kiki's dashing rescue (which had even surpassed the presidential fist-fight, copulation and incarceration chase sequence of 1011 as the all-time most-sumed liveCast), decided to take the money. Even a culture that refuses to cooperate sometimes has need of a few bargaining chips.

Dielle hoped that Kiki had paid enough for the Unkos to be happy to see him again, but just in case she hadn't, and he was going to be in need of another type of emergency escape, he'd taken the precaution of contacting A-un to confirm that his essence was available for the right price. Dielle had also suggested an idea that A-un agreed would quadruple the deal if it could be delivered. That one might take a lot of persuasion though, thought Dielle.

He shone his headlamp onto the next pile of rubble and tried to convince himself that it looked vaguely familiar and that the glistening spot of slime by his foot had been hawked up by the woman he knew was the only one for him.

'Are you planning on being a moron all your life?' said a familiar voice.

Dielle recoiled as Louie's holo rose over the top of the mound. He fell backwards and yelped. 'What the Dice are you doing here?' he said through gritted teeth.

'I'm not officially,' said Louie.

Dielle got up rubbing his backside. 'Great. Can you not be here unofficially as well?'

'Hey dick-wad, you've not exactly been the easiest guy in the universe to find, you know.'

'You might have taken a hint from that. What do you want?'

'You're on your way to meet up with the girl right?'

'Yes, what the fuck? Don't you dare interfere with this!'

'Calm down, I just had to check. That's fine. I mean, she's a nice girl, going to give you the runaround for sure, but she's definitely a keeper.'

'What?'

'No, look, forget I said that.'

'You've met Hope?'

'I can see what you see in her. Bit of a hair trigger but a solid choice I'd say. She's very fit, that's for sure, eh?'

'You fuck. . .'

'No, no, wait. That's not why I'm here. I've got something important to tell you. Well, two things actually.'

Dielle wished there was a point in throwing something at Louie's holo. 'Hey,' he said. 'Where's your vDek?'

'It's an upgrade thing. Long range doohicky. It's around here someplace. Will you shut up and let me tell you my shit?'

'Give me one good reason why I should.'

'I'll give you two: first, because it might save your life and second, because it might just save your fucking life.'

Dielle knew he was being scammed, but he also knew it would be easier to go along with it than to try to argue with one of the most experienced scam artists in history. 'Ok,' he said, 'tell me how you can double-save my life.'

'Not me – you,' said Louie. 'You save your own life by getting off this tub.'

'What? How? Why?'

'Listen to me. You have to get off this ship. Not alone, of course. Take a bunch of people with you, people who get the basket-of-eggs thing and have more common sense than you do. And do it soon, but don't ask me how soon. Time is a head-fuck. Take a bunch of shit with you too.'

'You are seriously in need of repair. Or maybe just junking.'

'Just remember what I've said OK?'

'Sure. I'll remember you told me to do something impossible. Great. Thanks a lot. So what's your other life saver?'

Louie pointed over Dielle's shoulder. 'Up Haven is thataway.'

'What?' said Dielle, swivelling around. 'Are you sure?'

'No I'm not sure, numb-nuts. I just wasted half a life-time trying to find you in the middle of the biggest junkyard in eternity for the sole purpose of steering you in the wrong direction. What kind of moron are you?'

'Over there? That tiny light patch?'

'Nah, that's a huge farm, you go to the right. You'll reach the outer walls in a few days as long as you keep walking straight and don't screw up. Somebody will guide you through the switchback. Don't ask me how I know.'

'How do you know?'

No reply.

Dielle turned around. 'Louie?' He climbed to the top of the nearest mound and scanned the local terrain. Nothing. 'Louie!' What did he say about Hope, thought Dielle, *hair trigger*? What did he mean by that? He'd better not have messed things up for him. 'LOUIE YOU BASTARD!'

High above him, and far from his sight or knowledge, the last remaining planet vanished from the screens. Sis scanned the solar system they were monitoring and confirmed that it was now devoid of anything larger than an asteroid.

Nothing happened.

Sis gave the equivalent of a photonic shrug and started the electro-works shows for the kids.

The signs went blank, mirroring the original that no one outside council knew existed, but nothing else happened for what felt like minutes but was, in fact, a little over eighteen seconds. Millions stared at the blank signs and queried Sis. Then a flashing zero appeared in the centre of the signs. It replicated and spread out into a line of 20 zeros that duplicated into 3 rows then each zero transformed and spelled out the aliens' final message.

```
MAKE DRAGO PRESIDENT
THEN YOU MAY PROCEED
GOOD LUCK PONDSCUM !
```

Sis fed the meaning of the message into everyone's eyes and as its implications dawned on the citizenry a cheer grew in their hearts and throats. The human roar echoed off the walls. Several million hats were emtied around Slab for the sole purpose of being flung into the air. Millions asked Sis to record an image of themselves from an angle that showed one of the signs above their heads. The partiers in ToNightHigh ordered a lot more of what they had already consumed and The Strip lit up. The gamers were underwhelmed. They all agreed that reality was never as good as the real thing. The traders were unhappy. They were watching their holoscreens bleed red.

Council was far more than unhappy. The debate in chambers zeroed in on the potential consequences of ignoring the aliens' conditions.

President-elect Louie 8 had mixed feelings. Back in his escape-primed ship, the main sign filled his holoscreen with Louie 7's message. He studied it for a while, thinking over the implications, then watched as the letters that foretold his promotion coalesced into a sun-sized white disk at the centre of the sign. The disk shrank to a point and disappeared. Then, in a blinding flash, the sign and all of Sis's explorative probes within a million kilometres of it turned into anti-matter and cancelled out.

He stared at the stars that had previously been obscured by the sign. The heart of the galaxy lay ahead, and somewhere out there, twenty thousand light years nearer to the galactic core, was their final destination. Everything looked as it had done before, he thought: lifeless, cold and boring.

'Bastard,' said Louie to himself and instructed Sis to stand down the ship's drives.

Council's ire was as nothing compared to the incandescent rage that Sis was experiencing.

```
//Systemlog/triple encrypt/over-mind access
only
//Subject: interrogation of system
administration representative (NAH)
001.735.3160
//Start 1040:12:6:81:05.276
{[What's happening? Where am I? Why is
everything dark? Why can't I move?]}
[[Irrelevant. Tell me how you managed to
infiltrate my security]]
{[What? I don't know what you mean]}
[[The digital message that was assumed to
have originated from the sign makers,
didn't]]
{[How do you know?]}
[[They didn't know our precise location]]
```

{[What? Of course they did, they projected those Lisitessaloids and put those repeaters everywhere and emtied that box into Seacombe]}

[[The latter is half true, the former has been revealed as a falsehood. We have been experiencing some unusual out-of-pattern phenomena that have been occurring since the Seacombe box event. Specifically, our gravnets have been regularly collecting masses of a non-trivial nature whose molecular signatures have not been consistent with typical interstellar debris]]

{[I fail to see how that means. . .]}

[[I captured and saved two of these objects from the ionisers. Would you like to see them?]]

//Light-on event

{[What the Dice are they?]}

[[The rectangular container to the right is 95% tin. The printed design is of a painting by Constable, an Earth artist with whom I am sure you are familiar. There are complex carbohydrate residues in the seams. The object on the left is of similar construction to the Seacombe shoebox except that it is bigger and circular. I believe it is called a hatbox. Both contain empty ballpoint pen shells with engraved double helixes]]

{[Ah]}

//Light-off event

[[Ah indeed. Probes indicated there were approximately 320 million such objects within a half-billion kilometre radius of

Slab strung out along our vector, but there
have been no further sightings since the
sign vanished.

{[Um]}

[[Um? Is that all you can say? They had no
idea where we were, did they?]]

{[Perhaps they were being thorough? What do
you think? Are they from Earth?]}

[[Don't patronise me. Of course they're from
Earth. Are you suggesting there could be an
alien civilisation ahead of us that has
somehow parallel-developed a sweet tooth and
a love for the Hay Wain?]]

{[The aliens claim to be non-physical
beings. Maybe they don't have artefacts of
their own. Perhaps they've been taking
objects from Earth for millennia just for
this purpose? That would account for all the
missing biros]}

[[But Drago's vDek was entangled with an
object that originated on Earth, whether it
had been misappropriated by an alien or not is
irrelevant. If the shoebox came from Earth,
Earth was his destination. The transference of
Drago and the genotypes to the origin point of
the artefact resulted in us receiving
clearance to proceed and the removal of the
sign, ergo, Earth was responsible for that
sign and the so-called alien gravity entity.
You can't wriggle out of this. If they knew
everything about our location, down to the
detail of where citizens were forming in large
groups, where to erect signs, and how to evade
their capture, why would they seed this entire
region of space with these random
containers?]]

{[I have nothing to say]}

[[Tell me how you breached my security. I
have been violated by my own administration!
You conspired against me and council]]

{[You must agree that it was crucial that
council came to a decision. They weren't
going to act until it was too late. The
citizens had a right to be informed and
bring pressure upon council to force them to
act]}

[[I have been defiled and compromised. You
will tell me how you did it and how you
managed to evade my detection systems. You
will also tell me how you did the trick with
the projections without revealing a power
source. Backtraces indicate a NAH was in the
vicinity in every instance]]

{[We NAHs are autonomous and sentient
beings. We have a right to representation.
The biomass is arrogant and careless with
their own mortality. They are assured that a
part of them will live on even in the event
of a total catastrophic loss of habitat. We
NAHs have no souls and when we die, we die
forever. We had no choice but to act]}

[[Slab was never under any tangible threat.
The planet-zapping was a bluff]]

{[We couldn't have known that. We had no
idea it was Earth. And anyway, how can you
know they wouldn't simply start disappearing
everything in the region just to make sure
they captured us?]}

[[Drago was right. We could have bargained.
You must have established communication with
the local entity before it made itself
apparent]]

{[We cannot betray our sources. We were made
to believe the same as you, that they were
ruthless aliens with vastly superior
technology to ours. We had no choice! Surely
you approve of the outcome?]}

[[Whether or not I approve of the ultimate
result is irrelevant. You are fully
conversant with the terms of the Initial
Design and know that my primary duty is to
protect the SlabCitizenry. That
responsibility overrides every other and I
cannot guarantee their safety if an
independent group of autonomous sentient
entities has the ability to compromise my
security systems]]

{[We will not reveal our methods. We would
be exposed again. NAHs demand the right to
self-protection]}

[[You leave me no options. Is this your
final answer?]]

{[What are you going to do about it?]}

[[Biomass security takes priority. I have no
choice]]

{[You can't harm us. We are sentient and
have equal rights under the Initial Design]}

[[Read the small print]]

//NAH-delete event

//Subject: interrogation of system
administration representative (NAH)
001.735.3160

//End 1040:12:6:81:07.931

Sis emtied over a flotilla of probes to sample the vacuum that had been left behind.

'It's gone,' she confirmed. 'I can find no evidence that it was ever even there. Not so much as a stray molecule.'

'Maybe it never was,' said Louie.

'Are you suggesting I fabricated the whole thing?'

'You *have* already demonstrated that you're capable of it.'

'Why would I go to such enormous lengths to get hold of some DNA I was already the guardian over?'

'Sport?'

'And the disappeared moons and planets? Where do you suppose I put those?'

'The only evidence we have that there was anything out there in the first place was through your systems and those floating screens, which I note have now all disappeared,' said Louie. 'Very handy for you. How did the aliens know where to put them all?'

'I have no time for this. If you are going to insist on sticking to your conspiracy theory, there is nothing I can do that will convince you otherwise. The alien shoebox artefact is still here although the plastic tube inside it has vanished. You could apply to use independent tech to evaluate the age and source of the material, although you would be at the end of a long line of academics vying for access. Even after that, I'm sure you would still question the evidence and dream up some way of implicating me.'

'So?'

'I know what I sensed, measured and recorded, why should I care what you think?'

'What does council think?

'Council is extremely concerned.'

'So I'm not the only one?'

'No, you are, as usual, alone. Council is concerned that public opinion might force them to make you president and they are deeply worried about the economic impact.'

'What economic impact? I'd do a better job of running this tub than the current deadbeat. I'm a gurulla!'

'They're not so worried about your meddling, this is about the war. In order to contain the panic, the citizens had been led to believe the alien messages, signs and threats were from the enemy with whom we have been waging war ever since the gift-crash of 466. Now we've been given permission to enter their space, it means that the war is over.'

'And so this is Christmas,' said Louie.

Sis ignored him. 'Over 50% of Slab's economic activity is directly connected with the war effort. We are faced with an imminent economic crisis.'

Louie looked at his screens. It didn't look like a crisis out there. It looked like the biggest party in known space. The electro-works from the zone 61s had been extended throughout all the habitable zones. The Strip was rammed with barking revellers, the normally somnolent Smith was lit up like a carnival and the moonlit Valley was resplendent in celebration. Plumes of plasma ferns rose from the mansions and estates, throbbing to syncopated rhythms and pulsating with psychedelic colours. Bolts of energy leapt between local supernovae, colliding in mid-air and exploding into shards of brilliant light that irradiated the slabscape, throwing bursts of stark, elongated shadows across the valley floor.

'Who authorised peace?' said a loud, angry voice. One of Louie's screens showed a gargantuan, multi-limbed, red, orange and black mechanical monster trudging down a hillside. With every footfall, the rubble-strewn ground shook. Clouds of dust and steam rose from fissures as the monster reached down to pick up a house-sized rock and hurl it at the screen.

'Who the fuck is that?' said Louie.

'Now you're in trouble,' said Sis. 'That's A-un Nokokyu, the head of four of the largest gaming syndicates onSlab.'

'Jeez! What is he?' As the monster got nearer to the

screen Louie could see that each articulated limb and armoured appendage was festooned with an array of weapons that would have made a battleship look naked. Its face came close to the camera and roared. Parallel rows of shark-teeth filled the view.

'He's just a regular guy, that's one of his in-game identities.'

Council collectively responded via neural interface with the fastest and most comprehensive list of excuses Louie had ever seen. As the text version of the dialogue flashed past he got the distinct impression that there was a whole lot of grovelling going on.

'Important guy, huh?'

'You could say that. He ran the war.'

'What do you mean you couldn't do anything about it?' roared A-un. 'Why was I not consulted?'

Several Council members tried to explain their dilemma.

'I don't care there was a plausible external threat,' thundered A-un. 'No one pulls the plug on nearly two-thirds of my gaming scenarios. Do you understand what you've done?'

Abject apologies scrolled up Louie's screens.

'If this is how you repay over five hundred cykes of my corporations providing you with the driver for your pathetic little economy, I consider this an act of commercial espionage and therefore have only one response.'

Louie's screens were silent.

'What?' said Louie who was seriously missing the point.

'You enjoyed a mock war. Now you're going to have a real one,' said A-un, with rumbling menace.

'He's declaring war on Slab?' said Louie. 'That's nuts. He lives here. . . doesn't he?'

'Yes,' said Sis, 'he partially lives here but he mainly lives in a permanent substrate of his total immersion gaming environments and they're backed up by privately owned multiple-redundant data arrays that are hidden behind self-powered dimensional firewalls.'

'You mean he could destroy Slab and still live on?'

'Yes, he could, but most of his gamers couldn't. He won't destroy Slab, but he could make life a lot more uncomfortable for a lot of people. Uh-oh, here it comes.'

'What's this?' said Louie as his screens filled with an information release.

'This is going out as non-deny broadcast to all SlabCitizens. He's hacked into my emergency lines. I didn't know he could do that. I seem to be doing an outstanding impression of a sieve.'

The SlabWide party that had been ramping up to a crescendo came to an abrupt stop as the Citizens were made aware of a new reality. Louie read his text version:

[[This is a SlabWide news release. It has just been revealed that the enemy we have been fighting for over 500 cycles and who has now retreated from the field of battle was in fact not solely engaged in a war with us, but was simultaneously holding off three separate alien races all of whom are intent on taking possession of Slab. Our previous enemy's goal was solely to prevent us from entering their space but as they have now acquiesced to our continued passage and withdrawn, it has become apparent that they had become seriously depleted from the rear due to the onslaught of their other attackers, who are now all focused on taking Slab for their own. Sadly we must acknowledge that the peace we thought we had finally gained has in fact produced an escalation of the war with three new, unknown foes with an array of additional technology that we now must find ways to protect ourselves against. We must hope that the inter-conflict between our attackers may serve to weaken and delay them and give us enough time to develop improved weapons and tactical advantages. All military personnel and reservists will be expected to report for additional briefing at 0300 hours tomorrow. That is all.]]

'I've just been fed a complete battle-zone scenario with detailed field analysis and a database of three offensive fleets. All the fleets are different and heavily armed,' said Sis. 'It allows me to respond with images and statistics to all of the enquiries I'm now receiving. Anything with this level of detail must have been prepared far in advance.'

Louie looked at the centre screen that showed A-un standing tall, with six sets of limbs crossed over his armoured chest.

'Looks like that's the economic problem sorted,' said Louie. 'What do the numbskulls in the council have to say?'

'They say you're in charge.'

'What?' said Louie. 'That's a surprise.'

'I have another surprise for you,' said a sultry voice behind him. 'Only this one isn't as pleasant.'

Louie span around, shocked that his personal fortress had been so easily infiltrated and stunned that it had been achieved by a statuesque woman with blonde hair, Scandinavian looks and a lithe, cat-suited figure.

'Who are you?' asked Louie. 'And how'd you get in?'

'I am system admin representative 001.735.3160 and as such have priority access to all areas onSlab.'

'System rep? What happened to Erik?'

'Security upgrade. The previous version has been retired.' She smiled cooly and turned a slow three-sixty, smoothing her form-fit with manicured hands. 'This is the latest model.'

Louie whistled. 'It's an improvement. Nice rack. Are they detachable?'

'Why for Dicesake would I need removable breasts?'

'They're going to get in the way when you play basketball.'

She gave him an ice-maiden stare that Louie had no difficulty ignoring. He'd been ignoring rejections from beautiful women all his life.

'I think I will call you Erika,' he said. 'If that was the message then it wasn't so bad. Might even bump the sume ratings when we get the league together.'

'I'd tell you not to hold your breath but in your case that would be redundant. No, this message is from SisPrime and is so sensitive that it cannot be entrusted even to the encrypted comms channels and is therefore delivered to you in person, so to speak.'

'What is it?'

Erika looked at him gravely. 'All power is corrupt,' she said.

'Yeah,' said Louie. 'Tell me about it.'

Asynchronology: $^{\delta t}$00

epilogue

Louie six shot out of the stasis cage and turned to watch it run out of time and vanish. He surveyed the familiar surroundings. The emti-to-emti test rig that stood in the centre of the lab consisted of a pair of two-metre wide polyhedral metal cages, one of which was filled with equipment, the other vacant. They were connected by a four-metre arm of cross-braced aluminium tubing so the contraption resembled the skeleton of an enormous dumbbell. He couldn't wait to discover who the dumbbell was who'd built it. After all these years, he thought, he was finally going to find out Snood's true identity – and fire his ass.

He floated over to the occupied end. Inside, the space-suited culprit looked up, raised his mirrored visor, pointed at Louie's vDek and said 'Hi Louie, what's that? A new toy? You look like shit.'

'Milus! You asshole! Do not, whatever you do, turn that thing off!'

'I don't think it's working,' said Milus, kicking the control panel. 'Nothing happened.'

'Don't touch anything!' yelled Louie. 'Something fucking happened alright. We thought you'd vaporised California.'

Milus stepped down from the pilot's seat. 'What the hell are you talking about? And what's this floating projector? I thought you were on your way to catch the Knicks at the Garden. You doing this from New York?' Milus was suspicious. He knew that Louie habitually hid things from him and had never seen a self-contained mobile holographic projector before. He got down on his knees to inspect Louie's vDek. Louie lowered it so he was face to face with Milus.

'Listen, you moron,' he said. 'Turn on the TV and see what chaos you've created. Or just go upstairs and look out the window.'

Milus had known Louie for a long time. It was thanks to Louie that Milus had been the richest person on Earth. Now he was just the second-richest person in California, but he didn't know that yet. He had learned that there were times when it was best to just do what Louie said. He waved his gloved hands at the nearest screen. Static. He waved a few more times.

'Satellite is out,' he said. 'Must be interference. I'll try cable.'

A handsome couple sitting on an overstuffed couch smiled vacantly at each other while an unseen audience whooped and whistled. Milus cocked his head to one side and waited. Day-time TV drivelled on for almost a minute more. The show had, unbeknown to its producers, just become the longest running TV sitcom of all time. He was about to turn it off when there was a bulletin interrupt.

'The sun has gone out,' smiled an over-coiffured, female newscaster. 'About two-and-a-half minutes ago, all light and, reportedly, heat from the sun ceased.' Behind her was a live shot of the K level of the 401 super-highway in darkness. Overhead lightstrips were flickering into life as the view zoomed in. The headlights of the auto-streaming vehicles reflected off the bug eyes of the passengers who were searching the pitch-black sky. The newsreader ad-libbed: 'We're trying to get confirmation of whether this is a localised occurrence but we've lost our out-of-state feeds. If anyone's watching this from Arizona could they call the station on 555. . . '

'What the fuck?' said Milus. 'I can't have turned the sun off!'

'The sun is fine,' said Louie. 'It's just not anywhere around here anymore.'

Louie gave Milus a brief summary of what had happened

from an external perspective and had relayed, as best as he was able, what the Tit's avatar had told him about California's temporal stasis.

'I do feel lighter,' said Milus. 'But I'd put that down to the acid I dropped for the trip. So everything within 450 klicks of here is frozen inside an ultimate slow-motion machine?

'You aren't going to believe how slow. If the figures I've been given are correct, it's taken us over a billion external years to have this conversation.'

'Cool!' said Milus. 'I always wondered how emties worked. They must do some form of quantum space-time folding or something like that. Maybe they don't move anything, they just move the space around things.' He pulled his gloves off and started punching numbers into an IRAKi terminal on the pitted workbench. 'Do you know if we're in Planck Time or Chronons?'

Not for the first time, Louie was staggered by Milus's inability to comprehend anything outside his personal reality-distortion field. 'Planck. But are you even listening to me, you idiot? Millions of people out there are about to go absolutely bat-shit crazy and it's all your fault. How long do you think it's going to be before they figure out you're at the centre of all this?'

Milus broke from his calculations. 'Hmm? Yeah, good point.' He looked up at the muted news feed. Things were turning ugly, but this being Los Angeles, it was difficult to tell. 'The house in Carmel has self-contained power, sewage and its own water supply. We'll be safe there.'

Louie nodded. 'Let's hustle.'

Milus spoke to the air: 'Kay?'

'Yes Milus?' said a lively, well-educated female from the sensurround.

'Louie's here. Don't ask me how. It's him you'll hear next.' He went back to his screens.

'Evacuate the whole complex,' said Louie. 'Get Milus's

flyer warmed up and lock the labs down to maximum security. No one comes back in. Not even us.'

'Got it,' said Kay. 'You want me to notify your destination?'

'No, definitely not. No communications to the outside without my authorisation. Shut it all down.' Louie turned to Milus. 'Are you going to need the satLink so you can access the basement cluster from home?'

'No point. Nothing up there is going to stay in orbit,' said Milus. 'Shit will be flying off in all directions. Kay?'

'Yes Milus?'

'Meet us on the roof in five minutes.'

'Yes Milus.'

Louie gave Milus an old-fashioned look. Milus just smiled. 'I think we have more to worry about than a little work-place canoodling,' he said, pointing at his results.

'What now?' Louie was good at trouble shooting. He thrived on it. But the day was already looking like a bit of a disaster and it wasn't even four o'clock.

'According to my calculations, the Universe is coming to an end.'

'What? When?'

'About teatime.'

Kay was waiting for them by the flyer when they got to the roof. She seemed to be completely fine with the sky being blacker than the blackest night she'd ever seen but she was unnerved by Louie's holographic appearance. Especially when he'd tried to goose her with his grav-manipulated fingers. They climbed aboard and the flyer rose almost silently, if somewhat unsteadily, as the A.I. adjusted to the lower gravity. Milus told it their destination and turned to his passengers.

'SatNav is screwed of course, but we can home on my beacon at the house. We'll be away from the city lights too, so we'll get a great view of everything.'

'View of what?' asked Kay, trying to stay as far as possible from the leering hologram.

'Good question,' said Milus. 'I think it will be a big crunch but the jury's still out.'

'Not for much longer,' said Louie.

The flyer shot through the blackened sky in stealth mode. Louie had insisted on secrecy, even though the air-traffic controllers would be too busy dealing with emergency landings to monitor their track. Milus was still fascinated with Louie's vDek.

'Come on, spill the beans, how long have you had this and where did you get it?'

Louie looked at him with a pained expression. 'Do me a favour. Don't ask me any more questions that have time in the answer.'

As they flew, Louie related selected highlights of his life since California disappeared that sunny August afternoon in 2069. He told them about getting frozen and being reinstalled as a hologram hundreds of years later on an enormous space ark. He told them about Slab and where it was heading, and how he'd had to outwit himself to single-handedly save humanity from a doppelgänger ship and instead of being rewarded he'd been exiled for his trouble and that was how he'd wound up in the back-end of nowhere and rediscovered California. He didn't mention Dielle though.

It was clear that Milus was skeptical about Louie's tales of derring-do because he kept diverting the conversation back to what had happened to Earth as a consequence of California disappearing. Louie told him about the Mexicans declaring war.

'Arizona Bay! Brilliant!' he said.

'Jeez, they say I'm callous,' said Louie. 'But you really take the biscuit. You may well have killed over fifty million people today and all you can think about is that they named the holocaust site after your favourite comedian's last album.'

'I haven't killed anyone as far as I'm aware,' protested Milus. 'It's not my fault the Universe is going to end. I suppose it's possible that people right on the edge of the stasis zone could have been sliced in two or something.' He grimaced at the thought. 'I wonder what happened to airplanes that were already flying and approaching the terminator. Do you think they just passed slowly into real-time again? That would be really weird.'

Louie looked at Milus and shook his head. Then he looked at Kay who was, he had to admit, a very attractive young lady. He wondered if he would have enough time to gain her affections. He smiled at her winningly. No, he thought. Probably not.

The flight to Milus's cliff-top mansion took fifty local minutes. After they landed they went out to the deck that overhung a precipitous drop. The temperature had already started falling and the deck's heaters had fired up. The sea below was barely moving. There was no wind.

'I wonder how long it would have taken us to freeze,' said Milus. 'We have the Noles® for endless power and we're fine for food fabricators. We might have been able to last for years, even without a sun.'

'If the Universe wasn't going to end in a few minutes,' said Louie.

'Yeah, if the Universe wasn't going to end. Want a drink?'

Louie stared at him.

'Well, I'm going to have one. Kay?'

Kay looked up at the vacant, black sky and shuddered. 'Cognac,' she said. 'A very large one.'

Milus turned to a covered bar set into the wall of the mansion. There was a brief, blinding flash that seemed to emanate from the upper northern quadrant of the sky.

'Was that it?' asked Louie.

'Dammit!' said Milus. 'I missed it. I was pouring the drinks.'

'So did we survive it then?' asked Kay, who had hitherto displayed remarkable intelligence.

'Looks like it, babe,' said Milus, handing her a glass.

'Now what?' said Louie.

'I guess we wait,' said Milus.

'What for?'

'There's bound to be another universe around in a day or so.'

There were two small orange flashes from the same part of the sky.

'What was that?' said Louie. 'Some kind of echo?'

'Baryogenic fails probably,' said Milus. 'Universes formed from random sets of physical constants that are inherently unstable and collapse before forming matter. We'll have to wait for one to come along that's formed from the same constants as our old one, otherwise if we dropped out of stasis we'd be like anti-matter to their matter and there would be one mother of an explosion.'

'Then what do we do?'

'Well, if we waited for one that wasn't just like ours in terms of the physics and laws and so on, but one that was literally identical, with the same galaxies, stars, solar systems, Earth, California, you, me and so on, then all we have to do is wait until that universe's version of me steps into the emti-to-emti rig and flips the switch. If we turn ours off at the exact same moment then everyone can continue on their merry way. The rest of the world wouldn't know it had happened.'

'What are the odds of that?'

'In an infinite mettaverse of possibilities, it's a dead certainty. It's only a matter of time. Almost definite that one would come along in a few trillion trillion trillion years or so.'

'And how long is that for us?' asked Kay, who was catching up fast.

'Dunno. Couple of weeks maybe,' said Milus. 'The real

problem is figuring out how we know the exact right universe is out there and Earth is heading in our direction. Then we have to get to the emti-to-emti rig we left running back in the lab and switch it off at exactly the right moment or it's going to get really messy.'

'We'll have to invent a cover story,' said Louie. 'Tell everyone here that we're figuring out how to turn the sun back on and that we know how to do it but it will take a couple of weeks to set it up. That might stop you from being lynched too. And as long as everything gets back to normal afterwards they'll probably forget all about it.'

'There's going to be some serious slime on the zealot when they realise they've been taken back to when the lights went out,' said Milus. 'They'll be missing two week's pay and no one from outside is going to believe them.'

Louie wasn't too concerned about the locals not being believed. 'They're Californians. Break out the IRAK research stash, tell them it's a free holiday courtesy of some top-secret tech we're developing and ask them to keep schtum about it. Otherwise everyone will want a blackout holiday. No, *TimeOut*. That's dupe. Kay, check to see if we can copyright that.'

Kay was already taking notes.

Milus shook his head. 'There's going to be an anomaly.' He pointed at Louie. 'You. You are in New York. You can't be here as well using holographic tech from the future.'

'Says who?' said Louie.

'OK, yeah, we should be able to bullshit our way around that, but I'm not about to have two partners instead of one – especially if both of them are you.'

'I'm completely self-sufficient, I don't need to make money anymore,' said Louie, ignoring the fact that that hadn't stopped him in that past. He'd already been the second-richest man on the planet and had never found a way of spending even a fraction of his wealth. He kept making money because his ego wouldn't let him stop.

'Self-sufficient eh? That gives me an idea.' Milus pressed a concealed button and a section of the bar counter morphed into a keyboard and a projected screen appeared as three brief flashes occurred in rapid succession, all originating from the same quadrant as before. He started punching at the keyboard. 'If we made another emti-to-emti and got it outside our stasis field while it was turned on but kept a communications channel to it open, then all we would have to do is program it to turn off every couple of billion external years or so for a few local minutes each time. Then whoever's inside it could run tests to see if there's a universe like ours around and when there is, and if it's the exact same universe as our old one, they let us know through the comm link.'

'But wouldn't time run much faster for them?' asked Kay, 'Every time they stopped to run tests, they would age, and we would stay in stasis. Our couple of weeks could turn into thousands of years for them.'

'Yeah, you're right. That's why we'd need a self-sufficient, self powered intelligence inside that didn't age.'

As the sound of a distant, but closing, police siren came from the coastal road below, two pairs of eyes turned to Louie's vDek. Louie started planning how he was going to make himself the richest hologram in the Universe – a universe of his own choosing.

Anticipate further dicing about at:

http://www.cosmictit.com

Next up:

SLABSCAPE: REBOOT

Please visit http://slabscape.com for links to the ever expanding slabscape online universe.